'IKE PĀPĀLUA

ʻIKE PĀPĀLUA

Science Fiction & Fantasy Stories
from the Hawaiian Islands

edited by

SAM FLETCHER

Mutual Publishing

Copyright © 2023 by Mutual Publishing
Cover image © 2022 by Solomon Enos
"Puowaina" copyright © 2009 by Alan Brennert
Authors retain sole and individual copyright to their respective stories.

No part of this book may be reproduced in any form or by any electronic or mechanical means, including information storage and retrieval devices or systems, without prior written permission from the publisher, except that brief passages may be quoted for reviews.

All rights reserved.

ISBN: 978-1-949307-40-5
Library of Congress Control Number: 2022950639
Design by Jane Gillespie & Courtney Tomasu
First Printing, May 2023

Mutual Publishing, LLC
1215 Center Street, Suite 210
Honolulu, Hawaiʻi 96816
Ph: (808) 732-1709 • Fax: (808) 734-4094
email: info@mutualpublishing.com
www.mutualpublishing.com

Printed in South Korea

CONTENTS

FOREWORD | CHRIS MCKINNEY vii
INTRODUCTION | SAM FLETCHER.. xi

LEHIWA AND THE
    NAME THIEF | DENAROSE FUKUSHIMA............................ 1
THE LOOKOUT | JOHN CHAMBERS 11
THE LAST CHIEFTAIN OF MOLOKA'I | GREG PATRICK...........16
BLUES OF EU | SAM FLETCHER...20
PUOWAINA | ALAN BRENNERT 36
KITES AND ORCHIDS | GEORGE S. WALKER.......................60
BENEATH THE IRONWOODS | C.B. CALSING 73
PILI KOKO | LEHUA PARKER 80
FOR ALL THE HEARTS
    WE BURIED | KRYSTLE YANAGIHARA 91
PELE IN THERAPY | DARIEN GEE 112
CINDY AND MICAH | PHILLIP RILEY 126
EATING RAINBOWS | MELISSA YUAN-INNES 135
WHAT GROWS
    MAY BURN | JOSH POOLE & TRAVIS WELLMAN............147
CHARGE! LOVE HEART! | RHIANNON RASMUSSEN 158

WHAT WE YIELD | TOM GAMMARINO 164

MANUAL OVERRIDE | JEFFERY RYAN LONG 167

THE SWEET SPOT | A.M. DELLAMONICA 186

A GUIDE TO THE
    FRUITS OF HAWAI'I | ALAYA DAWN JOHNSON 213

MAWAENA NĀ HŌKŪ | JAMES ROSENLEE 243

MAUKA ON MARS | A. A. ATTANASIO 261

HĀNAI | GREGORY NORMAN BOSSERT 270

CONTRIBUTORS 312

FOREWORD

[CHRIS MCKINNEY]

Since the beginning, storytelling and the fantastical have gone hand in hand. The *Epic of Gilgamesh*, considered by many to be the oldest written tale, is an epic poem about the supernatural odyssey of a half-man, half-god. It was chiseled onto clay tablets four thousand years ago in Mesopotamia. Ancient Greek writer Lucian wrote of traveling to the moon and witnessing a war between its king and the king of the sun. He is credited by many as the world's first science fiction writer. Perhaps the most iconic example of centuries old speculative fiction is *Arabian Nights*. Both fantasy and sci-fi are represented in this eighth century collection of stories originating from Persia and India. Flash forward to 1818, and we get the first science fiction novel. What else is *Frankenstein* but a blast of sci-fi about artificial intelligence? Since our beginnings, we seem to have gazed up at the cosmos and wondered "what if?" We've also looked within ourselves and questioned our scientific limitations, or lack-thereof, and we reveled in creating legends and monsters that we claim to have once walked this earth. Whether it be Grendel from *Beowulf*, the *El Naddaha* from Egyptian myth, or Japan's *Momotaro*, folklore, religion, entertainment, and speculation have always crossed lines in just about every culture.

Today, science fiction and fantasy have become multibillion dollar cottage industries. The Marvel Cinematic Universe has dominated film for the last fourteen years. J.K Rowling, the first billionaire author, has sold over half a million books worldwide. *Harry Potter and the Deathly Hollows* is the highest rated book on Goodreads. Which pretty much means, according to Goodreads users, it's the greatest novel ever written. Like everything else in this world, story has become monetized, and when it comes to story, nothing is as lucrative as the business of science fiction and fantasy, whether it be in film, gaming, or the book industry.

But it should be more than a commodity, right? It's supposed to be art, too. And the scaffolding of art that holds a piece of sci-fi or fantasy together is often the imagining of cultures. Here in Hawai'i, there's no shortage of culture. There are Native Hawaiians and other Pacific Islanders. There are white Americans. There are also many Americans, a majority in fact, with East Asian roots—Japanese, Chinese, Filipino, and Korean, to name several. Hawai'i is the only place in the world where, as a person of mixed race, I've never felt like a minority. When it comes to writing science fiction and fantasy, it may be that knowledge of different cultures is an advantage. And as writers in Hawai'i, we may have more cultural sensitivity than most simply because of all the exposure we get living here.

Both sci-fi and fantasy often involve the collaboration or warring with different people and cultures. In *The Hobbit*, elves and dwarves do not see eye-to-eye even though both can agree to hate orcs. In *Dune*, the Atreides and the Harkonnens are on the verge of war over who gets to run a colonized planet populated by a fierce native people. A lot of this stuff reads like allegorical histories of Hawai'i. Among my favorite sci-fi novels of all-time are David Mitchell's *Cloud Atlas* and Dan Simmons's *Hyperion*. Coincidentally, Hawai'i is represented in both in certain chapters. In *Cloud Atlas*, the reader is transported to a post-apocalyptic Big Island where members of an "advanced" civilization occasionally visit to learn the ways of the island people.

FOREWORD

In *Hyperion*, there's a planetary tourist trap called Maui-Covenant that is ultimately destroyed by the military when it puts down an anti-tourism insurrection. Sound familiar or relatable?

I think writers in Hawaiʻi, and some who are connected to it in some way, are beginning to catch on. We are less likely to get snared into the trappings of certain sci-fi and fantasy tropes or maybe approach them with more intellectual sensitivity. The white messiah. The disastrous first contact. Colonization. Interspecies romance. The perils, and courage, of traveling vast distances. The peaceful co-mingling of different cultures. The presence of the spiritual entwined with every named place. Firsthand knowledge of these things is advantageous when it comes to world-building, and writers in and connected to Hawaiʻi are beginning to use these advantages.

This anthology is a representation of writers who are connected to Hawaiʻi in various ways and write sci-fi and fantasy with wisdom and verve. Alan Brennert, who many readers here may be familiar with via his bestsellers *Molokaʻi* and *Honolulu*, is represented here. He contributed a short story titled "Puowaina." It's set in the early twentieth century and is about a ten-year-old Hawaiian girl who can sometimes see the future. Alaya Dawn Johnson, who won a Nebula and a World Fantasy Award, contributed "A Guide to the Fruits of Hawaii." It imagines a world in which vampires have taken over, and the Big Island is a blood bank populated by prey and collaborators. Tom Gammarino, a brilliant fixture in Hawaiʻi's writing scene and author of *Kings of the World* and *Jellyfish Dreams*, contributed "What We Yield." In this story, climate change has gotten so bad that houses in Manoa are appraised at $110,000. Can you imagine?

There are other, new writers represented here as well. Born and raised on the Big Island, Denarose Fukushima opens the anthology with "Lehiwa and the Name Thief." It's a terrific precontact story about a brave girl who seeks to find her lost older siblings. In Krystle Yanagihara's "For All the Hearts We Buried," a woman is forever shaken by a peculiar remembrance left by her grandmother. Sam

Fletcher, who took on the Herculean task of putting this anthology together, contributed "Blues of Eu." It's speculative fiction that reimagines the desperate attempt to save the F-4 submarine, which sunk off the coast of Oʻahu in 1915.

If you are searching for fire-breathing dragons or knights in shining armor, you won't find them here. Nor will you find wizards, jedi, superheroes, Fremen, or Dothraki. Instead, you will find an astonishingly wild mix of island myth, alternate history, horror, ecofiction, dystopia, and futurism. I suppose that's what we've always been good at here in Hawaiʻi—mixing things. Despite spanning hundreds of years, from a precolonial past to a Mars centuries into the future, where the original Polynesian wayfinders are honored and remembered, *Ike Pāpālua: Science Fiction & Fantasy Stories from the Hawaiian Islands*, is definitely a Hawaiʻi book. Even though it races from past to present to the far distant future in a fantastical manner, this collection of short stories by twenty-one different writers always feels familiar. It always reads like home.

INTRODUCTION

[sam fletcher]

A trip up Mauna Kea may take a wandering gaze toward Kapaʻau, where King Kamehameha I was born beneath the passing of Halley's comet in 1758. Legend said a feathered light in the sky would announce the birth of Hawaiʻi's greatest chief. Westward, you might spot Kealakekua Bay, where Captain James Cook first arrived during Makahiki, the peaceful harvest season honoring the god Lono. But wartime would come, and it was that same location where Cook was stabbed under High Chief Kalaniʻōpuʻu's order. On a clear day, you can catch Maui's shield volcano, Haleakalā, where Māui the demigod lassoed the sun's rays making the days longer. Legend says Māui's to credit for the Hawaiian Islands' emergence in the first place—he caught the ocean floor with a fishhook.

Hawaiʻi's history is so rich it can be hard to believe everything happened across such a small archipelago. These stories are rarely far away and don't usually have a commemorative plaque. Every square inch—from the luscious, downpouring Mount Waiʻaleʻale of Kauaʻi to the harsh, acidic Kaʻū Desert of Hawaiʻi Island—is packed with stories. Naturally, some are speculative.

Among the twenty-one science fiction and fantasy stories to follow, Greg Patrick takes you to Molokaʻi—where the Priest Kamalō once struck a deal with the shark god, Kauhuhu—to meet a warrior's final battle, leprosy, during missionary days before King Kamehameha V exiled 8,000 victims of the disease there.

In the fiery caverns of Kīlauea—home of the volcano goddess, Pele—a widow searches for answers surrounding her husband's prototypic jetpack accident in George S. Walker's "Kites and Orchids." But, no Pele. She might just be seeking advice—or giving it—in a therapist's office in Kona, according to Darien Gee's "Pele in Therapy."

Ancient moʻolelo tell of many battles occurring in Hāna on Maui. Some to rule the entire island, others to rule the entire archipelago. In Melissa Yuan-Innes "Eating Rainbows," the town is now a place for Menehune to play tricks on naïve tourists.

Early visitors of Lānaʻi dubbed it the "island of the ghosts," understanding it was run by the goddess Pahulu and her flesh-hungry spirit minions. In Josh Poole and Travis Wellman's "What Grows May Burn," it's now run by Pineapple Humanoid Organisms, just one byproduct of ecological damage caused by pineapple monoculture. The author duo sums up the transition best: "Lānaʻi had once been an untouched paradise haunted by man-eating ghosts chased off by a Mauian prince. That night, it became clear that the prince missed a few."

Off Oʻahu's Kāneʻohe Bay—where the hula goddess Hiʻiaka was attacked by a moʻo and triumphed, the severed tip of its tail forming the islet Mokoliʻi—a local high schooler and "kind of a huge dork" just might have discovered love after first discovering secret military equipment in Rhiannon Rasmussen's "Charge! Love Heart!" On Oʻahu, like many Hawaiian Islands, weather changes with the landscape. As peaks of the Koʻolau cut into the sky, the blue turns gray, and mist cascades down loose vines and tangled vegetation. In this jungle pours Sacred Falls, where it is said that Kamapuaʻa the hog god still dwells. He doesn't make an appearance in Phillip Riley's "Cindy and Micah," but two other playful hog shapeshifters do as they decide if they are adversaries or lovers.

INTRODUCTION

Mark Twain visited Hawai'i March 18, 1866—just after adopting the pen name—and spent four months corresponding for the *Sacramento Union*. After mooring in Honolulu, one of the first things he noticed were the cats. The second paragraph in *Mark Twain in Hawai'i* reads, "I saw cats—Tomcats, Mary Ann cats, long-tailed cats, bob-tailed cats, blind cats, one-eyed cats, wall-eyed cats, cross-eyed cats, gray cats, black cats, white cats, yellow cats, striped cats, spotted cats, tame cats, wild cats, singed cats, individual cats, groups of cats, platoons of cats, companies of cats, regiments of cats, armies of cats, multitudes of cats, millions of cats, and all of them sleek, fat, lazy, and sound asleep." In Jeffery Ryan Long's "Manual Override," Honolulu is now ruled under the Republic of Contributing Citizens. It's been through climate disaster and totalitarian overthrow, but not everything is unrecognizable from old stories. "M was really thinking about was how mystified and entertained the citizens were by the cats on the screens of their devices," the author writes, "while in certain abandoned parts of the city there were neighborhoods of cats, domiciles infested with cats, cats with nicked ears and bald patches on their cheeks, and no one wanted to get near them."

As you continue up Mauna Kea's peak, land fades away before sky and cosmos. Hawai'i's earliest inhabitants (save the Menehune) were never limited by eight islands and 129 atolls and islets. They looked on, guided by the stars.

Being the most isolated archipelago in the world, Hawai'i's sky reveals stars to the naked eye invisible in other parts of the world. The early travelers of the Pacific used no instruments, simply drawing maps of the sky. During the day, the sun indicated east and west. During the night, they used star lines—constellations—to determine the canoe's direction.

They established four main lines symbolizing ancient stories, some of which may seem familiar. The first constellation is Kekāomakali'i, the Kona chief who threw all the village's food in a net up into the sky creating seasonal fluctuation. Kaiwikuamo'o, the backbone, joins the North Star to the Southern Cross, which was compared to the location of the islands. Kamakaunuiamaui looks like a giant fishhook, named for the one Māui used to pull the Hawaiian Islands up. The fourth constellation is the tangled kites of cousins Kawelo and Kauahoa, called Kalupeakawelo.

It makes sense why science fiction writers speculate about Hawai'i as a leader in interstellar travel. In A.A. Attanasio's "Mauka on Mars," the futuristic human species Homo frigus of Triton can tour Mars hosted by a zobot "assembled from trillions of self-organized nanoparts." Even then, these tourists remember from where they distantly came. "The great navigators on Earth risked everything to cross the immensity of the sea, seeking islands they didn't know were there but that were always there, far out of sight, connected to the stars, wind, and ocean currents. Those first explorers met the mysterious outer world with their hearts, bravely. They won deep intimacy with the planet and its elemental powers—and with the islands that were always there."

In Gregory Norman Bossert's "Hānai," Hawai'i is again an independent republic and now a space station too. "Lono drones" provide rain to Kaho'olawe.

Ensign Hōkū was born "in the right place at the right time" in James Rosenlee's space opera "Mawaena Nā Hōkū." "We were the first Earth nation to make contact with aliens," the author writes. "The first child born in space was to a Hawaiian astronaut couple. There are various Star Union Academies scattered throughout the galaxy, but the oldest and most prestigious one was built in…you guessed it! Hawai'i."

Be it the squid-esque alien overthrow in A.M. Dellamonica's "The Sweet Spot" or vampirism in Alaya Dawn Johnson's "A Guide to the Fruits of Hawai'i," Hawai'i will endure apocalypse. Vampires won; the islands now hold concentration camps—graded by blood quality—of the remaining humans to be harvested. The most represented form of apocalypse, it seems, is climate catastrophe. "Manual

INTRODUCTION

Override" isn't the only story with toxic waters and a rising Pacific. In Tom Gammarino's "What We Yield," the principal of a private high school on Oʻahu faces the slow, grueling impacts of a changing climate.

In these stories dwell a diverse cast of personalities and experiences across Hawaiʻi. These include military personnel, from ancient warriors in Molokaʻi enacting the orders of their chief, to a Navy Diver salvaging parts offshore Honolulu from the first U.S. submarine to sink, to Johnny Kua, a Native serving in the 25th Infantry Division during World War II. On and on to rebel defenders against alien invaders and officers among star fleets.

Shapeshifters, too—goddesses like Pele, tricksters like the moʻo, lost lovers like Cindy and Micah. Not all shapeshifters do so by choice. Some get swept up by riptide and cursed by a shark god. In C.B. Calsing's "Beneath the Ironwoods," a child finds more in common with a school of goatfish than his own family.

Next are kahuna, formally guiding a mother through prophesied childbirth in John Chamber's "The Lookout." But kahuna persist informally too—offering advice, communicating with spirits, providing medicine. Some may not call themselves kahuna. Some may not even know.

In Hawaiʻi, all that outnumbers the supernatural are eyes to bear witness. Interacting with the spiritual has been passed down each generation. In Denarose Fukushima's "Lehiwa and the Name Thief," communing with spirits is common. But only Lehiwa, it seems, can channel the voices and truly understand them. In Lehua Parker's "Pili Koko," young Ahe starts hearing spirits when his Papa Keola passes on. Kaleialoha only finds closure after her grandmother makes the transition, too, in Krystle Yanigahara's "For All the Hearts We Buried," by way of paranormal gifts.

Nani MacGillvray in Alan Brennert's "Puowaina" feels that this is all a curse, the ability to see the supernatural, and see terrible things before they occur. The beautiful and charming is to follow, as well as the strange and disturbing. These characters find strength in this unknown, and imagination proves a powerful source of discovery. Brennert, through Johnny Kua, puts it best:

"We Hawaiians live in two worlds, Nani," he said gently. "This world you see around us, that's just the first layer, like the skin covering our bodies. There's another layer underneath, like you and I have blood and bones beneath our skin. My tūtū said the ability to see this second layer of reality is called 'ike pāpālua: it means 'twice knowing.' Seeing events that haven't happened yet—or things happening now, but at a great distance—that's a special gift you have, Nani. The haoles call it 'second sight.'"

"So I'm…not being bad when I see things?"

He laughed. "No, just the opposite. Your gift is pono—a very good thing."

LEHIWA AND THE NAME THIEF

[DENAROSE FUKUSHIMA]

Pinea had been missing for three days. She had gone in search of the ʻawa plant and never returned.

"She must have slipped and fell."

It was the only logical reason that Kekua could come up with for his older sister's disappearance. A small search party had gone to look for Pinea to no avail. Everyone assumed the worst.

Except for young Lehiwa, who stared at the steady drizzle from her place at the foot of a tall, thick tree. All around her, ʻōhiʻa trees, ti leaves, and mountain apple trees glistened in the rain, droplets sluicing down large, healthy leaves. The sky was a hazy gray.

"She's not dead," Lehiwa whispered.

Kekua glanced down at her for a few moments before speaking up. "What makes you say that?"

"I can feel her ʻuhane out there. She's not dead, she's lost."

Kekua turned to look in the direction that Lehiwa faced, as if he could gain her insight by doing so.

Lehiwa sat with her knees drawn up to her chest, waiting patiently for her brother to answer. She was younger than Kekua by many years, but while Kekua heard conflicting voices guiding him down many different paths, Lehiwa heard only a few voices within herself and knew which one to follow.

"I'll speak with Grandfather tonight," Kekua said, "and in the morning, I'll take Manu and go search for Pinea."

"I don't feel that you should."

He sighed. "Lehiwa, why do you say this? Is it your inner knowledge or your hurt feelings?"

It amazed Lehiwa how far her brother could be from the truth. He assumed, incorrectly, that she held a grudge against Pinea, that she didn't want her back. Lehiwa closed her eyes and said nothing. It would be deceitful to claim there was no bitterness in her heart.

The next morning, Lehiwa clutched her mother's skirt and watched as Kekua and his closest friend, Manu, set out on the same path that Pinea had taken just days before. The nights had already been miserable without her presence, but Lehiwa had slept even less worrying for her brother and his aikāne.

In the dead of the night, when the spirits were louder, Lehiwa realized that she should have kept the information regarding Pinea to herself. She had only meant to alleviate her brother's worry but should have known that he would try to take it upon himself to rescue Pinea. Even though Kekua had the lean, strong muscles of a man, he still had a long way to grow.

Silently tears rolled down her cheeks. It wasn't Kekua's job to save Pinea; it was hers. But some scared, foolish part of her hoped that someone else could do it, and now she might lose Kekua too.

Her grandmother turned and wrapped her in a hug. "Don't cry, child. Your brother will be back soon." She cradled Lehiwa in her arms until she fell into a numb slumber. When darkness came, Lehiwa arose and crept out of the hut. Pinea was the only one who would have woken up when she walked out. She was lost now; she couldn't stop her.

Into the quiet night, Lehiwa walked, head high, her dark, curly hair trailing down her shoulders and back, a gourd clutched in her hand. Walking in the light of the full moon, she prayed to the goddess Hina for protection.

In the days previous, Lehiwa had left out many leis and danced hula in front of the shrine dedicated to her family's ancestral guardian spirits. Only now did she feel the 'aumakua were appeased.

A small, spotted pig ran out of the bushes, squealing as it charged toward her. Before she could even think about running away, the pig went silent and lay still at her feet.

A middle-aged, dark-skinned man sprinted out of the darkness after the pig, hunched over to scoop it up. He stopped when he noticed Lehiwa, and she recognized him: the kahuna who once helped her overcome a fever. She greeted him politely.

"So young to be facing Hakau," he breathed.

"Hakau?" Lehiwa asked.

"The one who has your siblings. Listen closely, child, for you will be dealing with a tricky and powerful mo'o."

Lehiwa's blood ran cold. Her family had fought against the mystical lizards for generations. If it was a mo'o, it would show her no consideration.

"You will have no trouble reaching him if you continue the path you're taking," the kahuna said. "He will appear to you not as a mo'o, but in human form, and he will be persuasive. No matter what, you must not give him your name. If you do he will take it, and you too will be lost."

"Thank you," Lehiwa said as the kahuna picked up the pig.

"Your brother managed to wound the mo'o before he became lost. Hakau is injured and relies on the stream to rejuvenate himself."

She sucked in her upper lip and thanked him again. He nodded and watched her walk away.

Lehiwa continued to walk, gently parting the tall grass. She strained her ears, listening for clues or signs about where her siblings might be. The steady sound of the stream would normally soothe her, but tonight it masked footsteps. Lehiwa approached, heart pounding in her chest. Her first test began now; her confidence wavered. She was only a girl, after all. A girl who was small for her age with no one to help her if things went badly.

A thin waterfall maneuvered down a cliff of rocks, pooling into a stream. A young man was visible from the torso up. The moonlight highlighted the taut muscles of a warrior, full lips, and a strong bone structure. But she could not quite see his eyes.

"Hello, little sister," the man said in a silky voice. "You're out late tonight. You are lost."

"No," she answered.

The man chuckled. "Only those who are lost find their way here. Give me a few moments, little sister, and I will help you."

"I will wait by the ferns down the path," Lehiwa said, dread tumbling in her stomach.

"I shall call for you," he said with a smile, his grin showing like a second moon in the night.

Lehiwa was no fool, and she heeded the anxious, shaky sensation in her body. The man in the stream was not to be trusted. She quietly continued down the path.

A mournful, ghostly wail shivered through the forest. The grievous noise cut into Lehiwa's heart, and she strayed from the path. Lost spirits were said to wail through the night, but this was the first time Lehiwa heard it. She couldn't help herself; she had to help.

Tumbling toward the noise, she caught glimpse of its source. The spirit walked as if in a stupor, body swaying languidly. He wandered in no particular direction, eyes half-open, mouth stretched wide as he wailed. It was Manu.

"Manu!" Lehiwa called. "Manu!"

He did not move, did not react to her call. She dropped her gourd and ran up to him, steering him away from a tree.

"Manu," she said, arms on his elbow. "Manu, come to your senses."

"Manu?" he said, as if the word was unfamiliar.

"That's your name, Manu."

The boy shook his head. "I have no name. I am simply aikāne."

"You're more than Kekua's aikāne." Lehiwa waited, but though a spark of familiarity swept over Manu's face, he only shook his head again.

"Only aikāne…"

Pity welling up within her, Lehiwa left him and returned to the path. He really was lost. There was nothing she could do.

The warrior was sitting on a large rock farther down the stream, a yellow malo twisted around his hips. She still couldn't see his eyes. "It was very dangerous of you to wander off, little sister."

"Forgive me; I thought I heard a cry for help."

"You mustn't listen to the 'uhane that wander along these parts. They are dangerous."

"How do I know that you are not an 'uhane?"

"I did not try to lure you deep into the unknown with the ghostly wails of the damned." He laughed. "Come, I will take you across the stream where my family resides. You can rest your head for the night."

Lehiwa suppressed a yawn. She was tired; she couldn't lie about that. She had to find a way to get away from him tactfully, as he might grab her if she refused.

"I would love nothing more than to sleep for the night," she said with a sweet smile, "but I'm afraid that I left my gourd when I went to look for the 'uhane."

"We could come back for it tomorrow, when there's light out."

"This is a very special gourd. What if someone takes it before I can return? I would be devastated. I have to go back now; I'll come right back."

"Go fetch your gourd," he snapped. "But obey my words and do not trust the spirits you may hear. They are only trying to trick you. I will wait for you here."

She nodded and walked back toward the forest, glancing over her shoulder. Still he hadn't moved.

The salty smell of sea spray lingered about the trees, a scent that clung to her brother's skin no matter how long he stayed away from the ocean. His heavy, burdened footsteps thundered about the ground. He flickered into sight, running frantically through the forest, his spear clutched tightly in his fist.

"Kekua," Lehiwa whispered, hesitant to yell. She couldn't catch up to him; he was far too fast. And if she yelled, she might attract more dangerous spirits.

"Kekua!" she whispered again, chasing. He glimpsed her and slowed; she could almost keep pace with him.

"I am only kāne," he said, voice hollow. "That is all I am." The words were heavy, leaving sadness around them. He stopped and sat on the ground, his brow furrowed and his eyes wide. Lehiwa ran to him.

"You are so much more than just a man. Don't you remember?"

"So many pathways twisting into so many different directions. All leading everywhere, anywhere, nowhere. I can't choose. I can't choose..." Kekua's words broke into mumbles. Then, "Aikāne..."

"You mean Manu," said Lehiwa. "He's more than your aikāne. Which path is Manu on?"

Kekua stared down a trail. "There," he murmured, suddenly aware. "Manu. Manu! I have to get him. But..." He glanced down at his little sister as if noticing her for the first time. "You need my help. I can't leave you and Pinea."

"Don't worry about us," Lehiwa said. "You've done all you can against the moʻo...Find Manu and wait at the top of the trail."

"You have to return by sunrise," Kekua said. "This place is different during the day. Those who can't regain their name are stuck. You can only enter and exit at night."

Lehiwa nodded. "Go." Her brother turned and ran down the path.

It wasn't long before whispers settled into the forest. "She hasn't lost her name." The voice was frail, old, far away.

"She restored the boys." The voice was a woman's, just a stone's throw away.

"He will come after her next." The voice was a girl's, right beside her.

"Run. Run, child, before Hakau the name thief comes for you!" The voice echoed and tingled against her ear.

Cold sweat beaded Lehiwa's skin like fresh morning dew. Despite the warnings, Lehiwa did not run, she walked. Snapping branches rang throughout the forest, a large beast's rampage.

Not far from where she stood, the cracking stopped. The warrior's face appeared in one of the higher branches. His eyes were not only visible, but glowing: round and yellowish, lizard-like but shining like an owl's. It started to rain, making it hard for Lehiwa to look up at him.

"You should have just gone home, little sister," he hissed.

"I am not your sister."

"Then what am I to call you?"

Lehiwa stared up at him, taking deep breaths, trying to stay steady.

He chuckled. "Smart little child. Why have you ventured down to Hakau's abode so late at night?"

"You know why I am here, Hakau."

Lightning flashed, illuminating a large lizard twisted around the tree, its head exactly where the man's had been. Large, angry gashes covered its skin, still fresh from his encounter with Kekua. Then the forest was dark again.

"Curse the gods who have revealed my true nature!" Hakau cried. His thick tail slithered out of sight, trailing blood.

Lehiwa walked away, but the snapping branches followed close.

"You ought to turn around now, girl, before something terrible befalls you." His whisper lingered in her ear. She didn't reply. "Even if you were to find her, how could you possibly hope to save her? You, who are just a little girl lost in the night."

Lehiwa focused on putting one foot in front of the other, keeping her breath even. Hakau's words were her fears verbalized; they wounded her. Her knees shook with fear. All she wanted was to be with her siblings again.

Lehiwa took another deep breath, shuddering on the exhale, and she entered a meadow, a clearing. Her heart dropped. Pinea was curled up at the base of a great tree, beneath the light spray of rain. Lehiwa rushed forward, placing a hand on her shoulder. It was cold.

"Pinea," Lehiwa breathed.

"She has been lost for too long." Hakau's soft voice almost seemed mournful. He was right behind her. "She was an interesting soul."

"How can you pity her? You did this," Lehiwa spat.

Hakau shook his head. "She was free to leave. Did you forget? You can only come here if you're very, very lost."

A knot formed in the pit of Lehiwa's stomach. Pinea had been callous and cruel to her, pinching her and ignoring her. She had tried to understand what she might have done to deserve her sister's ire. Each time she confronted her, she was met with hurt.

Lehiwa stepped forward and kneeled to face Pinea. Gently, she brushed the soft, curly strands of hair away from her face.

"The first day you went missing," Lehiwa said, "I should have been worried. Or scared. But I didn't feel anything. I wasn't happy that you were gone; we have our memories, but I didn't miss you. I felt nothing."

Hakau's loud yawn sounded. Lehiwa glanced back; he was seated on a nearby stump, resting, uninterested.

When Lehiwa turned back to her sister, her eyes were open, but she stared vacantly ahead, unaware perhaps of Lehiwa's presence.

"Pinea."

"Am not Pinea..." she mumbled. "I am only wahine..."

"You are more than just a woman. Do you remember me at all?"

Pinea closed her eyes. Lehiwa shook her again, but Pinea did not stir.

Lehiwa's throat became tight as she continued to frantically shake Pinea. Large tears welled in her eyes and fell with the rain.

"Are you really so lost?" Lehiwa crumbled on top of her sister, holding her now, and wept. "I've found you, Pinea. Please, please come home."

"There is one way you could save your sister." Lehiwa straightened up at Hakau's words.

He was back to his human form, eyes large and brown.

"What do I have to do?"

"I can't free her. I am just strong enough to lift her binds if you take her place."

The thought shook her. Part of Lehiwa wanted to leave Pinea where she was.

She thought back, before all this, to images of playing in the surf, dancing hula, talking late into the night. A happiness burned. Her breath was slow. "I don't believe you."

"You'll damn her here? Leave, then. There's nothing more you can do."

"He's wrong, Pinea. Do not believe him. You came here because you were searching for something."

"Shut up!" Hakau screamed, and the forest trembled with lost souls. Men, women, and children of all types stared back at Lehiwa, wide-eyed, scared.

"All of you came here because you were lost," she said. "You are more than what Hakau says! You can leave!"

"No! The girl lies! Do not listen to her!" Hakau's roar ripped through the air, and beams of light shot through the forest, ricocheting off trees and rocks and launching upward. The forest lit with the bright souls fleeing the moʻo's hold, their wails sending Hakau to his knees.

Amid the flashing lights, Pinea sat up. She gazed upon the souls with wonder for a few moments before her eyes rested on Lehiwa.

"Lehiwa," she breathed, voice cracking.

Lehiwa stood as the forest returned bleak. Her sister held on to her, burying her head into her shoulder.

"I'm sorry we've grown apart," she said, eyes downcast. "I don't know why I'm like this."

"You're going to be ok," Lehiwa said, giving her sister a tight squeeze before stepping away. "Follow the path up. Kekua and Manu are waiting."

"Where are you going?" Pinea asked. "You can't stay. The sun is about to rise!"

"Trust me," Lehiwa said. "I'll be there."

Taking a deep breath, Pinea nodded. "Be safe, little sister."

Lehiwa watched to make sure Pinea did as she was told before heading off to the sound of the gurgling stream.

The great lizard was lying there again, water running over his scaly body. He tilted to face Lehiwa with a sneer. "Haven't you ridiculed me enough?"

The moʻo waited for her to speak. "Why did you steal my family away?"

Hakau managed a laugh. "It's my nature."

"I was afraid you would say that," Lehiwa said. She looked up at the sky. "The sun is about to rise."

"Then you had best be on your way."

"How long have you been here, Hakau? Can you even remember?" He stared into the water, saying nothing. "Perhaps one night you can leave and see the sunrise."

"Away with you," the moʻo hissed.

Lehiwa turned and continued on the path without trouble. The forest seemed quieter, peaceful. Manu, Kekua, and Pinea were waiting at the forest's edge, as promised, and together they walked, sun guiding them home.

THE LOOKOUT

[JOHN CHAMBERS]

Uʻilani clutches her swollen belly. "But why does it have to be us?"

Her husband, Mikala, peers through the curtain into the night. The darkness has soaked up the charge of the heavens. Even from here it tingles his skin.

Mikala takes a moment to respond, gathering his thoughts. Everything about Mikala is deliberate and measured, which earned him the respect of the village. His status weighed heavily during the choosing of the host.

In the distance, the flicker of torchlight. "They're coming."

He steps away from the window. Takes his wife's hands. His are rough, those of a fisherman, but to Uʻilani they are more comforting than the softest pillow.

"It's a great honor for us to be chosen," he says, not for the first time. "The alignment will bestow great blessings upon our child."

"Our child deserves a normal life, with parents who love him. Can't that be enough?"

Mikala pulls away from her. "He'll have a better than normal life."

"And what if he doesn't want that?" Uʻilani tugs at the plumeria pinned to her hair. "If I have to have a child, I want him to grow up to be a fisherman like his father. To climb the same mountains and dance in the same fields."

Mikala smiles. "He can still do those things, my love. When his duties permit. You've made your feelings on motherhood clear, but I promise this is for the best."

Uʻilani wishes she had been born under the sign of the Welo, boar, like her husband. Maybe then she would share his resolve. Instead, she is an Ikiiki, artist, prone to anxieties.

A knock at the door. Mikala opens it.

"It's time," the kahuna says.

With great effort, Uʻilani stands. She inhales deeply and attempts to swallow her dread. She nods and follows the kahuna outside. The night is like any other. She takes no notice of the wind whipping at her pāʻū or of the electric atmosphere. She resists looking toward the heavens, afraid of what she'd see.

A palatial carriage made from bamboo and woven with fronds and flowers sits on the grass, stout men with work-hardened muscles standing at the ready. Uʻilani gazes at them a moment, the stiff breeze thrashing her hair. She blinks and walks past them. Mikala is about to speak before he seems to think better of it. He motions to the men to follow behind them with the carriage.

But the kahuna cannot help himself. "Please i wae ʻia, the way is long, and the ground treacherous."

"I have walked this path since before I was old enough to speak. It is my right to carry myself in the manner I choose. You will not deny me this."

The kahuna acquiesces, and they proceed up the trodden path. Uʻilani's bare feet go unbothered by the occasional lava rock, her soles thick and calloused from two decades of daily exposure.

Her friend Kailani is there to meet them at the trailhead to the lookout. She spreads her arms and embraces Uʻilani, who returns the hug with a blank expression. "I'm so excited for you," Kailani says.

Uʻilani sighs deeply and fakes a smile.

"You made the right choice. You'll see. And not just because of who your child will become. Being a mother is more rewarding than anything. You'll understand soon enough."

"That's what everyone keeps telling me."

They continue up the narrow trail as it twists and weaves through the jungle, cutting a path through the mountains, the occasional torch lighting their way. They reach the lookout and find the rest of the villagers already gathered. Uʻilani spies the raised stone slab near the edge of the cliff. The wind is even stronger here, and she treads carefully to keep her balance.

The kahuna directs her to lie down on the slab while he prepares a tincture of herbs. Mikala and Kailani each hold one of Uʻilani's hands. For the first time, she gazes up at the starry firmament. The sky that once filled her with wonder now seems cold and merciless. Is it a comfort or a curse to know something else oversees your destiny?

The kahuna lifts Uʻilani's head and brings a coconut shell to her lips. Uʻilani slurps down the bitter concoction. When the shell is dry, the kahuna sets it aside and addresses the crowd. "My friends, we are gathered here to witness…"

Uʻilani tunes out the rest of his words, focusing on a tiny pinprick of light, and tries to steady herself. Eventually her nerves calm, either by potion or meditation.

"Something's wrong." Her husband's voice sounds distant and hollow.

The kahuna frowns. "The herbs are taking longer than they should."

"Great Kahuna, the stars are shifting," Kailani says. "The alignment will not—"

"I know, girl," the kahuna says. "Mikala, bring me a machete. Hurry!"

Mikala nods and runs off.

"What's happening?" Uʻilani asks. "Is something wrong with my baby?"

As the kahuna finishes rubbing a new compound on her belly, Mikala returns. Her abdomen goes numb. The kahuna takes the blade from Mikala. "Hold her."

Mikala and Kailani do as instructed. The kahuna glances nervously at the sky, then slices into Uʻilani. The machete cuts her flesh, but she feels nothing.

"The window is passing!" Kailani cries.

"Cut faster," Mikala pleads.

"Almost there…"

Uʻilani lifts her head to see the child emerge. She sobs with relief. It is a beautiful, healthy—

The ground trembles beneath them. The great stone bucks and cracks, tossing her into the night. The wind carries her several feet before dumping her to the ground. A fiery pain blasts through her body. She is surrounded by shrieking and wailing but she can't make out speech over the roar of earth and sky.

She manages to pull herself to her feet, clutching her midsection, arms soaked with blood. Where is her baby? Her head thrusts left and right.

Her eyes land on the kahuna, still holding her son, but the child is unnaturally bright, glowing. The kahuna looks to have captured a star, except instead of twinkling white it pulsates an angry red. Barbed wings tear from the baby's shimmering flesh. He opens his maw, revealing rows of jagged teeth surrounding a pit of infinite darkness. The kahuna screams as his soul is sucked from his body. His flesh sack drops to the ground, but the child stays hovering in midair.

"Hurry my love, we must leave!" Mikala cries.

Uʻilani pushes him off. "I'm not leaving without my baby."

"I'm sorry," he cries. "I'm sorry. This wasn't supposed to happen."

As her monster child soars over the terrified villagers, cutting off their escape, she laughs. He opens his mouth, releasing a torrent of black flames that engulf half the crowd, reducing them to burning cinders. Kailani tries to rush past their charred remains but is cut down by a bolt of crimson lightning. The rest of the panicked villagers are herded against the cliff's edge. Uʻilani watches passively.

The creature takes position next to his mother. Still hunched over, she looks up, greeting her offspring for the first time with a warm smile.

Mikala says, "Uʻilani, my love, please help us."

She cocks her head. "I am helping, dearest one." She grimaces, drops to her knees. "I'm letting our son be what he was meant to be, like you wanted."

The child unleashes another round of flames, forcing the remaining villagers over the edge. Uʻilani holds her husband's gaze; he plunges to his death.

At last, wind and earth go silent. Uʻilani looks to her son. "Come, my beautiful baby boy. You have a destiny to fulfill."

THE LAST CHIEFTAIN OF MOLOKA'I

[GREG PATRICK]

The affliction, the leprosy, ate away slowly and inexorably. For one accustomed to the fury of wading into battle and striking down two warriors at a time with one sweep of the koa club, the wasting of my body was terrible to endure. It was a day black with ashen skies in the aftermath of an eruption when I could no longer wield my club. First gaunt, then emaciated.

To be slain in battle would have been honorable, redeemable in the eyes of gods and mortals. I think back on my exploits. I remember when I cast off from shore to defend my chieftain's honor. I arrived from the dolphin-escorted wake of my outrigger canoe and stood at the coral atoll, a dark shrine of volcanic rock enduring a tense interval of tides. This site was where interisland rivals fought under scavenging birds, before the submerging tides roared over final groans and battle cries.

Our rival's sail flew, a crimson banner against the cerulean sky. I awaited, waves lapping at my soles. Sharks sensing death sailed with him and trailed the wake of the canoe, heralded by a conch horn's sonorous brays. The sail drew ever nearer. Tattoos and adornments boasted of accomplishments in hunt and battle.

I cupped sand into my palms to enhance my grip, allowing the dark grains to sieve through my fingers. Below me, through the stirred waters, the crab-picked bones of our predecessors littered the blood-red coral. My rage a force of nature like those that consumed ships and men, baring my teeth and brandishing my club.

I confronted the warrior under the punishing sun with a stroke of the shark-toothed club. I eviscerated him, into the sea. Blood wept down my face like warpaint. He looked up at me submerged, crimson trail bubbling up as he sunk. The sharks were insatiable.

Water rose to my shanks, sharks still ravenous, impatient. One reared at me and fell just short. It lacerated itself as it thrashed back to the water. The others turned on the wounded shark as a consolation. It writhed in its final throes as it was devoured alive in the explosion of red I stood in. It met my eye, jaws gaping, baring its teeth futilely.

I lingered there, chest heaving, then slumped into the canoe before the waters rose high enough to envelope me. I did not trouble with the paddles, allowing the currents to bear me away. I closed my eyes into the sensation of floating in ghostly passage. Like a dark music, the eternal sigh of the waves swept my soul. I passed over the sunken whaling ships, their torn sails swaying in the tides.

Above me a myriad of stars, the aerial charts by which the great mariners navigated. I recognized the beckoning constellations and the fragrance of flowers calling me back to the island. Torches lined the shore. Drums throbbed. I was expected.

I waded ashore triumphant, steeling myself to stride rather than stagger to them. The chief's daughter draped my neck with a lei, the dark spell of her eyes sweeping over me like a wave smiting the night shore. I knew again the intoxication of basking in them. I felt invincible, then immortal, and for that arrogance perhaps the gods sought to humble and punish me. Later a cut from an enemy crossed my guard in battle, and I felt no pain. I knew the affliction had me. In a terrible rage I lashed out, and his head flew free of his torso. My world spun.

When she knew and recoiled, that was my death. I lingered on in body only. The revulsion in her eyes scathed me more than any wound had.

My spirit was crushed and left me. I am a corpse warrior now.

I sought isolation in forbidden places where none ventured. Heights of cliffs overlooking the crushing brink of sea and the depths of remote coral reefs. In exile from the tribe that once hailed me.

I remember when the tiki idols were vandalized and defiled by the missionary's decree. I had felt the axe blows on them, a phantom pain. My eyes smoldered by the torches and the blood-chant of my heart. The splintering throws echoed into the dark forest as I ran.

I implored the gods, seeking them in the windswept heights of dormant volcano craters, towering above the clouds and in the depths of spirit-haunted woods.

Yet my cry merely fell in the void. And the cold, dark fathoms of the sea could not equal my sinking despair.

When I stood at the crushing brink at a remote island within sight of shore, jagged coral bit into the soles of my feet creating tide-pools of my blood. I waited, offering myself to the rising tide.

Dark shapes, attracted by the aroma of blood, circled me. I closed my eyes, arms spread wide, welcoming the waves and unrelenting will of the gods. I chanted the sacred songs. A masted ship approached and hailed me, a missionary ship from across the horizon.

They "rescued" me, and my affliction claimed them on our voyage.

And I stood looking out at the red horizon defiantly as I stared down enemies across the dark ground of battle. The sunset a reopened wound reflecting into the sea. Eerie cloud formations, the art of a mad god, reveled across the skyline of vog-enshrouded mountains.

My grim face was lit by volcanic eruption. The seas behind me steamed at the red veins of lava flowing in, and a sinister plume of smoke rose. I closed my eyes to escape into the realm of dream. I envisioned her next to me, eloping into the dark horizon. It was kapu yet, under the spell of eyes whose fires rivaled Pele's.

I caressed ash from her sweep of raven hair like an endearment whispered to the night.

My eyes opened, and the cry of present seemed disembodied. It had felt so real. I stood at the helm of the derelict ship looking back at the island beyond the biolumined wake, a sultry gust sweeping a lament that swayed the palms.

One last horizon over the silvery, white-crested waves.

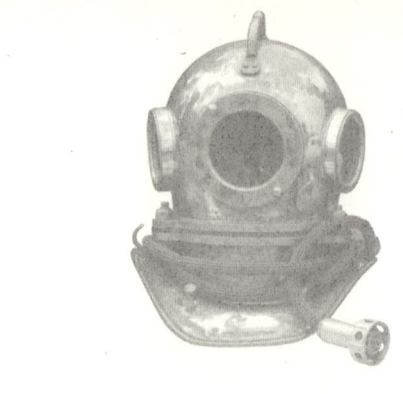

BLUES OF EU

[Sam Fletcher]

Howard Kriley knew already how heavy the gear was. His only glimpse outside was a small, grated window, like that of a jail cell. It wasn't so different, actually; he'd die inside if his mates didn't unlock him. He knew how cold the water was, how dark it could be past fifty fathoms. What surprised him was how good it felt.

He walked in line with the other hard hats, distantly leashed to the compressor, hearing the loud, annoying, perpetual whir keeping him alive—more than alive. He felt tranquil, comfortable. Like he was supposed to be down here, like he wasn't supposed to go back.

The water was oily, shimmering murk. One-hundred and forty-three feet of iron and steel lay before him, 340 tons that sunk quick enough. But it was the slow trickle of water that turned the F-4 submarine to a coffin, consuming twenty-one sailors over several desperate days. It must have been a painful wait, knowing of the ships on the surface and their blissfully unaware crews, without a sliver of daylight to pacify them in their fleeting hours. They must have been rationing supplies in the small hope that they would not starve, and that there was any possibility of rescue. Who knew what got to them first—the stale air's turn to carbonic acid, or simply water crashing

Image © Aliaksandr Klapkou | Dreamstime.com

in? The thought didn't scare Kriley anymore; he couldn't hear their screams over his whirring helmet.

The vessel lay at the base of a steep underwater mountain. The plan, as soon as they could, was to tow it to shallower waters if not the surface. Navy Divers waddled along the shell, brushing it with rubber fingertips. The sharp, silver lines of the submarine waved with the current. Kriley blinked rapidly, trying to keep his crew from multiplying. It was hard to focus on anything down here, let alone slabs of metal a grappling hook might catch. The first time setting boots this deep, today was mostly testing gear.

He stomped the ocean floor, and a patch of garden eels retracted into the pearly sand. Solid blue surrounded him, pulling it to dunes, miniature sandstorms far as sight. He locked onto a white stone wavy as all else. He didn't have time for souvenirs, but it must have been as valuable as a moon rock.

It was April 1915, a month since the F-4 sank, and the sea had already claimed her. Fish had been exploring here while the NDs couldn't; coral had been sprouting closer and closer in. A splotched, green eel folded itself beneath the light hull. Parrot and triggerfish meandered about; striped tangs kissed submarine walls up and down.

Colors down here were limited, but they were vibrant and pulsing. The slightest movement, real or imagined, pulled Kriley's attention all over the wreckage. In his corner sight, something emerged, odder than all else, a person—not an ND, not in a hard hat, not ballooned up with air, but... a free-diver. A *woman*. He jerked his neck to see, vision blacked out in the space between the front and side windows of his helmet. He squinted out the smaller window, and she disappeared with the shimmer of a flickering tail. It was gray, black tips, like that of any reef shark. A blur and then gone.

His heart drummed his ears through the whir. Was it really a shark? A dolphin? Wide eyes seared through the blue, glomming onto any hint of movement. Where did she go, and why? Great shadows lurked in the distance, swimming in circles, back and forth.

But—Kriley knew none would believe him—she was a human. Even as the tail flicked, it seemed less like any ocean dweller and more like two tied legs, as foreign to this depth as he.

He couldn't discern Chief ND Wilbur's staticky words in the shabby communicator, but he knew it meant it was time to ascend. Kriley hobbled his way back with the others, who waited their turn grabbing hold of the thick mooring line and pulling themselves up.

Wilbur continued to bark about nothing Kriley could pay attention to. As buoyant as they were, it didn't take much strength to rise. But Kriley made up for it when he set first boot onto the ship ladder, taking the suit's 200 pounds of copper as he broke through the surface of the water. Each step was more difficult than the last, and he suppressed grunts, heaving onto the stern. Crew walked him to the bench and unscrewed his helmet.

The daylight stung; Kriley's head pulsed. But as he shed the fifty-five-pound hat and eighty-five-pound weight belt, he realized it wasn't the gear making him feel so terrible. It was the surface; it was the sobriety.

After debrief and showers many NDs met in the mess hall in their civvies for chicken soup, biscuits, and canned green beans. Dry clothes and warm food can bring anybody to a new state of mind, but most the team seemed like they just woke up from a nightmare. "Just knowing it could be months before we lift the thing, before we get anybody out," said Deeth. "Months of work beside a pile of bodies."

"Haunting, seeing her that close," came Wells, cheeks rounded by dry bread. "A hulk of a thing."

"The first to sink ever, right?" Deeth asked.

"Not conquered by anything," Wells said. "Not punctured by some German battleship. They were just doing routine training."

"I heard the iron sides hit some rock, and the crew died when the water rushed in."

"I didn't see any crump-hole. At that depth the pressure could have crushed her."

"Let's hope," said Lunger. "Drowning's a better death than suffocation. They could have run out of air, you know? I heard water got into the battery compartment."

"No one knows how," Wells said. "The sea took her like nothing. No dignity. Those sailors thought they'd be back by lunch." He swallowed his food. "We weren't alone down there, did you notice? Something big was close by, circling."

The F-4 arrived to Hawaiʻi in August of 1914. Seven months later, mysteriously she became the first Navy submarine to sink. Service learning mentioned the mana folks felt setting foot on the archipelago. Something was strange about this wreck; they all must have sensed it.

"Anybody feel drunk?" asked Lunger. Everyone on the long table nodded. "What was that?"

"It's the nitrogen," said Deeth. "At depth, such high pressure, we must have been down there too long."

"I still feel loopy," Lunger said. Tile lines waned by Kriley's feet. He did too. "We need to look again at the deco tables before we go out there. They might not be right. You alright? You haven't said much, Howard." Kriley looked up from the floor, blinking dramatically. "You feel alright?" Lunger asked him.

"I—saw a mermaid," Kriley said, "I think."

A few divers were able to crack smiles, some audibly. Lunger remained serious, solemn even. "This a gas? You didn't, Howard."

"I need to go back down there. I need to find her."

The statement got him admitted to the medical center. The Naval doctor checked his heart rate, his tonsils, and ultimately gave him water and told him to rest. Kriley didn't feel ill anymore, though, nor dizzy. He just wanted back down.

Thomas Wilbur entered the narrow, white room while he was still sitting on butcher paper. "How is he?" Of course he was still on base, Kriley thought. The man never went home.

"Pumped with nitrogen," the doctor said. "He'll be alright."

"Chief," Kriley nodded, "what are you doing here?" Thomas Wilbur was the only one on the team who wasn't shipped here for this salvage. Rumor was his wife Genevieve disappeared off a vessel one night a couple years ago, body never found. He'd been pretty focused on work here since.

"Team told me you were pretty shaken. Everybody was."

The doctor looked down at his clipboard and stepped into the hallway. Kriley shook his head. "When are we going back?"

"A week at least. Stillson's going to tamper with air mixture to lengthen the dive time. We learned a lot today." He pulled a pack of Camels out and offered one to Kriley.

The ND shook his head, so Wilbur shrugged, put one between his lips, stowed the pack, and lit it with a match. "I need to go back in tomorrow," Kriley said. "Chief, you won't believe me, but a woman was down there. We can do it after duties tomorrow, if you'll take me."

Wilbur smiled. "Lunger mentioned something about that," he said, filling the room with his exhale. "He talked a lot about how dizzy everyone was. We have a lot to figure out, diving at that depth. Everyone reported the same conditions—it's going to be difficult to make any progress until we improve them."

Kriley's head kept shaking. "How long have you been on the island?"

"Six years."

"No family on the mainland, right?"

"No family anymore."

"The longer I'm down there, the better chance we have in retrieving those men. The whole team is still on the mainland with their wives and kids. They get out of the water and think about their other life. Me, I'm like you. I'm here. I have this."

Wilbur's nod was slow. "We'd have to fit all the equipment on the patrol boat. I'll be done by 1600 tomorrow anyway. That's when we'll have to leave port to be surface level by sundown. You're aware of the risks, and we follow Stillson's tables exactly. I'm not going to stop you from volunteering, Howard."

"Yessir. Thank you."

With only two of them, Kriley had to don his gear while the ship was moored, before they left Pearl Harbor. He bent over the bench, and Wilbur tied the laces on the back of his legs to keep air from getting in. The chief lifted the breastplate over Kriley's head and threaded it on. Next he tightened the perimeter of nuts, locking it onto the canvas. Kriley stood and shimmied his feet into the lead boots. The weight belt came after.

It was a hot hour out even with the high winds, and Kriley was anchored to the bench the full time. Passing the coastline's fancy hotels, shallow waters splashing with surf-riders, they headed toward Diamond Head. Three miles from shore, where all of that became a memory, Wilbur tied onto the mooring ball.

Kriley kept his chin tucked as his chief came over and quarter-turned the metal helmet onto his breastplate, tethering him to the compressor by his umbilical. He stood, shuffled his way to the stern while Wilbur plopped the ladder down.

"Deco limit is ten minutes at depth," Wilbur shouted through the thick helmet walls. Kriley gave an exaggerated nod, and Wilbur tapped the dome twice while the whirring started. His next words came from the communicator. *Go find your mermaid.*

One leg out, Kriley took a large stride into the ocean. Suddenly his world opened as he plunged through this doorway to new colors, creatures, and rules. He ignored the ladder entirely, instead grabbing hold of the mooring line and shuffling down as if it were a fire pole. The water was colder today and darker with each fathom passed.

He looked out around him, not called to the graveyard below. Squinting, he could already make out dark shapes moving on the horizon. It couldn't be the narcosis—he hadn't even reached depth yet.

The deeper he went, the more it felt like he was attached to some craft floating out into the abyss of space. When he set boot on sand, he did his best not to kick any up, but the patch of eels vanished anyway.

He glared about the murk, waiting for one of these shadows to show itself again. When it did, he followed it with his gaze. Back, forth. Back, forth. Gone, back. Gone, back. He couldn't count the shapes, couldn't tell if it were one or several.

His world started bending again. Finally, one of these shape's fringes solidified as it moved in. It was smaller. With each meter this blob took crisper shape and color. The stupor had to have been kicking strong; Kriley felt no fear whatsoever as whatever it was came to investigate him.

Slimmer and slimmer the shadow became, until Kriley could make out a head and a body. He knew what it was before he'd be able to testify. This was no fish—a diver. Long, thick hair spread through the water, and she emerged finally, a woman. A mermaid.

She moved with gentle expertise, gliding her way up to Kriley's window. Soft features, tan skin, wide nose, and the deepest auburn eyes Kriley had ever seen. His heart was beating so hard looking at her he listened for its clank against his breastplate.

Lines of her musculature became curves, all directing the eyes to a fishtail starting at her hips. Though covered in gray placoid scales, it blended with her human skin in both color and texture. Her tail fin was vertical, like that of a shark, the tips of them looking like they had been dipped in ink. Similar fins rose from her forearms, too. She was magnificent.

And she just floated there, staring deeply back into his window, perhaps looking too for the color of his eyes. She brushed the canvas on his arms with tame hands, then moved up to the cold copper of his helmet, and Kriley realized she must have been just as mystified by his presence as he was of hers. No man had ever set foot this deep. There was a chance he was the first she'd ever seen. The two couldn't draw back their stare even for a second, both myths to the other.

Kriley had forgotten completely of the submarine next to him, about the large figures circling about it. He thought only of her, saw nothing but her face. Holding onto her hand, he tried not to blink, not to breathe, not to interrupt a single moment of it.

Wilbur's static wasn't so kind. Kriley sighed, then broke gaze back to the mooring line. He had to go.

As he took small, backward steps toward it, the mermaid remained just as close, staring still with those large eyes, not letting go of her curiosity for a moment. It took everything Kriley had to drop her hand in place of the rope.

But she wouldn't let him. She grabbed hold of his free hand, gripping it tightly. He rubbed back with his rubber thumb, but he knew he had no choice. For each minute he spent down here now, the more likely he'd never make it back.

He started pulling himself up, forcing her to let go. But her hand was still outstretched toward him, in case he might change his mind. Her haunting eyes remained too as he lifted himself, as did a crippling sadness.

The farther he rose, the worse he felt, as if he were watching a lover tied to train tracks. He broke surface with a pulsing head, and the whole experience felt hazy, dreamy—he knew it was real, but how could it be?

Wilbur grunted as he helped Kriley up the ladder, sat him down and heaved the helmet off his head. Kriley didn't say a word, just kept staring out at the rippling surface.

"You ok?" Chief asked. "You look like you saw a ghost."

Not a ghost, a mermaid, Kriley told him. He didn't tell him that he wasn't haunted—he was heartbroken.

Wilbur couldn't have believed Kriley's stories in the slightest. But he met him at the shipyard the next day, 1600. He never balked at the mission, never made fun of his ramblings. It must have been a good couple hours' break from the job. Perhaps the first in years. It must have been nice to spend it with, over a subordinate, a buddy.

He did play along, though. Wilbur asked Kriley how he knew the mermaid would show up. Kriley didn't know how, he told him, but he knew.

And she appeared right away, before his boots touched sand, as if she had been waiting. Kriley danced about with her, not minding the coral, sea cucumbers, and eels at his feet, and she danced too—easy with waves as anyone on land.

Her skin seemed a bit paler today, her hair a tad shorter. Yesterday's memories were faint, though. She seemed happy, anyway.

He had so much to say to her, if only they could talk. Where did she come from? Were there others like her? How did she grow up? How did she find him? If she could speak, would he be able to understand her? Unlikely.

And so, they read each other's cheekbones, dimples, freckles, wrinkles, and peach fuzz. It didn't answer specifics, but it told a lot about expression, a lot about how they felt presently. Her eyes were wide, blinks were slow. She was here, with him. Neither wanted to be elsewhere.

And then came Wilbur's command, and grabbing the line was no less painful today. She held onto his glove just the same, wishing, begging for him to stay.

Halfway up the rope, they broke contact but not gaze, and she fell back down. When she was half-buried in the submarine's exhaust, Kriley wondered why she couldn't have come with him. It was as if he wasn't the only one limited by umbilical. She seemed just as tethered to something there, at depth. Her time somehow just as limited.

When he saw her next, her scales had climbed a bit up her torso. Her fins seemed longer, stronger, and those black tips cried down into the gray. Her breath fogged up his window. To Kriley, she looked more beautiful than ever.

He couldn't tell if the distant figures had been moving closer, but he could almost discern what they were. If not great sharks, whales undoubtedly.

He felt something in her grace, the looseness of which she moved about. She loved the sea as much as he did. Of course, she spent her whole life in it, but this energy meant pleasure. She didn't have to take so much joy in this environment, as he did. It's how he found himself in the Navy in the first place.

But her infatuation in him, he thought, implied something more. Some version of herself. He couldn't quite pin it down.

He didn't have to fight her off this time. When the static from the surface vibrated Kriley's helmet, she grabbed onto both of his sleeves and kissed his window with big, full lips. Kriley forgot to breathe, forgot to blink. It took all he had to not rip his helmet off then and there.

Wilbur's commands kept coming. That's right; he couldn't. This suit was jail, and this was no more than visitation divided by glass.

Kriley didn't sleep that night. Large, brown eyes drifted farther and farther into the murk of his mind. With each image came turning, writhing, and each twist rocked his frail metal bed frame.

Deeth, aligned with the wall over, clenched his pillow tight around his ears. Kriley must have been driving him insane, mumbling about mythical creatures through the night. He probably thought the sea had consumed his mind. The more time Kriley spent down there, the less time he spent with his mates, the less he spoke of anything but this woman.

But he had just discovered a mermaid, a real one, and she was in love with him. To not devote his life to that would be crazy, he thought. Crazy that his mates weren't doing it too.

He woke with a heavy face and dark rings around his eyes, throwing on his uniform as groggy as usual. Deeth proceeded with about the same speed. No one complained; mornings normally felt like this.

The men gathered in the dive detachment warehouse. Chief Gunner George Stillson stood among scattered parts from disassembled Mark IVs. Umbilical coils and service equipment added to the pile. The techs had been up early, it seemed, or late last night.

Stillson wore his service dress, a bit more formal than the rest of them. He spoke the way he dressed, with authority and seriousness. He'd lowered the nitrogen levels in the air mix a few points, he said, but the divers couldn't be beyond 300 feet a second over twelve minutes. That meant they didn't have time to go up the rope single file. They'd dive two men at a time to observe a precise slab of submarine before reporting back to the next pair of divers at the surface. Smooth as a relay race. Still, they were looking for areas on the F-4 a hook might snag, and it required diligent observation—if there were no great areas, Stillson would design clamps custom to its exposed parts.

Wilbur caught word with Kriley as the rest of the NDs divided into pairs and met with the chief gunner to split submarine jurisdictions. "That means we're off for tonight," he said.

"Hm?" Kriley was half paying attention, as he had been since he left the water.

"Stillson said no more recreational diving. Next week is our team test. The more nitrogen you take at depth, the less likely you'll be able to go. Don't forget why you're here, Howard."

"I could have that whole submarine surveyed by next week."

Wilbur shook his head. "Damn it, Howard, it's not safe."

Kriley's eyes were sore. They stung and watered from lack of sleep, from saltwater. There was no façade, no shame, no ego anymore. There was the sea only. "Let me go one last time."

Wilbur sighed, and his face sunk. Stillson was calling for the both of them. "There's really a mermaid down there, huh?"

Kriley focused on keeping a firm chin. He nodded.

"1600. Say goodbye to her."

On the stern, through his helmet window, Kriley looked down at the ruffled portal to the other side, the 300 feet of space separating her from him. It was clear. If he tried, he could already see silhouettes circling about the wreckage.

He let his weight do most of the work on the way down, hardly using the rope as a break line. He hung onto it today only so the current wouldn't take him. His quickest descent yet.

On the seafloor, he did a 360-degree patrol for his love. As always, a distant figure came closer and closer. Kriley squinted at the shadow focusing in through the murk. The hulking mass didn't appear less intimidating as it approached. Finally, the diver could make out what it was. Not a whale—a shark indeed, a gargantuan seven meters at least, a submarine itself coming right toward him. But it had never been a silhouette. Girth and shape in all cases indicated a white shark, but there was nothing white about it. The beast emerged as one solid color, the same shadowy appearance it held from afar, black as the deepest crevices on the planet.

He strained his neck to keep eyes on it as it swam overhead, feeling the dense wind of its tail. A second shark wasn't far, meandering through, circling back, not shy today. Kriley became stressed, impatient, as the minutes counted. Where was she?

Behind the oceanic ogres, finally she emerged. Slowly the girl found her way to her diver. When Kriley saw his mermaid, the great black sharks dropped from his memory.

She looked even stranger today. Her skin was now gray, blending completely with her tail. Her hair had vanished, replaced with skin smooth and scaly as the rest of her. The fins on her arms had grown and sharpened, and the color black climbed halfway up her tail and her arms and was starting on her head.

Kriley wrapped her in his arms and squeezed her as tight as he could. Her heartbeat mixed with his; through the thick canvas he could feel it. He shifted his arms around her back, which now had a prominent, half-black dorsal fin.

She pulled back only enough to look into his eyes. Her auburn had left in place of a dark, almost black, blue. Her soft smile slightly sunk, attention for the first time pulled elsewhere. Something was happening; she was trying to tell him. She opened her mouth to speak, and Kriley tilted his ear in, knowing it would be useless against the whir and walls separating them. Perhaps he could read her lips.

"Mo—"

Chief Wilbur's barking overlapped. *No*, Kriley thought. It can't be time already.

"Mo-oh—"

A word in her native tongue, perhaps. What could it mean? *I love you?*

"Mo-oh-ah—"

Minute eleven. Kriley's eyes welled with tears. The dark behemoths paced back and forth around them. He couldn't leave. He couldn't leave her with them.

Something donned on him looking at her scaly body, the way her curves caved from woman to fish, that when he was to return, she may not resemble a woman at all. A shark may completely take her place. Just like the F-4, just like himself, the sea had been claiming her too. Perhaps her love wasn't stemming from curiosity, from wonder, but from longing. From some desperate grasp to a fleeting humanity.

She never felt so different from any woman he would meet on land, any of these locals, surf-riding, fishing, sunbathing. Things were changing fast here, had been for a long time. If the sea is no longer fed sacrifices, perhaps she takes them. Perhaps this woman wasn't a mermaid at all. Not so different from Genevieve Wilbur, a sacrifice.

Minute twelve. The submarine lay still as ever. There was nothing he could do for those men. They were gone. The sea had already taken them. The woman blinked, eyes shimmering with the low levels of daylight that made it down here. Her, he could still help. Or at least he could be with her.

Minute thirteen. *Shut it, Chief.* What was he going to do, cut off his air supply? She looked between Kriley and the rope. She knew it was time too. She didn't let go of him. She wouldn't. God, he wished he could be with her. He'd sacrifice anything.

Fourteen. There was nothing up there for Kriley. Nothing at all beyond her. Nothing beyond the sea. The lines of her body waved with the current's pull. He would stay down here with her. Forever, if that's what it took. *Please.*

Her focus seemed pulled too. The sharks closed in with each circle. As long as she didn't let go, he wouldn't.

And she didn't let go. But as the sharks began retreating to the shadowy horizon, she went along as if she were yanked. What they would do to her if she didn't come, he had no idea, but Kriley was determined to stop it. He let the woman drag him across the ocean floor until his umbilical was pulled tight.

Minute twenty-five. Wilbur's cries were music now; the colors before him danced to it. She kept her grasp, but Kriley could go no farther. The deeper the sharks disappeared into the black, the harder she pulled.

Kriley's lifeline was bound to snap. His air supply would cut, and he would drown. Right now, stretched between the ship and his lover, nothing broke his euphoria. He prayed this moment would go on forever.

Through his side window he looked again at the F-4 and the twenty-one dead sailors within. Tangs were still kissing the metal. Peck, peck, peck. An article in his newspaper in West Virginia after she sank said those fish flashing by portholes must have been fatal reminders to the dying sailors that there was free life thriving down here, out in the open. Kriley looked forward, at the girl's smooth, ink-dipped face. Similar feeling.

As she pulled, he tapped the bastard nut on his breastplate, the lock keeping his helmet fastened. With rubber fingers he mimicked the motion of loosening it. It took both her arms, but she did it without hesitation.

Kriley took a final blissful gasp, and the depth's pressure smacked him. His suit rushed with water as he lifted the helmet off, icy crispness making him feel alive. Beyond alive, he'd never felt better. As if he could live down here, breathe in water just fine, just as she could, if he decided so. He didn't care if these were delusions, didn't care that he had but minutes left.

The helmet dropped to the sea floor. He was exposed fully now, and the woman let go of him; the sharks stopped too before reaching the darkest waters. In the center of the formidable black before them, two eyes emerged, blue as the woman's but bigger than the sharks' whole bodies.

This wasn't darkness at all. This was a thing, a being.

Straining, Kriley could make out the edges of its Goliath shape, two arms thicker than anything man could possibly sink, a dorsal fin rising like any mountain peak. *God*, he thought, the only word that came to mind.

The woman coiled into his torso, cradled by his every human muscle before they would turn cold, then raw, then flake off into the sea. With a final jolt of lucidity Kriley grabbed tight onto her hand, understanding everything. The sea had not taken Genevieve

Wilbur, nor those twenty-one sailors. She had not taken the woman in his arms, and she would not take him either. His soul bowed to the unending entity before him. There was no sea, never had been. There was *Moʻoaliʻi*.

△▽△▽△

PUOWAINA

[alan brennert]

Here's a story I've never told before, in all my long years—maybe I've been afraid to, afraid no one would believe. No, it's not about the Marchers of the Night (though I did see them once, at Ka'ena Point, and ran like the wind before they could abduct me into their spirit ranks). It happened a long time ago—back when I was just a skinny little Hawaiian girl, ten years old (yes, I was skinny back then! My sisters used to joke that "even poi won't stick to Nani's ribs," and it was true). America had entered the First World War the year before, and the sleepy little Honolulu of my childhood suddenly woke up one day as a bustling seaport. Anchored in the harbor were the dreadnoughts of many navies—American, British, Japanese, Australian—and the once-uncrowded streets were now filled with servicemen on the prowl for bathtub gin and bedroom eyes. My mama volunteered on the ladies' food-conservation committee, and as a good Victory Girl I gave up my weekly nickel to see the movies and pledged it to the war effort; but my parents had only daughters, no sons, so this was the closest the Great War came to knocking on our door.

We lived up on the furrowed slopes of Punchbowl Hill, in a big plantation-style house necklaced by a white picket fence, overlooking the green taro fields and glistening silver rice paddies of the Pauoa

Valley. Mama was Kānaka Maoli, pure-blood Hawaiian; Papa was a haole from St. Louis, Missouri, who'd come to Hawai'i as a young man and found success as an engineer for the Hawaiian Electric Company. When I think of my father, I think of fire: he had an Irishman's red hair and florid complexion. When I think of Mama, I think of cooled lava: her hair, black as the volcanic ash of the hill we lived on, was usually piled like stones atop her head, but sometimes tumbled in a rockslide down her back. My two sisters favored my father, with light complexions and russet manes; I was my mother's daughter, tawny skin and black hair, only worn shorter.

I was a bit of a tomboy, you see, and long hair got in the way when I'd scale the heights of Punchbowl's craggy ridges. All the neighborhood keiki climbed it, cutting our own trails that wound their way up to the five-hundred-foot summit. Sure, there was a road for cars to go up, but where was the fun in that? Leave that for the tourists and the soldiers on leave, come to take in the view. Back then, the view was just about all there was up there: the inside of the crater was a brown plain, sparsely decorated with lantana scrub, koa trees, the prickly panini cactus that flourished like a weed, and balloon plants, whose blossoms were round, hairy, and seemed to strike the neighborhood boys as hysterically amusing. But usually I'd go up alone—though I was never completely alone at the top. As I'd hike across the crater, I'd pass poor Hawaiian families squatting in sad little shacks and lean-tos, wives doing laundry in buckets as their children played with yappy little poi dogs. They might be stringing shell-and-seed leis for sale to tourists at the wharves, but otherwise had no jobs, nowhere else to live; when I could, I brought them fresh fruit from our garden.

On the southern rim of the crater there was a lookout, a tiny spur of land jutting like a raised eyebrow from Punchbowl's massive crown. I'd sit on the edge of the lookout and gaze down at the city spread out below me, dollhouses scattered amid orchards of toy trees. It was hard for me to imagine that thousands of years ago, rivers of fire had spilled down these slopes to the sea. I'd try to picture the molten lava boiling away the ocean, but the scene was just too peaceful from up here—from Punchbowl's equally placid volcanic sister, Diamond Head, on the left, to the slumbering mountains of the Waiʻanae Range on the right, and across the ocean to mysterious Molokaʻi wrapped in clouds on the horizon.

One day as I was sitting on the brow of the crater, I had a feeling—not a start or a fright, just a simple awareness—that there was someone standing behind me. I'd had this feeling a lot lately: I'd be alone in our backyard when I'd *know* that my sister Moani was standing in the doorway, and when I'd look up, there she was, asking me if I wanted to come and play jacks. Or I'd sense that my teacher was going to call on me to answer a question a split second before she did. It happened often enough that I was beginning to accept it as routine. I turned to see a man—Hawaiian, maybe twenty years old—standing behind me, wearing the drab, olive-colored uniform of the United States Army. He had a round, gentle face and smiling brown eyes. "Aloha," he called out to me.

I returned the greeting.

"Some view, eh?" he said as he approached. "Mind if I share?"

"Sure."

He sat down a few feet away and extended a hand, something most adults didn't bother to do with a little keiki. "John Kua. Friends call me Johnny."

I shook his hand, feeling very grown-up. "I'm Nani. MacGillvray."

"You know why I like this side of the crater best, Nani?"

"Why?"

"'Cause I can see the house I grew up in from here." He pointed into the middle distance, toward the crowded tenement neighborhoods of the Pālama district. "Right down there, on Cunha Lane. Little white-frame house sitting under a monkey pod tree."

I squinted into the distance. "I can't make it out."

"Eh, neither can I." He laughed. "But I know it's there." Despite his good humor, there was something sad in the way he said it.

I asked, "You just get home from the war?"

He shook his head. "No, I'm stationed here on Oʻahu. Schofield Barracks."

"How long you been in the Army?"

"Oh, I joined up even before we declared war. Saw the writing on the wall, figured we were going to get into it eventually. You come a lot to Puowaina?"

I was confused by this. "You mean Punchbowl?"

"Punchbowl's the name the haoles gave it when they came," he told me. "The old Hawaiian name is Puowaina—means 'hill of sacrifice.'"

"Why did they call it that?"

He hesitated for a moment, then explained, "Long time ago, there was an altar up here—like in church, yeah? Except on this altar, people were put to death for violating the kapu—the rules—laid down by the chiefs. Or they might be offered up as a sacrifice to the gods in exchange for something, like to end a drought."

My eyes popped at that. "Honest?"

"Honest! Not for a long time, though." He winded. "We know better now."

"How do you know that's what happened?" I said dubiously.

"My tūtū used to tell me stories about long ago, back when the slopes of Puowaina were covered with pili grass." He took note of my skepticism. "You want to see where it happened?"

Well, what keiki wouldn't? He got up and led me over to a large, impressive pile of perpendicular stones that looked, if not like an altar, then definitely like something that used to *be* something. "The chiefs would bring the victims up from the town," he said with an expansive wave of his hand. "Sometimes they'd drown them in the ocean before they brought 'em up here…and that's when they were feeling *kind*. Other times they'd bring 'em straight up and put them in that fire oven, over there" —he pointed to another, smaller pile of rocks not too far away—"built especially for burning men alive."

I gasped. To think that a place like Punchbowl, which I thought I knew as well as the back of my hand, could have such a hidden, and bloody, history! Needless to say, I was thrilled.

Johnny went on to tell me a few other legends about Puowaina—how the side of the crater had once opened up and poured fiery lava on a band of warriors who had cruelly destroyed a helpless village on Kaua'i—but, as fascinating as I found it all, eventually I looked at the fading sunlight and said, "I better go, I'll be late for supper. Nice meeting you, Johnny,"

"Yeah, same here. Maybe I see you again sometime. Aloha, Nani."

Well, after that, I saw Punchbowl in a whole new way. A little scary way, to tell you the truth. I'd think about climbing it, then look up at the brooding summit, imagine men burning in fire overs, and think, *Eh, maybe I stay home*—and I'd go play in my own backyard. That was where I was, late one afternoon, when I looked up from my game of hopscotch and noticed something funny in the sky above a neighbor's house. The sun was already behind Punchbowl, throwing its dying light onto a big cloud, making it glow like embers. But it was the shape of the cloud that was funny: a long "body" thinning at one end into a curved tail, and at the other end fattening into a diamond-shaped head. It looked exactly like a mo'o, a lizard, breathing fire into the sky above the home of Mrs. Fereia, a widow who lived across the street.

Then my mother called me in for supper, and at the table I happened to mention what I'd seen. Mama seemed unusually interested in what I'd said.

"The cloud looked like a mo'o?" she asked me. "Are you sure?"

"What's a mo'o?" my little sister, Moani, asked.

"*You* are," my big sister, Cynthia, taunted.

"Am not! I don't think."

My mother hushed them both. I told her, "It was lit up like it was on fire!"

"And it was directly above Mrs. Fereira's house?" Mama said.

"What's so all-damned fascinating about that?" my father asked, finally looking up from his bowl of clam chowder.

Mama instantly seemed to regret her interest in the subject. She explained, reluctantly, "In the old days, the appearance of a moʻo was thought to be an ill omen, for women especially. It augured the worst kind of misfortune."

Father let out a derisive snort, as we all knew he would.

"Superstitious claptrap," he declared. "There are thousands of lizards on this island, and what do they do? Augur? Portend? No. They stick to ceilings, leave their droppings everywhere, and womankind is none the worse off for their presence, unless it's to clean up after them." He shook his head disgustedly and returned his attention to his soup.

In fairness it must be said: Papa would have been equally likely to pronounce as "claptrap" a sighting in the clouds of the Virgin Mother. He had no patience for any kind of religion, whether it was Christianity or the old, so-called pagan Hawaiian beliefs. My mother gave me a look that told me, subject closed.

Father believed in science, especially as it was represented by his beloved 1915 Ford Model T Roadster—the first model to feature electric headlights. Each morning he would patiently hand crank its engine, then proudly—and, it must be admitted, a bit speedily—drive it down the steep hills of the Pauoa Valley to the offices of the Hawaiian Electric Company on King Street. And nearly every day he would inquire of his daughters, "Who wants a ride to school?"—but because so few of our classmates' families owned automobiles, we feared being seen driven to school, lest our friends accuse us of being stuck up.

Sometimes, though, Papa would smile devilishly at me and whisper, "C'mon, Nani—I'll let you drive," and my hesitation would disappear like the new moon. I would sit in his lap as he disengaged the parking brake and opened the throttle, and we would hurtle down

Pauoa Road as if on a roller coaster. Then, when we reached level ground, Papa would turn off onto a quiet side street with no traffic, carefully place my hands on the steering wheel, and allow me to "drive" the Tin Lizzie for an entire block (his hands rested lightly but reassuringly on the top of the wheel, in case he needed to take control). It was always a thrill for me, and well worth the occasional stink-eye I might get from a jealous classmate.

"Mum's the word, eh?" Papa would say as he dropped me off at school, and as I nodded readily he would race off, with a squeal of his transmission, to work.

Two weeks after I saw that fiery cloud above her house, Mrs. Fereira died unexpectedly of influenza, as so many people were these days. It was very sad; she was a nice lady, still young, and her Portuguese sweet bread was divine. But I didn't really think of it as having anything to do with what I'd seen in the sky. I'd almost forgotten about what Mama had said about bad luck and lizards.

I don't think Mama forgot, though. After she learned the news about Mrs. Fereira, Mama gave me the strangest look all day.

It wasn't long after that I had the most awful nightmare. It started out nice enough: I was soaring like a gull over the sea, though the shadow I seemed to cast on the water was much bigger than a bird's, the wind raking pleasantly through my hair. But then night and fog darkened both sky and ocean, and soon I felt myself dropping like a stone, unable to see a thing in the foggy dark…until the very last moment, when the fog blew away to reveal treetops looming up below me, and I crashed into them with a sound like crumpling wood and metal. Suddenly my whole body was drenched—not with water, but with what smelled like gasoline. Its acrid odor filled my lungs and stung my eyes.

I yelled so loudly it woke me up.

Cynthia and Moani tried to quiet me but couldn't. I was a dervish of anxiety. Only Mama, hurrying in from her bedroom, could quell my night terrors. "Sssh, sssh, it's all right," she said, taking me up into her arms and rocking me. "It was just a bad dream."

"I *fell.*" I told her breathlessly. "I was flying and I *fell...*"

"You fell into bed, safe and sound," Mama said with a smile. "See?" As I calmed down, I told her a little more about what I'd dreamt, and she reassured me that I was home and safe. But though I felt better when she finally left, I still didn't get much sleep the rest of the night.

By the time I got to school the next morning I'd mostly forgotten about it. But the teachers were all talking to each other about a story in that morning's newspaper about two aviators named Clark and Gray, who had just made the first interisland airplane flight in Hawai'i. The pair had taken off from O'ahu in a seaplane, landed briefly on Maui before heading for Hilo on the Big Island—and then promptly disappeared, and were feared to have crashed.

When I heard this I began choking again on gasoline fumes, so overwhelming that I had to flee into the bathroom, where I gagged over the sink.

When I got home that afternoon, Mama was looking at me strangely again. "Nani," she said, "tell me again about your bad dream."

I repeated what I'd told her last night, then said I wasn't feeling well and asked if I could be excused from supper and go straight to bed. She put a hand on my forehead, said, "Yes, of course," and tucked me into bed. Once she left the room, I wasn't so sure I *wanted* to go to sleep, after all; but eventually I did.

That night I dreamt calmer, though still exotic, dreams: I found myself walking through a jungle of algaroba trees and *maile* vines, feeling hot and sweaty and hungry, but oddly unafraid. There were no jarring crashes, no smell of gasoline, just heat, humidity, and a dull ache in my belly. This time I didn't wake up from it with a shout, just drifted out of it into other, less interesting dreams.

The next morning, over my breakfast *poi,* I calmly told my mother, "It's all right, they're alive. They're walking out of the jungle, that's all."

"What? Who?" my father said.

"The two men in the plane," I replied casually.

Mama looked stricken.

"It's nothing," she told my father. "Just a story Nani made up."

"That's nothing to be spinning yarns about," Papa chide me. "Those poor devils are probably lying at the bottom of the ocean."

But Papa was wrong. That day, against all odds, Harold Clark and Robert Gray emerged unharmed from the thicket of the Kaiwiki Forest on the eastern slopes of Mauna Kea, where their seaplane had crashed two nights before. They had walked away from the crash and then kept on walking through the jungle, without any food, for the next two days.

I thought Mama would be happy to learn this, but when I got home she took me aside and told me, sternly, "Nani, you must stop doing this."

This was the last thing I expected to hear. "Doing what?"

"*Seeing* things. In the clouds, in your dreams."

"But I'm not *doing* anything," I protested.

"You're telling your father things you can't possibly know! He won't understand."

"He will if I explain it to—"

"No!"

Mama seldom raised her voice to me, and it stung. "You asked me about my dream and I told you," I said. "I didn't do anything wrong!"

"No, you didn't, I know that," she said, softer. "But from now on I won't ask you any more questions, and I don't want you to tell me anything about what you—see. You understand?"

"But what if I have another nightmare?"

My mother looked pained at the thought but said nothing.

Angrily I turned and ran out of the house, without any real idea of where I was going. Then I glanced up at the slopes of Punchbowl and I sensed, somehow, that if I went up there now I would find Johnny Kua. I picked some mangoes from our tree, put them in a sack, then began climbing the trail to the summit, baffled as to why Mama was scolding me for things I didn't have any control over—what I saw in the clouds, or dreams that came to me in the night. I ate one of the mangoes on the way up, then when I reached the top I gave the rest to one of the squatter families and hurried across the crater to the lookout. Sure enough, Johnny was standing there, once again gazing down at the city.

He turned, saw me, smiled. "Well, if it isn't Nani MacGillivray. Aloha."

"Hi," I said, sounding pretty glum.

"What's wrong?"

I was suddenly reluctant to tell him for fear that he might have the same reaction as my mother.

"'Ey," he prodded gently, "what is it, what kind of pilikia are you in?"

We sat down and I told him everything: the moʻo in the clouds, Mrs. Fereira's death, my dream about the two aviators. To my relief, he didn't laugh or even look at me cross-eyed, but seemed to accept my story at face value. I told him about Mama scolding me, half afraid he'd scold me too. But he just smiled.

"Nani, there's nothing the matter with you," he assured me. "What you dreamt is called a 'revelation of the night.' You have a gift. Your mama knows it too, even if it scares her."

"A gift?" That wasn't the word *I'd* have used to describe it.

"We Hawaiians live in two worlds, Nani," he said gently. "This world you see around us, that's just the first layer, like the skin covering our bodies. There's another layer underneath, like you and I have blood and bones beneath our skin. My tūtū said the ability to see this second layer of reality is called ʻike pāpālua: it means 'twice knowing.' Seeing events that haven't happened yet—or things happening now, but at a great distance—that's a special gift you have, Nani. The haoles call it 'second sight.'"

"So I'm…not being bad when I see things?"

He laughed. "No, just the opposite. Your gift is pono—a very good thing."

"It doesn't feel good," I said.

"That's because your mama is afraid of it, or she's worried your father will be afraid. The important thing is, don't *you* be afraid of it."

"Johnny, do *you* have—'twice knowing'?"

He shook his head. "No, I joined the Army early on a hunch, not a vision. I'm not like you."

I thought about that a moment, and as I did I could see Johnny glancing down at the city again, and I knew he was looking at his family's house in Pālama.

"Johnny?" I said. "Can I ask you something?"

"Sure. Shoot."

"Why do you look so sad when you look down at your home?" I didn't need second sight to see it.

He smiled sheepishly. "Long story. Maybe I tell you sometime."

"Can't you go back there and visit your 'ohana?'"

He smiled and said," I think maybe you're the one who needs to go home…your mama's probably worried."

We got up, and then he squatted down and put his hands on my shoulders. "Just remember, Nani: it's pono. Don't be afraid of it, no matter what happens."

But something in the way he said that only made me feel more afraid.

For the next few weeks, I tried not to remember my dreams and even did my best to avoid looking up at the clouds. One weekend Papa took us all for a Sunday drive to Kailua, though this was not as restful as it sounds: Papa took the hairpin turns at his customary brisk clip up the windward side of the island. But we did have fun, stopping to watch the geyser of water erupting out of the Hālona Blowhole, and later Papa bought us all ice cream cones at the Elite Ice Cream Parlor.

The following day, I was playing tag in the schoolyard when I got tagged by Annabel Lucie—a girl I hardly knew—her fingertips just barely grazing the skin of my arm. All at once I had a familiar feeling—like when I was in the ocean, bodysurfing, and a wave pulled me under. It felt like I had a wave sitting on top of me and I didn't have more than a single breath in my lungs, but I didn't dare open my mouth to take another. The air of the playground actually began to thicken, to *liquefy*, as if it were turning to water all around me. I could still see the other girls playing tag, but now they were running in slow motion in the water, their hair floating up from their faces, oblivious to what was happening around them. I felt the sting of salt in my eyes; I couldn't hold my breath much longer and was on the verge of taking in a deep swallow of ocean when…

"Nani? You ok?"

It was my friend Beverly's voice, and the touch of her hand on my arm caused the water to evaporate, just like that. I was no longer bursting for breath.

"Nani? What's wrong?"

"Nothing," I lied and returned to the game, though steering clear of Annabel after that.

I went to bed that night with the salty taste of the ocean still on my lips.

The next morning, as my classmates and I filed into the schoolroom, I cautiously skirted past Annabel as she settled in at her desk, two rows behind me. I didn't touch her, didn't come close, but in my nervousness I bumped into her desk as I passed, and that was apparently enough to trigger it.

With the same absolute clarity that I'd dreamt of falling like a meteor from the skies above the Big Island, I now found myself treading water off Waikīkī—I could see Diamond Head off to my right, and some dozens of yards in front of me, a line of surfers rode a break I recognized as the one called Castle's Surf.

But the fact that I could see the surfers' backs meant that I was too far out. My leg cramped suddenly; I flailed in the water like a fish without a fin. I tried to call out to my family on the beach—not my family, I knew, but Annabel's—and to her older brothers, swimming closer to shore. I didn't know if they could hear me, couldn't tell whether they saw me frantically trying to get their attention. A wave suddenly slapped me in the back, knocking the wind out of me as it pushed me under water and held me there. I knew I had only a single breath in my lungs, and I started to panic as I fought the reflex to open my mouth, and...

A boy's hand clasped my arm, pulling me up to the surface.

No—a boy jostled me as he passed me in the classroom, startling me from my trance. I was no longer drowning; I was back at school, in my classroom.

I took a deep gulp of air and hurried to my desk.

I sat there wondering what had happened. Had—would—Annabel be saved by someone, one of her brothers, maybe? Or had it just been me who'd been rescued, by that boy's brief contact? And should I warn Annabel, tell her not to go swimming at Waikīkī—or at least not to swim beyond the surf break?

My first instinct was to do just that. But then I worried: What if she didn't believe me? What if she told the teacher I was trying to frighten her? What if the teacher told my mother, or, worse, my father?

Paralyzed with anxiety, I fretted over the question all week and into the next. And that Monday morning, Annabel came to school breathless with the news that she had nearly drowned in the surf off Waikīkī and had only been saved at the last minute by a surfer paddling by on his board.

She had certainly not been saved by me, and, as relieved as I was that she was all right, I was also angry at myself for doing nothing.

I thought of what Johnny had told me: "It's pono." But I knew that what I had done, or failed to do, was not pono.

That night, alone on the slopes of Puowaina, hiding behind some kiawe brush, I wept in frustration. I was just a little keiki, why did I have to make such important choices? I didn't want to see these terrible things! *Go away, dreams,* I commanded them. *Go away and leave me alone!*

To my relief and amazement, this actually seemed to work, at least for a while. The dreams and visions of other places, other people's lives, all stopped—as if my conscious mind were stubbornly refusing to take messages from my unconscious. Weeks went by without anything odd or disturbing happening to me. My dreams were all placid, benign: clouds that looked like clouds, flying that didn't end in a tailspin, frolicking in the ocean, but not nearly drowning.

So at first it seemed typically peaceful to find myself dreaming one night that I was on the beach, building sand castles as I listened to the rumbling sigh of the surf behind me. As in any dream, there were things that made sense only in a dream, so it didn't surprise me when I looked up to see a group of tanned young Hawaiian men wearing old-style malo cloths walking up the beach—and carrying lit torches, though it was the middle of the day. I heard drums, too, but when I turned around to see where they were coming from, I saw an outrigger canoe coming ashore. And the young men were now carrying a long bundle, about six feet long, wrapped in tapa cloth. They stopped in front of me and lowered their burden for me to look at.

I was startled to see that it was my father bundled up in the tapa cloth, his eyes closed, his skin looking unusually pale. But there was such a peaceful calm on his face, it didn't bother me. I asked him, "Papa, are you sleeping?"

"Yes," one of the young men said with a nod, "he sleeps the moe 'uhane."

I had no idea what he meant by this and somehow didn't think it important enough to ask.

The men lowered Papa into the hull of the canoe, now bobbing in the shallows, then pushed it away from shore. In moments the canoe bearing my father was being paddled out to sea, where the sunlight sparkling off the ocean made it seem as if the canoe were riding waves of white fire. It was beautiful to see, and though parts of this dream may have puzzled me, I didn't find it at all frightening, and awoke with a feeling of serenity and peace.

After breakfast, Papa again asked, "Anybody need a ride to school?"—and when Cynthia and Moani shook their heads, all he had to do was look at me with that devilish smile and I replied eagerly, "I do!"

I climbed into his lap and the Tin Lizzie took off down Pauoa Road. As usual, Papa took us onto a quiet little side street where I could steer, but this time I reached up and gripped the wheel in my hands—

And suddenly the car was spinning sideways—lurching off the road and down a steep embankment, though the street we'd been on a moment before had been flat as a board. The world literally turned upside down as the automobile rolled over with a crunch, jolting me out of Papa's lap. I fell, my head banging into the roof, which was now below me—and only inches from where a huge rock had torn a hole in the vinyl. I screamed as we kept on rolling and I was thrown like a beanbag around the passenger compartment. Then I heard a sound like tearing metal under me, and the whole world exploded in an angry roar. Flames were everywhere but we were still rolling, a fireball encased in metal. I continued to scream—even as I found myself suddenly, safely, in Papa's arms again.

"Nani, what is it, what's *wrong?*"

We were stopped in the middle of that quiet, level little side street—the car no longer tumbling end over end, no longer in flames. But the sudden normalcy and safety were anything but reassuring.

My screams died in my throat as I looked around me and realized that what I'd seen hadn't really happened.

Not yet.

I started to cry. Papa held me tightly against him. "It's all right, baby, everything's all right...." But it wasn't, because as I turned my tear-streaked face into the crook of his arm, I caught one last glimpse from inside the burning car—a man's hand lying limp on the crushed steering wheel. And though I dearly wished I didn't, I knew for certain whose had it was, or would be.

When I finally stopped crying, Papa asked me again what was wrong, what had happened. I told him I'd just gotten scared. It didn't sound convincing even to me, but in the absence of any other explanation, Papa took me home...and, after he had reassured himself I wasn't injured, he left me in Mama's care. She put me to bed, stuck a thermometer in my mouth, and left to make me some tea. I lay there terrified to tell her what I'd seen, yet terrified not to. I thought of Annabel—but that had turned out all right, hadn't it, even though I'd said nothing? Maybe this would too. How did I know what was the right thing to *do?*

Mama came back into the room to find me crying again. She sat down on the bed, took me in her arms, and asked, "What did you see, Nani?"

I looked at her fearfully.

"I know I promised I'd never ask you that again," she said gently, "but never mind that. What was it you saw in the automobile?"

"You won't be angry at me?"

"No. I swear."

I told her. She listened, looking concerned but not angry, even when I told her the last image I'd seen, the man's hand—the hand I knew belonged to Papa.

"You—you never saw your father's face?" Mama asked hopefully.

"Not this morning," I said.

"What do you mean?"

"I…I had a dream last night." I went over every detail: playing on the beach, the Hawaiian boys carrying torches, Papa sleeping as they carried him….

Mama was looking increasingly agitated. "But he was—just sleeping?"

"Yes. I asked one of them, and he said, 'He sleeps the moe 'uhane.'"

She nodded. "'Spirit sleep.' When someone is deeply asleep, their soul travels outside of their body. What happened next?"

"Then they put Papa into a canoe and took him out onto the ocean."

She could not have looked more horrified had I said that Papa had been stabbed with a whaling knife in his back.

My heart was racing now. "Mama? Did I say something wrong?"

She sat, pale and silent, for the longest while, then finally worked up the nerve to tell me: "A dream of a canoe is a dream of death. Your father was sleeping the spirit sleep and was making the final journey…to the next world."

"Are you sure?" I said. "Maybe the canoe was just going to—to Maui, or the Big Island…."

Tears filled her eyes.

"A dream of a canoe is a dream of death," she repeated, and began to weep.

Now it was my time to comfort her, holding on to her, offering her hope. "There's still time, Mama! We can warn him about what's going to happen…."

She shook her head. "He would never believe us, Nani. He would deride it as—'Hawaiian mumbo jumbo.'"

"But we have to do *something*, we can't just let him die! What can we *do*?"

She looked more shaken and afraid than I had ever seen her.

"I don't know," she said miserably. "I don't know."

Later, trusting an instinct I wished I didn't have, I hiked up the trail to the Punchbowl lookout, where of course Johnny Kua was again waiting for me. "Funny how you're always here when I come," I said.

"Or maybe you only come here when I'm here," he pointed out. "You're the one with second sight, 'ey?"

But I really was glad to see him. I told him about what had happened in the car, the terrible fate that seemed to await my father, and I desperately sought his advice. "Johnny, can I—can I change the things I see?"

He considered that. "Sometimes, I've heard, you can. Sometimes, what's seen in the 'ike pāpālua is just what's *possible,* not inevitable."

"So I should warn Papa? Tell him not to drive so fast, to be more careful, or he'll…he'll…"

Gently, he put a hand on mine. "Tell him."

I tried to hold back my tears of worry and hope. "I can save Papa?"

"You can't if you don't try."

"Are you sure?"

"Yes. Tell him."

I thanked him and scrambled down the hill in record time.

When I got back, my father was already home—he'd left work early out of concern for me—and so I couldn't speak freely to Mama. When Papa tried to give me a little kiss on the cheek, I couldn't help myself; I flinched a little, afraid that his touch might plunge me into another vision of his death. This only made him fret more about my own health, and over supper he stole worried glances at me; I could see a similar worry in Mama's face as she gazed at Papa.

After supper I insisted on helping Mama wash the dishes, and once alone with her in the kitchen I could tell her that we had to do something to warn Papa, we had to *try.* She had apparently come to the same conclusion because she said, "I know we do. I could never forgive myself if I didn't."

"Do you want me to go tell him what I saw?"

"No, you leave that to me. I'd rather he be angry with me than with you. I'll talk to him after you leave for school tomorrow."

I went to school the next day filled with excitement and hope that we would be able to prevent this horrible future from coming to pass. I could barely keep my mind on my schoolwork, and when we were dismissed for the day I ran like a banshee—one of Papa's favorite expressions—all the way home. As I neared our house I could see Mama sitting on our lānai in a big wicker chair. I pounded up the steps and onto the porch and asked her breathlessly, "Did you tell him?"

Only now that I was so close did I notices the distant look in her eyes.

"Yes," she said, her tone flat as a broken piano. "I told him."

She wasn't looking at me so much as past me.

"You told him about the car accident?"

"Yes."

"Did you tell him about Mrs. Fereira?"

"Yes."

"And the two pilots? And Annabel Lucie?"

She said tonelessly, "Coincidence."

I blinked. "What?"

She sighed like a balloon losing the last of its air. "Your father says that was all just coincidence."

"But I *saw* his car go off the road," I said. "I could *feel* the flames!"

"It doesn't matter what you felt." There was a bleak surrender in her voice that I had never heard before.

"Did you tell him about the canoe?"

She broke into a short, sour laugh. "Oh, yes. The canoe. He especially liked that."

She looked straight at me now, and I saw the exquisite, unbearable hurt in her eyes.

"He told me I was acting like a… 'superstitious native whore,'" she said, and though I didn't know the word, I could feel the shame in her voice as she spoke it aloud. "That I was filling my daughter's head with ignorant pagan nonsense…making her throw a fit in the car. He said if I didn't stop it, he'd leave me, and he'd take you and your sisters with him."

I was shocked not just by Papa's cruel words, but that Mama had even repeated them to me. It was the first time in my life that a grown-up had shared such a thing with me…such a raw, adult pain.

I went to her and hugged her, and she held me to her for a long while as we sat there on the lānai. Then finally she said, sadly, "There's nothing more we can do for him, Nani. We did our best."

That night, Papa sat me down and explained to me the laws of physics and the inviolate rules of science. He didn't scold me, just warned me not to let my imagination get the better of me, and never to credit any of Mama's "fairy tales."

After that, he also stopped offering me a ride to school. I think he was afraid that being in the car would trigger another "wild burst of fancy," as he put it.

Two months later, Papa was on his way to work, driving too fast down a steep hill, when he lost control of his beloved Model T and plunged into a ravine. The last of the series of rolling impacts punctured the ten-gallon fuel tank under the front seat, which exploded, killing him instantly.

When I think of my father, I think of fire.

Those were sad days for our ʻohana. Papa's body was burned so badly that his casket had to remain closed during the services at the Nuʻuanu Funeral Parlor. I had never heard a Hawaiian kanikau before, a lamentation chant; the mourners cried the traditional wail of "Auwē! Auwē!—Alas! Alas!"—as I stared helplessly at the coffin, unable even to kiss my papa goodbye. But this was so much harder for my sisters, because Papa's death had come as such a complete shock and surprise to them. Mama and I had been more prepared, and shared our own secret sorrow, our inability to prevent what we'd known would come to pass.

But in addition to my grief, I also felt a budding anger at one who'd given me, I felt, a false hope.

After Papa's burial I didn't even bother to change out of the black dress I was wearing before I went charging up Punchbowl Hill. I got my dress torn and dirty, black ash soiling black lace, but I didn't care. I raced across the crater's desolate face to the lookout, where, of course, I found a uniformed soldier standing with his back to me. Johnny turned as I approached; his eyes were sadder than the saddest kanikau. "I'm sorry, Nani," he said.

I ran at him and began pummeling him with my fists, screaming. "You *told* me I could save him!"

He winced, but it wasn't from my blows, I'm sure. "I told you to *try*."

I kept pounding at him, ineffectually, with my little fists.

"What's the good in seeing what's going to happen," I cried, "if I can't change it!"

"Nani, listen, listen to me." He squatted down, took my hands in his, and closed his big fingers around my balled fists. "You *did* change something."

"I didn't change anything!"

"You did. You *did* save someone."

"Papa's dead."

"But you're not. You saved *yourself*, Nani."

I stared at him, not comprehending. He let go of my fists. I let them drop helplessly to my sides.

"I swear, it's true," Johnny said. "After your mama told your papa what you saw, he stopped asking you to ride with him to school. Didn't he? And if he hadn't, you would've died with him in that car."

Disbelievingly, I said, "Me?"

"He's thanking you for it, Nani. Can you hear him? He's thanking you for telling him, so his little girl didn't die with him."

I couldn't hear Papa, and I didn't know how Johnny could, either.

"You—said you didn't have 'twice knowing.'"

"I don't. But I know, in a different way, that there are some things in the future you can change, and some things you can't. What happened to your papa was one you couldn't, and I'm sorry—but there'll be others that you can. Don't give up, Nani. Your gift saved you—it can help save lots of other people too."

He stood up, and as he did, I heard a kind of low thunder rumbling in the distance behind us.

"You hear them, don't you?" Johnny asked.

"Yes," I said, baffled. "What is it?"

"Something else you can't change," he said sadly.

In moments there were dozens of airplanes—more than I'd ever seen, in strange unfamiliar shapes—roaring above us. They were flying so low that I could see the markings on their sides—a bright red circle, like a burning sun at daybreak. They thundered on, swooping low over the harbor, where they began dropping torpedoes on the ships at anchor there. The explosions were deafening, even from here, and they turned mighty destroyers into flaming wreckage within minutes. Columns of thick black smoke rose from the ships like grave markers. Wave after wave of planes came, until there were so many they almost formed a cloud that resembled the lizard I'd seen in the sky—but this was more like a dragon breathing bursts of fire onto the land.

Johnny stood there on the lookout, as flames leaped and smoke rose behind him, and smiled his gentle smile.

"There's nothing you can do for me, either," he said, adding fondly, "Aloha, Nani. Use your gift wisely."

And then I blinked, and he wasn't there any longer. Neither were the airplanes, or the burning ships in the harbor. Not knowing what was real and what wasn't, I walked slowly to the edge of the crater and peered down at the city. Honolulu—the Honolulu of 1918—lay dozing peacefully below me, as if what I had just seen was only a bad dream the city was having as it slept.

I would see this carnage again, of course…though not for another twenty-three years. But I never saw Johnny again.

As Honolulu's day of destiny approached, I did try to warn the authorities about the Pearl Harbor attack, even though Johnny had said that it couldn't be prevented. I wrote letters to the Navy, but they all went unanswered. In the month leading up to the bombing, it seemed as if every other week the local newspapers were full of speculation that the Japanese might attack or invade Hawai'i, so I'm sure I appeared to be just another vocal alarmist. The few officials I managed to meet with in person dismissed me as well, and even had they believed me, they were at such a low level in the chain of command that they probably could not have made any difference. The Japanese planes came, and the rising sun breathed its dragonfire onto Honolulu. All I could do was to warn people I knew personally and try to get them to safe havens where they might survive the aerial assault.

This is what I've tried to do all my life, what Johnny wanted me to do: to use my gift wisely. He was right: if there were some things I couldn't change, there were others that I could. Sometimes that meant warning a friend away from a certain place at a certain time, avoiding an accident that would have claimed his life; sometimes it was telling a neighbor family that a fire would break out in their apartment the following day, or warning a pregnant woman that her baby was backward in her womb and would need special medical attention if it was to be delivered safely. Some people heeded my advice; some didn't. I've never counted the number of lives that have crossed mine in this way, but I imagine it would be nearly a thousand over the long course of my life, and I am proud to say that a majority of those lives were improved for having touched mine.

I'm grateful now for this gift I've been given as well as for the young man who crossed so huge a gulf to help me understand it. Once a year, in his honor, these old bones of mine make a solitary pilgrimage up Punchbowl Hill. Of course, it looks considerably different that it did when I was a girl: today the crater is graced with lush green grass and tall white monuments to the thirty-five thousand fallen souls who now abide there. One of the most beautiful of these monuments bears an inscription—a quotation from Abraham Lincoln—with words I've always found ironic in this place that was once known as Puowaina:

> *The solemn pride that must be yours*
> *to have laid so costly a sacrifice*
> *upon the altar of freedom*

When this National Memorial Cemetery of the Pacific was first dedicated, the many graves were marked with thousands of small white crosses, each like a tiny sapling whose life was cut short too soon; but today these have been replaced with simple flat headstones. I make my way slowly across the serene expanse of lawn, carrying a plumeria lei to one particular grave located not far from the lookout where I first met my old friend, in sight of his onetime home. And now, as I bend down, tears fill my eyes, as they always do, and I drape the lei across a granite marked that reads:

JOHN ROBINSON KUA
HAWAII
PVT 25 INFANTRY
WORLD WAR II
MAR 2, 1920 – DEC 7, 1941

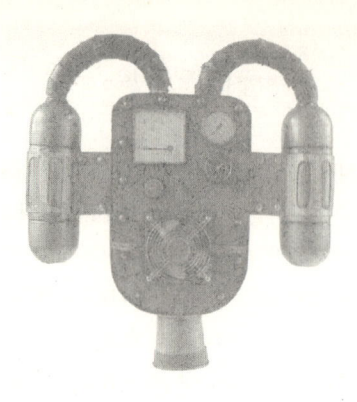

KITES AND ORCHIDS

[GEORGE S. WALKER]

"So safe a girl can fly it to school without the governess."
— Nikola Tesla, before his tragic jetpack accident

At least Tesla hadn't left a wife behind to mourn him. Leilani leafed through Kekoa's journal. She tried to blink back tears, but they dripped onto the pages, raising tiny welts of misery. The ahe blowing through the house refused to carry away her sadness.

She closed the journal and returned to her workshop next to the house. It smelled of burnt metal and vulcanized rubber. Long folds of colorful silk-asbestos weave draped from bamboo kite frames off the rafters. On her workbench lay the fused remains of the jetpack recovered by the Queen's Guard. The Queen had been overthrown decades ago. Territory police refused to investigate Kekoa's death, but out of a communal sense of kōkua, Leilani's relatives from the old Queen's Guard had come. Men climbed into the mouth of Kīlauea, using ropes and grapples to recover what they could. Leilani had refused to view the charred remains of his body. She would not remember her husband that way.

The police had found his Ford Model A truck at the end of the volcano road, one kite and a jetpack secured in the truck bed, the other missing. Until the Queen's Guard had found it in the caldera with what was left of his body.

Why had he flown alone? She'd read the final pages of his journal looking for clues. There was no hint that he'd decided to kill himself, as the police report concluded.

The next morning, she brushed her long black hair, put an orchid in it, then went down to the sugar mill. She began handing out "Day of Action" leaflets to the workers entering the mill. The union had been Kekoa's passion; she felt this was something she should do for him.

Ten minutes later, one of the haole bosses came up to her. "What the hell are you doing here? Picketing is against the law."

The ahe from the fields blew against the leaflets in her hands, hiding her shaking hands. "Giving out papers."

"Where's the guy who's usually here? Drunk in bed?"

"Dead."

He seemed ready to say something, but the tears in her eyes must have stopped him. After a moment he said, "You have to leave. Otherwise I call the cops."

She made no move, clutching her leaflets.

The boss shook his head and walked back to the mill. She continued handing them out. The police didn't come. She ran out of leaflets. Most of the workers, Hawaiian, Filipino, or Japanese, couldn't read anyway.

She walked home alone through the sugar cane fields, into the streets of town, where tall pālamas swayed. Out past the territory defense batteries, a zeppelin cruised above the ocean.

In the house, she opened Kekoa's journal again. When he was alive, he'd kept it locked, but the tiny lock was easy enough to jimmy. She was unwrapping his life backward, day by day. He wrote in a messy script; the ink from his fountain pen blotted in places. Mostly he used initials instead of names. She knew some of them, but not all. L. was her, of course. A. was Mr. Anderson, the union lawyer. Kekoa spent part of his time at the union hall, some at the courthouse or jail, and some in the fields.

A. talked of patience. He wants to postpone the Day of Action for six months. He's a good man, but why doesn't our cause burn in his veins?

A few pages earlier, she found an entry about herself.

L. is sweet and kind and oh, so naïve. To her the world is about tourists and lū'aus, kites and orchids. I love her dearly, but what did I expect from a girl whose family grew up in the palace?

That brought tears again, just when she thought she'd grown stronger. She closed the journal and made her way out to the workshop. This was where she worked her loom, weaving silk and asbestos into colorful patterns for kite fliers. That was how she'd apprenticed, but because she spent so much time with the fliers, she'd become an expert on jetpacks as well. The Tesla-engineered mechanisms were precision-built in Switzerland. The Swiss called them *moteurs alcoolisées* because they ran on pure alcohol. Or here on the islands, 190-proof distilled cane or pineapple juice. As her stern ʻanakē said, "If all the alcohol from stills went into jetpacks, kites would blot out the sun."

There were no clues to be found in the jetpack recovered from the caldera. It was a barely recognizable ruin of fused metal. She looked at the other unit, the one found in the Model A. It was one of hers. Why had Kekoa taken two jetpacks and kites? Had he been expecting someone else? A woman? Maybe he committed suicide when she didn't show? Leilani's mind was trapped in a Möbius strip of guilt and grief.

The jetpack had fuel in it. Not much. Certainly not enough for an ascent up Kīlauea. But it wasn't drained, either. She normally kept them empty when not in use. Either Kekoa had started to fill the tank and been interrupted, or he'd flown the pack and landed before using all the alcohol.

He hadn't left the key in the truck and hadn't left a suicide note. It must have been an accident. Had his kite broken? No way to know since it hadn't survived the lava in the caldera. Leilani might have nursed a broken kite to safety. Kekoa was a less experienced flier.

She was no detective. She didn't even know any policemen. When she'd gone to the station house, she'd informed them she was a hoahānau, cousin of the queen, to stress the importance of the matter.

"Those days are gone, Queenie," said the desk sergeant. "American men run this territory."

She'd marched back the next day with Mr. Anderson. They'd listened to him and given him forms to fill out.

And still, nothing had come of it.

The case was closed for the police, not for her. There was no journal entry for his last day. What had made him strap on a jetpack and fly into the mouth of Kīlauea? Her relatives had no idea. She needed to talk to people who worked with Kekoa.

Leilani walked to the lawyer's office.

Because she had no appointment, Mr. Anderson made her wait in the outer room with his secretary for twenty minutes. Makamae smiled sympathetically before resuming her work. She sat at a typewriter, type bars clacking against legal paper. The office looked expensive. Everything had come from America by steamer. Nothing was Hawaiian.

She'd tried to rehearse what she was going to say, but when Mr. Anderson called her into his office, the words came out in a jumble: all her frustration with the territory and the mill and not knowing what had happened on Kekoa's last day. The lawyer listened from behind his great desk, his cravat held in place with a diamond stickpin. As she fought back tears, Mr. Anderson pulled the silk handkerchief from the pocket of his suit jacket to hand to her.

He listened for a long time but finally looked at his gold pocket watch and held up his hand.

"Now, Leilani, there can't be anything harder for a woman than losing her husband. But cruel as it is, it's no fault of the territory. I spoke at length with the police at the station house and they assured me they'd looked at this case from every angle. Sometimes we can persuade the territory that there's been an injustice. When the McBryde plantation underpaid their workers and Kekoa had me go to court, I got back that money for him. But for an accident, there's no one to blame. Do you understand?"

She forced herself to nod. It wasn't that she didn't understand. She'd failed to persuade even a man sympathetic to her plight.

"You're still young," he said. "Move on with your life. It was an accident. A most unfortunate accident."

She neatly folded the handkerchief and laid it on a corner of his ornate desk. She stood, recovering her dignity. "I thank you for your time, Mr. Anderson."

He shook her hand cordially, and Makamae escorted her out. Leilani shuffled back through town. In the distance, a column of steam rose from Kīlauea. She missed Kekoa desperately.

At the house, she opened his journal again.

Bartered ration coupons with J. Damned unfair trade! Meat and cheese and other coupons in exchange for a single rubber goods coupon. But L. needs fuel line tubing to repair a jetpack. I would do anything for her.

It was a funny world, where silk and pineapples were abundant, and you had to bicker with dirigible companies for a bit of rubber as if it were platinum for a Tesla coil.

Met with A. about the McBryde plantation settlement. M. tried to flirt again. A. said the territory ruled in the workers' favor. But he wonders if we'll ever see the money. So I went to the mill to demand it. A boss from McBryde, irate, told me arrangements would be made. I'm sure he was lying.

The lawyer had just told her he'd given the money to Kekoa. This journal entry was from a week ago. There was no later entry about the payment. Had it happened on his last day? If so, where was the money? At the union hall?

She took Kekoa's death certificate to the bank. But as Kekoa's bank ledger showed, there'd been no deposit. He must have taken the money to the union. She could have dropped the matter then, but this was something she wanted to do for Kekoa. She went to the union hall.

"We never saw no money," said the union chief, shaking his head. "And we won't never."

No one at the union hall had talked to Kekoa on his last day. But that's when he must have received the money. Why hadn't he told them? Why hadn't he told *her?* She'd have to ask Mr. Anderson when the money had changed hands.

Mr. Anderson wasn't at his office. "He's at the courthouse for the rest of the day," said his secretary. "Could I help?"

Leilani remembered the journal entry about M. trying to flirt with Kekoa. M. must be Makamae. "No," she said coolly.

"I'm sorry about your husband," she said. Leilani shrugged, turning toward the door. "Did you know he came here that last day?"

That turned Leilani's head. "What?"

"He came for the money."

"Money?"

Makamae nodded.

"What do you know about it?" asked Leilani.

"The McBryde settlement."

"Yes. What happened to it?"

Makamae's eyes widened. "Didn't he give it to the union?"

"No."

Now her brow creased in worry.

"What happened when he came here?" asked Leilani.

She looked down at her typewriter. "You'll have to ask Mr. Anderson."

"He's not here. What happened?"

"Well, they both left."

"Together?"

"No. Kekoa, then an hour later, Mr. Anderson. He said he was going kiting."

Puzzle pieces snapped into place. She remembered the other kite and jetpack found in the truck, the pack's tank nearly empty. "I need to see for myself."

"See what?"

"I'm going kiting. To the summit of Kīlauea."

"But Leilani, police said it was an accident."

"They never went up to Kīlauea. Only the Queen's Guard did, and only at my insistence."

"You're going alone?"

Leilani nodded.

"You shouldn't, not in your state. I've seen you crying."

Leilani's cheeks burned. "I have to know."

Makamae looked at the stack of papers by her typewriter, then at the grandfather clock. "Let me come with you."

Leilani shook her head. "This isn't your problem."

"But it is! Something happened. This is something I should do for Kekoa."

Leilani felt a swell of anger at that. She didn't want strangers doing things for Kekoa. Not now. It was too late.

"Have you even flown before?"

"A few times."

"Likely not to the mouth of Kīlauea."

"But I feel responsible. What about the money? I need to know what happened after we gave it to him. Please."

Leilani looked at the grandfather clock, torn by indecision. "Alright. I'll load the truck and drive to the base of Kīlauea at 3 p.m. Come alone, understood?"

Makamae nodded gratefully.

She walked home, imagining what had happened to Kekoa. It must cost a fortune to maintain an American lifestyle on the islands. Where did it come from? If Mr. Anderson had invited Kekoa to take a celebration ride up to Kīlauea... She shuddered.

In her workshop, she fueled two jetpacks and lugged them to the bed of the Model A. Then she tied down two kites. One was hers, a bright pattern of purple and yellow silk interwoven with asbestos. The other was a drab olive color that looked like it had come from the U.S. Army but hadn't.

More and more, she regretted telling Makamae she could come along. She would only be in the way. What could she find that Leilani couldn't? There was probably nothing to find anyway. She decided to drive off before Makamae arrived.

But as she was backing the truck away from the workshop, there she was. "You're early," Leilani said, as Makamae opened the passenger door of the truck.

"I wasn't sure you had a clock."

What a condescending thing to say! Of course she had a clock, though not as fancy as the lawyer's.

Leilani shifted gears and set out through the plantation toward the mauna looming ahead.

Makamae had changed out of her stylish muʻumuʻu into a blouse and high-waisted trousers. They were much finer than the work clothes Leilani wore. Mr. Anderson had high fashion standards for his employee.

"This is probably a waste of your time," murmured Leilani.

"You want to know; so do I."

"I don't think there will be anything there."

"Did you know that Mr. Anderson has a pistol? An American Colt."

"A gun?" She imagined Kekoa shot out of the sky like a wild goose. Her hands tightened on the wheel as the car bumped over ruts in the road.

"We might find spent shells."

Climbing the volcano road, she downshifted. The motor growled up the incline. The road eventually petered out in a box canyon littered with volcanic cinders. She pulled to a stop and set the brake. The sky was overcast. Not the best kiting weather, but as she told tourists, "Anytime it's not pouring is good for flying."

While Leilani untied the kites and jetpacks, Makamae took off her stylish hat and laid it on the seat of the truck.

As she had for so many tourists, Leilani helped Makamae strap on her jetpack. She pumped to pressurize the tank on Makamae's chest and checked the hoses leading to the catalyst coils of the twin jets on her back. Then she unwound the electric cable from the Tesla igniter and handed her the control grip.

"You've done this many times," Makamae said.

Leilani nodded, then went to fetch the army-green kite.

She adjusted and tightened the bamboo kite frame to Makamae. "Now remember, you balance here. Even if your jetpack fails, the kite will ride you down."

Makamae nodded.

Leilani strapped on her own jetpack and kite, then looked up at Kīlauea, steam and smoke rising from the summit. "I'll start first. Do what I do. If you have any doubts, cut power and sail down."

The jetpack was heavy with the full tank. She loped forward awkwardly. When she squeezed the hand grip for the Tesla igniter, the catalytic jets screamed, lifting her up by her shoulders. She held onto the balance bar of the kite as the jetpack flew her out of the little canyon and up Kīlauea's flank.

After a minute, she glanced over her shoulder.

Makamae was airborne, following. The roar of the jetpack made it impossible to hear anything else as she climbed. She knew where Kekoa would have flown: a ledge on the rim that fliers called the Balcony. She'd flown there many times with him. It was a difficult landing spot, and she smiled, fondly remembering the first time she'd taken him. He'd botched the landing and she had to grab him before he fell off the ledge. They'd tumbled, scratched, bruised, both laughing. He'd kissed her.

The hot backwash of the jets whipped the fabric of her trousers against her legs. She jetted over barren, rocky terrain. Glancing at the pressure gauge on the tank, she saw her fuel was half-gone. Most tourists didn't fly this high; they kited along the coast, watching for a great naiʻa or kohalā breaching in the waves.

She crested the summit and cut power, gliding toward the Balcony. The mouth of Kīlauea stretched out below her, a hellish wasteland. Lava glowed through cracks in the caldera's crust. Venting steam drifted over the floor.

Makamae's jetpack roared behind her, but her own flight was silent now. The fabric of the kite rippled and snapped with the wind. She steered toward the Balcony, unfolding air from the silk to control her descent. She landed with legs flexed, then jogged to slow herself as she bunched up silk to keep from blowing off the ledge.

She turned to see Makamae approaching, jets still on, coming in too fast. She finally cut her jets, struggling with the kite's balance bar. Leilani stepped to the side of the Balcony to give her room to soar for another pass. But she came down like a fledgling from its nest. Too fast, she was going to land and then drop from the Balcony. Leilani sprinted forward, catching her just before she staggered over the edge. They both fell to the rocky ground just short of the cliff.

"You saved me," Makamae panted, struggling to her feet.

As Leilani helped her gather the kite silk, the secretary surveyed her blouse and trousers, frowning as she touched torn fabric at her knee.

"A seamstress can—" Leilani offered.

"No, it's ruined," Makamae said. "New York clothing isn't like one of your homemade kites, to simply patch and think no one will notice."

"I'm sorry."

"That's what Kekoa said."

"Pardon?"

"I told him he could have chosen better, that he still could, he said he'd married a princess. But you're not. You're a cousin who thinks growing up in a palace makes you better than everyone else."

Where did this anger come from? "Why are you—"

Makamae looked over the edge, at the caldera hundreds of feet below. "Kekoa brought me here the first time. He had to catch me the same way, and I was in his arms." She hugged her arms around herself.

"What?" Leilani's throat tightened. "When?"

"Many times." Leilani's mouth hung open and the secretary laughed at her expression. It was not a pleasant laugh. "No, unfortunately only once. The day he died."

Leilani's heart felt like it was tearing apart. "What happened to Kekoa?"

"He said no. Too many times no. I told him I wouldn't give him the McBryde settlement until he brought me up here. And then he could stop saying no."

Leilani felt her brain was stuck in low gear.

"Kekoa would have been happier with me," said Makamae. "We could have shared that money, traveled to America. He said no. How could he say no?"

"What did you do?!" Leilani cried.

"I put the money in my bank. Maybe not the smartest thing. Mr. Anderson would turn me in if he found out. And you, Princess, you ask too many questions."

Makamae was facing away, and now she whirled on Leilani. She had a pahi in her hand, a pig-gutting blade. She lunged.

Leilani jumped back, but the blade slashed a rubber hose off the fuel tank on her chest. The alcohol sprayed over her shirt. She screamed as she staggered backward over the edge of the cliff, falling from the Balcony.

In that moment of panic, she almost squeezed the hand grip, triggering the Tesla igniter. With the hose slashed, the jetpack was dead weight. Tumbling through the air, she yanked the fire emergency cord on the jetpack harness, shrugging out of it. It fell away and she fought for control of the kite. Air unfurled the silk, billowing as it righted her. She leaned on the balance bar, swerving away from the cliff, out toward the center of Kīlauea.

Then came the vengeful shriek of Makamae's jetpack.

Leilani gasped for breath, wishing she could go faster. She was gaining lateral speed at the expense of altitude. With the alcohol evaporating, her chest felt like she'd climbed into an icebox. Glancing over her shoulder, she was blind to where Makamae was because of silk blocking the view above her. She gasped for breath, trying to think.

She aimed for the center of the caldera where glowing lava sent columns of smoke and steam billowing skyward. That might hide her for a bit, buy her time. Her only hope was that Makamae would run out of fuel before catching up to her. Just kite-to-kite, the advantage was Leilani's. The secretary wouldn't understand thermals well enough to kite up over the rim.

Leilani reached one of the steam columns. Smoke and sulfur stung her eyes, blinding her, but she caught the thermal, spiraling upward like a leaf in a chimney. As the alcohol on her shirt kept fading, the air in the column warmed like a cooking pit. The jetpack screamed past, missing her. She kept her eyes closed, wheezing hot air as she flew by feel. She could hear Makamae's jetpack re-approach below and blinked long enough to see the kite.

She had to avoid her until she ran out of fuel.

But then what? Even if Makamae couldn't kite out of Kīlauea, she'd hike out. Eventually she'd make it back to town, where she'd tell more lies to Mr. Anderson. Lies about Kekoa.

Fear became fury. Leilani banked out of the column, blinking to clear her eyes. Makamae was below, jets full on, climbing. She couldn't see Leilani because of her kite.

Leilani furled silk, releasing air, dropping. Aiming her descent, she plunged feet-first into Makamae's kite, slamming into her back. She kicked hard, felt her foot catch a fuel hose beneath the fabric and kicked again.

With a whoosh, alcohol exploded, flames flaring out from all sides beneath the fabric. Makamae screamed. Leilani pushed up away from her, catching air in her kite.

The secretary's kite crumpled, spinning toward the lava.

Leilani rode her kite upward, the ahe of the thermal carrying her away from the pyre of Kīlauea.

Living, that was something she would do for Kekoa.

△∇△∇△

BENEATH THE IRONWOODS

[C.B. Calsing]

Water fascinates the boy. He obsesses over it. He wishes he had the words to tell his mother and his teacher and the one classmate who is nice to him how much he loves the ocean, but he does not know how. He can't make his mouth or his brain do the right things at the right times to *share*.

At school he categorizes cards with pictures and Velcros them to words that match. He sorts cards with letters and numbers on them to spell his first name, K-O-A, and his mom's phone number, even if he can't remember the phone number in an emergency. This frustrates him. If he does these tasks enough times correctly, he gets Play-Doh. He wishes they would let him use the water table instead. Or even just wash his hands at the sink. He could watch the faucet flow forever.

At home he must have Sister with him to go to the water. Koa cannot swim, but Sister knows he likes the water even if he can't *share*. Sister is older; Sister is also what people call "normal" when they think Koa isn't paying attention. Koa is not normal, he knows. If he were normal, he could say his name and tell his mother's phone number, among other things.

Image: https://commons.wikimedia.org/wiki/File:FMIB_51636_Red_Goatfish,_or_Salmonete,_Pseudupeneus_maculatus_Bloch_Family_Mullidae_(Surmullets).jpeg

At the beach Sister holds his hand, and then he can wade up to his ankles and sink his toes in the wet, dark sand. This lights joy in him that lasts a day or two, even with all his frustrations about how the world doesn't work for him. He has heard older people say, "the sea calls to me." He thinks, though, that those people aren't listening at all. The sea does speak to Koa, and he so longs to speak back to it. But that would take time, time Sister never gives him.

"Come on," she says and yanks impatiently at his hand. Koa stands with his eyes closed, feeling the warm water lap against his ankles, listening. But Sister pulls him back toward the dry sand, back to where they left their slippahs.

Their house—where they live with Mom and Dad, cousins and Auntie, Grandma and Grandpa—is a few blocks from the beach. Today Grandpa celebrates his birthday. The family will barbeque and listen to music. Friends will come over.

The guests come, beer is drunk, and everyone eats. Dusk arrives, and Koa sneaks away when no one is paying attention. He goes down to the beach, and each step he takes causes his heart to beat faster. He wears shorts and slippahs and nothing else. His fingers are sticky from Chantilly cake frosting.

The sky is red as he sinks his feet into the wet sand. The beach is empty, but a few surfers out near the reef catch the late afternoon glass-off. Koa watches the waves on the reef and wonders what they would feel like crashing over his body. Giddiness fills him, and he wants to shout it out across the water, but the words that mimic the pictures in his head won't leave his mouth. Instead, he repeats one of the few utterances he has perfected, louder, more rapidly, again and again. It is a line from a video Sister watched and showed him.

"What are those?" He points down at his feet in the water. "What are those? What are those?"

The words, being meaningless, put into sound everything he wants to share.

And across the water, he receives a response. The surfers are gone; the sky has darkened. But he *hears* something.

In the quickly waning light, he sees a figure—no, two figures—standing out on the point where the land wraps around and meets the end of the reef. They lurk beneath the ironwood trees, holding hands. Too short to be adults. Koa takes a few steps in their direction but stubs his toe on a jutting piece of lava rock beneath the water. Pain lances up his leg, and for a moment he panics, realizing that if he hurt himself for real, no help would come.

He glances down at the dark water. *Bleeding?* He can't tell. When he looks up again, the figures beneath the ironwoods have moved closer, standing now in the half distance. Koa squints. *Did they float there?* No moon shines, but the two figures seem to glow in the gathering gloom.

They drift closer, like flotsam on the surface of the ocean, shifting left than right, speeding up and slowing down, following some current of the air only they can navigate. Finally, they hover an arm's distance from Koa.

Koa looks at them. "What are those?" he says quietly to himself, confused. He knows he is not normal, but if he's just "not normal," what are these two standing before him? Their hands are still clasped together. Koa cannot tell boy from girl, if there is indeed that distinction. Their bodies are bluish-gray and dappled purple, their eyes large and black and ringed in yellow. Long, fleshy whiskers protrude from their chins, and their skulls are as smooth as the rest of them. They resemble reef fish Koa's seen in books at school, fish he has also seen on the hibachi. Fish he finds to be beautiful.

Fish he desperately wants to see up close in the water.

They smile at him, showing sharp rows of tiny teeth. Heart beating hard beneath his thin, bird-like chest, Koa smiles back. He has practiced smiling, yet he knows it comes out wrong.

The toothy, lipless gaps in their faces widen with encouragement.

He knows what they want. Without words he can tell what they expect of him. Are they in his head? Magic, Koa thinks. He feels the tension in his smile loosen as if it has become genuine, normal, not practiced. One of the creatures reaches out, takes Koa's hand. He acquiesces happily. They will swim together. Koa will be able to see the fish—moano kea! That was the fish these creatures resembled. The largest of the goatfish in these waters. Pretty purple and yellow. Sister likes that goatfish almost as much as parrotfish, but parrotfish, with their strong beak for crushing coral, scare Koa.

The goatfish children pull Koa toward the water, and excitement courses through him. He does not fear. They walk together toward a small channel of sand that runs out into the deeper water, surrounded by old lava flow. Hand-in-hand-in-hand the trio descends into the soft brine. The reef here blocks most of the waves, leaving a large, calm cove rimmed in lava with a black, sandy bottom.

Koa feels as if he has finally found those with whom he belongs. They do not speak to him or each other. Words don't work underwater, do they? Unlike the classroom and the family who insist on talking, talking, talking. Koa could never talk story like them.

They are up to Koa's waist now in the water, and his shorts feel odd and unnecessary. The goatfish do not wear shorts. They pull him down, and he floats on his stomach, his head above water, just barely. They glide away from the beach, effortless, and Koa thrills at the sensation of the water against his flesh, the firm grip of the goatfish children pulling him forward. Then he puts his face in the water; water fills his ears. He grins, then panics for a moment. He lifts his head to take another breath.

"Koa!"

He hears his name from the beach, and he turns, sputtering, trying to get his feet down on the sand beneath. He has a moment of panic when his feet do not touch, but the goatfish children are there, and they hold him, confused by the pause in their journey. Koa can feel their bewilderment, their disappointment. He feels back at them. *Sister is calling me!* Sister stands on the shore, a silhouette in the dim light, dark against the dark.

"No, I don't want to!" This was one of the few phrases Koa learned to express his feelings. He could say it when he meant that, or when he just meant *no* or other similar objections. He could also say "Yes, I want to" when the opposite was true, like when he wanted chocolate instead of white milk in the lunch line. Right now, "No, I don't want to!" means "I'm with my friends. Stay there. Everything is fine. I don't want you to get hurt." But of course he can't say any of that, and Sister doesn't seem to understand him the way the goatfish children do.

Clear as a bell, he knows what the goatfish children want. They want Sister to come. They cajole and reassure Koa. *Let her come. Let her come.*

"No."

The goatfish children understand him and renew their soft reassurances. *Swim with us.*

Tension tears at Koa. He squeezes his eyes shut, trying to think. He wants to be with those who understand him, to have a flow of communication, to know what it means to be human even if those he is with are not. The goatfish children have given him that. Sister, though, has tried to look out for him. He would love her if he could, if that emotion were something within his understanding.

His sister splashes toward them, shouting and calling to him. Koa opens his eyes, shaking his head frantically. He looks left and right. The goatfish children on either side of him glow softly in the darkness, a muted beacon. Their faces are split in wide grins, showing oh-so-many teeth.

Sister swims, only yards away now.

The goatfish children each reach a hand toward Sister, still supporting Koa with the other. They cannot hide their desire from the boy. He knows exactly what they want.

Eat with us. Koa feels a cloud of warmth at his crotch as he pisses himself. This is not abnormal for him; he still has to wear diapers to school because the teacher and the aide haven't figured out a way to understand when he needs to go. He has never pissed himself in fear, however. He's seen that in movies and TV shows, but it is a first for him. This emotion is the purest and most vibrant he's ever felt. In a moment, it changes him.

His fear is not for himself but for his sister. She is normal. She can't understand what the goatfish children really want. She wants to save him, but she cannot. He wants to save her, but he cannot. There is no way to *share.*

Too soon, before Koa can do anything, she is there. She reaches out for him, trying to pull him from the grasp of the goatfish children, but their strong, scaled hands grip Koa.

"Let him go!" she pants, struggling to keep her head up.

Then they wrap hands around Sister, bringing her into their fold. They all descend. Water closes over Koa's head, and he realizes for whatever reason that he does not need to breathe. Magic again, he thinks. He tries to fight the feeling that he is home, that he is one of these children with the glowing skin and sharp teeth.

Sister fights, kicking, pulling, trying to get back to the surface. The surface is dark above; the sand is black below. Disorientation takes over, but the goatfish children, hanging in the in-between are in their element. Exuberance and expectation radiate from them like rays of the sun. Koa feels their hunger. It grows to become part of him as well. The cove and reef around him thrum with life, with meat.

Sister, there in their tangle of limbs, vibrates the loudest, her distress and panic adding a piquant flavor to the water. Koa's stomach roils as he realizes what he now wants.

Once he heard a family member say, "You can't choose your family."

Where is my family?

In the dark water, Koa can see as if he wears goggles. The goatfish children are bright next to him, their grins wide, their hunger for Sister and welcome for Koa radiating from them.

Sister is a tangled mess of long black hair, her party dress, and flailing limbs. Koa knows she needs breath.

He also knows she will never draw another breath. He cannot fight that reality.

The goatfish children must know he has made his choice. Each move in and sink tooth-lined jaws into Sister's flesh. Koa pushes away and squeezes his eyes shut. He cannot escape the smell of blood that permeates the water, billowing up from his sister's wounds. Nor can he retreat from the joy radiating from the goatfish children.

Eat with us. This he cannot do.

He hangs there in the in-between as his sister stops struggling, her body going limp. Her limbs stretch out, her face upturned. Her dark hair surrounds her head, and her fingers trail the darkness.

The goatfish eat.

Other small nocturnal reef fish come out from their hiding places among the coral and lava. They swim in the cloud of blood surrounding the kill. Then, timid, they dart in to take up the little bits the goatfish children miss, shreddings of flesh and offal. The free-floating stomach contents of laulau, smoked meat, and Chantilly cake. Koa watches.

When finally satiated, the goatfish children turn to Koa and reach their hands out for him again. They seem disappointed he didn't eat, but they will find other kills. Ones easier for him.

They swim toward the reef, toward the break in the lava that leads to the open sea. Wide-eyed, Koa watches the world slip past beneath him, basking in the soft glow of his compatriots.

His hands, gripped by his new family, itch as the first opalescent scales begin to push through the pruney skin.

△▽△▽△

PILI KOKO

[Lehua Parker]

The last time I saw Papa Keola alive he was already dead. He was lying in our family room in a rented hospital bed. His broad shoulders that had carried me beyond the breakers at Keikikai Beach stuck out like bird bones from his chest. His big, coconut-twisting hands and lūʻau feet were blue like they'd been dipped in ink. Weirdest of all was his face, swollen like bread dough on Sunday afternoon.

He didn't look anything like the grandpa I knew. *My* Papa Keola sat in the backyard under the plumeria tree waiting for me to come home from school. Most afternoons he'd be there with his ʻukulele, strumming the chords to "Little Grass Shack" and "Pineapple Princess."

"Eh, Ahe," he'd call. "Come sit with me, and I'll teach you. Everybody needs a kanikapila song in their back pocket, plus one more for a hana hou," he'd wink. His fingers were giant next to mine on the fretboard. "This is C," he said, positioning my fingers. "And this is G7. Strum like this: down-down-up-up-down! Good!" We'd practice for a while until my fingers were sore and I begged him to play. He'd close his eyes and send his ʻukulele pick dancing across the strings like rain on a hot sidewalk, his calloused fingers too fast to follow.

Image © Cristian Storto | Dreamstime.com

But last year Papa Keola started to cough. Then he got thin and tired, with purple bruises under his eyes and ashy hollows in his cheeks. "Shhh," Mom scolded us. "Kulekule! Papa had a treatment today. Go outside so he can rest."

Papa Keola had gone to the hospital, but now he's back.

Last night Papa Keola motioned me up on his bed, wrapped me in his arms, and pulled my forehead to his, nose to nose. He whispered, his hā rising from his lips to my lungs. "Ahe, my moʻopuna. No worry, Ahe. Papa's gonna be fine. And even if you no can see me, I still going be there for you. Always. We're pili koko. Blood. Never forget."

As I stood in a corner of the living room surrounded by ʻohana, all eyes on the bed in the middle of the room, I don't think that's a promise Papa Keola can keep. It's the kind of thing grownups tell kids to protect them from the truth.

But I already knew.

It was suffocating in the house. All the windows were open, but too many people pressed close. Aunty Doreen's perfume was working overtime, strong enough to gag a cat, but not enough to cover the faint smells of Papa's urine and sweat. Tears rolled down Mom's cheeks, but she ignored them. Like everyone else, her attention was locked on Papa's breath as his hā traveled to and from his lungs, rising like an ocean swell in his chest.

It sounded like he was drowning.

Tūtū Kari was sitting in a chair next to Papa Keola, holding his hand and wiping his face with a damp dish cloth. Like a thunderclap from a clear blue sky, her sudden voice boomed over the muffled weeping. "Outside," she announced. "Papa wants to be outside."

Uncle Albert and Uncle Joe exchanged glances.

"Under the plumeria tree," Tūtū said. Everyone held their breath, except for Papa who continued to wheeze like a kettle on the stove. "Now!" Tūtū shooed, her hands flapping like church fans in August.

Mom jumped up and threw the lānai doors open. Cousins grabbed the pūneʻe from the hallway where it'd been pushed and carried it out to the backyard. My sisters Lisa and Joanie grabbed pillows and bedding from the bedrooms and made a nest. When they were done, Big Uncle removed the heavy blankets from Papa Keola, baring his legs and tattoos. Uncle Albert stepped forward. "Let me help," he said.

Big Uncle shook his head. "He weighs nothing now. Go help Mom." Uncle Albert turned and took Tūtū by the arm and led her outside. Uncle Joe took her chair.

When the way was clear, Big Uncle leaned down and gingerly slid his arms behind Papa Keola's shoulders and under his knees. "One last time, Pops," he whispered. "You'll see the sun, feel the wind. You'll know the way home."

In and out, the breath pulled from the world into Papa Keola's body was held longer and longer, the loudest sound in the universe.

When Papa Keola was at last lying under the plumeria tree, a canopy of yellow and white blossoms swaying above, his body eased. Tūtū said, "Everybody hold hands. E pule kākou." As we bowed our heads to pray, I whispered to Mom, "Shouldn't Papa be in the hospital?"

She shook her head and wiped her eyes. "No, Ahe. There's nothing they can do. It's better this way."

Aunty Lena was singing "Aloha 'Oe" for the second time when the ocean in Papa Keola's chest rose no more.

There was a funeral; I remember that. I saw the casket draped in lei, the church filled with people with sad eyes and casserole dishes. There was a hole in the ground and a dirt mound covered with artificial turf that was rolled up and put away once the hole was filled. At home after the pastor left, there was lots of laughter and *remember the time* and more smiles as stories ebbed and flowed like waves upon the sand.

Somewhere around midnight, tired of the noise, of being told I looked just like him, of not knowing where to sit or what to say, I walked into the backyard and stood under the plumeria tree. As I looked at the stars through the branches, I saw something move high in the treetop. I shaded my eyes and peered closer.

Papa's swollen face sneered down at me, his gigantic head bobbling on a too thin neck. His twisted and scrawny body was perched like a mynah bird on a branch, and when he stood, I could see he was wearing only a ragged malo. His tattoo lines of shark's teeth and kalo were blurred beyond recognition. I drew breath to scream, but my throat closed like a big blue hand gripped it tight. *Ahe,* said a voice like the rusted hinge on the garden shed. *You're mine, Ahe. I'll never let you go.*

"Go away, Papa!" I squeaked, the sound weak like a flat tire.

His broken glass laughter shredded my ears. *That's right. I'm Papa. You can't make me leave, Ahe. We're pili koko. Come join me in the tree.*

"No!"

He leapt from branch to branch, tumbling through the tree until I felt his fetid breath on my face. *Ahe. My moʻopuna. We'll be together forever, just like I promised.*

"No," I shouted and shoved with all my might. The next thing I knew, I was on the ground, the sunlight warm on my face, a ti leaf clutched in my hand.

After that, I saw Papa constantly. His tiny body with its swollen head leered at me from the back of the school bus. He watched me eat my lunch in the cafeteria, licking his yellow rotted teeth with a swollen black tongue. He hovered over my bed when I tried to sleep, cackling nonsense.

Worse was when he'd whisper in my ear.

The Chang girl thinks you're ugly, he said. *I can tell.*

Nobody wanted you on their team. They just picked you because they feel sorry for you.

Why bother? Even your teacher knows you're stupid.

You think that's good? Look at Lisa's. It's way better.

You know Joanie's is the favorite, right?

You're a waste of space.
They'd be better off without you.
Everyone would be happier.
You'd be happier.
Come join me in the tree.

I stopped eating. I stopped sleeping. When I looked in the bathroom mirror all I saw were Papa's dying bruises under my eyes and hollows in my cheeks. *Go away, Papa,* I prayed, but no one was listening.

Come join me in the tree.

Aunty Nora noticed first. "Hey, sis," she said to Mom, "Ahe—"

Mom held up a hand. "Ahe's fine. We all grieve differently, Nora. Ahe will figure it out."

Aunty raised an eyebrow. "How are you doing?"

"I'm dealing. I'm fine. I just wish Ahe—" Mom sighed.

"It's hard," said Aunty Nora delicately. "You want me to—"

"Leave it, Nora. Ahe's fine. We're all fine."

The next day Aunty Nora brought chocolate dobash cupcakes and kūlolo, my very favorites, and frowned when I didn't eat. "Ahe," she said, "are you alright?"

"Yes, Aunty. I'm fine."

She tipped her head to the side. "You can tell me, you know."

You're such a tilly, Papa growled. He hovered near the ceiling. *Look how you're making Aunty worry over nothing.*

I swallowed the lump in my throat like a ball of rice after a fish bone. "It's fine. Everything's fine," I said, giving her a hug.

Behind her, Papa floated over to the table. He stuck his fingers up his nose, then dragged them through the kūlolo. My stomach twisted. Like he was reading my mind, Papa laughed. He climbed on the table and lifted his malo, dragging his saggy 'ōkole across the chocolate frosting.

Aunty Nora felt me tense and pulled me close. "What is it?"

"Nothing," I stammered.

Loser, sang Papa, licking his fingers. *Everything would be better without you. Mom wouldn't have to worry if you weren't around.*

A blue hand tightened, strangling my heart.

Aunty rubbed my shoulders. "You miss Papa Keola so much," she said with a sad, slow smile. "You two had such a special bond." She tipped my chin until I looked in her kind eyes. Like sunbeams, the light and aloha I remembered from Papa Keola pierced the fog I felt around me.

I thought of how Papa Keola stood firm in the shore break and taught me how to hold my breath and grab for sand when the big waves came. How he held me up to put the Christmas star on the tree, and how we had hot fudge Mondays, Tuesdays, and Fridays because ice cream was for every day, not just Sundays. How he'd sneak me Life Savers at church when the pastor droned too long, and how he told me stories about Māui and the sun and great ocean sharks and fire that lived underground.

My eyes welled.

Yes, I missed *my* Papa Keola with an ache worse than a sore tooth. It was endless and niggling and—

Bobble-head Papa bounced over Aunty's shoulder. *Boo!* he shouted.

I burst into tears.

Aunty held me tight. "It's ok, Ahe. Let it out."

Yeah, Ahe, whispered Papa, *Let it out, cry baby. Tell her. They'll put you in a house for crazy people. We'll have lots of fun then!*

I gasped and pulled away, wiping my face on my shirt. Aunty Nora reached into her bag. "This is for you," she said and dropped an ʻukulele pick into my hand. "Papa wanted you to have it."

The minute the koa wood pick touched my palm, I felt peace. I turned it over and over, the smooth shape soothing my soul, the sharp edge lancing the darkness. For the first time since I saw Papa in the plumeria tree, I felt like I could breathe.

Aunty Nora closed her hand over mine. "That's the pick Papa made when he was a kid—you know his uncle taught him ʻukulele and slack-key guitar? He wanted you to have one of his ʻukuleles, too. I'll bring it bumbye."

I nodded, unable to speak.

She squeezed my hand one last time before letting go. "Ahe, an ʻukulele pick is small and easy to carry. Keep it with you to remember the good times. There's no need to be sad. Pili koko. Our ancestors are never far away." She shook her finger at me, laughing, and turned me toward the table with a little shove. "Now eat!"

I looked to see where Papa was, but he was gone. When I went to the table, there wasn't a mark in the frosting; the kūlolo was untouched. I forced myself to take one bite—oh, so ʻono—then devoured the rest.

Later, I slipped the koa wood pick into my pocket, and whenever I felt anxious the rest of the day, I touched it, feeling calm and peace.

I didn't see Papa again until bedtime. He popped into the misty edges of the bathroom mirror as I brushed my teeth.

Miss me? he smirked. *Loser. You ate all the kūlolo. What a pig. Big Uncle didn't even get any.*

I dropped my toothbrush and stepped back. Tears threatened, so I sucked my lip tight.

Oh, baby's gonna cry, he wailed, mocking me with his gnarled fists rubbing black hole eyes. He tsked. *Such a sensitive waste of space. In the tree there are no feelings, Ahe.*

He's right; I'm too sensitive. Maybe things would be better in the tree.

His face filled the mirror as a pilau grin fissured his face like a rotten mango. *Face it, Ahe. We're all worm food. It's the best thing about you.*

The tears fell. "Why do you say things like that? I thought you loved me! I missed you so much! I wanted to see you, but now I don't—not anymore! Go away!"

He slithered through the mirror like an eel through the reef. *Who am I?* he giggled, his breath like hot tar in August.

I flinched.

Who am I?!

"Papa!" I groaned.

That's right, he sneered. *Papa. I told you we'd always be together. Blood. You can't get rid of me!*

I ran to my room and scrambled for the pants I'd left on the floor. Like smoke, he drifted after me. *What are you doing?* he said. I ignored him and kept digging in my pocket. *Stop that!*

Wrong one! I switched to the other pocket.

I said stop!

Got it!

I held the ʻukulele pick up to his face, brandishing it like a cross. "Go away, Papa! You were never like this before. The Papa Keola I knew was kind—you're cruel!"

The ground trembled as a conch shell blew in the distance. I turned and ran for the backyard and didn't stop until I was standing beneath the plumeria tree.

The grass was thin and dry, scratchy against my bare feet. Dead plumerias littered the ground, the sickly-sweet smell nauseating in the cool night air. I looked back to the house, as the earth shook, shook, shook, but no one else came out—Mom, Tūtū, and the rest must have gone out the front. Fresh flowers fell like sugarcane ash. I wrapped an arm around the tree and held the ʻukulele pick tight. I closed my eyes and thought of my grandfather, my true grandfather.

I thought of his joy when Big Uncle brought him ʻopihi plucked fresh from the rocks and the way his face scrunched when he laughed. I thought of his footsteps down the hallway in the middle of the night as he peeked into our rooms, and how he'd listen patiently to Joanie's endless stories. I thought of the sound of his voice like water over the reef, and how he'd close one eye when I sang off-key. "Eh," he'd tease, "you sure you Hawaiian?"

When I opened my eyes, my Papa Keola was standing before me.

He was young and strong, tall and proud. A feather cloak stretched across the mountains of his shoulders and fell in waves against his tree trunk legs. In one hand he held a long spear with a marlin bill lashed to the tip. His tattoo lines were sharp and clear, his malo crisp and 'ehu-tinged in the moonlight. He smiled, his eyes squinting with delight. *Ahe,* his voice like water on parched land, *who am I?*

"Papa," I breathed. "You're my Papa Keola."

No! shrieked the creature with the too big head and twisted body. *Ahe's mine! He chose me! Pili koko!*

Papa Keola's eyes narrowed. *Is this true, Ahe?*

"No!" I shouted at the creature in the top of the tree. "You're not my Papa! I don't want you around!"

The ground rolled like breakers against the shore. I clutched the tree with both arms, but Papa Keola threw his arms wide, tossing his cloak over his shoulders. Bringing his spear forward, he crouched in a warrior's attack. *You heard Ahe. Be gone, foul creature! Trouble him no more!*

The creature reared its ugly head and hissed. *By what authority?*

Papa Keola looked at me and nodded. I swallowed hard and found my voice. "Mine!" I shouted, my words crashing like a tsunami. "Leave and never come back!"

The creature howled, his head splitting like a melon and running down his withered body, dividing and folding onto itself until there was nothing left but the faint stench of rotten eggs.

The earth stilled.

I turned to Papa Keola.

He stood relaxed in the moonlight. *Maika'i, Ahe,* he said. *Well done. Never forget, the living always trump the dead. The unliving cannot hurt you or remain in your presence unless you let them.*

"I don't understand. I told it to go! Many times!"

No, he said gently. *You told me to go. You prayed for Papa Keola to stay away. You didn't see clearly, but now you do.*

"But you said you'd always be with me."

Papa Keola knelt and leaned on his spear so he could look me in the eye. *I did say that. And I am. But that creature was not me.*

"Why? Why did it come?"

You fed it with your fear and sadness. For creatures like that one, those feelings are the most delicious and delightful food on earth. Your feelings, Ahe, the things it made you ashamed of, are especially powerful. They are intoxicating to creatures like that. It would never have left you alone until you made it.

I held out the 'ukulele pick. "This. It was afraid of this. This pick is powerful. Is that why you left it for me?"

Papa Keola laughed. *It's an old piece of wood, Ahe, nothing more. But it reminded you of who I really am, and that was enough to chase the darkness away. Use it, save it, lose it—the 'ukulele pick doesn't matter. What matters is that you remember how this feels.*

I put my hand to my belly in wonder. "Bubbles and light," I said, "like a full belly with a calm heart. Aloha! Papa Keola, this feels like aloha."

'Ae, Ahe, it does.

The conch shell sounded again in the distance. When I looked to the mountains, I saw torches lining the ridges. "You have to go," I said.

Papa Keola nodded. *One last thing, Ahe. Your eyes are open now, but I don't want you dwelling on this. Ancestors are always with you, cheering you on and defending you when necessary, but it's your life to lead. Live it!* Papa Keola stood, gathered his cloak, and hefted his spear. *I'll see you soon, Ahe.* He winked. *But not too soon.*

"Wait! Can I give you a hug?"

He laughed. *Every time you strum an 'ukulele, you'll feel my arms wrap around you. Aloha e Ahe!*

The wind rose and blew the last plumerias from the tree as the torches on the mountains blinked out and Papa Keola slipped into the night.

"Aloha 'oe, Papa Keola," I sighed.

"Ahe!" called Mom as she ran through the lanai door. "Thank goodness! We couldn't find you! Why did you run to the back yard? Are you ok?"

"I'm fine," I said and laughed, because this time I meant it.

Mom cocked her head at me. "Are you sure you didn't hit your head or something?"

"No." She narrowed her eyes and felt my forehead. "Really, Mom, I'm fine."

She clucked her tongue. "If you say so."

In my hand, the 'ukulele pick pressed against my palm. I rubbed it between my fingers. "Hey, Mom," I said, "you think we could stop by Aunty Nora's tomorrow? I want play Papa Keola's 'ukulele."

FOR ALL THE HEARTS WE BURIED

[KRYSTLE YANAGIHARA]

It feels strange to be back here again.

My home.

The once beautiful and full carpet of grass in the front is now a dried-out patch. Even the paint on the walls, a remnant of family bonding time, has faded and begun peeling at the edges.

I don't know why I'm here. Everything has been packed up and shipped off, the property sold, with the deeds transferred and finalized more than a week ago. But something is calling me, a pulling, a pleading; I can't ignore it anymore.

Grandpa didn't want to come, saying he was too tired, too sore, but I know the reason why. The memories that lurked behind every corner and closet would hurt too much to relive. I don't blame him.

I thought grandma's funeral would bring me some resolution, a closing of a chapter that would enable me to move on with my life, but the hollow ache in me only grew larger. A simmering sort of resentment and anger building up in secret like a sinkhole under my feet.

Why did she have to die so soon?

I have so many questions still festering within me the older I become. Now I will never get answers.

My grip is loose and unsteady around the key. Today is the last day to turn it in, and I need to let go. With a swift click and a push, the door opens, and I cross over the threshold. I close my eyes, thinking of all the memories that could come rushing up to me like a frantic crowd of people, but there's nothing. Only silence.

Just get this over with, I chide myself.

Opening my eyes, I make my way through the house. Past the kitchen where my grandma made all her delicious meals. She did everything old school. No recipes, only measuring by feel with her hands.

The walls are startlingly bare, and the floor is bereft of the soft, beige carpet that used to tickle my feet as I walked.

I peer into the parlor, missing all the strange knickknacks she kept in here, like the frightening oni mask she hung on the far wall; the sneering red face and horns made me want to hide behind a chair in fear. Or the giant decorative fans she insisted were family heirlooms but were really choice purchases made from our next-door neighbor's garage sale.

But those are gone. Packed away to be sold.

I turn and make my way down the long hallway bisecting our house. My old room is at the end on the left. I don't even bother.

Then my grandma's on the right and the bathroom all the way at the far end. This is the one place I don't want to be. I struggled cleaning out her room, every keepsake like a claw tearing away a piece of me.

So why am I here? I had been proud of myself after the funeral to not have shed a tear. Not one. Not even a hiccup. I survived, have been surviving, with only this dull, hollow ache, which is manageable. Preferable.

Stupid me.

I can do this. I can do this. But no matter how many times I say this mantra, the grief seeps in, threatening to throw me into the black hole that is eating me whole. I suck in a breath and wait for the memories to emerge, but there is only me and the empty chasms of this house.

The soft yellow of sunlight filters through the jalousie windows, and I enter her room.

I stand in the center. Watching. Waiting. Expecting. And I am met with silence and stillness. Somehow, I feel the pain of disappointment even when I had told myself not to.

Then I see it: a box flush against the back of my grandma's closet. How did I miss that? I had cleaned out everything from here. *Everything*. Frowning, I pick it up.

The box is simple, a small wooden rectangle no bigger than both of my hands placed side by side. There are no carvings, no embellishments, just a metal latch and a lacquered finish. What is this?

There's not much weight to it, more akin to a floppy paperback than a thick hardcover. I run my fingers over the top, then tap, before skirting around the latch. Do I open it? Do I dare?

I press my lips together, mind coming to a decision. My inability to give up the keys, my draw to come back here, and the lingering doubts and feelings of unfulfilled closure can only mean one thing. There's a message to be answered.

So, I open the box.

It flies out of my hands and floats in midair, dispensing three items that hover in front of it: a kokeshi doll, a green tassel, and a letter. All the hair on my body stands up, and I scream.

I bolt out of the room, racing for the front door. What the fuck is that? How can an object just *fly?* I need to get out of this place and shove it into the memory bank of things never to be opened again. My skin crawls, peppered with rising bumps, and I am almost free of this house, hand on the knob. But something stops me.

Grandma had never believed in ghosts, scoffed at it. Every time I whispered my fears to her after I had watched a frightening movie, she'd chide me saying I watched too many stupid shows.

This is the same woman who told me of how our ancestors spoke to us in our dreams. How she was visited by her in-laws after the birth of her son, how she had been crying and struggling, and a soft gentle breeze filtered through, carrying the scent of sandalwood and a touch of warmth to give her strength.

No, I would not run away.

Grandma wants me to know something. It must be her. She is the only one I can't let go of, and whatever she says I'll take all of it. Words are precious, even if she can't speak them. I will listen to her.

I return to her room, back straighter, steps firm, wondering briefly if this had all been some conjured fantasy, but when I peer in, the box and items are still there. Floating. A soft, yellow aura envelops them, and they hover in place with no movement.

A faint smell of jasmine and rose permeates through the room. *Grandma?*

Hands shaking, I grab the first object.

The doll.

The kokeshi doll is small and fits perfectly against my palm. The wood is smooth and weathered and shiny. Two dots of pink mark the doll's cheeks, eyes crinkled in a smile, arms at her side, her oblong body wrapped in a pink kimono dotted with sakura blooms.

I wish I could be as cheerful as this toy.

I don't have time to inspect and admire. The world around me darkens and I am pulled into a world of hazy gray.

Voices erupt into being, and I am standing in my grandma's room. Two figures are in front of me, both standing, and in the middle of furious argument.

Grandma!

She's younger. Her eyebrows are still drawn on with perfect, neat arches, and her hair not yet cut into the bob she later favored. I want to reach out to her, to touch her, to cry and apologize over and over again, how I hadn't done more for her when she had been alive, but she's nothing but an illusion that wavers when I step closer.

This is a memory.

Across her stands a man with thick, straight eyebrows, round nose, and a ruddy face. My father. He towers over her, voice booming, but my grandma isn't intimidated, she stands right up to him, pointing an accusatory finger at the center of his chest.

I don't know if I'm supposed to feel excited, hopeful, distressed, or sad at his appearance. But honestly I feel nothing. I don't care. He's been there but mostly not. I can recall less than ten instances when he stayed more than a month, but the shouts, and the fights, and the destructive rages I can count more than the years I have been alive.

"How can you expect to take care of a baby?" Grandma demands, hands fanning out wide.

"I can!" my father roars back, but I know the real answer.

This scene must be about me. Is this how my grandparents found out? A sudden confrontation in the dark of night?

What an unwelcome surprise.

"How? How can? You no more job. You didn't even finish school! You not even home all the time!" She throws her words like she's attacking him in court, trying to indict him on all the guilt and resentment that has been festering. And then she throws it out, the final hook. "What are you even doing? Drugs?"

The accusation hangs heavily in the air, but my father doesn't back down. He doesn't even hesitate.

"You watch!" he yells defiantly. "I thought you was my family. But you can't even support me!"

I flinch. Grandma's face breaks countenance just for a second, her eyes turning bright before she hardens. "Get out!"

"Mom—"

"I don't want to deal with this right now! OUT!"

The scene shifts. I'm in the room again but my father is no longer there. Expected.

My grandma looks tired. Her face is pale and thin. There's a weariness to the way she carries herself as she slumps into her chair. A deep sigh erupts from the roots of her bones.

"Hello?" *a voice calls out in the direction of the door, marked with hesitation.*

This voice, soft and tentative, makes my heart pound and I whip my head around. Could this be? But I can't see her—my mother—she's hidden by the memory, cloaked in shadow and filtered with blur.

No! Please... let me see her, just once...

But that's not what my grandma brought me here. The identity of my mother is not important to her message. Yet, the yearning and the desire to possess such knowledge rises up, something I thought I had buried, thrown away, and forgotten. Why didn't she tell me?

"No." *A long pause.* "Come in."

She enters. My mother is carrying me, a bundle in carefully cradled arms. I can only see her hair, dark, thick, and curly, brushing the top of her arms. Her skin is a shade or two darker than my own. I am so close yet so far to touching the piece of me that has been harbored and hidden. I can only swallow and watch.

"Do you want to hold her?"

Grandma stiffens, looks up at her, eyes fluttering between a decision. If she holds me, the barrier will crack. Then she looks down at me and there is a glimmer of hope there, a spot of happiness, and finally she makes a terse nod.

My mother slides her gently from her arms and into my grandma's. My eyes are bright and dark, like beads of prized pearls freshly strung onto a necklace. My cheeks are so round, I wonder how I'm able to even move them. It should be strange to see a version of myself so young and free of the constraints of life, but I am more intrigued than revulsed.

There is a moment of pause, the press of tension and expectation all wrapped up so tightly together, until baby me smiles, breaking into a giggle. My mother stands to the side, watching, waiting for something

I can't puzzle an answer for. But when I look back at my grandma, I can see the strands of anger slowly begin to unravel as she pulls me closer, bringing me tighter to her heart.

There's movement, a pudgy arm reaching up for grandma's face, tiny fingers outstretched. Tears well in her eyes, all the resentment snapped in an instant as a new emotion forms there now. Hope. She smiles so broadly with all the warmth and adoration she can muster, the beginning of love seeping into her countenance.

I lean back against the wall, hands pressed around my cheeks. I still remember the quiet moments when it was just her and me, and she felt safe enough to share, how she had tried so many times over and over to have another child again, a girl. But her efforts were only rewarded with one child, my father.

Grandma reaches out to her side and grabs something from her dresser. The kokeshi doll. The kimono and dots of pink are visible from here. She coos and places it in my open hand. My first gift, my first toy.

I am flung mercilessly back into reality, my grandma's room swarming up around me. I don't know how to take this information. I sit down and put my pounding head into my hands.

My grandma was so happy, something rarely seen from her. She didn't express much except when she had to make her displeasure known. I could count on my fingers how many times I had seen her cry; it wouldn't take all ten of them. Her joy, her longing, had been reflected in every action. It makes me think I'm wrong for having this rising sort of conflict inside of me, these views that are clashing and baring teeth at each other.

But then I remember a time I was on the playground in elementary school. I can't pinpoint my age, only that I was young, not even into the double digits. Even then this memory sticks in my mind like scalding water from the faucet.

During recess a boy had come up to me. He was lanky with wild hair that never seemed to know whether to lie flat or rebel into random spikes. I thought he was going to ask me to play with him, but I was wrong. This was a boy who had the reputation for blurting out everything he thought.

"Why's your name weird?" he asked.

I frowned. "What do you mean weird?"

"Kalei? Kaleialoha? That doesn't sound Japanese," he insisted.

"It's not. It's Hawaiian."

He scrunched up his nose, eyes narrowed as he stared at me like I was some sort of bug. "You don't look Hawaiian."

I froze, astonishment seeping into my veins. How could I not be Hawaiian? Everyone told me so, even my grandma had said so, and she had no reason to lie. But doubt was creeping in.

"I *am* Hawaiian," I said with all the force I could muster, back straight, chest out, and hands on my hips.

"Oh, yeah? Then prove it! Who's Hawaiian?"

"My mother!" I shot back, nearly screeching.

"Where is she? Show me then I'll believe you."

All of my bluster, my indignant rage, deflated at that moment. "I…I don't know."

He cocked his head, a smirk on his face. "What do you mean you don't know? Everyone knows where their mother is."

I couldn't respond to that, didn't know how. Everything in me searched and searched but nothing was offered. Had my grandma told me where she was, and I hadn't remembered? Was she dead? This couldn't be. She had to be somewhere, right?

"I don't know!" I screamed at him, face hot, vision blurry.

The boy made a note of dismissal and turned away, leaving me with an uncomfortable weight of knowledge. I stood there for a long time staring at my hands and wondering what would make me look more Hawaiian. What if my skin was browner like all the others? Or maybe my hair? What if I made it long, curly, and thick? But when I turned my hands over, all I saw was pale skin. Not Hawaiian. Only Japanese.

I hid them from my sight in disgust.

Later that day when school was finished and all of us were waiting to be picked up, I saw that same boy. He stood, backpack on and hands, clutching a small bag that held his home lunch, not acknowledging the others around him. His earlier words rang in my head, and I seethed with every sting they left on me. I hated him, *hated*. I wanted him to trip and fall right into the dirt, face ugly and scraped.

But his squeal of excitement ripped through my vicious thoughts and had me reeling at what I saw.

His parents had come, broad smiles and open arms. He ran to them, and a chasm opened up within me—a different sort of pain slipping into its place as they enveloped him with a type of love I could only observe.

Why couldn't I have that? Why was I so different? I looked at my pale hands once more and sneered.

When my grandpa arrived not too long after, his old car chugging away in loud spurts, he greeted me with his usual restrained, quiet demeanor. I frowned.

"Did you have a good day at school?" he asked me in the car. A matter of routine more than curiosity. I bit my lip and stared at my feet, then the gray panel of the glove compartment. "Kalei? Are you alright?"

"Nothing! I'm fine," I snapped, turning away from him to stare out the window, lips firmly sealed shut. This was the first time I realized something wasn't quite right with my family.

***

Hānai. An informal adoption of a child into a family. In the olden days, it was done by the grandparents. Usually wanted, usually known to all.

But I didn't know, and even after my research on the subject—*much* research—my newfound understanding didn't stop me from feeling abandoned. Unwanted. Unloved.

The kokeshi doll is still gripped in my hands. I wish I could emulate its beaming smile. What sort of answers am I supposed to derive from these memories? I am drawing empty circles, and the thing that I wanted to see most of all, my mother, is being withheld from me. I can't even see her face.

I asked my grandma about her countless times. Her response was always a shift in body posture, eyes that wouldn't meet mine. "I don't know where she is," she'd say softly each time, firmly, with no leeway for probing until I just stopped.

Trembling, I place the doll back in the box and stare at the other two objects left before me. A tassel and a letter. Do I even want to continue? So far all I've experienced is pain.

I'm not going to pick the letter. I'm not ready to address the sneaking suspicion I have carried with me for all these years. I pluck the tassel from the air.

I giggle loudly, swaying on my feet. The night is sticky with humidity. The world around me seems to dance in bright lights, and I crash into the side of my house. Oops.

I manage to get inside, door clanging behind me. I cringe, but that feeling is quickly consumed by the idea of lying down and taking a nap. I think I need to sleep, or maybe I just need to feel the soft carpet tickling my skin.

I roll around. There's a pressing weight at the back of my head like a migraine, and I am not so amused anymore. I yawn. Maybe washing my face and brushing my teeth would do the trick. There's a lingering sour taste on my tongue, and I'm sure it expands into my breath.

The lights are on in my grandma's room, the first in the hallway. Shit.

My room is at the end, where the bathroom is, and where I need to be. But I have to pass the cavern of the fire-breathing monster first. I stick close to the wall, take small steps, and hope I can sidle on by.

But my balance wavers, and I stumble into the doorway instead. My grandma is up in an instant, eyes flashing. I can practically see the rage pulsating from her. I'm in big trouble.

"About time you came home," she says, words sharp enough to leave a gash. "Where have you been? Do you know what time it is?"

I do. It's precisely 2:13 in the morning. Far past my curfew, that's for sure. But I keep those words in check because I don't want to get smacked. "Yeah," I say, hoping she'll be nice and let it slide just this once. "I'm home now."

Her expression tells me she's not impressed. She strides over and—crap, crap, crap—she leans down and takes a sniff. I'm done for. If she was mad before, she is absolutely melting me with the heat of her stare now.

"Have you been drinking, Kalei?"

"Only a little…" I say, although we both know that is not true.

"Don't you lie to me! I can't believe you would do something so stupid, so dangerous—"

"It's fine!" I snap. Why does she always ask me questions she knows the answer to? Just say it already so we don't have to go through this back and forth. I swear sometimes she does this so she can catch me slipping up and sink her teeth into me and tear me apart for my transgression piece by piece.

"It's NOT fine, Kalei! You aren't even eighteen yet and you're drinking? And driving? Do you know how dangerous that is? You could have gotten someone killed!"

I flinch at the rise in her voice. But Grandpa isn't going to come around, he never does when we argue, choosing to sit back and have my grandma deal with it. I couldn't ask him for support.

"Well, I'm here now, aren't I?" I say.

"No, that's not ok! Some friends of yours, let you drink and drive home drunk. Shameful!"

A spike of anger shoots through me. Sure, I may have done some drinking, but it was the smallest amount, never out of hand. I know what I'm doing. I'm not stupid. She can't slander my friends like this. How dare she? They've done nothing wrong. "Don't say anything about my friends! They're good people!"

"Obviously. They're so good friends they let you drive home drunk! Who knows what else you could be doing with them!"

"Nothing! I am an adult! I can go out with my friends if I want!" My head is about to burst with adrenaline, the fog of alcohol stripped away. The migraine is in full force now, throbbing in my temples and forehead.

"You're not an adult! You're not even eighteen! Keep going, and you'll turn out just like your father."

Her words cut into me instantly, the next responses dying on my lips. Doesn't she trust me? Doesn't she know I would never do things like that? All I did was hang out with friends, talk story, eat food, and go home. It's not like I had been out robbing stores or snorting lines. Tears burn my eyes.

"Give me your keys," she says, reaching for my hands.

"What?" I say, yanking back instinctively.

"You're grounded. And you won't get to drive my car until I say so," she states, ripping the keys from my fingers.

"This is unfair!"

"Well, you shouldn't have done dumb things then."

"I hate you!" I explode, all emotions escaping at once. Her words ring in my ear, and they slap me repeatedly, reminding me of how much I'm a failure to her. "I wish I'd never been born!"

At once my grandma's face crumples but I don't look back. I storm past her and slam the door with vibrating force. The sound echoing long into the night.

I'm thrown out of the memory at once. I rub my face roughly, not wanting to cry, but my last words sting. Even then I had regretted those words as soon as they left my mouth.

But things once said can't be returned. I hadn't meant it. In the depths of my heart, I knew what I was saying was wrong, but I couldn't stop myself from relishing in the spite I wanted to throw at her. She had taken away something important from me—my agency, my freedom, my friends—and I wanted her to feel just as badly as I did.

Apologies are easier to say in reflection, in the dark of the night, not when they are needed. We were taught to never bow and show weakness, so neither one of us spoke them.

If I knew then how little time I had with her, I would have said them loudly to show her how much I cared, how much I loved her. It's too late now.

I glance down, and the tassel glows brighter, yellow light seeping through the cracks between my fingers, and I'm thrown into another scene.

Grandma grips me to her side, her touch gentle, and I smile broadly for the camera. There is a mountain of lei around my neck, a colorful cascade of flowers, candy, ribbons, and carefully folded bills of money. Grandpa stands next to me, bringing out a begrudging smile for the picture. He hates being in places where there's lots of hubbub and commotion, but he suffers through it for me.

The cataclysmic fight we had only a month earlier seems to have faded away, replaced with tense atmospheres and stiff interactions. We spoke not a word to each other for nearly a week, but when my graduation date came near, my grandma began to thaw, her resentment melting away, as she bustled around in her excitement. Clothes, hair, makeup. All had to be perfect for this momentous day.

Grandma is effusive today, pride practically bursting from her. Her eyes are bright, and she looks at me with pure joy. I finally realize how important today is to her.

I am her star, her shining achievement. The second chance that she had been given, an opportunity to remold all her past mistakes into one of success. All the pain and regret she held, the failures she thought she committed in raising my father, are free from her now. I have done the things she could only have wished for him.

Education, so held as the pinnacle of prestige and status for her back then, would be mine. Growing up poor, raised by parents who had been brought in to work countless days and hours in the plantation fields, this diploma is a promise of more. A pathway upward that she had never been afforded.

Later on, when the celebrations have settled and I have taken more than a day to recover, I wander into my grandma's room.

A cloying smell permeates the air, and I see the heap of lei still sitting on her chair. Why hasn't she thrown those out already? A lot of the flowers were wilting; some even had patches of brown. I also love and cherish each one in that pile, as they came from a friend, a family member, or even a classmate who cares. Someone who thought I was important enough to remember. A weighty sentiment, yes, but surely not when they start to go bad?

"Come," she says, indicating the low table at her side. "We need to start writing thank you cards."

I groan inwardly. This is too much. Aren't my hugs and thank yous said that day enough? But I pick up my pen and begin rifling through the list of names and addresses.

Looking up, I see my grandma fondly touching the frame of something. I squint; it's a picture. All three of us are beaming for the camera, the rare moment when pure happiness and joy is captured on film for all eternity. The pride I can see gleaming from their eyes is evident. I have never seen them so exuberant.

How quickly had she developed that thing? My graduation was only a few days ago. She must have rushed off to the photo developers as soon as we came home.

She cradles my green tassel lovingly in her hands, holding it flat in her palm. Her fingers run the length of it with gentle caresses. Had she taken that straight off my cap? Grandma fondly gives the tassel another pat and drapes it over the corner of her picture, a smile curving her lips.

"I'm so proud of you, you know?"

The soft-spoken words fade away. I blink and stare at the tassel in my hands, the long strands of green thread brushing my skin.

I wonder if I'm broken. If I'm heartless. I should feel touched, but I can't. I'm just numb. That moment was one of the few times I ever heard her praise me. Yet her words ring hollow in my ears.

Not too long after, we had dinner parties for all our extended family members and friends. Grandma wanted me to be present at each one, to give smiles, hugs, and quaint speeches about how happy I was to have everyone there. I hated it.

There is still something missing, something off about the picture. I can't help but feel the slightest bit of resentment, a piece for envy and a piece for yearning interlocking into one puzzle. Even if my grandparents loved me, a normal family has parents there. A father. A mother.

I always wondered what they would have thought about me. Graduating, growing up to become the better iteration any of them could be. Yet there must be a reason. An answer as to why my mother could not be here, why my grandma guarded the answer so closely like a treasure box in a dragon's cave.

Or maybe I just don't want to accept it. I stare at the one remaining item hovering in the air, the letter. All the secrets may be cracked open once I take it, escaping out of their confinement in a rush, bringing epiphanies I'm not sure I am ready for.

I suck in a deep, shuddering breath, place the tassel in the box, and grab the letter.

The paper has yellowed from time, thin and crispy in my fingers. One flick and I'm sure it would crumble. The ink is legible but faded. The handwriting consists of big, looping letters in neat, uniform heights. Not my grandma's handwriting, small and dainty. No, it must be my mother's.

I admire the penmanship, wishing mine was half as pretty. There are darker blotches on the paper, spread out with no real pattern. Circles with fuzzy outlines. Teardrops.

And then I am pulled into the last of my grandma's memories.

A woman stands in front me. Her hair is a curtain of thick black with a sea of curls. My mother? Instantly, I reach out to grab her shoulder, wanting to turn her around to face me but my hand merely goes through her form. Like a ghost wishing they could still be alive.

No, please. You can't be keeping her from me now.

Grandma enters the room. She sees my mother and gestures for her to sit. They take up space on the bed and I can hear myself as a baby, gurgling and then giggling.

The room shifts and, like a panorama unveiling in slow motion, I am finally able to see my mother. Not her eyes at first, not her rounded cheeks and square jaw, but the drawn eyebrows and expression of fatigue.

Her skin is brown. She smiles briefly, a mere lifting of the lip at the corner, and talks. There is so much of her that I can't see in me, from the lines of her face to the sweet lilt of her voice. None of that was transferred to me; all I am reminded is how much I look like my father.

"Do you know where Marcus is?" Grandma asks, holding out her arms in offer.

"No," my mother says, sighing. Glancing down at me, she slides me over and continues, "I haven't seen him in over a week actually."

"I'll talk to him."

My mother shakes her head. "Don't bother. It won't make a difference."

There is truth in the silence, and neither of them look each other in the eye. My mother's gaze is intense, watching as she observes Grandma's every touch, every whisper, every emotion. There seems to be a storm brewing within her, dark and furious, as she struggles to come up with a solution.

"Do you love her?" my mother breaks into the moment suddenly.

Grandma tips her head, glancing back at me. "Of course I do."

My mother swallows, taking a moment to gather her courage, before asking another question. "Would you do anything for her? Even if I'm not able to?"

"Yes, anything." Grandma frowns. "What a strange question. You'll be a good mother, Māhea. Not everyone is perfect at this from the start."

I start. Māhea. My mother's name. I form the letters on my tongue and with the press of my lips. Ma-he-a. Strange and awkward when I voice them. Yet, I can't help but linger on the last words my grandma has said. I wonder if she's echoing her own experiences as a mother.

Despite the support and words of encouragement, my mother shrinks into herself, looking more crestfallen than when she had first come in. And then I know. She made her decision.

The image melds with the present. The walls of my grandma's room surround me, and I suck in a deep breath, clutching at the letter firmly. With a loud exhale, I stare at the words, waiting for the pull back in.

My mother is gone. I can hear my grandma rushing down the hallway calling out for her, delaying the inevitable. There's a heavy pang in my heart. I don't want this next scene to play out, but I know what's happened.

Grandma runs into the room, picking up the phone to dial my mother's number. But only silence. I want to reach out to her, to touch her, to tell her it will be ok. But will it?

She slams down the phone and frets, pacing, putting her fingers to her lips, then pacing again. Until she sees the letter, a small folded up piece of white paper left on the side of her bed. Grandma reaches out and grabs it with trembling hands, sinking down into her chair before she starts to read.

I am in her eyes now, seeing all that she sees but not what she feels. Inserting her fingers into the fold, she slowly brings the letter flat. And then she reads.

Dear Mrs. Hiromi,

You've realized it by now, haven't you? I'm gone. Probably have been for a while. I've thought about this decision. Agonized over it. But I could not come up with any answer that would not bring pain to either of us. This is the easiest, and only path, moving forward.

I know I'm not what you wanted. An unwelcome surprise, I guess. I can't hold it against you. I would react the same way if I were in your position. Thank you for opening your heart and home to me. I am forever grateful.

But this is where things must end.

You've asked me about my parents. And the answer is the same. They haven't budged. They refuse to acknowledge my daughter's existence and accept what my reality is now. Our fights have only grown more heated, more angry, and I can't take another one. I'm much better than this, they say.

If I continue with this path, they've told me that they'll cut me off. I won't be a part of their family anymore. And... I can't do that. I need my family. It hurts me so much but if I were to stick with you I will always second guess, always wonder, and even though you've been as kind as you can be to me, it can't replace my family. I'm meant for more than this. College, a career, a life ahead of me without the stigma of a teenage mother.

I'm sorry.

I may come to regret my decision in the future. In fact, I'm sure I will but this is what I have chosen. Do you remember when I asked you if you would love and support her no matter what? I hope that's still the case.

The best thing I can do is leave her with you, where she will be truly loved and cherished as she's meant to be.

The name you chose for her is perfect. I couldn't have done better.

Kaleialoha. The Beloved Child.
Please forgive me,
Māhealani

Plop, plop, plop. Tears, hot and stinging, drip down my grandma's face, as every piece of her heart slides down onto the paper.

My eyes burn, and I place a hand to my cheeks. They're wet. Teardrops fall in dark, oblong splotches next to my grandma's. But it's like a fissure in the ground, like lava erupting in belching spurts; I can't stop these loud, gasping cries.

This is the message grandma's left. Even through the pain of my childhood and my difficult, raging times, she's always loved me. Even when I was angry and blamed her for all the things I couldn't have, she still loved me. So much.

The letter flutters away from my grasp, floating to the ground, and I sob. I can't even see through my tears, and I try to stem them by pressing the back of hand to my face.

Warmth blooms around me like a thick comforter, and the scent of jasmine and rose is so strong I almost want to sneeze. "Grandma?"

There's the gentlest of touches, a brief press of fingers to cheek, and I hear a soft murmuring, a shushing in my ear. The pounding of my heart slows, calms, and I can take in one steady breath after another.

It will be alright.

And then she's gone. I feel her absence immediately, like an evaporation of smoke. I sit for a while, waiting for my tears to dry. My mind is buzzing, swirling, and I don't know what to do now. But at least I have answers.

As the sun begins to set and the room begins to darken from golden to the cool palettes of browns and purples, I gather the items around me. The kokeshi doll, the tassel, and finally, the letter.

I place them all into the box and with one last, lingering glance, I walk out of the house.

I'm at her grave. It's the first time I've been here since her funeral. There's a solid copper plaque with branches full of leaves around the borders. Her name stands out in thick, capital letters: HIROMI NAGASAWA. I no longer want to run.

Instead, I squat down and carefully place the bouquet of spring flowers into the holder. Brightly colored and beautiful. There are other offerings here as well: a cup of saké, a persimmon, all things she loved in life. Brushing away a few leaves that had fallen on top of her plaque, I run my fingers over her name. Gently, lovingly.

"Thank you," I whisper, hoping she can hear me. "I've received your message."

A breeze flows through my hair, bringing with it the scent of jasmine and rose.

△▽△▽△

PELE IN THERAPY

[Darien Gee]

My ten o'clock appointment is late. I'm sitting in the living room of the small condo I'm renting, waiting for a client who probably won't show. I know this because it's almost two o'clock.

But still I'm dressed and waiting, a fresh pad of paper and two glasses of water in front of me. I'm dressed and waiting because I have nothing else to do. I have been on this island for three months and have managed to burn through what little savings I have. I'll take any client I can get.

I glance at the calendar. Three months ago to this day I was sitting in a suite at one of the hotels on the Kohala coast with my husband, David. We were on our second honeymoon because we didn't really have a first—no time, no money—and before we knew it, twenty-five years had passed.

David surprised me with a trip to Hawai'i, but that's not all. On the night we were scheduled to catch the red-eye back to Seattle, he told me he was having an affair with his secretary and would be leaving me once we got home.

The next day, he flew back and I barricaded myself in the hotel room with our suitcases. The bellhops thought I'd gone insane. I opened the gifts I had so carefully and laboriously packed, upending everything. I swam among bags of Kona coffee and vacuum-packed macadamia nuts. I buried myself in tie-dyed pareos. I scooped white honey out of the jar. Dashboard hula girls and dolphin key chains littered the floor. The pīkake-scented soap set I bought for David's secretary was hurled off the balcony.

I stayed in the hotel four more days until David canceled the credit card. Then I packed and came up the hill to Waimea.

A pounding on my front door startles me. I should have come up with a way for screening people before they show up for an appointment—I imagine myself cut into small pieces with no identifying body parts. Nobody will know who I am or what has happened to me. I haven't made a single friend since I've lived here. The pounding continues and all I can feel is dread.

When I open the door, I see it's my landlady, Mrs. Fukumoto. She's Hawaiian but her fifth husband was Japanese-Hawaiian. She looks about eighty, crusty with an annoyed, disapproving look on her face. A lit cigarette dangles from the side of her mouth. Next to her is a little white dog, an annoying yapper that starts barking the minute he sees me.

"You're behind on your rent." Mrs. Fukumoto jabs a gnarly finger into my chest, poking me so hard it hurts. Ash falls from her cigarette onto the carpet.

"I know, I'm sorry. I should have the money soon." I look at my bare feet when I say this.

Mrs. Fukumoto lives in the adjoining unit and constantly boasts about how much property she owns on the island. She cranes her head to look inside my condo.

"What are those?" she demands.

My cramped 900-square-foot living area is overrun with boxes stacked to the ceiling. David shipped my things to me via slow boat, which means that after two months at sea they arrived the other day. That was the one blessing about not having children—it made the division of assets much easier. The only thing left is the house, which my lawyer says will be split right down the middle when it sells. We'll fight for alimony, too, but until we go to court, I'm on my own. I can't afford a storage unit, so here we are.

"They're just some old things," I say. I can't even begin to think of what's inside. I haven't opened them since David sent them, my name scrawled across each box like an afterthought.

"Take it to the dump," Mrs. Fukumoto says with a smirk. The cigarette has burned out but seems permanently stuck to the bottom of her lip. Her dog yaps in agreement.

The idea of hauling everything to the transfer station and adding them to the island's growing landfill holds little appeal for me. *What's left of my life is in those boxes,* I want to say, but instead I keep my mouth shut.

An odd-looking man hovers by my sign. Mrs. Fukumoto frowns.

"Too many visitors!" she snaps. By the way the man is squinting at me, I have a sinking feeling that he's my ten o'clock, four and a half hours late. Not a good sign.

"Mrs. Fukumoto, I told you. I'm a trained therapist, I see clients in my home." I do my best to sound like the professional I'm not. That's the problem with starting a career mid-life—I'm clueless. I don't have the business background or life experience necessary to build a successful practice—I just have a license to see patients and dispense advice and not much less. It's one thing to study psychology in college and grad school and another thing entirely to attempt it twenty years later.

"I don't want any crazies around here," Mrs. Fukumoto says loudly. The man looks nervous, eyes flickering between the two of us. "You know what you need? Better marketing. You need a hook, get good customers in. Forget these nut jobs." She thumbs my client's direction and throws him a surly look.

I don't say anything. As desperate as I am, I am not about to take marketing advice from my landlady.

"That reminds me," she says. "I need to leave my dog with you."

I look at the mangy white dog at my feet. He bares his teeth.

"I have to go out for town tomorrow for a few days. I'm almost out of dog food so you'll have to get some from the store. Take it out of what you owe me."

I start to protest but her eyes narrow and I find myself saying, "Fine, all right." I just want her to leave before I lose this client.

"Keep his water dish filled with the bottle on the counter. It's special."

"Yes, yes."

"He eats four times a day. Small meals."

"Four times a day. Small meals. Got it." I clench my teeth, willing her to go.

Mrs. Fukumoto nods, satisfied, and heads back to her place. Her dog follows her and glances back with a look that says he'd eat me if he were big enough.

I beckon the client into my home. He stares at the boxes in horror and then at the stuffing coming out of the couch, the mildew on the wallpaper. It takes me less than a minute to see he has OCD—obsessive-compulsive disorder. He's a neat freak. I don't expect our session to last long.

It doesn't.

The next day I decide Mrs. Fukumoto is right. I need a hook, a catch phrase that will draw people in. While I'm at it, I'd like to find a way to get the men to self-select out. I've already had two ask me out, which is inappropriate and a little creepy. I get the feeling that they're less interested in self-improvement and more concerned about having someone to go barhopping with on Saturday nights in Kona.

At Ace Ben Franklin, I wander the aisles. I spend the last of my savings on two folding screens, some needle and thread, a container of Clorox wipes. I add a packet of red adhesive letters. On the way home I stop by the gas station and pick up a musubi for lunch and some dog food.

Mrs. Fukumoto was gone this morning, her rusty Toyota no longer in the car port. I had filled the dog food bowl and poured water from the gin bottle on the counter, but the dog was nowhere to be seen. It's my secret wish that she took the dog with her and forgot to tell me.

When I step inside her place, I see both the food bowl and the water bowl are empty. I replenish them, whistling for the dog while hoping he doesn't come. He doesn't. I can only hope we continue to avoid each other until Mrs. Fukumoto returns home.

Back in my condo I push the boxes to one side and hide them behind the folding screens. I take the needle and thread and sew the couch as best I can. I wipe down the walls. Then I go outside and stare at my sign.

KATHERINE O'DELL, MFT
WALK-INS WELCOME

After a moment's hesitation, I use the adhesive letters to add:

DISCOVER THE GODDESS WITHIN!

I know it's silly, but people tend to be into this new age sort of thing. And it turns out that this town is already full of psychotherapists, not to mention real estate agents, so unless I want to call David and demand that he advances me some money, I need to find a way to differentiate myself.

Drivers and passersby turn their head to read the sign. My cheeks redden as I hurry back into the condo, near tears that I've had to sink this low. I'm forty-six and my parents are cajoling me from their assisted-living facility in Boca Raton to reconcile with David, a thought I entertain when I'm at the lowest of lows. So he cheated. Is that really a deal breaker? Can I overlook this unfortunate incident in exchange for a lifestyle of companionship and security? Independence is overrated. The affair was only going on for two years, a little less if you take out the days we were in Hawai'i and the other time we visited my parents for Easter. I never asked David to take me back, but maybe I should. Maybe it's time to face reality.

There's a knock on the door.

I feel a sudden rise of panic and consider escaping through the kitchen window. That's what I want to do—run. Hide. But where? I'm on an island in the middle of the Pacific. Where could I possibly go? I am stuck, like it or not.

When I open the door, there's a striking young woman on my doorstep, her dark hair pulled away from her face. She's wearing a dark red sundress, but you can see the outline of her sculpted body through the thin fabric. I can't even remember life before cellulite.

The woman is muttering under her breath, twisting a loose strand of hair around a slender finger. I want to say she's in her twenties, but she could be older. I can't quite place her age.

"Can I help you?" I ask.

"I don't have an appointment." Her face is dark.

My pulse quickens. "I'd be happy to schedule…"

"I'm having a bad day," she continues. "I saw your sign outside. Find your inner goddess or something?"

"'Discover the Goddess Within?'"

"Close enough." She steps into the condo before I have a chance to invite her in.

I ask if she'd like water or tea, but she waves the offer away. We settle in the living room which is more spacious and comfortable with the small changes I've made. The woman's forehead is puckered in a frown.

"My love life," she sighs. "It's on the rocks."

"I see." I nod and clear my throat. "I should mention that there's a ten-percent discount if you pay for your session in cash…"

She ignores me. "I think he's in love with someone else." She takes a breath and the whole room breathes with her. "He saw me in a moment when I didn't look like this…" she gestures to her body, her perfectly made-up self, "…and he fled."

Now she has my full attention. *Men!* I want to spit out, but instead I nod sympathetically. "I understand." I can't imagine how difficult it must be to always look so beautiful. People start to expect it, and the minute you have a bad hair day, their illusions are shattered. I pick up my notebook to look like I'm doing something. I write the day's date, the time, and realize I don't even know her name.

"I'm Katherine," I say. "And you are…?"

"I am sick and tired of everyone assuming that I don't want love!" The look on her face is explosive. She stands up and begins pacing, her red dress swirling around her. "I don't have time to be frivolous like everyone else. I have my own life, my own responsibilities. I do more than all of them!"

"Them? Who's them?"

"My sisters. Their responsibilities are nothing like mine. I have to do so much more." She tosses her head in defiance.

I nod in what I hope is a reassuring manner. "How many sisters do you have?" I ask. It's important to get the family history—it's elemental to who we are. At the end of the day, that's where most of our issues lie.

"Seven. Seven sisters and seven brothers."

I can see where this is going. The young woman in front of me is fiercely competitive and independent. Definitely not a first born or the oldest girl—this one's always had to fight for her place.

I write *Big Family* on my notepad. Then I ask, "Are you originally from Hawai'i?"

She flops down on the couch. "No. I came here some years ago. I didn't plan on being here exactly." She looks away, and I can tell she doesn't want to talk about it yet.

"I can relate," I say. "A lot of people seem to have that experience."

"I am *not* like everyone else!" she steams.

"No, of course not," I reassure her hastily. I add *Middle Child* to my notes with a question mark next to it. "Why don't you tell me more about what's happening in your love life? You said it's on the rocks?"

"I've never been great with relationships," she admits. She pulls up her legs, tucks them underneath her. "It's one reason my older sister and I don't get along. She was very angry at me for seducing her husband." She rolls her eyes derisively.

I try to hide my shock, but she notices my discomfort.

"What?" She arches an eyebrow. "We can't control whom we love. Or desire." She gives a slight smile. David said the same thing to me that night when he told me about Janine, his secretary.

It takes all my willpower to remember I am here to help her, not judge her. She's my client—there's no room for my personal opinion even if I find myself siding with her sister. "Have you ever been married?"

She nods, her face flat and indifferent. "It didn't work out."

I write *Commitment Issues* and tap my pen. "Did you try marriage counseling?"

She bursts out laughing. Even I can't help but chuckle. David wasn't interested in having couples therapy with his therapist wife. The question sounds asinine coming from my mouth.

She leans towards me. "Have you ever been to the volcano?" she asks. "Kīlauea?"

I nod. "Once. But it was pouring rain and foggy. I didn't see a thing."

She nods, not surprised.

I shrug. "It was fine. I'm more of a beach person anyway."

Her eyes harden. "Beach?" she spits out. "Kīlauea is alive, flowing. It's the most active volcano in the world!"

"We tried to see it. My husband and I—" I stumble, unsure if I should say *ex-husband* since our divorce is far from final but our marriage is clearly over, "—were hoping to see the lava flow. Maybe catch a glimpse of Pele in the lava." The concierge at the hotel told us that people sometimes saw the image of Pele, the Hawaiian goddess of the volcano, in the lava.

Her eyes flash with sparks of anger. "That's ridiculous!" she snorts. "Why would she reveal herself to just anyone? She would have nothing to gain from that."

"More tourists, maybe?" I suggest.

The woman shakes her head in disgust. "Just because a child sees an animal in the clouds does not mean that the animal is actually there," she says. "People see what they want to see."

Good point. "A goddess would probably have more important things to do with her time," I concede.

The woman grins. "Exactly." She reaches behind her head and removes a bone clip holding her hair in place. Long, gorgeous locks tumble down her back, dark as lava. "Now if she needed to vent for any reason, that would be different. But to pose for a photo op? I don't think so."

I remember something I heard. "What about Pele's Curse?"

"Which one?"

"I didn't know there was more than one," I say. "I only know about the one with the lava rocks—if you take a rock from the volcano as a souvenir, you'll have bad luck."

I can tell that she doesn't think much of this because she doesn't say anything, just casts her eyes around my condo, bored.

"I hear that every year park rangers are flooded with several thousand pounds of rocks that are returned to them," I continue. "People write letters explaining how they've had a run of bad luck and ask that the rocks be returned to their home. People sometimes make offerings of these rocks back to the goddess."

"Returning pōhaku that have been inappropriately taken in the first place is just putting something back," she sniffs. "It's hardly an offering."

"You seem to know a lot about this," I say.

"I know about a lot of things," she says.

I glance at my watch. It's time for me to feed Mrs. Fukumoto's dog again, but I don't want to end our session. "Can you excuse me for a moment? I'll be right back."

The dog bowls are empty and again the dog is nowhere to be seen. I refill them quickly.

When I return to my living room, I find her trying to set two of my plants on fire. Since one of them is plastic, she's got a good chance of succeeding.

"Don't do that!" I say, imagining the conversation I'm going to have with Mrs. Fukumoto and the fire department. I don't have a fire extinguisher, much less property insurance. I try not to panic as I hold out an ashtray.

She tosses me an annoyed look before blowing into her palm. The flame flickers then disappears. I place the empty ashtray on the side table.

I take a deep breath as I settle back into my chair. I jot *Pyromaniac* into my notebook. She's glaring at me, but I don't care. I add *Destructive to Other People's Property* and *Unremorseful*.

It's time to get this session back on track. I pull out a questionnaire I've printed from the Internet that identifies the specific goddess a person most closely resembles. I hand her the questionnaire and she skims it, guffawing along the way.

"It should only take you a few minutes," I explain. "Just choose the answer that most closely matches you." I hold out a pen, but she ignores me.

"Demeter, Aphrodite, Diana..." Her voice is a bored monotone as she skims the list. "...Athena, Hecate, Isis..." She perks up when she comes across the Hawaiian goddess we have been talking about. "Pele as Creator," she reads, and starts giggling.

"And Destroyer," I append.

"It's the same thing," she tells me. Her hair fans out over her shoulders. "Well, I think I'm done." She stands, and I'm struck by how tall she is. I didn't notice before.

I follow her to the door. While she's in better spirits, I don't feel like I've done much of anything. "Are you sure?"

She turns and gives me a serene look. "I don't have any money to pay you. I don't really have much to do with that sort of thing."

Great. My first real client and she can't pay. "Barter?" I venture. I had one person pay me in apple bananas. It's better than nothing.

She rests her hand on the doorknob as she thinks about this. "I don't barter," she finally says. "But I'll send you referrals. People who can pay."

I'm skeptical she'll send anybody my way, but you never know. It's my own fault for not discussing my fee up front—I'm going to have to work on that. "Ok. I appreciate that."

The woman smiles and leaves. I close the door behind her, then jerk my hand away when I touch the metal knob. It's so hot, it's glowing.

Over the next few months, my practice takes off. Women from all over the island compete for any available time slot. My bank account grows, as does my confidence. I start to lose weight. Not eating on a budget lets me make better choices and I buy organic salads, fresh fruit, and sprouted bread from the health food store and farmers' markets.

Mrs. Fukumoto does little more than grunt when she sees me, now that she's getting her rent money on time. She still disappears on random jaunts leaving me to care for her dog who makes himself scarce the minute I step into their condo.

One evening I find David waiting by my door. It's coming up on one year, our divorce almost final. We haven't talked in a long time, everything going through our lawyers. I can hardly remember what transpired in the past, it seems so long ago.

He steps forward and gives me a hug. "Hey."

He smells just like I remember, and for a second I forget who I am. I want to melt in his arms. "Hi," I say.

His eyes wander up and down my body. "Wow, you look amazing." He gestures to a stack of boxes in Mrs. Fukumoto's doorway. "I wasn't sure which place was yours. I brought over the last of your boxes. They were in the attic."

"Thanks." I feel the heat of a blush warming my cheeks. "Would you like to come in?"

Inside he tries not to look shocked at the boxes still stacked high behind the folding screens.

"I'll get to it eventually," I say with a shrug. "I've been busy with work." I casually open a bottle of wine, hoping that maybe we will have cause to celebrate. In some ways this couldn't be more perfect—I had to get away from David to find out who I am. Now I can come to him not needing anything other than his love. I light a candle and blow out the match, a smile tugging the corners of my mouth.

He accepts the wine glass. "It's great that you're doing so well," he says. He downs his wine in one gulp.

I'm having the strangest feeling of déjà vu. "You didn't come all this way just to give me my boxes, did you?" I ask. I refill his glass and perch on the edge of the sofa, crossing my legs. They're tanned and nicely shaped from hours of Pilates. I see David's eyes linger on them hungrily. "Let me guess: you have something to tell me."

He downs his second glass. He looks tormented and miserable, and I can't tell if I'm enjoying this or feeling a bit sorry for him. Both, I conclude.

"I'm getting married," he says. "Once the divorce is final. Janine is pregnant."

I'm certain David was expecting a repeat performance of my dramatics last year. Even I'm surprised by how calm I am.

"Twins," he gulps, and I can see that he's stunned by this development. David is a couple of years older than me, which means that he'll be changing diapers when he's fifty. He'll be well into his late sixties when his kids go off to college. Any hopes of an early retirement have just gone out the window. I see that he knows this, too.

"Oh, Katherine," he says, and I open my arms and take him in.

The condo is on fire. David is sound asleep—he's always been a hard sleeper. I wrap a robe around me and cover my nose and mouth. I shove him until he wakes up, his eyes filling with alarm.

"Go!" I say and point to the window. He stumbles out, half asleep, a sheet wrapped around his naked body.

In the living room my boxes are on fire, flames licking the ceiling. The furniture, the folding screens, the plants. Everything is being consumed.

I glance around frantically, knowing that I can save one, maybe two boxes. There are my client notes, my identifying documents. I gather them quickly, dark smoke already filling my lungs.

I hear David call my name, the siren scream of a fire truck. The unmistakable sound of a dog barking.

The fire is dancing on the curtains, the carpet. I touch my front door and it's hot—the fire is in the shared hallway but it's the closest way into Mrs. Fukumoto's condo. I drop to the ground and throw open the door, the palm of my hand scalded. The heat of the fire pushes me back. I hear the dog, louder now, a hysterical, angry yapping.

My body feels aflame. I crawl across the hall, my silk robe catching fire. It falls off my body like ash and I am naked, fire on my skin. I fling open the front door of Mrs. Fukumoto's unit and the dog races out and into my arms. We tumble down the stairway. A lick on my face, a tickle of fur. The last thing I see is the shadow of a woman standing over me before I black out.

The fire started in my living room and in Mrs. Fukumoto's bedroom. A fallen candle, a burning cigarette. Together we started a fire that burned down the place in which we lived and everything inside. I wish I could say I escaped with the clothes on my back but that would not be true. I lost everything.

When I woke, I was in the ambulance. When I asked about the dog, they tell me there was none. I fell to the bottom of the stairs with nothing in my arms. Mrs. Fukumoto, too, is missing.

Burns cover fifteen percent of my body, but they are second-degree burns. Almost all are expected to heal. The scabs will fall off as the new skin comes in.

David stayed with me for a couple of days before I told him to go back to Seattle, back to Janine and their babies on the way. It's true, I realize—we can't control whom we love. I still love him, but I no longer want him in my life.

When I was discharged from the hospital, I came straight to the hotel. I ended up in the same suite I shared with David a year ago, but instead of looking at the ocean, I cast my eyes toward the mountains instead. I'll stay here for a couple of weeks, a gift to myself, before I start looking for a new home in Waimea.

There is a knock on my hotel door.

"I don't have an appointment," she says.

I smile and step aside, and let her in.

CINDY AND MICAH

[PHILLIP RILEY]

The letter arrived from Micah, and Cindy glowed with vengeance to meet him. Under the humid, mossy ledges of the Koʻolau Mountains, she wore rugged blue jeans, a red plaid shirt, and her leather tan hiking boots. The thick air vitalized her steps as she recalled Mother's Day a decade ago, when eight people died at Sacred Falls, where she was returning. On that Mother's Day, she canceled her rendezvous with him, and possibly death. She imagined the victims that day singing "Ninety-nine Bottles of Beer" as they hiked to the falls as she had seen others do. They perhaps smoked Marlboros and tossed the butts at the base of koa trees, just when they looked skyward at the boulders falling upon them. Now, Micah teased her with an impish nerve. The letter beckoned her to meet him in the same spot on that same day. She ignored the "Keep Out" signs and marched into the site that had been returned to Mother Nature.

Cindy wore a tight mien upon her lips with a glare in her dark eyes, as if to display her determination against the odds she felt the world had placed against her. At four feet tall, her long hair wisped to

Image by Eric Tessmer: https://commons.wikimedia.org/wiki/File:Koolau_Mountain_from_the_Pali_%E2%89%A1_Eric_Tessmer,_Molokai,_Hawaii_-_panoramio.jpg her ankles. She could have advertised for Just for Women, with bountiful grey streaks streaming down shades of black. Her pale, sunless eye sockets framed beady, dark eyes that resembled a raccoon's. There was something ghostlike about Cindy.

She marched deeper into the valley, where wild plants and a rare native bird called. The ʻiwiʻi sang above Cindy. It wore scarlet plumage and a hooked needle beak.

"They took away from the land, and the land took back. They took away from the land, and the land took back."

"Shut up," said Cindy to the ʻiwiʻi overhead, without even looking up. Its repetitive message earned Cindy's disregard. She stared ahead shrouded like a monk with her drapes of hair. "Sacred Falls, ha" she mumbled, "some new age misnomer for a tourist industry. Damn bird."

She strode onward, heedless of her discomfort and dehydration, oozing determination yet possessing no plan. An undefined presence grew inside her like a virus.

The ʻiwiʻi overtook her and settled in the red flower brush of old ʻōhiʻa trees high above the trail. The roots of the ʻōhiʻa crawled like spiders on the high mossy pumice slopes. The sweet flowers fed the ʻiwiʻi with nectar and camouflaged their red brush tendrils.

"How far will you go, Cindy?" Its song twirled into the air.

She only muttered, "As long as it takes."

"Far enough" The ʻiwiʻi said. It fluttered like sparks into the dusky aura of the mountain valley.

A powerful sadness descended upon Cindy. The futility of the confrontation she sought consumed her, and she shrunk into her own hairy shroud. Just as suddenly, her sadness dried up, and she drew from inside a familiar rage. Marching forward, Cindy's aggression trailed behind her like a gown.

Cindy sought outlets to her rage, envisioning a satisfying release. She had attended the Kung Fu Academy in Mililani for years to channel her angst. She imagined an opportunity to use her training, playing violent scenes of victory over Micah. She didn't know why he called her again, but he fit a script to realize her rage.

"He will be here," she said under her breath. "Why else would that postcard say, 'Happy Mother's Day?' I could have been dead, pummeled like the others. He thinks it is a joke. We could have been ground like poi by the avalanche." She gritted her teeth.

"Coming here for you Cindy, coming herrrrrre," chirped the red, flashing 'iwi'i.

"Oh, shut up."

Then, a group of mosquitoes descended upon her mane as if the bird commanded them. Cindy settled with poise upon a rock and pulled out a tobacco pouch purchased from the Let's Roll place in Wahiawa. As she opened it, she swatted at the mosquitoes, swearing.

"Little shits." She twirled the tobacco between her thumb and forefinger and cradled the rolling paper into a u-shaped barrel. After filling the tube and rolling it, she licked the paper cylinder with cat-like quickness. Striking the sulfurous match and lighting her cigarette, a bluish wreath soon circled her hair. The mosquitoes hovered at bay, attempting to find openings at her ankles below the plumes. Within the fern-scented air, the mosquitoes were attracted to Cindy's blood. No amount of kung fu training would aid her against the little kamikazes. The mosquitoes were desperate. They had but one day of life to provide for their species, as billions of others had before them.

"Where is he?" the 'iwi'i teased again. "Cindy, Cindy, where is your adversary? The one who beckons you."

"Shut up," she repeated. The cigarette drooped from her lower lip. She stood up and once again strode along the trail that followed the stream. The scent of wild guava and mountain apple added to the valley's perfume. For the next half mile, she outpaced the mosquitoes. The trail descended from above the stream and now hop-scotched upon boulders at the same level. The 'iwi'i had flown ahead and gathered on another 'ōhi'a over the hundred-foot vertical lava walls shrouding the Sacred Falls pool. Once at their destination, it sang a sonnet to Cindy—

> *Cindy under the hairy mound of grey*
> *You chaff against the bridle you have bit*
> *Hosting a hard pride in your donkey bray*
> *The ancients chant from the volcanic cliffs*
> *Your adversary waits in jagged rocks*
> *You curse your footfalls upon mossy stone*
> *Absent with no bridge to others you walk*
> *A dogged curse to live always alone*
> *He invites you to finally unite*
> *And do battle with your own ocean deep*
> *Your oath of stubbornness cannot be right*
> *How surreptitious the waters do creep*
> *In the rainforest at Sacred Falls Pond*
> *With the demons you have held for so long*

Cindy relit her cigarette and rested by the cool glow of the pond. A mist drifted from the base where water fell over the mossy pumice walls. The meditative sound of water pattered into the pond, and the ripples rolled peacefully toward her. She blew a puff of smoke. "It must have been him, Micah, who sent these birds for me to follow. Maybe he sent mosquitoes. Where is he?"

Micah had started later and on the other side of the gulch, creating his own path. He scrambled from the heights of the ridge and stood in the shadows of the mountains. A pueo soared silently by, usually an omen. Watching it, Micah chanted—

I am the mighty Micah
Taking fate to the grey-haired witch
I am the mighty Micah
We shall be pigs in a watery ditch.

Proudly small, like Cindy, he displayed spotted skin and a protruding lower lip with a short mustache. His beady eyes, also like Cindy's, were set wide apart. He wore his old cutoff jeans, a ragged long-sleeved shirt, and high-top green sneakers.

"I am ready, Cindy. Even if afterward all that remains of me is a crumbled heap. Be that my fate, I care not. Hack away dear girl with your bitterness." Micah mumbled on somewhat romantically, driven by the part of the brain that tries to put things together like a jigsaw puzzle. He had been planning this meeting for a year, step by step. His short, firm legs bounced down the path like resilient shock absorbers. He was still far from his destination.

He stopped and gazed down the slope where the trail wound in lengthy switchbacks and knew it was time to change. He pulled out an iPad from his backpack. The solar sensor atop the pack constantly charged it, and so within seconds after pressing the "on" button, a topographical map glowed into focus. A small, blinking green light indicated his position, and a red light indicated the destination of Sacred Falls over two miles away. Micah would have to traverse a large valley of macadamia trees and then climb a steep ridge westerly. He had to pick up the pace if he wanted to arrive at the falls before sunset.

"It is time," he said confidently. On the mauka side of the trail, looking outward toward the ocean, he sat on a stone and with erect posture, setting his hands flat upon his knees. He closed his eyes and counted to himself as he took a deep breath for the transition. Then, he held his breath to the same count and released. He repeated the process for at least ten minutes. As his anxiety dissipated, he listened to the rush of the wind through the cavernous Koʻolaus. His nostrils discerned the sharp scents of mountain apple, guava, and lilikoʻi. Attuned to his surroundings, his mind floated out of his body and hovered above him, and he began to realize his choice, a four-legged animal that could navigate the terrain speedily—a pig.

And so, he transformed. First his torso compressed into a log shape, and then his arms and legs slowly shortened as if sucked into it. His skin then bulged with mottled blond bristle. His nose protruded and reshaped his head while his neck bent to the same circumference. Lastly, his ears rotated from a side position until they sat on the top of his head. He watched from above as his body completed the transformation.

His thick head turned left and right. Free from the imbalance of two legs, he did not need to follow the lengthy switchback trails. He thrashed through the ferns and vines in a direct line to the falls.

Cindy waited tensely by the pond as the day light faded.

"Where are you? I am ready now." She felt the cool radiance of the pond in contrast to her heat and tension. The sun had almost crept below the horizon and cast shadows as the green colors darkened.

The ʻiwiʻi sang a sunset chorus: "Cindy, you won't have to wait long."

"Shut up, will you?" Cindy shouted. Her dark orbs glanced upward, but the birds were merged with the hues of the trees. She rolled another cigarette from her Let's Roll pouch. Once again, the grey wreath encircled her head, and the mosquitoes breeding in the shallows of the pond hummed at a distance: Dusk gathered its melancholy darkness, overwhelming the forest. Cindy unfolded her pop-up tent seeking refuge.

Nearby and unseen, Micah scurried thirty feet up into the arms a macadamia tree. He found the crux between limbs to curl into just as darkness absorbed the colors. Mosquitoes did not venture to that height. The chirps of geckos sang like tiny birds in the black leafy curtains. The trade winds fluttered the elliptical leaves of lychee, guava, and a thousand hybrids like varieties of jazz brushes on drums. The respite before the battle sang a sweet tune, and they both slept.

A bird cacophony woke them at the first glimmer of dawn. Micah rustled urgently from the limbs of the tree for the advantage of surprise. At the same time Cindy, like an agile bug, leaped from her tent and quickly rolled it. She too sought the element of surprise and crouched even smaller than her four feet. Micah stalked toward the edge of the pond. His pig snout sucked in her smell. Her vibrations flowed through his sausage like form. The 'iwi'i, far above in the red 'ōhi'a, watched, hidden and quiet.

Micah crashed through the leaves to a slight bluff over the pond to surprise her. His eyes settled on Cindy's naked back in the pond for she had decided to bathe. Her white form undulated with water's deflection of light. Without turning she knew his presence, and as she did their eyes met. Micah grunted.

"So be it," said Cindy with a hollow stare seeing him in the form of a pig and knowing she too would turn. She dreaded the syndrome. Silently she cursed Micah.

Her transformation began as her long hair sucked into her body becoming a mass of bristles. Likewise, her white breasts shrunk into a hairy rotund pig's body. Her small nose puffed into a snout, and her ears moved to the top of her head where they flopped in triangles. As her arms and legs shortened, they lost touch with the pond bottom, and she had to paddle with her hooves to keep her nose above water. Two short white tusks sprouted under her nose and pierced the water's surface. Treading furiously, she looked upward.

Micah leaped off the shore's dark boulders and flew into the pond. With his most frantic effort, he managed only to keep his snout above waters. They approached each other in the middle of the pond.

"Great thought, idiot," snorted Cindy at Micah for adopting such a form in water. By the time their tusks met, they had exhausted themselves and wearily turned away from each other to seek opposite shorelines. As they reached the edges, their hooves stumbled upon the angular boulders. They shook their hairy hides and glowered at each other. Their cold bodies shuddered at the unsatisfying impasse.

The 'iwi'i now chirped notes resembling a funereal dirge—

> *May you wander alone like an umi fish*
> *May you conjure upon your unresolved wish*
> *You pined and imagined how you would meet*
> *To free your bonds of attraction*
> *All that energy and nothing to show*
> *Pride drawn to the water below*

After, Cindy and Micah slowly returned to human form. They peeked at each other during the process, pig bristles shedding into the water. As their snouts receded into their heads, the trade wind dried their skin. They ignored each other's nakedness and pulled on clothes. Micah rested in a bed of pine needles hidden from Cindy by an ironwood tree.

"Damn bugs," said Cindy, waving off mosquitoes on the other side of the pond. She hung another cigarette from her lower lip. Micah smelled the sulfur of her match and the scent of hand rolled tobacco. He saw the smoke clouds.

He stared upward at the tips of the mountains pointing into the clouds like green quartz crystals, wondering himself why he called Cindy here. The wind blew low notes, and he napped.

When Micah arose, he brushed off the dry pine needles and looked over the ironwood tree. Cindy had fled. He noted with some satisfaction how much she wanted to avoid him, and this only fueled his desire.

"I will wait until next year. Maybe we can be birds. Mynas, perhaps," he said whimsically to himself, marching out of the forest.

Mother's Day would return. Her ornery, determined countenance appealed to him. He could wait another year. Next year on Mother's Day, Micah's invitation would launch her fury anew. Mother's Day would bring her again to nature, and she would take another swing at Micah. They were attracted to each other, attracted to that energy. They were in love and didn't know it.

△∇△∇△

EATING RAINBOWS

[melissa yuan-innes]

"That's one weird looking rainbow, Gert."

"Maybe 'cause it's Hawaiian."

"No, I'm serious. You got to take a look."

"I don't got to do anything, Bert. That's the whole point of a vacation."

"I'm telling ya. It's worth opening your eyes, ok?"

"Ok, but... hey. That is kind of weird. I don't know what it is."

"I do. The red is all gone."

"Well, it's kinda—"

"No, look at it. There's orange, yellow, green, all that jazz. But no red."

"Maybe 'cause it's Hawaiian."

"What, you think the light is any different here? The raindrops bend 'em different?"

"Bert, you think too much on vacation."

I tried all the colors; red was the tastiest. Not the weird fake cherry flavor one might think, based on humans' horrible cough drops and licorice, but lighter, spicier. Like clouds spiked with pepper water. It undulates in my mouth, too. Makes me want to hum. I can't eat too much of it or I'll end up giggling and falling on my butt, and people think I'm a drunken dwarf with fluorescent paint plastered around my mouth.

Who knew eating rainbows could be so much fun?

Once upon a time, these islands were nothing but volcanoes: orange tongues and pools of live lava, cool, porous black shores of rock, and of course the goddess Pele-honua-mea, exiled by her father for her gloriously wicked temper and the seduction of her brother-in-law.

Each time Pele ignited a new volcanic home, her vengeful sister, the sea goddess Nā-maka-o-Kahaʻi, flooded it out. They battled from island to island until Nāmaka tore Pele into pieces on Maui.

Once upon a time, the only visitors were fern and moss spores drifting through the air, insect eggs cuddled in a piece of driftwood, and plants swimming in on the tide.

That was a long time ago.

"Look, that's what I thought. There aren't as many rainbows as there should be. See, someone wrote to the *Maui News* about it."

"Oh, boy, Bert. Must be true, then."

"Seriously, Gert. It's not normal. We got rain and then sun, but even when you're facing the right way…"

"Yeah, you told me, Bert."

"I was thinking of going to Hāna."

"Where's that?"

"The east side of the island. You know. The road to Hāna. It's in all the tourist books. One-way roads and bridges. You're supposed to honk so the cars coming the other way don't hit you. It's that narrow."

"Why the hell would we want to do that?"
"Well, it's still got forest, unlike the rest of the island."
"You're kidding me, right?"
"Supposed to be beautiful."
"We're here for the beaches."
"We got beaches in Florida."

Pele's bones make a hill near Hāna. But her spirit, ah. Can the earth ever contain a goddess of fire?

Some of the oldsters say we come from Pele's spirit. We may be small now, but we are mighty. We are tethered to the earth, a peace bond between Pele's fire and Nāmaka's sea.

On the other hand, some of the oldsters are full of it.

They think they're legendary because of their fishponds. Yeah, I admit those ponds are nifty. I especially like the kind bordering the sea. The walls curve into the shore at either end, containing the pond. Māhaka, "sluice gates," permit skinny young fish to swim in, but fat fish can't make their way out. After we built a few, the humans figured out how and made their own. They even improved the design on inland ones. Good eats all around.

But the oldsters don't seem to see how the humans slaughtered the fishponds. Farm silt, erosion, foreign plants, graffiti, neglect. Pick your poison. And anyway, the fish have been gobbled nearly to the last bone.

Humans used to be good builders. To be fair, some still are. But it seems like most of them are hell-bent on destruction instead. Even some of their concrete and steel cages are built to last only five years. Pass the code, turn a profit, tear them down. Spam lasts longer than their monuments.

"Dammit."

"It's pretty, in't, Gert?"

"No, it sure ain't, and I'm getting carsick. Where's my beach?"

"There are beaches in Hāna."

"What kind of beaches?"

"Nice ones."

"Hot ones? With sand I can dig my feet into while I lie on my back and you spread suntan oil on my front?"

"No. Different. Hey, check out that tree. It's got red and green and black stripes—"

"Different how?"

"I think there's a waterfall coming up. Keep your eyes peeled."

"Different how—goddamn it, that guy!"

"He didn't hit us."

"Why'd you shaka him? He almost hit us. Are you an idiot? And stop trying to change the subject. I know you. No sand beaches, right? So why are we doing this?"

"It's part of the history—"

"It's this rainbow thing, right? Ha! I *knew* it! Next time a car comes around, I'm gonna grab the wheel and shove you into it."

"You'd die too."

Humans aren't the only ones changing.

We are too. The Menehune. I'm the new and improved brand. I don't care if you recognize me or just use my name on your bottled water. I don't ache for the good old days. I tear down. I obliterate.

The only problem is I'm about the size of a ten-month old baby human. My appetite for destruction is limited—like that of mice and termites. Small but constant.

But I can make these tourists very uncomfortable. And once the other Menehunes join me, we'll be a force to reckon with.

"Look at this. I'm like Sir Isaac Newton."

"The guy who got hit on the head with the apple?"

"I'm not sure that actually happened, but yeah. That was the gravity theory. He did light, too. He used a prism to break white light into the colors."

"Like our glass coffee table does at home."

"Uh, yeah. Just like that."

"So that's why you bought some crystals at that Looney Tunes tourist shop? What does that prove?"

"I don't know. I just wanted to show that we can still make real rainbows out here. See?"

"Yeah. That is pretty, Bert. So now what?"

"Well, I dunno."

"Hmpf. Well, at least it looks nice."

This human is not the only one hunting me. I have meteorologists scratching their heads, children staring at oil slicks in rain puddles, science teachers braying at the sky. But for some reason, this one, Bert, intrigues me. Maybe because he's so fat, his belly seems like an appendage, but he has an intelligent look buried in the pouches around his eyes.

I approach his homemade rainbow and poke it. Like a real one, it has no material substance. Only magical beings can stroke the light, feel its warmth humming against their fingertips. This rainbow is so tiny, I can barely feel it. But I give the red a lick. It tastes a bit like a real one, a little more metallic. It tastes like trouble.

I suck down every last streak of red, then I scamper away before he returns.

"I don't belieeeeve it!"

"Shut up, Bert."

"The red's all gone here too! That's impossible. You saw it, Gert. I gotta take a picture. Look, even if I move the crystal, there's no red."

"I'm gonna go *crazy* if you don't shut up. Here. You gonna drink this or what?"

"Ok, ok. You see it too, though, right?"

"Right, right. Whatever you say, boss."

The next time I come back, he's scattered crystals all around the room. They're right there, soaking up the sun from the west. All of them glowing mini rainbows except the one I downed on Monday.

I like it. I even like the motion detector video camera he's rigged up. It probably wasn't easy to track it down that fast, even for a fat old rich guy like him.

I'm pretty sure I'm invisible to humans. I've walked right by while they keep on licking their ice cream cones and pulling thongs out of their ass cracks. Even babies keep staring into space or banging toys on the floor.

Dogs? It depends. The real inbred ones are almost like humans, clueless. But a few of them, especially the wolf-types, I watch out for. They sniff, and their ruffs go up, and they growl. I've got a cousin who had to skim up a palm tree a few decades ago. He still talks about it, especially when he gets drunk on moonbeams.

I've never heard of a Menehune captured on film. But I can't be too careful. Especially since these humans are getting so good at technology. Most of them suck at the important stuff, like nature and family. But they can build, and they can breed. I'll give 'em that.

I hesitate in the shadows. The camera is pointing right at the doorway, waiting to go off, while his little crystals' rainbows dance in the sunlight by the window. I couldn't attack them without risking the camera.

Unless I materialize through the window. Duh.

So that's what I do. A few of the red in the rainbows even taste ok, like cinnamon. I burp. The taste of cinnamon, chalk, cloud, and wonton wrapper flies back at me.

I wipe my mouth with the back of my hand and imagine leaving him the camera with blank film. Proof that I'm smarter than him. I sneak up on the camera, shut it off, and take it with me.

"Gert!"

"Shut up, y'old fart."

"This ain't funny, Gert!"

"Neither is your face this early in the morning."

"I told you. Don't mess with that room!"

"What, your goddamn rainbow room? I didn't touch it."

"Where's the camera?"

"I don't got it."

"I paid a big deposit on it, and I want it back. Now."

"You're going crazy, big boy. How many times do I got to say I don't got it?"

"Goddamn it, Gert."

"No, goddamn you, Bert. You used to be fun and now you're just Looney Tunes. Hey. Get out of my stuff! You're ripping my—hey! That cost two hundred smackers! Bert! Stop it! Bert!"

It takes me a while to make it back to the rainbow room. I had to take down some more of the big rainbows, just to make sure the rest of the world was paying attention. And the camera was a lot of fun. I ran the battery down trying to film my posse. On the playback, we were still invisible, but you could see the effects, so it looked like real poltergeist stuff: coconuts flying, clothes walking by themselves, that sort of thing. Interesting.

My cousin pointed out that I farted so hard my Speedo rippled. I laughed along with everyone else, even though my stomach's been bothering me more and more.

I decided to distract myself with big Bert. I made the time to come back.

It's still a rainbow room. More crystals. A chandelier, crystal animals, quartz, the lot. Cameras set up in the doorway, outside the windows, outside the main door. And the sort of booby traps a kid would think of: a strand of hair closed in the door, flour sprinkled inside the window, that sort of thing.

I'm kind of disappointed. Bert's not working at too high a level. But then I peek out the door and catch him passed out on the sitting room couch with an empty bottle of Jack Daniels beside him. I got it. Not many species are smart when they're tanked.

Or maybe that's a trap, too. You shouldn't underestimate humans. That's what my mama used to say. They know how to breed, they know how to kill, and they know how to plan. Nanny cams in teddy bears, that sort of thing.

A lot of tourists think we're like brownies or elves. We rub your back as long as you leave a dish of milk out. But the Menehune are not pets. We, too, have evolved over the past few millennia.

I don't want to take a chance with all that electronic equipment. I dematerialize, rainbows untasted, about to hurl. I have to come back with a better plan.

"I knew you'd come crawling back."

"I ain't on my hands and knees, Gert."

"Yeah, all right. Nice flowers, though."

"Yeah. I wasn't sure what to get a guy. So, you want 'em or what?"

"Sure. I was gonna get you some myself."

"Yeah. After you figure out your little physics problem, right?"

"...Sorry."

"Forget it. I have. So, you old goat, did you do anything besides drink until you puke?"

"You saw all the rainbows."

"Yeah. I can see you got that one weird rainbow and everyone's gonna think it's just the stone that's screwed up. You need more than that. Aw, go eat some of that health food store crappy bread I brought ya. Gert's on the case. I'm gonna fix this and then we're gonna get the hell out of Hāna."

"Gert. Thanks, but you've got no idea—"

"I know enough, Bert. I know enough. Stuff no one ever taught ya."

Well, at least he's trying.

Not only have the number of crystals doubled, but he's added artificial light so that even at night there are fake rainbows.

How sad can you get? We have a saying in Hawai'i: "No rain, no rainbows." Here's no rain, no sunshine, no life. I won't be snacking today. Good thing, too. My head is spinning, and now I'm burping up beans and lava. But at least I've got principles.

All of a sudden, it's like my stomach is trying to punch out a belly button. It tastes like mold and river slime and wine gums, and I'm shaking and heaving.

My vision clears. I wipe my mouth with the back of my hand. I stare at the mess, and suddenly I see their room like a little altar. They're trying so hard. In a way, they're replenishing rainbows. Not the way I'd like, of course. They're using more energy and electricity and trying to catch me on YouTube. But they're on to something. I'll give 'em that.

"This is impossible."

"Why, it ain't in your physics manual, right?"

"Did you do this? I can't figure out where the red light is projecting from."

"I can tell you one thing for sure. It ain't me making that rainbow in the middle of the room."

"You think it's a rainbow?"

"I know it is."

"It's beautiful."

"Yeah. It is that. Now you got me interested."

They've got a dog. Its bark pierces the air. I freeze, then force myself to relax. Dogs can't see me. They can't touch me.

Even so, a prickle of unease runs up my spine. I start to dematerialize out of the house before I'd barely cleared the drywall.

"So there you are, you lil' bugger."

The dog yips, but a skinny old white woman holds its collar with one hand while her eyes are on me.

Impossible. Humans haven't been able to see Menehune for generations, aside from kahuna. Certainly not white trash bearing crooked teeth and a worn-out nightgown with a teddy bear printed on the front.

"Figured you'd be something like that," she says.

I can't resist testing her, and not just because her shirt says "HUG ME" above the bear's head. Humans are deaf to us. Too much TV, iPhones, and science. I materialize fully inside the house and say in my normal voice, "Like what?"

"Little brown dude. I like the thing around your privates. Keeps you decent."

I glance down at my purple loincloth before I can help myself.

She laughs. "Don't worry. You got Bert's panties in a knot, but I'm not after ya. We got enough little bogies where I'm from. You just keep eating your rainbows."

A hundred questions trip over my lips. Where is she from? How can she see me? But the dog's nostrils quiver, and I started to dematerialize out of fear before I force myself to stand my ground. "You tell your man, if he wants the rainbows to keep up, we need green space."

She doesn't blink.

I open my mouth to explain how humans have ruined the earth, but she cuts me off with a nod. "I guess we could manage that, seeing as how we made our money in oil."

I wait for the fury to boil through my veins. Instead, for some reason, I suddenly feel like laughing. Quickly, I make a mysterious gesture and dematerialize. Just as I fade out, I spot my regurgitated rainbow. It's been redrawn into a pentagram on the wall, right where I'd entered.

What a witch!

It shakes me up enough to put me off rainbows for a while. Although, truth to tell, I've lost my taste for them. Right on cue, my stomach rumbles. I taste sulfur this time.

By dawn, I know exactly what to do.

I puke again, spewing light over Lāhainā for all the tourists to see on their morning jogs, whale-watching tours, golf tournaments, time-share spiels, and lūʻaus. But I don't just spray, I make sure I'm controlling the flow. Shaping it, just like Gert:

SAVE THE EARTH

My first rainbow graffiti.

The new Menehune, re-creating, re-designing the earth. It feels good. Better than fishponds.

A dog cocks its ears and digs its heels in the sand. Its owner tries to drag it along, but I'm turning cartwheels and laughing and crying and praying it's not too late. Meanwhile, my cousin starts drinking waterfalls, and another one, a real crazy one, starts to play with Pele's bones.

△▽△▽△

WHAT GROWS MAY BURN

[JOSH POOLE & TRAVIS WELLMAN]

I pointed the flamethrower's flickering end in the direction the noise came from.

"Just a bird," said Sergeant Evans, his face painted dark with camouflage.

"Just a bird," I repeated, and lowered my weapon, listening to its incessant hiss of ignited gasses as we moved deeper into the forest.

We'd inserted on Lāna'i through Shipwreck Beach on the island's north shore via amphibious craft the night before. A platoon of a hundred men armed with flamethrowers and automatic weapons. There was one matchstick in every fireteam. Sergeant Evans served as our fireteam leader for Alpha Team, and we had two soldiers on M240 machine guns: Velasquez and Thompson. I remembered our craft passing the barge just off the coast for which the beach got its name. It'd been chewed up and spit out by the wild current, until all that remained was a rusted can from World War II.

The island was much the same, its ecology corroded by an unsustainable pineapple monoculture until most of what remained was desert. What little water remained had been wrung out to feed the golf courses and resorts whose patches of green stood out on the satellite images we were briefed with. According to legend, Lānaʻi had once been an untouched paradise haunted by man-eating ghosts chased off by a Mauian prince. That night, it became clear he missed a few.

Our targets were mutants designated P.H.O., Pineapple Humanoid Organisms. They were human by appearance but their heads, which looked just like the fruits until they opened their mouths to reveal rows of shark teeth. Command showed us all a specimen on the carrier before we moored, a real nasty bastard caked in blood from whatever they'd been feeding it. Blind, mean, twice as strong as a soldier, and they look just like plants until they pop out of the ground. The P.H.O. were just as foreign to that world as the pineapples had been to these islands when James Dole started his plantation here.

The 3,000 residents had already evacuated to the other islands, and even from those distant shores I'm sure they could see the orange glow from firebombings a week prior. We scorched the old plantations, and as I watched the glow rise into the night air, I couldn't help but feel the redundancy in burning deserts to the ground. Our operations left the forests mostly untouched so there'd be at least something left to come back to when it was all over, assuming the threat could be neutralized. It shocked me to find pine trees there, but with the dry ground that was all that grew above patchworks of grass and hellish undergrowth.

We maneuvered through the conifers, staying close to the other fireteams as the brush grew too thick to see one another and a full moon hung in the canopy. Our platoon had split in two, with our objective being to secure an old plantation factory that was supposed to have been occupied by airborne paratroopers. They hadn't been in communication with command in several days.

"Bravo Team, get your goddamn comms up!" Sergeant Evans barked over the radio from behind.

"Got canned, probably," Thompson sneered.

In that moment I recalled the sickly sweet, syrupy taste of canned fruit. Tasted the upside-down cakes and the tropical punch I'd consumed all my life. No wonder they hated us so much.

We'd initially hoped that the firebombing would solve the problem, but the fires only killed the ones above ground. The stronger specimens made it through, and part of me wondered if they weren't toughened up by the whole bombing campaign. It was like fighting a strain that had become resistant to antibiotics. Harder to kill, impossible to eradicate.

We moved slowly, using night vision but leaving one eye naked for when the torches lit up. The brush had become fiendish, cutting at our legs through the fatigues. Sergeant Evans threw up a hand for us to stop. I listened over my pounding heart and shaky, uneven breath.

"Thirty meters, potential fruits," he whispered.

I moved up to the front of the team, pointing the torch straight ahead.

"Confirming, Alpha Team has point? Over," Sergeant asked.

"Confirmed, over," came the delayed responses of several other teams.

"Bravo Team, confirm? Over," Sergeant asked, his voice distilled and calm.

The noises drew closer, and I could hear them just beyond the pines. It was a straight shot with the torch, with gaps between trees large enough for me to do a pass or two through them and have the entire area coated. Sarge gave me a nod; we couldn't wait to hear back from the Bravo Team. I engaged the gas and propellant.

"Torch it," Sergeant whispered.

I didn't feel anything when we released the fire but adrenaline. My head was clear as I pulled the trigger, closing the eye that stared through the night vision to avoid the blinding flash. The fire arched through the undergrowth, bursting in a conflagration. I felt the heat burn at my face and hands, wanting to let go of the weapon and take cover with the others. Then, I heard the screams. *Human* screams.

I knew what I'd done, listening as what remained of Bravo Team wailed in the fire.

"Friendly! Friendly!" I heard as a soldier burst through the pines and onto our position.

He collapsed, his pack on fire.

"Matchstick is lit! Get down!" He yelled as he rolled over the ground.

I tried to put out the fire attacking his equipment, his words not yet having cleared customs in my brain. I didn't have time to process them before Brave Team's torch exploded like a volcano no more than ten meters from the rest of us.

I woke up staring at the night sky, watching as the moon looked down on me like a portal in a ceiling. Orange, glowing walls surrounded me; I tried to find my bearings.

"Private Dalton!" I heard a voice but couldn't see anything. It was all dark or all bright, nothing in between.

A pair of hands grabbed me by the pack straps and craned me up to my feet. Still dizzy, I checked my kit for any fires, not wanting to suffer the same fate as Bravo Team's torch.

"We're moving back to the ridge line! Open cover!" one of the M240s barked in my ear, but I could barely hear her.

I nodded, following close as we maneuvered back away from the fire that quickly engulfed a small section of forest. My team and the lone survivor of Bravo Team grouped up, trailing behind the others as we closed in on the ridge. From there, Sergeant Evans took charge, dispensing the other teams to secure a hundred-meter perimeter while we stationed ourselves in the skeleton of a fallen pine. I could see the gunner from Bravo Team, but I couldn't look him in the face.

Sarge touched base with command once the perimeter was secured. I could overhear everything from the radio but did my best to let him relay the information as he saw fit. I had plenty of fuel left, judging from the weight on my back. Still it only offered six or eight seconds of burn time, and if a pack of those things fell on us, I'd go through that in the first or second wave. The M240s could tear them apart like any other animal, but P.H.O.s were hard to hit, and the noise made everyone in the squad deaf.

"We've got incoming hostiles picked up by aerial recon. Eight to twelve closing in, three hundred meters out and moving quick. The fire must be drawing them in, but they've probably got our scent by now," Sergeant Evans said, shoving his helmet up to wipe the sweat from his brow.

The Bravo Team gunner checked his weapon; he hadn't fired the first shot since we'd hit the beach three days before. Most gunners hadn't. The woods were crowded, and that was the first time we'd been able to see more than fifty yards ahead. All the teams cracked red glow sticks to show their positions to the others and prevent any more incidents of friendly fire. I could see the outlines of pineapples.

Somehow, the creatures could see bright lights. When we were briefed on their capabilities the explanation was that, like most plants, they could sense the sun. Low light, especially with a red filter on it, was safe to use.

"Hostiles approaching from the southeast, maintaining visual," Thompson relayed, and Sergeant Evans repeated over the comms to the other teams.

I looked down into the hollow below, oscillating between my naked eye and night vision. I saw nothing, killed the flame on the torch, knowing the creatures would lock onto it and rip me apart if the gunners didn't do their job. I didn't have a reason to trust them yet; I'd never been deployed with them. We waited for what felt like hours, but may have been no more than a few minutes, before I finally discerned their shambling forms moving among the pines.

They looked just like us but a bit thinner and completely naked. I watched their jaws open, lapping the air with their tongues and homing in on our location. They moved so quickly, I'd never seen anything like it, and they maintained that speed without making the slightest of sounds. The gunners orchestrated a coordinated volley over the comms, and once Sergeant gave the signal, all hell broke loose.

A dozen M240s and 249s roared to life all around me, cutting through the quiet night air with a fully automatic crash that roared down through the trees like a crashing wave. I watched as the tracers sprayed in such high volume that they illuminated the surrounding trees and the carnage that befell the creature's exposed bodies. I felt bad for them, no matter how mindless or horrible they were. Nothing deserved to be ripped apart like that.

When the volley ceased, I heard only the ringing in my ears and the distant, muffled shrieking of those that somehow still clung to life. The engagement wasn't over. It was my time to shine.

"Move in, torches up front," Sergeant Evans ordered.

I maneuvered away from the fallen tree accompanied by three gunners. Velasquez swapped out her belt. A gunner team would normally have two, one to reload and the other to spray, but we weren't a normal platoon. With the suddenness and speed at which threats propagated on the island, command deemed every unit should be armed. That was the reasoning we were given, at least. I still don't think it made any sense.

The creatures' wails became more disturbing as we moved within range. Their bodies writhed as I engaged the lines and covered them in fire. Adrenaline coursed through my body, numbing my face and hands to the heat. The other matchsticks didn't bother, conserving their fuel for the next engagement, while I dumped half of what I had left.

Command radioed in with Sergeant Evans, a disembodied voice coming through crisply. "Aerial recon suggests all hostiles have been eliminated. No others visible in the area. Consider immediate surroundings secured until further notice. Proceed to the initial objective when ready."

"Copy that, over," Sergeant Evans replied, slinging a rifle over his shoulder.

We pressed on with the other teams along a different route, still heading toward the old plantation factory where they'd last heard from the airborne teams. The factory was surrounded by twenty acres of desert, open terrain, perfect for securing a position and maintaining visuals on all sides. There, we would group up with the rest of our platoon that at that time was likely finishing their sweep along the dirt road off Shipwreck Beach.

I had a feeling of what we'd find there, considering it'd been days since anyone had heard from the airborne troops. At the same time, I knew we had orders of magnitude more firepower and intel, as they'd been deployed before a live specimen had even been secured. They hadn't radioed anything unusual in their last transmissions, having set up a large perimeter and establishing a base of operations inside the factory that was supposed to be one of the major command centers for the whole operation. After that they just vanished, ghosts in the darkness.

It was a two-mile hump to the desert's edge, but we made it without incident even as we jumped at every cooing bird and crawling insect. At the edge of the scalped earth I saw nothing out of the ordinary, and the satellites hadn't picked up any unusual activity. The factory loomed in the distant night, as formidable and gargantuan as the wrecked barge we passed coming in. Our fireteams grouped up, with Sergeant Evans taking point as we crept onto the cracked dirt.

It was unclear whether the ground had been desiccated from the incendiaries or if it had been ruined long before military operations began there. It felt like walking on dinner plates, with each step breaking up the brittle ground. I was up front with Sarge and the others while the Bravo gunner had receded back with the bulk of our troops. My nerves were shot, but Velasquez flashed me a smile that I could only see in the night vision. For a moment, it didn't feel like I was unraveling at the seams.

When we made it to the factory we went through the open loading dock, finding all the heavy doors closed but unblocked. Sergeant nodded at Thompson, who kicked open a heavy metal door and pointed the business end of his M240 through the opening.

"Clear," Thompson declared.

We moved inside, finding nothing except the rusted remains of a long-abandoned factory. A conveyor belt ran serpentine throughout the metal husk, and steel beams held up the second level, accessible only by two sets of metal stairs. None of the lights worked.

"What the hell?" Sergeant Evans muttered.

All the fireteams pressed through the door, securing the ground while Alpha Team secured the second floor. Velazquez and Thompson were with me, and we set up shop in one of the offices while Sergeant Evans set up a comms station across the room. The office was nearly empty, cannibalized long before the mutations occurred. The farming had done worse things to the ecology of the island than we ever could. For the first time, I was at the epicenter.

For something as malevolent as industry, the factory felt empty and without conscience. Even the air smelled dull, like business as usual. I had a realization then that it was indifference that made for the worst catastrophe. At least when someone means evil, they know the consequences and others might manage to mitigate them. Nobody tries to burn down forests, but millions of us will toss our cigarettes into the grass without a second thought.

Dust had accumulated as thick as a book across most of the surfaces, and we moved carefully to not disturb it. Particles like that would interfere with the night vision, and our naked eyes were next to useless in those black corridors.

"No contact with the paratroopers," Sergeant Evans relayed to command.

"What the hell happened here?" Thompson asked. "Didn't they secure this place?"

"I don't know," Sergeant Evans replied. "There are no reports on any activity spotted by the satellites or aerial recon after last contact. From everything we know, nothing happened here."

"Something happened," Velasquez protested, looking around the room like she was going to find the answers written on the walls. "There a basement?" Velasquez asked, her eyes settling on the sergeant.

"Not on any of the prints I had of the building," Sergeant Evans shrugged. "Worth a look though."

"Permission to search the ground floor for basement access?" Velasquez asked while Thompson and I readied up to join.

Sergeant Evans nodded before returning to his comms station. We geared up and moved back down to the ground floor. Our boots fell heavily on the metal stairs as the other teams finished setting up their positions behind busted out windows. There was coverage for 360 degrees around the building, a great defensive position against anything that didn't have artillery or air support.

"Why the hell would they leave this place?" Thompson muttered.

I checked all the offices and side rooms, engaging the torch to allow its orange tongue to flick about in front of us. There was nothing to indicate that the paratroopers had ever been in the building. Nothing to suggest that *anyone* had been inside the building for decades. The dust hadn't been disturbed, and there was no equipment lying about. No blood, no shell casings, no bodies.

"Wait," Thompson broke our silent operation. "Do you feel that?"

I paused but felt only the gentle vibration traveling through my weapon. As a few seconds ticked by, I could sense something else beneath my feet. The sensation went faintly through the soles of my boots, but it was there. Then, what had been only a minute vibration a moment before roared into cacophony.

"Contact!" Zulu Team yelled. "Multiple hostiles approaching from the south!"

"Contact! Northeast!" Foxtrot yelled shortly after.

"Contact! Oh, shit! We're surrounded! There's hundreds of them!" another voice screamed.

I moved to the wall to look out of the windows, finding only a sea of creatures storming across the open desert as every gunner but the ones with me began firing. With a dozen machine guns roaring inside the building, I might as well have stuck my head inside a thundercloud. Everything became disoriented; I could hear the yelling and the firing, but I couldn't find my bearings. Everything flashed.

I stumbled backward, away from the wall and onto a section of floor that collapsed beneath my feet. There was the feeling of weightlessness, and then the sensation of all the air being squeezed out of my lungs with the impact.

"Shit!" Velasquez yelled, looking down at me from above. I must have fallen ten or twelve feet.

My night vision had been dislodged from my face, but as I regained my composure, I realized that the entire sub-floor was basked in a pale, fluorescent lighting from a single overhead tube.

"What's going on?" I heard Thompson scream over the gunfire.

"Oh my god," I struggled to speak.

"What's going on?" she cried out again.

"Air support! We need air support!" Sergeant screamed. "I don't give a shit! Drop it on our heads! We're dead anyways!"

I looked around, surrounded by dozens of clear, plastic barrels. Each one of them canned the bodies of paratroopers or civilians. I made it to my feet, peering into one of the barrels as the chaos unfolded on the floors above. The body wore a paratrooper's uniform, but its face had already started to undergo the transmogrification into a P.H.O. Before I could check any others, there was a sudden flash and a horrible sound; an airstrike hit the factory.

Private Dalton adjusted his tie, looking over the long table that had been set for everyone at the company picnic. The sun was out in full force, blasting over the entire party with noonday heat.

Nobody else had survived, and he'd only been spared by having been in the basement when the shelling hit. Every factory on the island had similar production facilities, places where the P.H.O had collected dead bodies and started the transformation process. Nobody knew how it started, with the debrief claiming it was some freak immunological response of nature righting itself. He looked around, seeing all the friendly faces of people who had no idea of what happened on Lāna'i, of what happened to him there. He hadn't told anyone that story in six years, not since he'd been debriefed on the aircraft carrier.

He looked down at the table without a soul standing anywhere near him. The pineapple stood harmlessly among all the other fruits and appetizers, and his plate remained empty.

△▽△▽△

CHARGE! LOVE HEART!

[RHIANNON RASMUSSEN]

Sometimes when you're lying awake in bed and pretending to be asleep because it's way too late for a high school student to be up, you can hear 'um: a series of bass thumps, more felt than heard, the footsteps of a giant. They're not what people tell you—a semi compression-braking on the highway, definitely not the warrior ghosts of the Night March (the huakaʻi pō make no sound as they pass), not even artillery testing (those exercises mostly happen during the day). I can tell you, but you have to promise to believe me and not share this around.

Ok, to start with, I'm kind of a dork. There's no shame in that kinda thing anymore; the revenge of the nerd days are way over. Everyone here grew up on Kikaida and that kine toku anyway; we all know about Bijinda's bust lasers (pink, heart-shaped) and Mazinger and Astro Boy. They're practically household words. So that means I'm an expert on what I saw, yeah? This story isn't about that kind of Internet dick-measuring, anyway, who's what kind of nerd or whatever. *This* story's about how I met my girlfriend.

The first time I saw her—well, ok, *noticed* her—was across the lunch table. I was sitting in the shade; she was sitting in the sun. We had the same lunch— time slot, not food—everybody had the same cafeteria food. It was chili and cornbread, but not in a good way. I elbowed my friend Kimo and asked him who was *that* girl. Kimo knew everybody. He squirted the packet of mayo he'd just opened all over the table instead of into his chili like he'd been aiming for and then elbowed me back hard. I handed over my napkins sheepishly.

He squinted across the concrete tables while he wiped mayo off his tray. "Who, Erika? She's from Big Island. She's my girlfriend's cousin."

"No shit?" Just then, the eagle charm at the end of her necklace glinted in the noon sun. I got up, and Kimo swiped my mayo packets too. I ignored it; I was on a mission.

"What, you gonna ask her out?"

"Maybe."

The eagle had made up my mind. I marched over. Like twelve girls with perfect frizzless hair and hella makeup stared back at me and my resolve pretty much died in my throat. "Hey, is it cool if I… hi. Sit here?"

"What, James, you got something to talk about other than League of Legends?" That was Kimo's girlfriend, and it was good enough for me.

"Yeah I do!" I said, offended. I sat down, not so close to Erika that it was creepy or anything.

Erika was looking at me, her fork paused mid-air. She was way cute even up close— no offense, but some girls aren't—round face, lips pursed thoughtfully in my direction. She was wearing a spaghetti strap top, and I followed the strap down the curve of her shoulder to the bra—I yanked my gaze back up to her face and stammered. "So… um… Kamen Rider, you a fan?"

"Huh?"

Behind Erika, Kimo's girl mouthed *Ka-men Ri-da* slowly.

"The eagle?" I prompted. The whole table full of girls was staring at me. They'd even stopped eating, and two or three of them had these smug girl-smirks on. I kind of wanted to die, or at least crawl back under my table and wait for the lunch bell to ring. Instead, stupid words spilled out of my mouth. "It's uh, the SHOCKER symbol, from Kamen Rider… First?"

"This?" Erika held up the charm, looked from me to her hand. Kimo's girl covered her mouth, which did basically nothing to muffle her laughter. Erika shrugged graciously. "I dunno, sorry. My dad gave me it?"

"Oh," I said. "That's cool." Stay cool. Pretend you're not into the shit her old man was into. That charm was gonna go straight into a drawer when she got home and never out again, I knew it. "So, hey, you know Kimo, right?" I waved back toward him. His face was full of mayo chili. "I'm James. I'm, like, his best friend."

She leaned around me to check, then back. "Yeah, I guess I know Kimo. I'm Erika."

"Uh… you paddle board? Stand up?"

She thought about it. "Not like… a lot."

"You wanna come with me and Kimo and a couple of the other guys on Wednesday? We go every week, leave at noon during study period."

"So what, like, Hickam?"

"Nah, we're heading down Kāneʻohe."

"Shoots, sure," she said.

There was a hoot from the table. "Hooo, Erika, you go girl!" Big change from all that tittering earlier, eh? But it made my face burn just as bad.

"Cool, I'll meet you in the parking lot. Wednesday, yeah?"

She nodded, little smile lighting up her face, and I retreated back to Kimo's table in the shade.

"You *actually* asked her out?"

"Yeah," I breathed. My hands were shaking. Kimo shook his head and returned to his chili.

So that Wednesday we all piled in the back of the truck and went down Kāneʻohe side to paddle down to the sandbar off Heʻeia. It'd been a pretty cool winter—don't laugh—and the surf had been high, which was great for the lolo surfers and not so great for us less extreme stand-up paddle boarders, otherwise we woulda been up North Shore. We parked at beach access on the Marine base and started to walk down to the sand when I heard the thumps again. I grabbed Kimo's shoulder. "Oh man, you hear that?"

"It's the artillery, brah."

"No way."

I listened close, but all I heard now was the surf and the clap-clap rustle of fan palm leaves in the breeze.

"Aren't they filming *Godzilla?*"

"Shut *up,* man." I turned around and almost ran into Erika. She'd changed into a pair of really tiny hibiscus swim trunks, and I had to pull my gaze up and then up again quickly. Thankfully she didn't seem to notice.

"Ey, James, what's up? You look like you saw a ghost."

"You hear that *thump?*" I asked her.

Her eyes got wide. "Man, I heard that the first night I got here! I was like, the hell is *that?*"

I glanced left and right. Big wet clouds were rolling in, and we'd get soaked if we went into the surf or not. Kimo and his girl had run off to make out in the naupaka bushes on the other side of the beach. I dropped my voice to one low whisper. "You wanna go check it out?"

She glanced left and right too, then dropped her voice. "Shoots," she said.

We'd gotten about three miles off base, across the freeway, and over a chain-link fence into a live ammunition zone alongside the quarry road before the elation wore off. I realized this was a real stupid thing to do whether Erika was with me or not. I was pretty sure the military didn't shoot people on sight anymore, but we'd hopped the live ammo zone fence and I'd heard they still had land mines for one reason or another. I mean, the military, right? They kinda just had landmines around, didn't they?

I didn't mention any of this to Erika, but I did start doing a weird half-trot hoping that I'd hear the landmine click before lifting my foot and then exploding.

She held her hand out to signal that I should stop. "I dunno if they have landmines," she whispered. "Gotta be careful."

We helped each other across the scrub, increasingly paranoid, until the ground was so rocky that they'd have to drill a hole to stick an explosive into there. I checked my phone for the time. My phone was dead. I groaned and shoved it back into my pocket.

"Mine's good," Erika said, but I barely heard her because there was a noise so loud I barely registered it as the *thump* until it had passed. I ducked, and so did she. "That's it!" She pointed. "I saw it!"

"Saw what?" I didn't see nothing. I followed her finger with my gaze up to the sheer cliff face above us. I craned my neck, but Erika leg'um up the mountain into a bunch of scrawny haole koa trees right before the rock got just about vertical. She climbed up there and then she vanished into the scrub with a little yell, just gone, outta sight.

"Hey!" I called after her.

No answer.

When I caught up, I saw it wasn't a little bit haole koa, it was a big ol' pile of California grass covering one gaping puka in the lava rock. I peered into the hole and saw a thin light way down in the cave. Erika's cell. I patted my useless one in my pocket and seriously considered just ditching her and walking back off down the highway to the beach before some Menehune or whatever lurked in mountain holes got me. But man, she'd trusted me enough to hop in a truck that morning. I crouched to see how well I fit in the hole. Pretty well. Even my shoulders were skinny.

"Come on!" Erika called. I took a deep breath and crawled in. The pāhoehoe dug rough, but not sharp, into my hands so I scooted forward fast instead of careful. I almost ran my head into her butt, and she shined the cell light in my face and then laughed, I guess at how red my face was. I apologized and she laughed more; "you can't see back there at all, huh?"

"No way," I said. The crawl wasn't too long, which was good for our knees, coz even with that little crawl they got scraped bloody. Take my advice, man, don't spelunk in board shorts. We squeezed out the other side, in the shelter of a copse of koaia, but not into the other side in Maunawili like I expected. The sky was getting dark, and it was raining, big walls of rain passing through every few minutes with the trades. The clouds cast mottled shadows over the bare stone walls, but the alcove kept us dry. Erika shaded her eyes to squint into the dusk.

We'd found a little valley carved into the actual mountain, like a knife had cut down the sides and lifted one slice of mountain-cake out and away into the sky. Netting and new plants sheltered the valley from the air. Built into one side, just like the old World War II bunkers, was a towering concrete launch pad, and on the launch-pad stood a machine big as an apartment building and probably as heavy as one. It was painted mottled grey and green, pixelated camouflage. Long antennae like Lü Bu's helmet swept back from the machine's crested head, red mud splatted all up the bulky legs. It looked like a person, if a person looked like a tank. When it started up, it musta been noisier than the jets over Hickam.

You wouldn't think they could hide something that size on an island. But they do.

Erika and I stared down at it, from our vantage on the cut-up mountain. I was too dumbfounded to even start to put words together, but Erika wasn't.

"Holy shit," she said. "It's an actual freakin' mech."

We've been going out ever since.

WHAT WE YIELD

[TOM GAMMARINO]

When the king tides flooded Waikīkī and box jellyfish floated along Kalākaua Avenue, I failed to understand that it had anything to do with me. But two years later, when the number of applicants to the private high school where I was principal had declined by nearly fifty percent, I began to feel the stings.

I was struggling to replace that third of our faculty who, having seen the writing on the wall, had left these islands behind. If I were smarter, or less stubborn, I might have followed them, but after a long, steep climb up the career ladder, I couldn't bring myself to abandon my position so easily. So, we proceeded to weather a half-decade of more flooding, voracious hurricanes, ocean acidification and coral bleaching, plummeting real estate, an eviscerated tourist industry, widespread bankruptcy, and escalating crime, before our board of trustees—all living abroad now—shuttered our school indefinitely.

Luckily my wife, Janet, was from a well-to-do family that had been living in these islands as long as any haole family. Pride in my self-reliance had always prohibited me from wanting any piece of their coffee fortune, but now that we faced genuine existential risk, some of my core values were turning out to be negotiable. That June, on a day that happened to be the hottest on record in the entire history of Oʻahu's weather records, we locked up the house in the lush Mānoa Valley that, at well over a million dollars, was supposed to be the biggest investment I ever made—the latest assessment put it at a hundred and ten thousand—and we flew to the Big Island to move into a two-bedroom bungalow and learn to farm.

For exactly eight months, we got to believe we were going to live out our lives insulated from the tragedy that was playing out in the rest of the world. Manhattan was underwater, to say nothing of the Maldives and Bangladesh. California was perpetually on fire. Earlier summers had been favorable to tick populations, and Lyme disease was reaching epidemic proportions on the east coast of the U.S.. Latin America was a gigantic dust bowl, and border skirmishes were in the news daily. Only China seemed to be doing relatively ok because, aside from having led the world in switching to renewables in the twenties, they had sufficient land to accommodate massive internal migration. Mind you, this was just the humans. Other species suffered genocides by the hour.

Now that it's so true, people no longer seem to use the expression "When it rains, it pours," but I can't think of a better phrase to describe that otherwise lovely, mid-winter day when I went out to the farm to discover the first signs of a fungus called coffee rust on the season's crop. Two hours later, Janet came home from the doctor's office, where she'd gone to complain of a persistent cough, to announce with admirable equanimity that she'd been diagnosed with one of the new, mosquito-borne viruses for which there was yet no vaccine. Science's best guess was that the virus had been locked up in permafrost somewhere for millions of years, but as with all the rest of this Pandora's box of a world, human activity had set it free. He predicted liver failure within six months, and that was with dialysis.

So each day now, I tend to Janet and work with her younger brother to establish our crop higher up the mountain. It's slow, tedious work. We walk the rows in our farmer's hats, handpicking the mature berries, throwing away the rusty ones, and then we take them inside and roast, package, and ship them.

Our premium arabica orders come mostly from Toronto, which has been the center of the banking world since Wall Street went under. The cruel irony is that most of these folks who are ideally situated to survive this apocalypse got rich in part by denying that it was even happening. And they're still doing it. No one can in good faith pretend that Miami or honey or hope still exists, but they can keep on insisting that humans had nothing to do with it. Denialism might as well be the wealthy set's religion now, long since having eclipsed Christianity. Meanwhile, Janet feels like there's an anvil on her chest.

It so happens we have in our backyard a silverleaf cotoneaster tree. The berries look not unlike coffee berries, and I know from watching my neighbor's dog have a seizure that they're poisonous. I doubt the poison survives roasting and brewing, but whenever the big accounts come through, I make sure to throw in a few of these berries for good measure. I'm under no illusions that there will be heroes in this story, but we do what we can.

△▽△▽△

MANUAL OVERRIDE

[JEFFERY RYAN LONG]

M didn't know how he felt. He only knew it wasn't like the other days. The clouds still glowed with a greenish tinge, as they did every afternoon. A yellow smear suggested the sun, barely shining through, toward the west. The air was heavy and moist. Out of habit M wiped at his brow, damp as ever. Below his feet the senseless waves splashed against a reef of rubber and rusted steel, submerged automobiles lost to the risen sea.

M stared at a car that had once been parked on a street, not yet so sunken that the ocean had completely washed it away. On days when M was confused, he usually went to the water and looked at the cars, at crabs crawling through the window holes and over the hoods. His mother had told him that, long ago, citizens would dive to salvage the scrap metal and tires. But no one was allowed in the water anymore.

M wasn't thinking about the poison waters or the cars underneath. He'd been remembering what his supervisor, T, told him earlier in the day, before the protectors took him away. Before they played T's song.

"I just want to see one more sun come up," T had said to M, quietly, grabbing his arm. "Just one more."

It was T's retirement party. T had contributed for twenty years, and now he was finished. The protectors would play his song, and he would go on contributing after death.

"Sure," M told him and withdrew his device. He searched "sunrises" and scrolled through the fingernail clips on his screen until he found a particularly majestic sun, orange and sphere-shaped, lording over some remote desert. He held his device to T's face and pressed play.

T knocked the device away. "I'm not talking about a stupid computer," he said. "A real sunrise. When you see it in the sky."

M stopped the device and slid it back into his pocket. "It doesn't come up like that anymore," he said.

"It will happen again," T said. "The sun will rise."

"That's not possible," M said, before he saw two protectors approaching. As the protectors made their way through the crowd of citizens eating cakes on small plates, showing one another clips on their devices, M's coworkers grew quiet, each citizen's attention drawn to his own device.

"Honored," T said, greeting the two protectors as they stood before him.

"The honor is ours," one of the protectors replied, removing his black cap as he nodded deeply to T. "To accompany one who has contributed for so long—it is a great privilege."

"You're coming with me, then?"

When neither protector responded, T simply said, "Never mind. Let's get it over with."

"What's your song, citizen?" a protector asked M as the other led T away.

"I'm called M." He passed his card to the protector. M's song was imprinted in code on the middle of the card.

The protector read M's song with a device he drew from this hip. The screen flashed, and he handed the card back to M. "I've made an appointment with a physician tomorrow. Directions will be received shortly. I advise you to be prompt."

With that, a pleasant vibration accompanied a gentle chime of the device in M's hand. The physician's office, just a few blocks from the factory.

For the rest of the party, M ate the ceremonial noodles and cakes reserved for retirements of the most esteemed. He exchanged clips with his coworkers. Since they curated the clips that everyone watched on their devices and on larger screens in their domiciles, each of the workers was allowed to reserve five files from the archive that were not disseminated to the general public. Most often these were short videos from films that neither could be made nor seen any longer, glimpses into stories the workers could only imagine. A man alone in a room between rows of empty benches yelling at the ceiling before bowing his head. A black-garbed demon commanding the equipment in a machine room to separate from its moorings and fly toward his opponent, all with a wave of his red electric sword. A giant tearing a sink from its place set into the floor, water rushing around his ankles as he hurls the sink through a caged window in a room full of sleepers. M didn't know why these particular clips moved him the way they did. In most cases, he wasn't even sure what was going on. But he played them over and over on his device until these miniature vignettes were memories.

Any of the workers who accessed more than five uncirculated clips on their devices or downloaded video images of kissing or any other unauthorized bodily contact would be involuntarily retired by the protectors.

Near the end of the party, M had watched as T pulled one arm from the protector's grasp as he was led away. A second later, shoulders slumped, M's supervisor began sobbing as he followed the protectors out of the conference room. That T, who M emulated not only in his work and discretion, but also in his austere life habits, should resist an hour as meaningful as retirement—well, it seemed inappropriate. Embarrassing.

Now M stood at the edge of the toxic ocean with its drowned cars and florescent octopuses and missed, for a moment, all that T had meant to him, understanding at once that he'd never see his supervisor again. It wasn't the first time M thought the impossible, the impracticable—what if T had been allowed to go on? To just go on? M grasped a piece of metal on the shore, some old corroded screw, and was about to cast it into the light waves when he noticed someone watching a ways off, from the corner of an empty building. Not a protector, M realized with relief, even though any citizen, for the safety of the populace, carried with them the obligations of the protectors. No, he'd seen this citizen before—someone from the factory, perhaps, though not in his division. He let the rust-swollen screw drop into the shore's powdery cement. If reported throwing things into the water he could be identified as troubled, and troubled citizens, according to the guidance, negatively affected everyone's ability to contribute.

♪ ♩ ♩ 𝄽

The line for the weekly charge of M's power unit extended several blocks. As he stood behind another citizen, M wished he hadn't wasted his time at the water thinking about T, who was now irrevocably retired. If only he could be on his bed in front of his screen, allowing time and moving pictures of animals to wash out his reflections. At the end of the line, with his power unit in his hand, he hoped no one could see his concern.

Fortunately, most of his fellow citizens held their devices close to their faces, the pallid light of the screens illuminating each unbroken gaze as the evening grew dark. Normally M would have taken pride at the clips of cats that were so popular among the citizens—cats batting at colored lights, cats placing their heads into spaces they could not conceivably fit, cats acting as if they were citizens themselves. Many of the clips M himself had developed at work, sometimes joining together disparate strings of archived clips featuring similar cats.

It enhanced their adventures so that each of their stunts were increasingly incredible. T had been impressed with these longer projects. Citizens watched them not once, again and again.

Not inclined to access his own device, M watched the citizens in front of him and the line that grew behind him, all of them with their hair close-cropped like his, all of them in the same gray clothing—a thin, short-sleeved shirt and equally thin pants, which were fairly comfortable in the humidity, and rubber shoes, which sometimes chafed but protected everyone's feet from the brackish water when the tide rolled into the cracked streets. Slowly he made his way to the charging station. Towering above him were what his mother had called office buildings, converted now into collections of free domiciles for contributing citizens, by the grace of the officials. Many of the outdoor walls of these buildings bore a digital screen that recycled, through the day and night, the guidance: *We Are All Men Now. To Love Yourself Is to Love What You've Been Provided. The Song Implant—Take Your Life into Your Own Hands!*

M didn't really see the signs—rather, they'd been so omnipresent in his life that they'd absorbed their way into his chemistry as a biological credo. *We Are All Men Now.* It was so simple and right. What M was really thinking about was how mystified and entertained the citizens were by the cats on the screens of their devices, while in certain abandoned parts of the city there were neighborhoods of cats, domiciles infested with cats, cats with nicked ears and bald patches on their cheeks, and no one wanted to get near them.

While M thought about cats, a disheveled citizen—black water stains from her ankles up the side of her body where she'd presumably fallen—must have noticed M without a device in his hand. Twitchy and harried, she stepped through the rising puddles to stand next to him.

"I'm not feeling well," she said to M. "I need to go home. I need to rest. I just need to lie down." Most domiciles could not be entered without a charged power unit.

For a moment M suspected she was not a citizen at all, but a denizen: non-contributors who traded the songs and power units of retired citizens. Who sucked up the resources of the contributors until the protectors eliminated them, by grace of the officials. M wished that he, too, had been watching his device.

"Please. I'm tired," she said, sweaty, looking back to the long line that reached for blocks behind M. "Please. I just need to lie down."

Something in M wanted to step back, to gesture to a space before him so she would be closer to the front of the line, closer to her domicile. In less than an hour he'd have his own power unit charged. But as he followed the citizen's eyes to the line behind them, he saw all the contributors who'd followed the guidance, who'd acquiesced according to the schedule. They were now, all of them, looking up from their devices, at M and this individual who was perhaps a citizen but nevertheless was of undetermined status in M's mind. Allowing someone to move ahead of his fellow citizens, no matter what their needs, simply could not be done.

"I'm sorry," M said, meaning "no."

Desperate, the supposed citizen seemed to hear M from far off, her frantic gaze already farther up the line. She rushed away, hoping to find a break.

At last, M withdrew his device from his pocket and idly swiped through his library of clips.

M heard the weeping when he'd almost arrived at the charging station. Turning his head slightly from the screen of his device, he saw the citizen pressed face down in the wet streets, three protectors standing above her. "Must have been a denizen after all," M said to himself and felt immediately better.

The charging station was a multi-sided obelisk: gray, sleek, and tall as a building. On each side of the obelisk a cradle was set to receive the power units, and once placed inside, the charge required only a few seconds to fully replenish the unit. While M waited for his charge, he idly thought about loving himself when he got home.

♪ ♩ ♩ ♩·

On his way back through the now saturated streets to his domicile (curfew for all citizens was 2000), a figure stepping from the shadow of an abandoned building doorway caught M by surprise. He was sure it was a protector—but for what? What had they seen?

"M," the citizen said.

He breathed with relief, seeing the figure in the clean gray and close-cut hair of all citizens. How she knew his name was another matter.

"We work together," she said. "At the factory. You put the clips together. I destroy the unauthorized material."

"Yes," M said. "I think I saw you over by the water earlier."

"I'm E," she said. "I wanted to tell you—the physician tomorrow. Don't let them into your head, M."

"My head? How did you know about the physician's appointment? What—what do you think they'll do inside my head?"

"Your song, M. They take it from your heart and plant it in your head, and then they'll control you. You know the guidance. The implant: take your life into your own hands."

"Everybody does it. It's supposed to be a simple procedure."

"Not everybody," she said. "We need you, M. Don't let them control your song." E quickly turned to the sound of splashing rubber shoes in the dark runoff from the tide, drowning the streets as the evening carried on. "I'll find you again," she said.

M entered his domicile with a swipe of his song card, the only possession allowed and required on his person, other than his device. When he set his refueled power unit into an electric frame in the wall, the bright white lights exposed a windowless room with a bed along one wall, a screen attached to the wall opposite. A few feet to the left of the screen a door led to M's bathroom—sink, toilet, and Love Tunnel, above which a smaller screen hung. As soon as he turned the faucet M began to weep, only through his eyes, which he'd done for years.

That evening, M wanted nothing less than to watch another set of clips. But he feared the protectors would assume he was doing something else: fomenting insurrection, perhaps. Loving himself outside of the Love Tunnel. So M lay on his bed and watched an hour's worth of clips (dogs catching frisbees and balls, mostly), then powered down his domicile. In the darkness he allowed himself to recall the citizen who'd caught up with him on the street, who'd warned him not to accept the implant. The officials stated that the implant was a means of taking one's life into one's own hands; it was the retired citizens who created the future. M, who often felt guilty, wondered if he should notify the protectors tomorrow. No, he concluded, he would not. Actually, he did like his head the way it was.

♪ ♩ ♩ 𝄽

M felt the device buzz in his pocket while stitching together panda clips, a fresh assignment from his new supervisor, who seemed to have no aesthetic appreciation of his unit's work. T would laugh, his heart warmed by the nutty exploits of pets as he stood over the shoulders of his employees. D, after introducing himself to the staff, had stated that cats and dogs were "over," and unless they looked forward to early retirement, the employees had better find another life form, preferably mammal, by which to enchant the citizens.

With their rotund bodies, small hands, and sympathetic faces, M thought pandas would generate a wealth of clips. But they were inherently lazy and did little except reach out and eat what was nearest them. Fortunately, their laziness brought a labored, clumsy quality to their more complicated movements, which M pulled from longer clips that were, generally, stagnant. He found it difficult to hang even two minutes of this panda business together.

At the buzzing of his device, M closed his editing program and left the factory, the protectors' appointment with the physician having already been transmitted to D. The physician's office, as indicated by the directions, was around the block, and as M made his way down the dried out, crumbling streets he saw protectors on the corners and in the doorways, searching for non-contributors. Even though M knew that the protectors knew he had a legitimate appointment with the physician, he still couldn't escape the feeling he'd done something wrong, that he'd thought something wrong, and that, regardless of any evidence, the protectors would take him away.

After he'd had his song card swiped by the citizen at the desk, M was directed to a small, white room with two chairs and a computer in the corner. Moments later the physician, dressed like M except for a white coat over his gray scrubs, entered and took the second seat before attaching his device to the computer.

"M has decided to take his life into his own hands," the physician said, turning away from the computer. For several seconds, he simply looked at M. "I knew the M before you," he said. "You're nothing like him."

"I never had the opportunity to meet him," M said.

"Obviously," the physician said. "So the protectors—the protectors have designated you as one of the increasingly small minority of citizens without the implant. Of course, you're a little older, and it wasn't a universal procedure at the time. So here we are. Mother? Father?"

"Mother," M said.

"Mother. The last vestige of a civilization who believed the obsolete assertion that citizens could be shaped into contributors by a parental figure. That folly has been exposed, naturally. Mother retired?"

"She cut her wrists," M said. "Above the sink. On a highchair so she wouldn't fall over and the blood would run into the sink. So she wouldn't make a mess."

The physician looked down a moment and shook his head. "If only the implant had been available then. But her sacrifice was undoubtedly noted. Those who pass before us allow us who follow the opportunity to better contribute."

It was M's turn to look down.

The physician took a deep breath. "As you are a citizen who has decided to take his life into his own hands, it is my pleasure to share with you the following information." He raised his hand as M was about to speak. "Even if you have heard all this before. After the Rise of the Waters and the Abandonment, the poisoning of both sea and sky, our officials of this island formerly known as Oʻahu of Hawaiʻi (now Republic of Contributing Citizens) understood that the limited resources of this place could not sustain unchecked population growth. The officials in their wisdom first regulated procreation which, aside from a minority of denizens (may they be rounded up and retired soon) has been executed to great success. Our citizens are healthier and more productive, contributors to their essences. Second, the officials gave to us the mercy of the implant, allowing citizens to secure a space for generations of succeeding contributors, with all the comforts of life provided by the officials. The implant has made it possible for all contributing citizens to want for nothing—food, entertainment, housing."

"Yes," M said. "I am aware—"

The physician raised his hand again. "How the implant works. It is a code, a series of notes, a song, the same song that gives you an individual identity as a citizen of the RCC. Though your place of business may know the numerical value of your song, the precise melody is known only to you, the protectors, and the officials. Once you've accepted the implant you will, at any time, be able to play your own song into retirement, after which you will be thanked for your services as a contributor. Your remains will be offered to the toxic oceans in hopes they might one day be redeemed. At retirement age, your song will be played, and your space in the RCC will be designated to another contributor. It is a cycle that resounds against itself beautifully. Otherwise, retirement is a messier process—hanging, usually, though you could perhaps follow in the footsteps of your mother."

"I understand," M said, though he was already panicked. Secretly, he'd always envisioned himself sailing away when it was time to leave, to some place where the waters were clean and the sun could be seen.

"The implant floods the body with barbiturates, while gently shutting down brain and heart function. You hear the opening notes of your song—and then, you are gone, your work complete."

"And is it absolutely required?" M asked.

The physician didn't respond as he turned his chair back to the computer. "Now that I've provided all the necessary information, we can get you set up—one week. Outpatient. You won't miss a day."

♪ ♩ ♩ ♩·

The tides had risen in the time M had been in the physician's office, and the sun, weak with a greenish pall behind the clouds, had gone below the city's gray desolate skyline. M no longer needed to contribute for the day. He stepped over deepening puddles on the puckering, gravelly sidewalk on the way back to his domicile.

An implant. Nearly everyone had them. It was just—they would go into your head. They would know your song. They could play it any time they liked, and it would be over.

"Your head is your own," a voice said.

M looked up from the reflections of the harsh streetlights in the wet ground and saw E.

"We can't be talking to each other," M said.

"We must," E said, stepping closer. "You don't have to do this. There's another way."

"They didn't say the implant was required."

"The moment you refuse the implant you lose all rights of a citizen. You're a denizen, a non-contributor, you're troubled. Both options are equally damning. There's another way, M."

M breathed deep, resigned. "What can I do?" he said in a harsh whisper.

E walked a few yards down the street and turned. "You aren't alone. Come with me. We will reclaim future."

"The curfew," M said, hurrying toward E, looking back toward his domicile.

"There's time yet," E said, touching his arm quickly and releasing it. "But not much."

City officials provided time after work, before check-in at each citizen's domicile, for foot travel, power unit charging, uniform maintenance, and hair-trimming—anything else was strictly prohibited.

"I can't do this. Not now," M said.

"Think of your mother," E said. "We knew her, M. She was one of us. She wanted something better not only for you, but for all of us." She began walking, and M followed. "Give me an hour, and you'll know everything."

♪ ♩ ♩ 𝄽

E led M to a domicile complex where she used her song card to unlock the entryway.

"I can't follow you in there," M said. "Guests are forbidden."

"Everything has been arranged," E said, looking around the block as she pulled M into the building.

At the entrance, a large citizen in front of a desk of computer screens commanded E to stop. M froze—what explanation would he give? His heart bounced between his ears, his breath short, sweating through the chest.

"It's alright," E told the citizen. "Thirteen."

The concierge stared at M over the readers low on his nose. "Thirteen," he said. "Careful on the stairs."

In most domicile complexes, staircases had been blocked by city officials. It was too difficult to monitor stairways, where lovemaking or any illicit transaction might take place. Elevators, with their static cameras, were less expensive to maintain. With a key she'd hidden between her device and its case, E unlocked the door marked EXCLUDED in great red letters. When the door closed behind them, M and E stood in complete darkness.

"Do not power on your device," E said, sensing that M had already withdrawn it. "The signal is scrambled, but as soon as you log in you'll be recorded in the mainframe."

"But I can't see," M said, hoping to access the Illuminator application.

"Follow my voice," E said, and M heard the scuff of her rubber sole on the first step. "Five at a time, then a turn at the landing. One, two, three, four, five, then turn. One, two, three, four, five."

M stretched his foot until it scraped the stairs. He began the ascent. One, two, three, four, five.

"The thirteenth floor is not registered on the elevator," E said as they climbed and turned, climbed and turned. "Even those who live here don't know it exists."

Pitch-black stairways, hidden floors—it was all something he may have dreamed before, some clip imprinted on his memory. Now he was trapped in the dream, both eyes open but seeing nothing, the darkness composed of his dread.

By the time he heard E make her final stop, M was long out of breath, and the dampness that had begun to spread from his chest had soaked into his armpits and back. A clicking noise was magnified by the blackness, and M recognized the turning of a knob, the light creak of a door opening.

If he'd entered the room from outdoors, M would have seen nothing before him, only an extended darkness. But his eyes had adjusted up the stairs and he could perceive, more feeling than seeing, a dim illumination in a chamber of unknown dimensions. As he followed E by the sound of her footsteps deeper into the large room, he saw the light source tended by someone—not a citizen, judging from her patched clothing—a single, small flame burning over a bowl of a fragrant liquid. Next to the flame a small mirror rotated, controlled by a small wheel M heard, but could not see, being turned. The mirror's face turned directly toward M, shining the flame in his eyes.

"Your song?" the tender of the flame said.

As M began to withdraw his song card, E spoke.

"Our songs are the songs of those who came before and those who will come after."

"O is ready," the tender of the flame said, and M heard the wheel spin. The mirror shifted direction, and as it turned and redirected the light M saw a seated woman—a woman—just a few feet away, flanked by two men in yellow robes. M knew she was a woman because of her long hair, which hung thick and white down her shoulders. The men on each side of her also had long hair, which they wore tied at the back of their heads. Beards as thick as garments grew on the lower halves of their faces.

"What is the Eleventh Principle?" the woman asked. With the aid of a staff that had lay across her lap, she took to her feet to look M in the eye.

"The Eleventh—the Eleventh Principle," M repeated, his mouth dry. Though he could not see beyond what the small flame and mirror revealed, he could feel the presence of others in the darkness surrounding him, all of them breathing at the same time, watching him, waiting for his answer.

"The Eleventh Principle," the woman said. "The damned thing is hammered in your skull from the time you are born. Played on a loop for not a one of us to forget."

"The Eleventh Principle. 'We are all men now.'"

"Now you tell me," the woman said, switching her staff from hand to hand as she removed her robe, "do I look like a man to you?"

M felt a foreign arousal as he stared at the woman's body. He'd seen such a thing only via the abstract distance of clips, bodies so perfect as to seem synthetic, engaged in all manners of stimulating activity. In front of him, glowing brown with the mirror's full face directed at it, was a real body: thick, discolored in spots, flesh sagging in some areas.

"Not at all," M said softly.

"Well, at least he's not an idiot," the woman said, slipping back into her robe. "Or too brainwashed to see the truth. Alright, kids, you can open your eyes now." She eased back into her chair. "My sons hate it when I pull that stunt. Embarrasses the hell out of them."

Soft laughter pulsed at the edges of the room, just at the threshold of M's hearing. The men on each side of the woman, M noticed, had lowered their eyes.

"I am O," the woman said. "My sons—K and W. We welcome all who acknowledge truth."

"I didn't want the implant," M said and nearly took back his naked words. If he'd said what he felt to a citizen, the protectors would be surrounding him immediately.

"Why should you? A method of control by officials to keep them in their lawns and their homes. Not 'domiciles.' You've seen their homes, yes?"

"Of course." The lawns, flawless green spaces at the edge of the city where the officials, for all they'd provided for the citizens, hit balls over gentle slopes, out of clean, white patches of sand. The lawns for which the penalty for trespassing was death. Not retirement, death. And the homes! Rooms for sitting, rooms for sleeping, elaborate furnishings and decorations from times past. With windows that looked out onto the perfect lawns.

"You don't know your story, M. The story of your people—or any people, for that matter. The leaders of this man-made hell call you 'citizens' and make you believe you have rights, that you are all equal, all of you 'contributing.' Another word they've corrupted. Before the United States came, before they left, before they ruined the oceans and the sky, this island—these islands, not the officials—provided because they were provided for. People—citizens, yes, but human beings first—took care of one another. It was—"

O sighed.

"Now I'm getting all preachy. I'm sure it never has been perfect. But this—this is an abomination. We have been in hiding, M. We have no allegiance to your officials and their devices and implants. We cannot be tracked like citizens, you who allow yourselves to be tracked and controlled. And we will take Hawai'i back, island by island. Soon. We are the people the protectors were meant to protect you from."

"But the officials—"

"Are dependent on the same technology upon which they've made you dependent. They just know how to use it more intelligently. Your mother, M, she was one of us. She worked in secret, like us. She protected you, and when they found out about her, she took her own life to protect the movement. So we could continue our work."

"How? You have some kind of supercomputer or robot army?"

"We don't need that crap," O said. She turned to one of her sons. "Stop me if I'm getting this wrong," she said. "I'm terrible at explaining these kinds of things. You see, M, all the bullshit—the devices, the domiciles, the protectors, the officials, the implants—all of it is maintained through digital information operating at a prescribed transmitted frequency. That's kind of the gist, ok? If you interrupt that digital transmission, even for an instant, the system goes offline. It doesn't work anymore, yeah?"

"But how could you knock it offline? Explode the information centers or something?"

"Jeez, this guy's got clips on the brain," O said. "This isn't *Die Hard*. Never mind. You see, M, interrupting the transmission is where you come in, where I come in, where we all come in. Call it a manual override. Every song assigned to a citizen has a set of notes, yeah? They've broken it down to code, but the song is much more than that, much more. What if one song was the key? One song to supersede all others, sung loud enough to blow the connections. They've prohibited music to supposedly protect their beloved citizenry—it is the weapon by which they've made you slaves. You live in fear of the song because it is inseparable from your life essence, and they've channeled that away from you. Every citizen has a song, and once their song is played, life is over. We will use the weapon against them. With our voices. We need all our voices, M. We need you."

M felt the eyes in the darkness on him, the collectively held breath, K and W staring stone-faced, O relaxing farther into her chair.

"And what song will I sing?" M said.

"The song of songs, of course. Our mele."

♪ ♩ ♩ ♩.

The Hana, as O and her followers called it, was to take place in one week, the same day M had been scheduled for his implant. While cutting clips at work he'd think that perhaps his life wouldn't be all that bad with the implant, that it would be much of the same, really—he would edit videos from the archive (the latest was rabbits eating) and go to his domicile, where he would love himself before falling asleep.

Those thoughts, though, dissipated in the presence of O, who taught him the mele syllable by syllable. The language, beautiful, infinitely expressive, was unfamiliar. But M took to the song easily, buoyed as he followed the gestures of O, by the chorus of voices in the darkness of the thirteenth floor. K and W's deep baritones added a solidity, a third dimension to the mele, which M could almost see as he sang.

For several days he visited the thirteenth floor after work at the factory, during the small window of time before check-in and the start of curfew. In his domicile he played the clips of which he knew the protectors were taking note, but as he watched he formed the words of the mele in his mouth, singing silently. M thought he could hear the voice of his mother whisper each phrase into his ear.

One evening, just before he was about to leave for his domicile, M saw in the light of the flame and mirror O sitting on the floor with a drum between her knees, pounding a slow, languid beat. She seemed to weep the words on top of the plodding drum, echoed by the voices in the dark. M was distressed to realize the only word he recognized was "Hawai'i."

"What is it?" M asked E.

"A piece from one of the great warrior-poets of the past," E said. "Kalākaua."

On the day before the Hana, M heard an explosion from his editing bay at the factory. Immediately he thought he'd missed some important part of the plan, some step from which he'd been excluded. All around him his coworkers looked up from their screens, eyes dilating in the indoor light.

"I'll be damned," M's supervisor, D, said as he moved through the factory, trying to calm everyone. "First time since I can remember," D hammered a code into his device, which immediately responded with a bell chime, "it's raining. Protect yourselves on the way back to your domiciles."

In the streets citizens fled the rain, trying to avoid the liquid dropping onto their skin, sliding into their eyes. Officials said the sky was as poisoned as the ocean, but to M it felt clean. He stood underneath the shower until he thought someone might notice. When he reached his domicile he didn't love himself, nor did he lie in his bed and search for more clips. He sat on the floor, set his ear against the wall, and listened to the falling rain.

♪ ♩ ♩ 𝄽

At roughly 1100 O, followed by her two sons, emerged from the darkened chambers of the thirteenth floor into a day that belonged to the sun, which held steady near the top of a blue sky framed with long, flat clouds on the horizon. They had only gone a few steps down the dry, cracked streets before a group of protectors rushed at them, waving their underutilized billy clubs. As the protectors' primary weapon had been, for so long, fear, they'd had little reason to train properly in the nuances of combat, and were quickly disposed of by O, who swung at them with her walking staff, and K and W, who were just as effective with their bare hands. Only slightly winded, O and her sons continued to walk toward the center of the city with open mouths to sing.

At which point M, palms sweating over his keyboard, heard a voice from the other side of the room, strong in the words he'd memorized. Around the singing citizen other workers, their eyes rolling to the back of their heads, collapsed from their chairs. M hadn't considered the effects of the mele on those with implants. Were they dying, or were they being released? Only moments after she began the mele, the citizen was set upon by four protectors, two of which fell senseless to the ground before they put their hands on her. The other two clubbed her on the head until she, too, fell.

Then, another citizen took up the song, and then another. Voices from the darkness. Computer screens flashed blue, and somewhere outside the factory M could hear the circular blaring of an alarm. Already the protectors were leaping over chairs and fallen citizens toward those who loudly proclaimed the song, the manual override, the mele.

M decided to withdraw. If it all turned out to be a failure, the officials would never know he'd been a part of the conspiracy. All he had to do was nothing.

He heard a voice next to him, another citizen taking up the song. Now, not only the screens were flashing—everything in the factory, it seemed, was flashing. Even the electronic wail from the bowels of the building could not cut through the voices conjoined in song. Bodies lay everywhere—protectors, citizens, and, standing among them, the carriers of the mele.

The citizen standing next to M, his song clear against the chaos, extended his hand. More protectors swarmed through the door. Another citizen silenced, beaten to the ground. At last M took the hand, and with it took up the song of his people.

THE SWEET SPOT

[a.m. Dellamonica]

"I'm gonna visit Dad." Matt is curled in the passenger seat of their antique minivan, scowling as offworlders tromp and slither past their front bumper. Shooting a glance at Ruthie through long, pretty eyelashes, he flips down the visor to check the mirror.

"Dad's dead, Matt. He can't see your haircut."

"Want to come?" Falsely casual.

"Can't." She throws the word through the driver's-side door; she's outside, waving merchandise: soda, water bottles, scented strips of leather and fur. "I have to pay off Security."

"You could trust Romano with that. You do it for him often enough."

"I could get a job in a feeler bar too," she snaps, then regrets it. So much for vowing to be more patient.

Matt gives up on finger-combing his curls. Coaxing a battery out of their aging solar charger, he checks the readout. "Did you use this?"

Ruthie winces. "An old lady paid me forty for half a charge. Her son just died."

A flat glare.

"Forty, Matt."

"So you get forty, I get half a visit with the old man."

"With an answering machine." He can dress it up all he likes, but the battery is just juice for an interactive video of their father. "Waste of credit, waste of time."

"You suck, Ruth." He edges out of the van, stomping off to the cemetery.

Ruthie reins in an urge to beg forgiveness. It's done; she'll grovel later. Instead, she climbs into the van, thumbing the air conditioning and leaning into the vent.

Since they came to Kauaʻi, her fantasies have been about winter. Deep breath, in through the nose, out through the teeth. As cool air chills her sinuses, she imagines snow melting through her mittens.

She mimes packing a snowball, rolling it across an unbroken plain of white. She barely has the bottom ring of a snow fort built when someone raps on the window.

It's Sam, a.k.a. Security, leering down her shirt through the tinted glass.

Ruthie shuts off the air conditioning, grabs the weekly payoff, and slides out into the balmy fist of the afternoon.

Sam is a spotty-faced redhead whose scarred right eye socket bulges with a cut-rate offworld prosthetic. Blue gel shot through with veins pulses at her, fronted by a lens that has the fluted edges of a poker chip.

"Morning, Ruth." Onion breath ruffles her hair.

"Hi." She holds out the weekly bribe.

He pockets it without counting. "We gotta talk. Inside?"

She shakes her head. "Graveyard. I'll have Romano watch the van."

"Please. You think I want a piece of your skinny ass?"

She shrugs. Not all the women on Vender's Row pay their bribes in cash. Besides, she doesn't want that onion smell in the car. "Gotta stretch my legs."

He's not thrilled, she can tell, but he follows her through the converted golf course to the high point of the cliff.

It's a scenic viewpoint, postcard perfect: ocean glittering silver-blue under swirled, fragile clouds. An anti-aircraft platform, purple-black in color and shaped like a rosebud, drifts lazily among the cirrus wisps, guarding the Kauaʻi channel and the offworlders' undersea military base there.

A hundred feet down, the aliens are splashing around the beach at the foot of the cliff, exuberant as children. They *are* kids, pretty much—barely grown, they were yanked from the seas of their homeworld to help the Democratic Army in its war against the Fiends.

"I never see anyone but you up here," Sam says. "Gawking at squid makes it hard to forget the war."

Ruthie leans on a sand-colored boulder. Below, the offworlder soldiers wrestle, dunking each other, spitting water and tootling, churning up the Pacific as they tangle themselves into knots and then slip free. "Is that possible, forgetting the war?"

"Who the fuck knows. Hey, want an apple?"

"In exchange for what?"

"My treat." He holds out the gleaming red fruit and Ruthie can't help but snatch it. It's tart enough to make her pucker, and she nearly moans at the first bite.

"So…" Sam glances around. "Army's decided to put in another databank for the graveyard."

Ruthie catches a dribble of apple juice on her chin, licking it off her thumb. "More storage…the Democratic Army expects more casualties?"

"Lot more. Fiends have been cleaning their clocks."

"What's that to do with me and Matt?"

"They're not digging up the green for no mausoleum."

"They're putting it in the parking lot?" The fruit in her mouth becomes rubber; she fights to swallow. "How big?"

"Arches, plaques, statues, flowers—the whole nine."

"The entire parking lot?"

"Half," he says. "I'm giving twenty vendors their walking papers."

Yet another crypt. She can already see it, a square, depressing monument to the endless grind of this war. The Fiends—Friends of Liberation, they call themselves—have been making headway in their drive to secure the whole planet.

"Kabuva's gonna have to send even more of them," she says, indicating the squid on the beach.

"Yeah. That'll happen," Sam grunts.

"We're never gonna beat them at this rate."

"It's cute, Ruthie, your belief in the great Demo cause. But I ain't here to debate strategy."

"You're right. Matt and I can pay more if you give us a chance. There'll be fewer vendors, less competition, more mourners. Can we stay?"

"Well…" Sam drawls, fake eye pulsing, snaggled teeth peeping out from under the skirt of his loose upper lip. "That depends."

The graveyard greens are lined with mosaic paths made of slate tiles. Each tile is inscribed with the name and signature of a Demo soldier, along with their mourning catalog code. Twining over the immaculate fairways, the paths lead to curls of hedge and stone walled alcoves, nooks constructed to offer privacy to visitors.

Near an erstwhile sandtrap is a bench and an interactive obelisk. Ruthie pulls up its menu and lets it eat five of their hard-earned bank credits to pay for power. There's a jack for a battery—it's cheaper to bring your own juice—but she only needs a minute.

Fog machines belch out mist and a micro-projector starts up, projecting an image of Daddy within the fog. He's young, the invincible father she remembers from childhood, and Matt has apparently set his defaults so he's proportionately big. She has to look up, way up, because she only comes to his thigh.

The giant face brightens as Daddy looks down. "You're starting to look like your mother," it says. "How old—"

"I'm looking for Matthew," she interrupts. "I thought this was your spot."

Dad scratches his non-existent beard, buying time as, elsewhere, computers process her statement. "Your brother's not on the system, Ruth."

"Since when?"

"Twelve days, ten hours, six minutes."

She sinks to the edge of the sand trap and buries her face in her hands. Ok, don't be stupid, don't be a baby. Where you been going, Matt? Little lying bastard...

The ghost shifts, sitting. "Shit day, kid?"

She remembers the phone call when he asked her that. She was in school; she'd failed an art exam. Through a teary haze she sees him flicker, resetting. He resolves on a chair near the obelisk, older now, normal sized. He's playing his guitar.

That does it...she melts down completely. Dad plays rock songs under the tree, burning cash Ruthie can't afford while she cries and cries.

When she's stopped carrying on like a diva, he tilts his head: "Want to talk about it?"

"You're an answering machine," she says. "Cobbled-together phone conversations, vidblog entries..."

"If you prefer, I'll direct you to my physical remains."

Remains. A dust-proof tube containing a DNA sample, buried under the slate tile that bears his name. "I'd prefer to talk to Matt."

"Sorry, hon. I don't know where your brother is."

She glares at the illusion. "We're losing our parking spot. No spot, no money. No money, no food. You get that? Matt told you how we live?"

"Yes."

It hurts to look at him, but the tears have carried her back to a hot, achy place where she can function.

"Sam will let us stay, but there's strings."

She can't go on. Demo Intelligence has to be monitoring these conversations, combing transcripts for damaging admissions. Exploiting people's grief. She can't tell him Sam's joined the Fiends. "Anyway, bribe's going up."

"Can you pay more?" Daddy asks.

"That's the question, isn't it?"

Matt turns up after midnight, slipping through the side door and delicately arranging his skin and bones onto their mattress. She doesn't bother pretending to be asleep. He wouldn't be fooled; they've lived this way too long.

"Where were you? I went to the sandtrap."

"It's a big boneyard, Ruth."

She pinches him. "You haven't been online all week."

He lights up. "You talked to Dad?"

"Where were you?"

He bites his lip. "I'm seeing someone."

"Oh." A flare of unease, somewhere in her marrow.

"Yeah, 'oh.' You want to know who?"

"Someone I won't like, I guess, or you'd have told me. But human."

"Yeah, human. I don't do squid, Ruth. It's Holly Scott."

"Oh." Holly's a Democratic war veteran, like Sam. She's royalty here on the Row—lives in a real camper, sells water and battery charges. She runs a good patter on the human and offworlder marks alike; her wares sell well.

She's old—thirty at least, twice Matt's age.

"That's all you have to say? No lecture on fucking the competition?"

He's spoiling for a fight, but Ruthie doesn't have one in her. "If I was that much of a bitch last time you had a girlfriend, I'm sorry."

"If?" He morphs from mad to scared. "No. You've been drafted, haven't you?"

"Worse." She laughs weakly. "Sam's with the Fiends."

"So? We knew there had to be a few on the Row."

"They want us to sing, Mattie."

That gets his attention—his eyes widen, and he lets out a peep.

"He called it a project," she tells him. "We sing, it draws the squid off Fry Beach. Fiends want to plant a bomb there."

"We're a diversion?"

"I guess."

He sits, toppling a stack of soda cans. "No way."

"Half the parking lot's getting demolished. Sam says we can keep our spot—"

"I am not helping those bastards commit murder."

"You think I want to?"

"You're considering it, aren't you?"

"Where we gonna go? We got a good thing here…"

"I remember what a good thing is, Ruthie, and this isn't it."

"You ungrateful shit. We're eating, aren't we?"

"You'd rather kill people than go hungry?"

"Hungrier?" But now Ruthie's ashamed of herself. She fumbles for his hand. "We'll offer more money."

With that, the resistance vanishes. Matt presses his forehead against hers, and they don't say any more.

Next morning they pull out all the stops, hustle-hustle, sell-sell-sell. Ruthie does a tune-up on the van, fills the fuel tank, changes the oil. Matt trades their heavy goods for lightweight stuff: touchables, music files, things they can hawk at any roadside. By dinner the van is ready to move. They have a few weeks of water and protein mallows laid by, just in case.

They're discreet, but the Row talks. Sam shows, a disappointed expression on his narrow face. "You pissing on my offer, then?"

Ruthie lets him into the van. Steady voice, she thinks, don't quaver. "We'll pay more to keep our spot—"

"Did I ask for more money?"

"We can't sing," Matt says.

"Can't?" Sam's gelatinous eye rolls in his direction, its false iris cycling wide.

"Take the payment, Sam, ok?" Ruthie pleads.

"No." Sam holds up both hands, making an "L" with his left finger and thumb, mirroring the gesture with his right hand so that his prosthetic leers at them through a rectangular space the size of a photoprint.

"What's that?" Ruthie says.

"Making sure I'm in the now," he says. "Kids, this is the moment when we become Friendly."

Matt puts up a hand. "There's no attitude here."

"No scam," Ruthie agrees. "We'll pay more, or go."

"It's just singing's impossible."

"And I'm—*we're* sorry."

"Gee," says Sam. "Can't I change your mind?"

The back of her hand tingles. Itches. Pinches. A tiny silver dot pimples up from under the skin behind her thumb.

She looks up, horrified, locking on Sam's flinty, half-alien gaze. Her flesh, around the metallic pinprick, is heating up. There are other itches now, too, a scattering of discomfort across her body.

"The apple you gave me…"

Sam smirks.

"What's happening?" Matt asks.

The dot behind her thumb begins to smoke. The burn's a candle-flame at first—and that's bad enough—but the fiery seed is getting bigger, glowing like the cherry of a lit cigarette, frying more skin by the second.

"Ruthie?"

Another of the itches, above her navel, goes hot.

Matt catches her as she doubles over. She can't squelch a growl of pain. Wasp-heat in her temple, the stink of scorching hair, makes her gag.

Matt is screaming now.

No, she thinks, he's hurting Mattie too. She tries to lift herself off the van floor, to fight back.

Sam is laughing.

And Matt's not hurt, she realizes. It's worse—he's begging. "Stop, you win, we'll do it, don't hurt her."

Tears stream down Ruthie's face—crying again, second time in two days, she thinks—as Sam grabs her hair. "That true, Ruth? You'll sing for us?"

"Yeah," she manages.

The seeds cool off, forming blisters.

"Saturday, dinnertime, at the Atlanta monument." Sam nudges her with a toe; she has his pants leg fisted in her hands. "Sing for at least an hour. Don't try running off—we're listening, we'll know."

He steps over her to the door, patting a furious Matt on the head.

"Sam…"

He turns, and she finds herself wanting to cringe, like a whipped dog. "We'll need our stuff."

"That so?"

"She's right." Matt says. "It was in storage in Koloa. Masks, instruments, sound system. Can you find it?"

"We can find anything." With that, Sam steps back out onto the parking lot.

Matt slams the door, throws the locks, and flicks the A/C on full. He yanks out their first aid kit, rummaging. "What do we do?" he asks, sounding like a little boy.

Shakily, Ruthie knots her fingers together in an approximation of a Kabuva tentacle knot. "Practice," she says, but the sign she makes is different; it's the squid word for deception.

"Isshy taught us the Kabuva folk songs back when he and Dad were living together," Matt says. He's standing beyond the bedroom door of Holly's camper. Ruthie is stretched out on the bed.

"Your dad had a sugar squiddy?" Holly pokes Ruth's shoulder with a stubby finger; she's using bootlegged med equipment to locate the fireseeds.

Ruthie nods. "By the time I was ten, we were a bona fide novelty act."

"Human kids who sing squid. I can see it." Holly's apparent lack of judgment annoys her. She wonders if this is playacting, if Matt already told Holly their secrets.

"Dancing monkeys, they called us," he says.

"Found another one." Holly eases the point of her knife into Ruthie's shoulder. "Over soon. Just breathe."

Matt keeps talking. "Isshy got on the wrong side of his superiors and got reassigned to The Sponge." He means the massive undersea installation the squid built in the middle of the Kaua'i channel. "Dad got drafted into the Demo Army. We moved here to live with a cousin, who got Dusted."

"Ok, doll, I got all the seeds. You doing ok?"

"Thanks, Holly." Ruthie reaches for her clothes.

"And now the Fiends want you to sing so they can crisp some calamari?"

"That's their plan, yeah."

"You want my opinion?"

"What, for free?" Ruthie says.

"Do as they tell you."

"Don't joke, Holly," Matt says.

"So not joking."

"But—you fought with the squid against them."

Holly steps out into her kitchenette, where she can see them both. "Democrats are losing the war. The squid'll give up on us."

"Holly, come on! What the Fiends want—it's terrorism."

"I don't want to cross the playground, Matt, I don't. But in another few years, Fiends'll invade the mainland. After that…"

"After that, what?"

"It'll take years. But Earth's gonna be all Fiend, all the time. They're gonna crawl over the whole map and eject every offworlder they find."

"There's gotta be some chance."

She shook her head. "Make some Friends, Matt. They're psycho, but they'll be running things."

"Switch sides? You wouldn't do that." He runs a finger down her face, stunned. Ruthie wonders: does he love her?

"This whole war's going in the squatter—"

"We aren't murderers, Holly."

"It's not like they're asking you to kill *people*."

"It is like that. Isshy was a mother to us."

"Squid momma left you here, grafting," Holly says. "For that you defy the Fiends?"

"We're not doing it," Ruthie says. "We just haven't figured out how to screw them yet."

Her brother's fingers come together, unconsciously expressing relief. Ruthie immediately feels better. Mattie's on board; she's still in charge. How hard can fooling Sam be? Being a Fiend doesn't make him smart.

"Thanks for patching me up, Holly," she says, then forces herself to add: "You two should get in some time together while you can. We may have to run for it."

Matt catches her arm. "You won't decide anything without me?"

"I figure something out, I'll text you."

With that, she heads for the beach path, vying with other scrabblers to sell touchables to the squid heading down to the water. She sells fake fur, fruit leather, perfumed gel, acting like everything's ok.

Squid are blind, their senses based in taste, smell, and touch—preferably all three at once. They'll stick a tentacle into any stinky moist thing they can find. Even the poorest scrabblers out here are wearing protective masks over their eyes and mouths.

Of course they'll pay you to take the masks off, to let them ramble their tentacles over your mouth and eyes, better yet into your pants. Every so often, a fry goes into the bushes with one of the vendors, bringing 'em back well-paid and covered in sucker marks.

Ruthie's not up for that, but she leaves her burned hand unbandaged, offering a taste of her blood.

It's over an hour before she gets what she's hoping for—a squid whose mantle veins go green with compassion when it tastes her wound. A bleeding heart.

Ruthie's fingers form the sign for help as the stranger's tentacle slithers over her…and before it can pull away, she passes it a KabuBraille note she's been coding, surreptitiously, this whole time.

It recoils, vanishing into the crowd. Ruthie starts coding another strip, hoping for another chance.

At sundown, she goes back to the sand trap. Dad is older when she boots him up: older, uniformed, hollow-eyed. "You look more like your mother every day."

"I need to get Matt somewhere safe," she says. "If Isshy boots you, will you tell him?"

"Isshy rarely—"

"I'm trying to get him a message."

More beard-scratching: it's processing again. "I know you're unhappy about Isshy and me."

She winces. "Stop. Play guitar—"

"It was love, you know—" He freezes.

Like Matt and Holly? Her face burns. "I'm over it, Dad. I'm sorry they broke you up."

The personality simulator is so good sometimes—he looked surprised, even grateful.

Steel up. Squash that rush of emotion. Ruthie's about to walk off when Dad starts strumming. She sinks to the grass, fixing her eyes on the anti-aircraft platform over the Sponge, the glimpse of ocean through the trees.

That evening Sam turns up with their old music trunk.

"You owe me back rent on that locker," he says. "Fifty, due after the concert."

"Yeah, yeah." They shut themselves in the van and Ruthie restrings her minicello. Matt warms up, warbling soprano Kabuva laments.

As they sing, they flash squid signs back and forth, piecing together a conversation the Fiend listening devices won't pick up. Ruthie tells him she's trying to contact Isshy.

Matt digs in his pocket for a balled-up sheet of seapaper. Ruthie runs a hand over the Kabubraille quickly; it is an advertisement for their concert.

Where? she signs.

All over the island. Throwing back his head, Matt lets out a string of notes, all too high and atonal to sound musical to human ears. It is one of the squids' favorites, a howl of despair about leaving Mother Sea for faraway, violent shores. Disaffected soldiers went nuts over it.

Ruthie joins in, again fighting tears. She never liked this piece; what's wrong with her?

When the song ends, she turns away, hiding her brimming eyes. "Let's take a break—do some planning."

"You're the planner." Sour. Talk about disaffected...

"I meant...wanna talk song order?"

"Up to you."

She fumbles the minicello, which feels small. Her hands have grown. "Matt, you're the one told Sam we'd do the dancing monkey on Saturday."

"I should've let him burn you to a crisp?"

Ruthie's stomach burns. She was stupid; she took candy from a stranger. "Fine, everything's my fault."

"Any song order is ok," he sighs. "Shits, I'm already tired of this."

"We ended up getting drafted after all, Matt."

"Just not by the side we thought?"

"At least our so-called friends are winning," she says, for the benefit of the listening Fiends.

"Now there's a silver lining." He smiles weakly, signing: *Are we gonna be ok?*

In response, Ruthie plucks through the opening notes of a Kabuva folk song. Its first line translates, roughly, to: "All we can do is hope."

Next day she is emptying out the minivan's squatter when two goons whisk her off to the cemetery. It's just as she imagined in her wildest paranoid dreams: there's a secret door within the mausoleum, then a long elevator ride down to dull, fluorescent-lit Demo offices.

The air is stale but cold—air-conditioned. Heavenly.

Matt is already there. "I told them everything," he blurts.

"It's ok—"

"Hurry up." Her abductor, a lanky blond Amazon in a Democratic Army uniform, cuts them off. "We can't have the Fiends noticing you're gone."

They're marched to a squalid concrete box that smells of body fluids. An interrogation room? Ruth tenses...

Then Matt cries out like a baby. Isshy is here.

Her brother hurls himself across the room, burying his face in the slime of Isshy's mantle, keening in Kabuva. Ruthie feels herself glancing askance at their captor. The woman's disgust is obvious.

That makes it easier. When Isshy extends a tentacle, Ruthie takes it without hesitation, pressing her knuckles into the gelatinous flesh of her father's one-time lover, then transferring a tentacle to her armpit so he can taste her.

"You're here to get us away?" she asks, hating that she sounds like a little kid.

Isshy's cap tightens, puckering.

Matt pulls his face out of the slimy hug. "Isshy?"

"I am getting immigration permits for you."

"Immigrate to where? Canada?" Her legs quake with almost sexual longing. Snow, she thinks. Cold.

"You've betrayed the Fiends, child. There's nowhere on Earth we can hide you."

"The Sponge, then?" Matt asks. "With you?"

The soldier grunts. "To a refugee city on Kabuva."

"Offworld?" Living away from Earth, on a wholly squid planet... Ruthie tries to imagine it.

"With you?" Matt repeats.

Isshy signs regret. "My term of service was extended. But Earthtown is a good place. It's on Blighted Sea."

Extended service: Isshy is buying their freedom with another tour. Ruthie shoves guilt aside; he got them into this, after all. "Can we leave right away?"

Matt startles. His face darkens.

"Or what, Mattie? Stay and die?"

"Can't we go to the Sponge?"

The alien caresses Matt's neck. "It's not allowed, spawn. We've been infiltrated, twice—humans have been banned from the base."

"I never heard that."

"It's classified," snarls the Demo officer. "Don't leak it. And before you go thinking there's some choice in this for you, let me lay this out. You do the concert for the Fiends, then you go to Kabuva. That's the deal."

Ruthie's jaw drops. "You *want* us to sing?"

"You're bait, child." Isshy is white now—angry. "They hope to catch the Fiends booby-trapping Fry Beach."

"Pardon me for trying to save some of your people, Sir. Fry Beach has state-of-the-art defenses, kids. If we find out how the Fiends plan to crack its security..."

"We can't go back out there." Ruthie says. "If they realize we've reported them, Mattie and I are dust."

"Life's a gamble. You sing, we bag 'em, you go to Kabuva."

"Or we stay and the Fiends kill us?" Ruthie says.

"Pretty much. We done here?" the woman asks.

She looks at Matt. "What do you think?"

"I think if there was any real choice, you wouldn't ask my opinion."

"Matthew," Isshy says, reproachful. "Your sister is doing her best."

Her brother turns red.

"Say your goodbyes." The woman mimes scrubbing her hands, as if they're dirty. "I gotta get the boy out of here."

"Leave Matt," says Ruthie. "I'll go first."

"He's been missing longer." She takes obvious pleasure in peeling Matt out of Isshy's grip. "We're taking you out near your favorite obelisk, son; far as the Fiends know, you've been visiting Daddy."

Matt clings to the outstretched tentacle until she has bundled him out of reach. Then he's gone, and Ruthie's alone with Isshy.

"Thanks for helping us."

"Child. There was never any question."

"We have to run all the way to your homeworld?"

Tentacles spiral in distress. "Our attempt to help your government is falling into disgrace at home; the number of casualties is catastrophic."

"You never lose. When you show up, the Fiends always retreat."

"Ruth, it may be years yet before we leave. But leave we will. In defeat, I fear. You, Matthew—anyone close to us—you won't be safe. Everyone with sense is getting their loved ones to Earthtown."

"Your pets?"

"I hoped you weren't angry with me anymore, spawn."

"Isshy, we're in the shits now because of you and Dad."

"I can't change the past," he says. "But this could be a better life. Do you want to spend your days jammed in a car, starving?"

"I want my goddamn father back," she says sulkily.

He fluffs his cap. "I wish that, too."

○

She spends the evening atop her cliff, watching the fry gambol in the tide. Dozing with her back against a tree, she dreams of being on the run with Matt. Her brother is a baby again, easily transported, too young to balk or argue. They hide in a blizzard, amid curtains of freezing snow. Ruthie feels safe, invisible, in control.

When she wakes, Matt is beside her, watching the sunrise. Light spills gold over the water; peach and magenta clouds unfurl, like streamers, across the sky.

His eye falls on one of her burns.

"Don't worry about me," she says, irked.

"Cast iron maiden." It is something Dad called her, before he went away.

"It wouldn't hurt you to steel up a little."

"Get cold," he says.

"Life hasn't been getting easier."

"Cut off human contact. Dump my lover without so much as a 'do you mind, dear?' Yeah, that's an answer."

Tears spring to her eyes. Her fingers twist, of their own accord, into a Kabuva sign: *hurtful, unfair.*

"Sorry. I didn't mean—" He reaches out.

She slaps his hand away. *One of us has to have a hard shell,* she thinks. You can't be an open wound all the time.

"I screw up, Mattie," she says instead. "I don't ask your opinion enough. But this mess—I didn't make it."

He forms a clumsy chain of signs. *We should run.*

Which is ridiculous. Instead of saying so, she signs: *How?*

Matt opens a bottle of water and takes a long, slow gulp. "Something terrible's going to happen," he says, in his clear, light voice and Ruthie feels her stomach dropping into a pit.

Detonate a Dust bomb on a windless day, and it will expand in a sphere before falling downward. The nanotech weapon disassembles everything it touches. If it falls straight down, touching bare ground, the crater it makes will form a hemisphere.

The Atlanta monument, like so many from this war, reflects this reality. Its focus is a copper-lined crater, big enough to stand in and half-filled with offerings: flowers, stuffed animals, photos of the dead. Carved into its rim are images of the city in various eras, artists' renderings of famous citizens and heroes from the Democratic Army. The Fiends reduced Atlanta to atoms.

It is a creepy place to stage a concert.

Ruthie and Matt set up their backstage in a nearby grove of magnolia trees, pitching a small tent and unpacking their gear: the electronic synthmasks that play their backup music, the minicello, and two mesh sheaths woven from strips of seaweed. It has been years since they performed, and Ruthie's sheath is a bit short. But they still fit; neither of them has gained much weight since the so-called good days.

Squid start arriving before they are set up, flowing up from the beach, arriving in flitters, in buses from the barracks in Koloa. First there's a half a dozen of them, then thirty, then fifty.

Sam breezes into the tent, leering. "Ready for the big day, kiddies? Where's your donation bowl? You're supposed to be singing for money."

"We are singing for money," she says. "How long do you need to do your thing? An hour?"

"That should do. I expect a cut, you know."

She goes through the motions of haggling. Finally she says, "I need to dress."

His plastic eye pulses. "Go ahead."

"Get out, pervert," Matt says, and to her relief he does. "You ok, Ruth?"

"No. I'm a big bag of emotion."

"It's not a bad thing."

"Bad timing," she says.

"It's always a bad time," her little brother says.

Wrestling with grief and fear, she peers outside.

In the time it has taken to play out the little farce with Sam, the audience has swelled. Hundreds of squid are out there, setting up seawater sprinklers, lying on kelp mats and each other. They smell of overripe seafood, and they are passing things around—touchables, food, scent packs, drugs. Vendors from the Row hawk goods avidly from the sidelines.

Disturbed, Ruthie wrings out the brine in her dress, slithering into the mummy-wrap of seaweed strips. She swallows a pill called *Hot Flash* that will send her sweat glands into overdrive, then tests the microphone and display screen within her singing mask. Her hair goes into a ponytail; then she slicks it against her neck with gel.

The waiting squid are hooting a tune, their flute-like voices tootling in the meadow. It is a song about death—that's all the fry seem to sing anymore—and it brings up the gooseflesh on her burned arms.

"Lament to Blighted Sea," says Matt. He is in his sheath, ready but for his mask. "You think we'll get to Kabuva?"

"Don't see why not," she lies, then surprises herself by hugging him. "If anything happens, we meet on the cliff."

"The high spot." With a half-smile, he pulls his mask over his face. She does likewise, adjusting her mic.

Tech check. The words appear just above her eyes.

A-OK, she texts back.

"Let's do this," Mattie says aloud.

They emerge from the tent, hand in hand, and the cacophony of singing toots turns into a one-pitch whistle. Matt steps up to the lip of the Atlanta monument. The weeds on his legs and arms flutter in the breeze, carrying scents to their audience.

Ruthie is almost too stunned to move. There must be a thousand of them. How did the Fiends do it? She sees officers here and there, trying to disperse the crowd, only to get slapped down by a dozen hostile fry.

Bad morale, she thinks.

Mattie is letting go with a piercing high note. She activates the synthesized accompaniment coded into her mask, and the air fills with a clatter of shells and stones in surf.

Don't let your mind wander onstage. Daddy's voice, so deeply internalized it feels real. She boots the minicello, playing tones and chirps as her brother works his way into the song. It is a bloody-minded kid's chant about newborn squid drifting below the skin of the sea, yanking birds down from the surface, devouring them.

The listeners are mottling, their caps turning beige and coral as they relax. Ruthie remembers opening with this same piece in dozens of clubs across America. Daddy intertwined with Isshy at the water's edge, Scotch and soda in his hand. A sick and twisted family, sure, but a happy one. Isshy believed they'd win the war. Matt loved it all so much.

They finish singing the birdhunter piece and warble through a transition. Maybe we can do this in Earthtown, Ruthie muses, be dancing monkeys on Kabuva.

Concentrate, her dead father's voice admonishes.

Another platoon of squid wriggles over Vendor's Row as Matt begins a piece about pressure hallucinations—squid hear ghosts when they swim at too great a depth. Ruthie opens her throat, pouring out accompaniment. The words are grim, but the alien harmonies ring true.

They segue into "Mad Moon," a more patriotic piece, and the audience pales.

Ruthie brings the song order up on her mask display, deleting several numbers. She switches the rah-rah stuff with bleaker material, and texts the revised list to her brother. Matt nods without breaking a beat. He cuts the last chorus of "Mad Moon" and starts an awful ballad about two doomed lovers who get poached out on a rock in the sun, because the tide refuses to come ashore and save them.

Yeah, they *love* that one. Morbid fucking aliens.

The crowd gets ever more dense. A few officers go through the motions of trying to curb their wayward troops, while clearly enjoying the show. The stick-in-the-muds have been dragged to the middle of the mosh, entrapped, their protests drowned out. The crowd is singing along, so loudly that Ruthie's mask vibrates against her cheekbones.

A thousand squid, she thinks. Why sabotage Fry Beach when they could just drop a dust bomb right here…

Her skin crawls. She misses a note. Matt, lost in song, doesn't notice.

We have time, Ruthie thinks. Sam's only ten feet away…if a bomb's going off, he'll get clear.

We have to get them away, she texts. *THIS is the trap.*

Matt doesn't answer; his eyes must be shut.

Dropping notes left and right, Ruthie calls up a menu of folk songs coded into the synthesizer. There used to be some old 'Follow the Leader' things, pieces they rarely played in clubs but…here. Matt knows this one.

First, they'll need to get these soldiers up. Watching Sam fearfully, she waits for the end of their current number, then wrenches her minicello through the opening of a jig called "Jump and Fly."

Matt jerks in surprise, then he starts in on the intro as smoothly as if they'd planned it.

We're the trap? He finally responds. *U think?*

Yes. Lead them to the beach.

A creeping chill on her neck makes Ruthie glance back.

It's too late. The fog generators in the graveyard are all running, pouring out an opaque, rolling cloud. Behind them, the ground is crawling with shadows.

So much for finesse. Ruthie stops playing. The crowd, which was beginning to dance, devolves into confusion.

"Run!" Ruthie screams, even as she hears the *phut* of the first grenade launcher.

Hundreds of the fry react, surging away from each other at shocking speed. Unarmed, out of armor, they can only flee as the first grenades pop overhead, coffee-colored Dust spreading in the air like bursts of fireworks before smearing into a deadly, downward-drifting haze. Squid who are fully enveloped by the brown wind vanish in a puff. Others lose body parts: caps, heads, tentacles.

The shrieking starts.

Grabbing Matt's hand, Ruthie runs crossways between the approaching Fiends and the roiling, panicked offworlders. She drags her brother toward the cliff. A mumble, an undertone, follows: she is praying. In Kabuva.

Fry surge onto the beach path, fleeing for the ocean and safety. Others charge unarmed into a row of flamethrowers at the front of the Fiend line—with predictable results. One cluster hurls fry over the wall of fire, up and into the oncoming wave of human guerillas. It is an acrobatic trick Ruthie saw performed in the same clubs where she sang as a child. The flying squid vanish into the graveyard, disappearing into the cloud of smoke and artificial fog. Human screams spread where they land.

One freaked-out squid slides toward them, whistling, and Ruth's idiot brother tries to jump in front of her. She yanks him to ground, shouting the word for 'Ally' in Kabuva. A line of old-fashioned bullets chops through the alien before she finds out if it heard her.

"Stop!" Matt yells. But Ruthie scrambles up, mulishly using her greater strength to force him to the high ground. If they can get around the Fiends, they might escape before the Sponge orders a strike on the whole cemetery.

"Ruthie!"

"All we can do now is get away!" The words run in her head: getaway, get away, git way. But Mattie breaks free, leaving her with a handful of seaweed rags as he pounces on half of a dead Fiend holding a grenade launcher.

Phut! He fires at the edge of the cliff. A Dust grenade digs out the edge, excavating a crater ten feet deep. He promptly fires two more, creating a scalloped incline within the rock, a crude slide, a new escape route to the beach.

Squid start pouring through the gap, making for the ocean. They don't wait for the Dust to settle, and so they bleed and lose tentacles as they flee.

Ruthie makes a grab for the launcher. "Someone's gonna mistake you for a target."

"Let 'em." His face is wet. Stupid, over-sensitive...

He still needs her.

"You've done your good deed; now come on!" A grenade detonates nearby, and they flee uphill. The high point of the cliff is in sight; they're clearing the Fiend line, almost at the rear. No chance to get to the van from here; the van's gone. She must write it off as she has written off her parents, an education, an ordinary life.

All Ruthie has left is her brother.

A Fiend comes up the path, methodically firing into the crowd of squid escaping down Matt's improvised slide.

It's Holly. Ruthie feels it before she truly recognizes the other woman. Holly has decided that she needs a Friend or two.

Their eyes meet, and Holly's lips move. Shouting Matt's name, but he can't hear it over the battle noise.

Stay quiet. He'll never know who was behind them. Damned cougar—Matt doesn't need her. Run for it, force the squid to send them to Kabuva. He'll never know.

It is an easy choice, the kind she's been making on his behalf for years.

Instead, Ruthie tugs his arm. Points.

Matt turns. Looks. Sees that his supposed girlfriend is in on the squid slaughter.

Ducking a flying piece of monolith, Matt sprints back. He and Holly converge, crouch with their heads close. She reaches for Matt's hand...

Ruthie clutches her chest. Will he take it? If Mattie leaves her, who is she supposed to be?

The ground turns to jelly underfoot.

There's an awful, impossible light, a glow on the horizon. A torch thrusts up from the ocean, burning white-hot to the clouds. It bulges, grows fat, frying the anti-aircraft platform to ash. And now the sound is coming too, a clatter and shriek, something tearing that was never meant to be torn, louder, louder. The sound bites like a saw into her skull.

On the battlefield, everyone—human and offworlder—freezes, staring in the direction of Oʻahu.

It's the Sponge, it has to be the Sponge, and how could the Fiends touch that? How could there ever be the slightest possibility of them being powerful enough to destroy an undersea squid—

Suddenly everything on the battlefield is after Ruthie.

No, she realizes, they aren't running toward me. They're fleeing to the high ground, like mice. That's right, there'll be a shockwave, won't there?

"Matthew," Ruthie shouts, before a scorching wind lifts her off her feet, ripping her mask off, flipping her ass over tea kettle through the air.

When she awakes, she is soaked, sore, and draped on a delicate arch of rock formed by the cliff's edge and the lip of a dust crater. She raises herself to hands and knees, pulling her seaweed mini-skirt over her ass and staring around.

Water has battered the graveyard, making pools of its many Dust craters. Seawater, she guesses, thrown by the explosion. The rush of water doused the Fiends' flamethrowers, giving the squid an edge in the battle—the offworlders seem to be winning now. Drowned and strangled humans litter the ground, along with Dust-proof tubes containing human DNA samples—coffin tubes—that jut up from the murk of the one-time golf course.

There is no sign of Matt or Holly.

Everything's quiet, Ruthie realizes. The battle is continuing in total silence.

"Actually, spawn, I think you've gone deaf." The words are Kabuva. Dad and Isshy are with her, flickering in the fog.

Isshy is right. She cannot hear a thing.

Her eyes find a column of black smoke rising in the east, where the Sponge was. "Isshy's dead then," she says, and it is a surprise how much that hurts.

"Is he?" Dad says.

"I must be," the squid says. "Child's right. Nothing could survive that."

"You're hallucinations," she says slowly. "The baby…I would know if Matt was dead, wouldn't I?"

"Oh yes," Dad says. "You would know. He's alive—oh, wait, there's his body."

She screams, curling up in the crater.

"That's not him, Ruth," Isshy says, in that annoyingly gentle voice. "Jacob, you're upsetting her."

Is it or isn't it? She crawls to the gristle lying face down in the bloody sand.

"What did I tell you, child?"

It is a stranger. He is lying atop an old machine gun. An extra cartridge of bullets is taped to his fist.

Ruthie crouches by the body, takes a breath, makes a snowball. She can see it, just as she sees Dad and Isshy loitering beside her. She tosses it into the pond, but there is no splash, no ripples.

Write it off, she thinks. The van, Isshy, escape, even my sanity. But not Matt. Never Mattie.

All around her, the skirmish continues, a disorderly cut and thrust. Down the cliff path, her intended route of escape, is a squad of Demo soldiers and armed squid, trotting up to join the fight. A trio of Fiends has set up an ambush for them. They've hidden behind a toppled cenotaph and are making ready to Dust the upcoming squad.

"What now?" Dad asks. "Dive into the fray looking for your brother?"

"What chance would she have?" Isshy replies. "One side or the other is bound to shoot her."

"He's right. Hon, you can't start looking until the dust settles. Pardon the pun."

"And you can't help your brother if you're dead."

"Shut up!" She covers her deaf ears.

"She should go to ground. Wait this out."

"Sure," Dad says, "and end up a prisoner of whichever side wins?"

"You've been drafted after all, Ruth," Isshy tells her. "Pick a side and go with it."

"The Fiends killed us," Dad reminds her. "They made you do the concert. Sam fed you fireseeds. Isn't that him over there, directing that ambush team?"

"The Fiends are winning the war," Isshy disagrees. "Her best chance for finding Matt might be to get Friendly. Holly thought so."

Is it that simple? Take up the gun, join the ambush? Start killing the Demos, or start killing squid?

"Hon," Dad says.

"Shut up," she says. "You're a hallucination." She looks from one parent to the other, Dad with his guitar and reproachful eyes, Isshy pale-blue with understanding. Who would Matt pick?

Impossible to say. His mom's a squid, his lover's a Fiend.

But she does know who she'd most like to kill.

"Ruth," argues Isshy. "The Fiends are winning. Your best chance to get offworld died with me. Forget the Democratic cause and join that ambush. Pick the winning team."

"They're not winning this battle, are they?" Dad counters. "She doesn't get off the cliff, today, she doesn't get to look for anyone."

Daddy's right. And the squid might be grateful if she pitches in; the Fiends just regard it as their due.

She pries the clip of ammo off the corpse and slithers up to the lip of the dust crater. She takes careful aim at the center of Sam's back, the sweet spot, as he prepares to slaughter the contingent of Demos and squid coming up from below.

"Ashes to ashes," she murmurs—and it is so weird not to be able to hear her voice, or even the pop-pop-pop of the gun as she signs up for the Demo cause, pulling the trigger and sending her alleged brethren to oblivion.

△∨△∨△

A GUIDE TO THE FRUITS OF HAWAI'I

[alaya Dawn Johnson]

Key's favorite time of day is sunset, her least is sunrise. It should be the opposite, but every time she watches that bright red disk sinking into the water beneath Mauna Kea her heart bends like a wishbone, and she thinks, *He's awake now.*

Key is thirty-four. She is old for a human woman without any children. She has kept herself alive by being useful in other ways. For the past four years, Key has been the overseer of the Mauna Kea Grade Orange blood facility.

Is it a concentration camp if the inmates are well fed? If their beds are comfortable? If they are given an hour and a half of rigorous boxercise and yoga each morning in the recreational field?

It doesn't have to be Honouliuli to be wrong.

When she's called in to deal with Jeb's body—bloody, not drained, in a feeding room—yoga doesn't make him any less dead.

Key helps vampires run a concentration camp for humans.

Key is a different kind of monster.

Key's favorite food is umeboshi. Salty and tart and bright red, with that pit in the center to beware. She loves it in rice balls, the kind her Japanese grandmother made when she was little. She loves it by itself, the way she ate it at fifteen, after Obachan died. She hasn't had umeboshi in eighteen years, but sometimes she thinks that when she dies she'll taste one again.

This morning she eats the same thing she eats every meal: a nutritious brick patty, precisely five inches square and two inches deep, colored puce. Her raw scrubbed hands still have a pink tinge of Jeb's blood in the cuticles. She stares at them while she sips the accompanying beverage, which is orange. She can't remember if it ever resembled the fruit.

She eats this because that is what every human eats in the Mauna Kea facility. Because the patty is easy to manufacture and soft enough to eat with plastic spoons. Key hasn't seen a fork in years, a knife in more than a decade. The vampires maintain tight control over all items with the potential to draw blood. Yet humans are tool-making creatures, and their desires, even nihilistic ones, have a creative power that no vampire has the imagination or agility to anticipate. How else to explain the shiv, handcrafted over secret months from the wood cover and glue-matted pages of *A Guide to the Fruits of Hawai'i*, the book that Jeb used to read in the hours after his feeding sessions, sometimes aloud, to whatever humans would listen? He took the only thing that gave him pleasure in the world, destroyed it—or recreated it—and slit his veins with it. Mr. Charles questioned her particularly; he knew that she and Jeb used to talk sometimes. Had she *known* that the *boy* was like this? He gestured with pallid hands at the splatter of arterial pulses from jaggedly slit wrists: oxidized brown, inedible, mocking.

No, she said, of course not, Mr. Charles. I report any suspected cases of self-waste immediately.

She reports any suspected cases. And so, for the weeks she has watched Jeb hardly eating across the mess hall, noticed how he staggered from the feeding rooms, recognized the frigid rebuff in his responses to her questions, she has very carefully refused to suspect.

Today, just before dawn, she choked on the fruits of her indifference. He slit his wrists and femoral arteries. He smeared the blood over his face and buttocks and genitals, and he waited to die before the vampire technician could arrive to drain him.

Not many humans self-waste. Most think about it, but Key never has, not since the invasion of the Big Island. Unlike other humans, she has someone she's waiting for. The one she loves, the one she prays will reward her patience. During her years as overseer, Key has successfully stopped three acts of self-waste. She has failed twice. Jeb is different; Mr. Charles sensed it somehow, but vampires can only read human minds through human blood. Mr. Charles hasn't drunk from Key in years. And what could he learn, even if he did? He can't drink thoughts she has spent most of her life refusing to have.

Mr. Charles calls her to the main office the next night, between feeding shifts. She is terrified, like she always is, of what they might do. She is thinking of Jeb and wondering how Mr. Charles has taken the loss of an investment. She is wondering how fast she will die in the work camp on Lānaʻi.

But Mr. Charles has an offer, not a death sentence.

"You know… of the facility on Oʻahu? Grade Gold?"

"Yes," Key says. Just that, because she learned early not to betray herself to them unnecessarily, and the man at Grade Gold has always been her greatest betrayer.

No, not a man, Key tells herself for the hundredth, the thousandth time. *He is one of them.*

Mr. Charles sits in a hanging chair shaped like an egg with plush red velvet cushions. He wears a black suit with steel gray pinstripes, sharply tailored. The cuffs are high and his feet are bare, white as talcum powder and long and bony like spiny fish. His veins are prominent and round and milky blue. Mr. Charles is vain about his feet.

He does not sit up to speak to Key. She can hardly see his face behind the shadow cast by the overhanging top of the egg. All vampires speak deliberately, but Mr. Charles drags out his tones until you feel you might tip over from waiting on the next syllable. It goes up and down like a calliope—

"...what do you *say* to heading down there and *sorting* the matter... out?"

"I'm sorry, Mr. Charles," she says carefully, because she has lost the thread of his monologue. "What matter?"

He explains: a Grade Gold human girl has killed herself. It is a disaster that outshadows the loss of Jeb.

"You would not believe the expense taken to keep those humans Grade Gold standard."

"What would I do?"

"Take it in hand, *of* course. It seems our small...Grade Orange operation has gotten some notice. Tetsuo asked for you...particularly."

"Tetsuo?" She hasn't said the name out loud in years. Her voice catches on the second syllable.

"*Mr.* Tetsuo," Mr. Charles says, and waves a hand at her. He holds a sheet of paper, the same shade as his skin. "He wrote you a *letter.*"

Key can't move, doesn't reach out to take it, and so it flutters to the black marble floor a few feet away from Mr. Charles's egg.

He leans forward. "I think... I remember something... you and Tetsuo..."

"He recommended my promotion here," Key says, after a moment. It seems the safest phrasing. Mr. Charles would have remembered this eventually; vampires are slow, but inexorable.

The diffused light from the paper lanterns catches the bottom half of his face, highlighting the deep cleft in his chin. It twitches in faint surprise. "You *were* his pet?"

Key winces. She remembers the years she spent at his side during and after the wars, catching scraps in his wake, despised by every human who saw her there. She waited for him to see how much she had sacrificed and give her the only reward that could matter after what she'd done. Instead he had her shunt removed and sent her to Grade Orange. She has not seen or heard from him in four years. His pet, yes, that's as good a name as any—but he never drank from her. Not once.

Mr. Charles's lips, just a shade of white darker than his skin, open like a hole in a cloud. "And he wants you back. How do you *feel?*"

Terrified. Awestruck. Confused. "Grateful," she says.

The hole smiles. "Grateful! How interesting. Come here, girl. I believe I shall *have a taste.*"

She grabs the letter with shaking fingers and folds it inside a pocket of her red uniform. She stands in front of Mr. Charles.

"Well?" he says.

She hasn't had a shunt in years, though she can still feel its ridged scar in the crook of her arm. Without it, feeding from her is messy, violent. Traditional, Mr. Charles might say. Her fingers hurt as she unzips the collar. Her muscles feel sore, the bones in her spine arthritic and old as she bows her head, leans closer to Mr. Charles. She waits for him to bare his fangs, to pierce her vein, to suck her blood.

He takes more than he should. He drinks until her fingers and toes twinge, until her neck throbs, until the red velvet of his seat fades to gray. When he finishes, he leaves her blood on his mouth.

"I forgive... you for the boy," he says.

Jeb cut his own arteries, left his good blood all over the floor. Mr. Charles abhors waste above all else.

Mr. Charles will explain the situation. I wish you to come. If you do well, I have been authorized to offer you the highest reward.

The following night, Key takes a boat to Oʻahu. Vampires don't like water, but they will cross it anyway—the sea has become a status symbol among them, an indication of strength. Hawaiʻi is still a resort destination, though most of its residents only go out at night. Grade Gold is the most expensive, most luxurious resort of them all.

Tetsuo travels between the islands often. Key saw him do it a dozen times during the war. She remembers one night, his face lit by the moon and the yellow lamps on the deck—the wide cheekbones, thick eyebrows, sharp widow's peak, all frozen in the perfection of a nineteen-year-old boy. Pale beneath the olive tones of his skin, he bares his fangs when the waves lurch beneath him.

"What does it feel like?" she asks him.

"Like frozen worms in my veins," he says, after a full, long minute of silence. Then he checks the guns and tells her to wait below, the humans are coming. She can't see anything, but Tetsuo can smell them like chum in the water. The Japanese have held out the longest, and the vampires of Hawaiʻi lead the assault against them.

Two nights later, in his quarters in the bunker at the base of Mauna Kea, Tetsuo brings back a sheet of paper, written in Japanese. The only characters she recognizes are "shi" and "ta"— "death" and "field." It looks like some kind of list.

"What is this?" she asks.

"Recent admissions to the Lānaʻi human residential facility."

She looks up at him, devoted with terror. "My mother?" Her father died in the first offensive on the Big Island, a hero of the resistance. He never knew how his daughter had chosen to survive.

"Here," Tetsuo says, and runs a cold finger down the list without death. "Jen Isokawa."

"Alive?" She has been looking for her mother since the wars began. Tetsuo knows this, but she didn't know he was searching, too. She feels swollen with this indication of his regard.

"She's listed as a caretaker. They're treated well. You could…" He sits beside her on the bed that only she uses. His pause lapses into a stop. He strokes her hair absentmindedly; if she had a tail, it would beat his legs. She is seventeen and she is sure he will reward her soon.

"Tetsuo," she says, "you could drink from me, if you want. I've had a shunt for nearly a year. The others use it. I'd rather feed you."

Sometimes she has to repeat herself three times before he seems to hear her. This, she has said at least ten. But she is safe here in his bunker, on the bed he brought in for her, with his lukewarm body pressed against her warm one. Vampires do not have sex with humans; they feed. But if he doesn't want her that way, what else can she offer him?

"I've had you tested. You're fertile. If you bear three children you won't need a shunt, and the residential facilities will care for you for the rest of your mortality. You can live with your mother. I will make sure you're safe."

She presses her face against his shoulder. "Don't make me leave."

"You wanted to see your mother."

Her mother had spent the weeks before the invasion in church, praying for God to intercede against the abominations. Better that she die than see Key like this.

"Only to know what happened to her," Key whispers. "Won't you feed from me, Tetsuo? I want to feel closer to you. I want you to know how much I love you."

A long pause. Then, "I don't need to taste you to know how you feel."

Tetsuo meets her on shore.

Just like that, she is seventeen again.

"You look older," he says. Slowly, but with less affectation than Mr. Charles.

This is true; so inevitable she doesn't understand why he even bothers to say so. Is he surprised? Finally, she nods. The buoyed dock rocks beneath them—he makes no attempt to move, though the two vampires with him grip the denuded skin of their own elbows with pale fingers. They flare and retract their fangs.

"You are drained," he says. He does not mean this metaphorically.

She nods again, realizes further explanation is called for. "Mr. Charles," she says, her voice a painful rasp. This embarrasses her, though Tetsuo would never notice.

He nods, sharp and curt. She thinks he is angry, though perhaps no one else could read him as clearly. She knows that face, frozen in the countenance of a boy dead before the Second World War. A boy dead fifty years before she was born.

He is old enough to remember Pearl Harbor, the detention camps, the years when Maui's forests still had native birds. But she has never dared ask him about his human life.

"And what did Charles explain?"

"He said someone killed herself at Grade Gold."

Tetsuo flares his fangs. She flinches, which surprises her. She used to flush at the sight of his fangs, her blood pounding red just beneath the soft surface of her skin.

"I've been given dispensation," he says, and rests one finger against the hollow at the base of her throat.

She's learned a great deal about the rigid traditions that restrict vampire life since she first met Tetsuo. She understands why her teenage fantasies of morally liberated vampirism were improbable, if not impossible. For each human they bring over, vampires need a special dispensation that they only receive once or twice every decade. *The highest reward.* If Tetsuo has gotten a dispensation, then her first thought when she read his letter was correct. He didn't mean retirement. He didn't mean a peaceful life in some remote farm on the islands. He meant death. Un-death.

After all these years, Tetsuo means to turn her into a vampire.

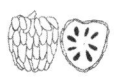

The trouble at Grade Gold started with a dead girl. Penelope cut her own throat five days ago (with a real knife, the kind they allow Grade Gold humans for cutting food). Her ghost haunts the eyes of those she left behind. One human resident in particular, with hair dyed the color of tea and blue lipstick to match the bruises under her red eyes, takes one look at Key and starts to scream.

Key glances at Tetsuo, but he has forgotten her. He stares at the girl as if he could burn her to ashes on the plush green carpet. The five others in the room look away, but Key can't tell if it's in embarrassment or fear. The luxury surrounding them chokes her. There's a bowl of fruit on a coffee table. Real fruit—fuzzy brown kiwis, mottled red-green mangos, dozens of tangerines. She takes an involuntary step forward and the girl's scream gets louder before cutting off with an abrupt squawk. Her labored breaths are the only sound in the room.

"This is a joke," the girl says. There's spittle on her blue lips. "What hole did you dig her out of?"

"Go to your room, Rachel," Tetsuo says.

Rachel flicks back her hair and rubs angrily under one eye. "What are you now, Daddy Vampire? You think you can just, what? Replace her? With this broke down fogie look-alike?"

"She is not—"

"Yeah? What is she?"

They are both silent, doubt and grief and fury scuttling between them like beetles in search of a meal. Tetsuo and the girl stare at each other with such deep familiarity that Key feels forgotten, alone—almost ashamed of the dreams that have kept her alive for a decade. They have never felt so hopeless, or so false.

"Her name is Key," Tetsuo says, in something like defeat. He turns away, though he makes no move to leave. "She will be your new caretaker."

"Key?" the girl says. "What kind of a name is that?"

Key doesn't answer for a long time, thinking of all the ways she could respond. Of Obachan Akiko and the affectionate nickname of lazy summers spent hiking in the mountains or pounding mochi in the kitchen. Of her half-Japanese mother and Hawaiian father, of the ways history and identity and circumstance can shape a girl into half a woman, until someone—*not a man*—comes with a hundred thousand others like him and destroys anything that might have once had meaning. So she finds meaning in him. Who else was there?

And this girl, whose sneer reveals her bucked front teeth, has as much chance of understanding that world as Key does of understanding this one. Fresh fruit on the table. No uniforms. And a perfect, glittering shunt of plastic and metal nestled in the crook of her left arm.

"Mine," Key answers the girl.

Rachel spits; Tetsuo turns his head, just a little, as though he can only bear to see Key from the corner of his eye.

"You're nothing like her," she says.

"Like who?"

But the girl storms from the room, leaving her chief vampire without a dismissal. Key now understands this will not be punished. It's another one—a boy, with the same florid beauty as the girl but far less belligerence, who answers her.

"You look like Penelope," he says, tugging on a long lock of his asymmetrically cut black hair. "Just older."

When Tetsuo leaves the room, it's Key who cannot follow.

Key remembers sixteen. Her obachan is dead and her mother has moved to an apartment in Hilo and it's just Key and her father in that old, quiet house at the end of the road. The vampires have annexed San Diego and Okinawa is besieged, but life doesn't feel very different in the mountains of the Big Island.

It is raining in the woods behind her house. Her father has told her to study, but all she's done since her mother left is read Mishima's *Sea of Fertility* novels. She sits on the porch, wondering if it's better to kill herself or wait for them to come, and just as she thinks she ought to have the courage to die, something rattles in the shed. A rat, she thinks.

But it's not rat she sees when she pulls open the door on its rusty hinges. It's a man, crouched between a stack of old appliance boxes and the rusted fender of the Buick her father always meant to fix one day. His hair is wet and slicked back, his white shirt is damp and ripped from shoulder to navel. The skin beneath it is pale as a corpse; bloodless, though the edges of a deep wound are still visible.

"They've already come?" Her voice breaks on a whisper. She wanted to finish *The Decay of the Angel*. She wanted to see her mother once more.

"Shut the door," he says, crouching in shadow, away from the bar of light streaming through the narrow opening.

"Don't kill me."

"We are equally at each other's mercy."

She likes the way he speaks. No one told her they could sound so proper. So human. Is there a monster in her shed, or is he something else?

"Why shouldn't I open it all the way?"

He is brave, whatever else. He takes his long hands from in front of his face and stands, a flower blooming after rain. He is beautiful, though she will not mark that until later. Now, she only notices the steady, patient way he regards her. *I could move faster than you,* his eyes say. *I could kill you first.*

She thinks of Mishima and says, "I'm not afraid of death."

Only when the words leave her mouth does she realize how deeply she has lied. Does he know? Her hands would shake if it weren't for their grip on the handle.

"I promise," he says. "I will save you, when the rest of us come."

What is it worth, a monster's promise?

She steps inside and shuts out the light.

There are nineteen residents of Grade Gold; the twentieth is buried beneath the kukui tree in the communal garden. The thought of rotting in earth revolts Key. She prefers the bright, fierce heat of a crematorium fire, like the one that consumed Jeb the night before she left Mauna Kea. The ashes fly in the wind, into the ocean and up in the trees, where they lodge in bird nests and caterpillar silk and mud puddles after a storm. The return of flesh to the earth should be fast and final, not the slow mortification of worms and bacteria and carbon gases.

Tetsuo instructs her to keep close watch on unit three. "Rachel isn't very… steady right now," he says, as though unaware of the understatement.

The remaining nineteen residents are divided into four units, five kids in each, living together in sprawling ranch houses connected by walkways and gardens. There are walls, of course, but you have to climb a tree to see them. The kids at Grade Gold have more freedom than any human she's ever encountered since the war, but they're as bound to this paradise as she was to her mountain.

The vampires who come here stay in a high glass tower right by the beach. During the day, the black-tinted windows gleam like lasers. At night, the vampires come down to feed. There is a fifth house in the residential village, one reserved for clients and their meals. Testsuo orchestrates these encounters, planning each interaction in fine detail: this human with that performance for this distinguished client. Key has grown used to thinking of her fellow humans as food, but now she is forced to reconcile that indelible fact with another, stranger veneer. The vampires who pay so dearly for Grade Gold humans don't merely want to feed from a shunt. They want to be entertained, talked to, cajoled. The boy who explained about Key's uncanny resemblance juggles torches. Twin girls from unit three play guitar and sing songs by the Carpenters. Even Rachel, dressed in a gaudy purple mermaid dress with matching streaks in her hair, keeps up a one-way, laughing conversation with a vampire who seems too astonished—or too slow—to reply.

Key has never seen anything like this before. She thought that most vampires regarded humans as walking sacks of food. What pleasure could be derived from speaking with your meal first? From seeing it sing or dance? When she first went with Tetsuo, the other vampires talked about human emotions as if they were flavors of ice cream. But at Grade Orange she grew accustomed to more basic parameters: were the humans fed, were they fertile, did they sleep? Here, she must approve outfits; she must manage dietary preferences and erratic tempers and a dozen other details all crucial to keeping the kids Grade Gold standard. Their former caretaker has been shipped to the work camps, which leaves Key in sole charge of the operation. At least until Tetsuo decides how he will use his dispensation.

Key's thoughts skitter away from the possibility.

"I didn't know vampires liked music," she says, late in the evening, when some of the kids sprawl, exhausted, across couches and cushions. A girl no older than fifteen opens her eyes but hardly moves when a vampire in a gold suit lifts her arm for a nip. Key and Tetsuo are seated together at the far end of the main room, in the bay windows that overlook a cliff and the ocean.

"It's as interesting to us as any other human pastime."

"Does music have a taste?"

His wide mouth stretches at the edges; she recognizes it as a smile. "Music has some utility, given the right circumstances."

She doesn't quite understand him. The air is redolent with the sweat of human teenagers and the muggy, salty air that blows through the open doors and windows. Her eye catches on a half-eaten strawberry dropped carelessly on the carpet a few feet away. It was harvested too soon, a white, tasteless core surrounded by hard, red flesh.

She thinks there is nothing of "right" in these circumstances, and their utility is, at its bottom, merely that of parasite and host.

"The music enhances the—our—flavor?"

Tetsuo stares at her for a long time, long enough for him to take at least three of his shallow, erratically spaced breaths. To look at him is to taste copper and sea on her tongue; to wait for him is to hear the wind slide down a mountainside an hour before dawn.

It has been four years since she last saw him. She thought he had forgotten her, and now he speaks to her as if all those years haven't passed, as though the vampires hadn't long since won the war and turned the world to their slow, long-burning purpose.

"Emotions change your flavor," he says. "And food. And sex. And pleasure."

And love? she wonders, but Tetsuo has never drunk from her.

"Then why not treat all of us like you do the ones here? Why have con—Mauna Kea?"

She expects him to catch her slip, but his attention is focused on something beyond her right shoulder. She turns to look, and sees nothing but the hall and a closed feeding room door.

"Three years," he says, quietly. He doesn't look at her. She doesn't understand what he means, so she waits. "It takes three years for the complexity to fade. For the vitality of young blood to turn muddy and clogged with silt. Even among the new crops, only a few individuals are Gold standard. For three years, they produce the finest blood ever tasted, filled with regrets and ecstasy and dreams. And then…"

"Grade Orange?" Key asks, her voice dry and rasping. Had Tetsuo always talked of humans like this? With such little regard for their selfhood? Had she been too young to understand, or have the years of harvesting humans hardened him?

"If we have not burned too much out. Living at high elevation helps prolong your utility, but sometimes all that's left is Lāna'i and the work camps."

She remembers her terror before her final interview with Mr. Charles, her conviction that Jeb's death would prompt him to discard his uselessly old overseer to the work camps.

A boy from one of the other houses staggers to the one she recognizes from unit two and sprawls in his lap. Unit-two boy startles awake, smiles, and bends over to kiss the first. A pair of female vampires kneel in front of them and press their fangs with thick pink tongues.

"Touch him," one says, pointing to the boy from unit two. "Make him cry."

The boy from unit two doesn't even pause for breath; he reaches for the other boy's cock and squeezes. And as they both groan with something that makes Key feel like a voyeur, made helpless by her own desire, the pair of vampires pull the boys apart and dive for their respective shunts. The room goes quiet but for soft gurgles, like two minnows in a tide pool. Then a pair of clicks as the boys' shunts turn gray, forcing the vampires to stop feeding.

"Lovely, divine," the vampires say a few minutes later, when they pass on their way out. "We always appreciate the sexual displays."

The boys curl against each other, eyes shut. They breathe like old men: hard, through constricted tubes.

"Does that happen often?" she asks.

"This Grade Gold is known for its sexual flavors. My humans pick partners they enjoy."

Vampires might not have sex, but they crave its flavor. Will she, when she crosses to their side? Will she look at those two boys and command them to fuck each other just so she can taste?

"Do you ever care?" she says, her voice barely a whisper. "About what you've done to us?"

He looks away from her. Before she can blink he has crossed to the one closed feeding room door and wrenched it open. A thump of something thrown against a wall. A snarl, as human as a snake's hiss.

"Leave, Gregory!" Tetsuo says. A vampire Key recognizes from earlier in the night stumbles into the main room. He rubs his jaw, though the torn and mangled skin there has already begun to knit together.

"She is mine to have. I paid—"

"Not enough to kill her."

"I'll complain to the council," the vampire says. "You've been losing support. And everyone knows how *patiently* Charles has waited in his aerie."

She should be scared, but his words make her think of Jeb, of failures and consequences, and of the one human she has not seen for hours. She stands and sprints past both vampires to where Rachel lies insensate on a bed.

Her shunt has turned the opaque gray meant to prevent vampires from feeding humans to death. But the client has bitten her neck instead.

"Tell them whatever you wish, and I will tell them you circumvented the shunt of a fully-tapped human. We have our rules for a reason. You are no longer welcome here."

Rachel's pulse is soft, but steady. She stirs and moans beneath Key's hands. The relief is crushing; she wants to cradle the girl in her arms until she wakes. She wants to protect her so her blood will never have to smear the walls of a feeding room, so that Key will be able to say that at least she saved one.

Rachel's eyes flutter open, land with a butterfly's gentleness on Key's face.

"Pen," she says, "I told you. It makes them... they *eat* me."

Key doesn't understand, but she doesn't mind. She presses her hand to Rachel's warm forehead and sings lullabies her grandmother liked until Rachel falls back to sleep.

"How is she?" It is Tetsuo, come into the room after the client has finally left.

"Drained," Key says, as dispassionately as he. "She'll be fine in a few days."

"Key."

"Yes?"

She won't look at him.

"I do, you know."

She knows. "Then why support it?"

"You'll understand when your time comes."

She looks back down at Rachel, and all she can see are bruises blooming purple on her upper arms, blood dried brown on her neck. She looks like a human being: infinitely precious, fragile. Like prey.

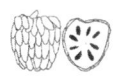

Five days later, Key sits in the garden in the shade of the kukui tree. She has reports to file on the last week's feedings, but the papers sit untouched beside her. The boy from unit two and his boyfriend are tending the tomatoes and Key slowly peels the skin from her fourth kiwi. The first time she bit into one she cried, but the boys pretended not to notice. She is getting better with practice. Her hands still tremble and her misted eyes refract rainbows in the hard, noon sunlight. She is learning to be human again.

Rachel sleeps on the ground beside her, curled on the packed dirt of Penelope's grave with her back against the tree trunk and her arms wrapped tightly around her belly. She's spent most of the last five days sleeping, and Key thinks she has mostly recovered. She's been eating voraciously, foods in wild combinations at all times of day and night. Key is glad. Without the distracting, angry makeup, Rachel's face looks vulnerable and haunted. Jeb had that look in the months before his death. He would sit quietly in the mess hall and stare at the food brick as though he had forgotten how to eat. Jeb had transferred to Mauna Kea within a week of Key becoming overseer. He liked watching the lights of the airplanes at night and he kept two books with him: *The Blind Watchmaker* and *A Guide to the Fruits of Hawai'i*. She talked to him about the latter—had he ever tasted breadfruit or kiwi or cherimoya? None, he said, in a voice so small and soft it sounded inversely proportional to his size. Only a peach, a canned peach, when he was four or five years old. Vampires don't waste fruit on Grade Orange humans.

The covers of both books were worn, the spines cracked, the pages yellowed and brittle at the edges. Why keep a book about fruit you had never tasted and never would eat? Why read at all, when they frowned upon literacy in humans and often banned books outright? She never asked him. Mr. Charles had seen their conversation, though she doubted he had heard it, and re*quest*ed that she refrain from speaking unnecessarily to the *har*vest.

So when Jeb stared at her across the table with eyes like a snuffed candle, she turned away, she forced her patty into her mouth, she chewed, she reached for her orange drink.

His favorite book became his means of self-destruction. She let him do it. She doesn't know if she feels guilty for not having stopped him, or for being in the position to stop him in the first place. Not two weeks later she rests beneath a kukui tree, the flesh of a fruit she had never expected to taste again turning to green pulp between her teeth. She reaches for another one because she knows how little she deserves this.

But the skin of the fruit at the bottom of the bowl is too soft and fleshy for a kiwi. She pulls it into the light and drops it.

"Are you ok?" It's the boy from unit two—Kaipo. He kneels down and picks up the cherimoya.

"What?" she says, and struggles to control her breathing. She has to appear normal, in control. She's supposed to be their caretaker. But the boy just seems concerned, not judgmental. Rachel rolls onto her back and opens her eyes.

"You screamed," Rachel says, sleep-fogged and accusatory. "You woke me up."

"Who put this in the bowl?" Kaipo asks. "These things are poisonous! They grow on that tree down the hill, but you can't eat them."

Key takes the haunted fruit from him, holding it carefully so as to not bruise it further. "Who told you that?" she asks.

Rachel leans forward, so her chin rests on the edge of Key's lounge chair and the tips of her purple-streaked hair touch Key's thigh. "Tetsuo," she says. "What, did he lie?"

Key shakes her head slowly. "He probably only half-remembered. It's a cherimoya. The flesh is delicious, but the seeds are poisonous."

Rachel's eyes follow her hands. "Like, killing you poisonous?" she asks.

Key thinks back to her father's lessons. "Maybe if you eat them all or grind them up. The tree bark can paralyze your heart and lungs."

Kaipo whistles, and they all watch intently when she wedges her finger under the skin and splits it in half. The white, fleshy pulp looks stark, even a little disquieting against the scaly green exterior. She plucks out the hard, brown seeds and tosses them to the ground. Only then does she pull out a chunk of flesh and put it in her mouth.

Like strawberries and banana pudding and pineapple. Like the summer after Obachan died, when a box of them came to the house as a condolence gift.

"You look like you're fellating it," Rachel says. Key opens her eyes and swallows abruptly.

Kaipo pushes his tongue against his lips. "Can I try it, Key?" he asks, very politely. Did the vampires teach him that politeness? Did vampires teach Rachel a word like fellate, perhaps while instructing her to do it with a hopefully willing human partner?

"Do you guys know how to use condoms?" She has decided to ask Tetsuo to supply them. This last week has made it clear that "sexual flavors" are all too frequently on the menu at Grade Gold.

Kaipo looks at Rachel; Rachel shakes her head. "What's a condom?" he asks.

It's so easy to forget how little of the world they know. "You use it during sex, to stop you from catching diseases," she says, carefully. "Or getting pregnant."

Rachel laughs and stuffs the rest of the flesh into her wide mouth. Even a cherimoya can't fill her hollows. "Great, even more vampire sex," she says, her hatred clearer than her garbled words. "They never made Pen do it."

"They didn't?" Key asks.

Juice dribbles down her chin. "You know, Tetsuo's dispensation? Before she killed herself, she was his pick. Everyone knew it. That's why they left her alone."

Key feels light-headed. "But if she was his choice...why would she kill herself?"

"She didn't want to be a vampire," Kaipo says softly.

"She wanted a *baby*, like bringing a new food sack into the world is a good idea. But they wouldn't let her have sex and they wanted to make her one of them, so—now she's gone. But why he'd bring *you* here, when *any* of us would be a better choice—"

"Rachel, just shut up. Please." Kaipo takes her by the shoulder.

Rachel shrugs him off. "What? Like she can do anything."

"If she becomes one of *them*—"

"I wouldn't hurt you," Key says, too quickly. Rachel masks her pain with cruelty, but it is palpable. Key can't imagine any version of herself that would add to that.

Kaipo and Rachel stare at her. "But," Kaipo says, "that's what vampires do."

"I would eat you," Rachel says, and flops back under the tree. "I would make you cry and your tears would taste sweeter than a cherimoya."

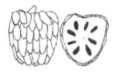

"I will be back in four days," Testsuo tells her, late the next night. "There is one feeding scheduled. I hope you will be ready when I return."

"For the... reward?" she asks, stumbling over an appropriate euphemism. Their words for it are polysyllabic spikes: transmutation, transformation, metamorphosis. All vampires were once human, and immortal doesn't mean invulnerable. Some die each year, and so their ranks must be replenished with the flesh of worthy, willing humans.

He places a hand on her shoulder. It feels as chill and inert as a piece of damp wood. She thinks she must be dreaming.

"I have wanted this for a long time, Key," he says to her—like a stranger, like the person who knows her the best in the world.

"Why now?"

"Our thoughts can be... slow, sometimes. You will see. Orderly, but sometimes too orderly to see patterns clearly. I thought of you, but did not know it until Penelope died."

Penelope, who looked just like Key. Penelope, who would have been his pick. She shivers and steps away from his hand. "Did you love her?"

She can't believe that she is asking this question. She can't believe that he is offering her the dreams she would have murdered for ten, even five years ago.

"I loved that she made me think of you," he says, "when you were young and beautiful."

"It's been eighteen years, Tetsuo."

He looks over her shoulder. "You haven't lost much," he says. "I'm not too late. You'll see."

He is waiting for a response. She forces herself to nod. She wants to close her eyes and cover her mouth, keep all her love for him inside where it can be safe, because if she loses it, there will be nothing left but a girl in the rain who should have opened the door.

He looks like an alien when he smiles. He looks like nothing she could ever know when he walks down the hall, past the open door and the girl who has been watching them this whole time.

Rachel is young and beautiful, Key thinks, and Penelope is dead.

Key's sixth feeding at Grade Gold is contained, quiet and without incident. The gazes of the clients slide over her as she greets them at the door of the feeding house, but she is used to that. To a vampire, a human without a shunt is like a book without pages: a useless absurdity. She has assigned all of unit one and a pair from unit four to the gathering. Seven humans for five vampires is a luxurious ratio—probably more than they paid for, but she's happy to let that be Tetsuo's problem. She shudders to remember how Rachel's blood soaked into the collar of her blouse when she lifted the girl from the bed. She has seen dozens of overdrained humans, including some who died from it, but what happened to Rachel feels worse. She doesn't understand why, but is overwhelmed by tenderness for her.

A half-hour before the clients are supposed to leave, Kaipo sprints through the front door, flushed and panting so hard he has to pause half a minute to catch his breath.

"Rachel," he manages, while humans and vampires alike pause to look.

She stands up. "What did she do?"

"I'm not sure... she was shaking and screaming, waking everyone up, yelling about Penelope and Tetsuo and then she started vomiting."

"The clients have another half hour," she whispers. "I can't leave until then."

Kaipo tugs on the long lock of glossy black hair that he has bluntcut over his left eye. "I'm scared for her, Key," he says. "She won't listen to anyone else."

She will blame herself if any of the kids here tonight die, and she will blame herself if something happens to Rachel. Her hands make the decision for her: she reaches for Kaipo's left arm. He lets her take it reflexively and doesn't flinch when she lifts his shunt. She looks for and finds the small electrical chip which controls the inflow and outflow of blood and other fluids. She taps the Morse-like code, and Kaipo watches with his mouth open as the glittering plastic polymer changes from clear to gray. As though he's already been tapped out.

"I'm not supposed to show you that," she says, and smiles until she remembers Tetsuo and what he might think. "Stay here. Make sure nothing happens. I'll be back as soon as I can."

She stays only long enough to see his agreement, and then she's flying out the back door, through the garden, down the left-hand path that leads to unit two.

Rachel is on her hands and knees in the middle of the walkway. The other three kids in unit two watch her silently from the doorway, but Rachel is alone as she vomits in the grass.

"You!" Rachel says when she sees Key, and starts to cough.

Rachel looks like a war is being fought inside of her, as if the battlefield is her lungs and the hollows of her cheeks and the muscles of her neck. She trembles and can hardly raise her head.

"Go away!" Rachel screams, but she's not looking at Key, she's looking down at the ground.

"Rachel, what's happened?" Key doesn't get too close. Rachel's fury frightens her; she doesn't understand this kind of rage. Rachel raises her shaking hands and starts hitting herself, pounding her chest and rib cage and stomach with violence made even more frightening by her weakness. Key kneels in front of her, grabs both of the girl's tiny, bruised wrists and holds them away from her body. Her vomit smells of sour bile and the sickly-sweet of some half-digested fruit. A suspicion nibbles at Key, and so she looks to the left, where Rachel has vomited.

Dozens and dozens of black seeds, half crushed. And a slime of green the precise shade of a cherimoya skin.

"Oh, God, Rachel... why would you..."

"You don't deserve him! He can make it go away and he won't! Who are you? A fogey, an ugly fogey, an ugly usurping fogey and she's gone and he is a dick, he is a screaming howler monkey and I hate him..."

Rachel collapses against Key's chest, her hands beating helplessly at the ground. Key takes her up and rocks her back and forth, crying while she thinks of how close she came to repeating the mistakes of Jeb. But she can still save Rachel. She can still be human.

Tetsuo returns three days later with a guest.

She has never seen Mr. Charles wear shoes before, and he walks in them with the mincing confusion of a young girl forced to wear zori for a formal occasion. She bows her head when she sees him, hoping to hide her fear. Has he come to take her back to Mauna Kea? The thought of returning to those antiseptic feeding rooms and tasteless brick patties makes her hands shake. It makes her wonder if she would not be better off taking Penelope's way out rather than seeing the place where Jeb killed himself again.

But even as she thinks it, she knows she won't, any more than she would have eighteen years ago. She's too much a coward and she's too brave. If Mr. Charles asks her to go back she will say yes.

Rain on a mountainside and sexless, sweet touches with a man the same temperature as wet wood. Lānaʻi City, overrun. Then Waimea, then Honokaʻa. Then Hilo, where her mother had been living. For a year, until Tetsuo found that record of her existence in a work camp, Key fantasized about her mother escaping on a boat to an atoll, living in a group of refugee humans who survived the apocalypse.

Everything Tetsuo asked of her, she did. She loved him from the moment they saved each other's lives. She has always said yes.

"*Key!*" Mr. Charles says to her, as though she is a friend he has run into unexpectedly. "I have some*thing*... you might *just* want."

"Yes, Mr. Charles?" she says.

The three of them are alone in the feeding house. Mr. Charles collapses dramatically against one of the divans and kicks off his tight, patent-leather shoes as if they are barnacles. He wears no socks.

"There," he says, and waves his hand at the door. "*In* the bag."

Tetsuo nods and so she walks back. The bag is black canvas, unmarked. Inside, there's a book. She recognizes it immediately, though she only saw it once. *The Blind Watchmaker*. There is a note on the cover. The handwriting is large and uneven and painstaking, that of someone familiar with words but unaccustomed to writing them down. She notes painfully that he writes his "a" the same way as a typeset font, with the half-c above the main body and a careful serif at the end.

Dear Overseer Ki,

I would like you to have this. I have loved it very much and you are the only one who ever seemed to care. I am angry but I don't blame you. You're just too good at living.

Jeb

She takes the bag and leaves both vampires without requesting permission. Mr. Charles's laugh follows her out the door.

Blood on the walls, on the floor, all over his body.

I am angry but. You're just too good at living. She has always said yes.

She is too much of a coward, and she is too brave.

She watches the sunset the next evening from the hill in the garden, her back against the cherimoya tree. She feels the sun's death like she always has, with quiet joy. Awareness floods her: the musk of wet grass crushed beneath her bare toes, salt-spray and algae blowing from the ocean, the love she has clung to so fiercely since she was a girl, lost and alone. Everything she has ever loved is bound in that sunset, the red and violet orb that could kill him as it sinks into the ocean.

Her favorite time of day is sunset, but it is not night. She has never quite been able to fit inside his darkness, no matter how hard she tried. She has been too good at living, but perhaps it's not too late to change.

She can't take the path of Penelope or Jeb, but that has never been the only way. She remembers stories that reached Grade Orange from the work camps, half-whispered reports of humans who sat at their assembly lines and refused to lift their hands. Harvesters who drained gasoline from their combine engines and waited for the vampires to find them. If every human refused to cooperate, vampire society would crumble in a week. Still, she has no illusions about this third path sparking a revolution. This is simply all she can do: sit under the cherimoya tree and refuse. They will kill her, but she will have chosen to be human.

The sun descends. She falls asleep against the tree and dreams of the girl who never was, the one who opened the door. In her dreams, the sun burns her skin and her obachan tells her how proud she is while they pick strawberries in the garden. She eats an umeboshi that tastes of blood and salt, and when she swallows, the flavors swarm out of her throat, bubbling into her neck and jaw and ears. Flavors become emotions become thoughts; peace in the nape of her neck, obligation in her back molars, and hope just behind her eyes, bitter as a watermelon rind.

She opens them and sees Tetsuo on his knees before her. Blood smears his mouth. She does not know what to think when he kisses her, except that she can't even feel the pinprick pain where his teeth broke her skin. He has never fed from her before. They have never kissed before. She feels like she is floating, but nothing else.

The blood is gone when he sits back. As though she imagined it.

"You should not have left like that yesterday," he says. "Charles can make this harder than I'd like."

"Why is he here?" she asks. She breathes shallowly.

"He will take over Grade Gold once your transmutation is finished."

"That's why you brought me here, isn't it? It had nothing to do with the kids."

He shrugs. "Regulations. So Charles couldn't refuse."

"And where will you go?"

"They want to send me to the mainland. Texas. To supervise the installation of a new Grade Gold facility near Austin."

She leans closer to him, and now she can see it: regret, and shame that he should be feeling so. "I'm sorry," she says.

"I have lived seventy years on these islands. I have an eternity to come back to them. So will you, Key. I have permission to bring you with me."

Everything that sixteen-year-old had ever dreamed. She can still feel the pull of him, of her desire for an eternity together, away from the hell her life has become. Her transmutation would be complete. Truly a monster, the regrets for her past actions would fall away like waves against a seawall.

With a fumbling hand, she picks a cherimoya from the ground beside her. "Do you remember what these taste like?"

She has never asked him about his human life. For a moment, he seems genuinely confused. "You don't understand. Taste to us is vastly more complex. Joy, dissatisfaction, confusion, humility—those are flavors. A custard apple?" He laughs. "It's sweet, right?"

Joy, dissatisfaction, loss, grief, she tastes all that just looking at him.

"Why didn't you ever feed from me before?"

"Because I promised. When we first met."

And as she stares at him, sick with loss and certainty, Rachel walks up behind him. She is holding a kitchen knife, the blade pointed toward her stomach.

"Charles knows," she says.

"How?" Tetsuo says. He stands, but Key can't coordinate her muscles enough for the effort. He must have drained a lot of blood.

"I told him," Rachel says. "So now you don't have a choice. You will transmute me, and you will get rid of this fucking fetus, or I will kill myself and you'll be blamed for losing *two* Grade Gold humans."

Rachel's wrists are still bruised from where Key had to hold her several nights ago. Her eyes are sunken, her skin sallow. *This fucking fetus.*

She wasn't trying to kill herself with the cherimoya seeds. She was trying to abort a pregnancy.

"The baby is still alive after all that?" Key says, surprisingly indifferent to the glittering metal in Rachel's unsteady hands. Does Rachel know how easily Tetsuo could disarm her? What advantage does she think she has? But then she looks back in the girl's eyes and realizes: none.

Rachel is young and desperate, and she doesn't want to be eaten by the monsters anymore.

"Not again, Rachel," Tetsuo says. "I *can't* do what you want. A vampire can only transmute someone he's never fed from before."

Rachel gasps. Key flops against her tree. She hadn't known that, either. The knife trembles in Rachel's grip so violently that Tetsuo takes it from her, achingly gentle as he pries her fingers from the hilt.

"*That's* why you never drank from her? And I killed her anyway? Stupid fucking Penelope. She could have been forever, and now there's just this dumb fogie in her place. She thought you cared about her."

"Caring is a strange thing, for a vampire," Key says.

Rachel spits in her direction but it falls short. The moonlight is especially bright tonight; Key can see everything from the grass to the tips of Rachel's ears, flushed sunset pink.

"Tetsuo," Key says, "why can't I move?"

But they ignore her.

"Maybe Charles will do it if I tell him you're really the one who killed Penelope."

"Charles? I'm sure he knows exactly what you did."

"I didn't *mean* to kill her!" Rachel screams. "Penelope was going to tell about the baby. She was crazy about babies, it didn't make any sense, and you had *picked her* and she wanted to destroy my life... I was so angry, I just wanted to hurt her, but I didn't realize..."

"Rachel, I've tried to give you a chance, but I'm not allowed to get rid of it for you." Tetsuo's voice is as worn out as a leathery orange.

"I'll die before I go to one of those mommy farms, Tetsuo. I'll die and take my baby with me."

"Then you will have to do it yourself."

She gasps. "You'll really leave me here?"

"I've made my choice."

Rachel looks down at Key, radiating a withering contempt that does nothing to blunt Key's pity. "If you had picked Penelope, I would have understood. Penelope was beautiful and smart. She's the only one who ever made it through half of that fat Shakespeare book in unit four. She could sing. Her breasts were perfect. But her? She's not a choice. She's nothing at all."

The silence between them is strained. It's as if Key isn't there at all. And soon, she thinks, she won't be.

"I've made my choice," Key says.

"*Your* choice?" they say in unison.

When she finds the will to stand, it's as though her limbs are hardly there at all, as though she is swimming in mid-air. For the first time, she understands that something is wrong.

Key floats for a long time. Eventually, she falls. Tetsuo catches her.

"What does it feel like?" Key asks. "The transmutation?"

Tetsuo takes the starlight in his hands. He feeds it to her through a glass shunt growing from a living branch. The tree's name is Rachel. The tree is very sad. Sadness is delicious.

"You already know," he says.

You will understand: he said this to her when she was human. *I wouldn't hurt you:* she said this to a girl who—a girl—she drinks.

"I meant to refuse."

"I made a promise."

She sees him for a moment crouched in the back of her father's shed, huddled away from the dangerous bar of light that stretches across the floor. She sees herself, terrified of death and so unsure. *Open the door,* she tells that girl, too late. *Let in the light.*

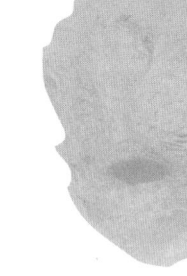

MAWAENA NĀ HŌKŪ

[James Rosenlee]

"Hōkū. Warp out of here right now."

"I can do this," I mutter, hands tight on the control panel. I try to steady them.

"Ensign Hōkū. *Now.*"

A couple hundred more kilometers, and I'll be in range to send out a tractor beam. I'm *almost* there. I send the ship into a tight dive to the right, narrowly avoiding a piece of debris hurtling from the collapsing planet. It ricochets off the lower hull, and I wince. *Oops.*

"Ensign Kahōkūlani, you are disobeying *a direct* order from your captain."

Yikes. I'm so used to being called "Hōkū" that hearing *Kahōkūlani* sends a spike of adrenaline through my system. My family only calls me that when I've really screwed up—like when I used to cut classes, or the time when I was six and fed cookies to the dog. Vaguely, I can tell I'm gonna be in *a lot* of trouble the second I get out of this mess.

"I can do this." I turn around in my seat and stare my captain dead in the eye. "I *know* I can. Do you trust me?"

Image by upklyak on Freepik

Captain Kōnane glares back at me with steely brown eyes, incredulous. *"No?* I thought I made that abundantly clear!"

"Uh… sir, should I remove Hōkū from the bridge?" Commander Lin asks in the abating silence. The short man fidgets uncomfortably, sinking into his seat. Disobeying a captain is almost unheard of in the Union, but I've always been good at going against the grain.

Kōnane grits her teeth and shakes her head. "We have no time, and they're our only capable pilot," she mutters quietly to him.

I grin. They can't replace me.

I catch Kerresi's gaze across our shared desk. She stares back at me, golden eyes frantically darting side-to-side in shock. She can't believe I'm doing this. Gods, *I* can't believe I'm doing this.

Please, I mouth at her silently. I hold my breath in the moments it takes her to form a response and practically watch the gears turn in her five-lobed brain. But, as always, she pulls through in the end.

"Dude, you *owe* me one," Kerresi whispers. With a quick, subtle flick of her clawed fingers, the ship's navigator feeds course-correction info from her holo-screen into mine. I absorb the information easily and start to make micro-adjustments to our spaceship's path.

"Ensign *Kerresi*—" the captain shouts, absolutely livid.

I tune her out. Almost there. We're almost there. The ship begins to shake as we near the gravity well of the star. My eyes flutter uncomfortably from the sun's light as the rocky planet slowly evaporates into its tight grip.

Watching a planet collapse into its star is a once-in-a-lifetime sight. It's what brought our entire crew here in the first place. It's truly beautiful, if you're a far enough distance away in the safe little bubble of a starship. Considering that I'm impulsively flying the aforementioned ship directly into said planet, that's not exactly our current situation.

Kerresi sucks in a panicked breath beside me.

I'm less than thirty seconds away. I steady my hands on the button, prepared. Another chunk of rocky debris skims our starboard side despite my best attempts to pull the ship away.

"Direct auxiliary power to the shields," Captain Kōnane orders behind me. My breath stills in concentration, vision going nearly white as I steady the ship.

"Yes!" I whoop, more relief than victory, as I lock onto the artifact with a secure tractor beam.

"Lieutenant, beam the artifact into storage with a level eight force field," I command with *completely* unwarranted confidence. My voice only shakes a little. Lieutenant Commander Njeri turns to the captain from her post, paralyzed.

Captain Kōnane glares daggers at me. "Do it, Lieutenant," she affirms.

"Shield at 12 percent," Commander Lin reads out from his holo-screen. "7 percent... 4 percent..."

As the remains of the shields falter, the ship vibrates from increasingly volatile shakes. I can barely keep my hands on the controls as I'm tossed from side to side in my seat. One particularly nasty impact hurls my arm into the gears of a nearby panel. *Ow.*

The tractor beam slowly, surely, pulls the artifact forward with a flurry of Njeri's fingertips. Within moments, it's securely within the belly of the ship.

"Hōkū, begin warp *right* now," the captain bites out. I need no convincing. Within a couple flicks of my fingers, the ship braces for the hyper-jump.

The bridge breathes a sigh of relief as we warp to safety with a familiar flash of blue.

The *'Oumuamua* steadies and sails forward smoothly as we re-enter empty space. I collapse back into my chair. On my right, Kerresi quietly lets out a string of curses that I know are less-than-nice in Imuni. I can vaguely hear the captain open a channel with Engineering, and Lieutenant Tayanita recites an uncomfortably long list of damages within the ship but confirms no one was seriously injured. Then a gruff acknowledgment, a couple of orders, and a light click signifying the end of the communication.

"Ensign Kahōkūlani," a voice repeats behind me, sharp enough to cut steel.

I groan quietly and attempt to melt into my chair. Well, I should've seen this coming.

"My ready room," the captain snaps with barely restrained rage. "Meet me there. *Now*."

I make the mistake of glancing at Kerresi, who stares back, wide-eyed. How comforting.

"See you on the other side," I mutter to her under my breath, hauling myself out of my seat.

"Yeah, if you *survive*."

I am so very, *very* screwed.

To make matters worse it's literally my second month on the job—what happened?

If I'm being honest, I have no excuse for not being a perfect human.

I'm Kānaka Maoli, born in Kohala, Hawai'i to a Union admiral and a spaceship architect. I grew up in a space travel *epicenter* during the Sixth Arc of humanity's exploration.

It goes without saying that Hawai'i is peacefully allied with all other Earth nations and alien civilizations within the Star Union. Exploration is by no means a race. But if it *was*…Hawai'i would be winning. We were the first Earth nation to make contact with aliens. The first child born in space was to a Hawaiian astronaut couple. There are various Star Union Academies scattered throughout the galaxy, but the oldest and most prestigious one was built in…you guessed it! Hawai'i.

It's really no surprise we're the leading pioneers of space. As a people, we've always kept our eyes on the constellations and our feet on the ground. Once, our ancestors were voyagers who relied on the stars to travel. And now, we travel *amongst* nā hōkū—the stars.

So, I was born to the right people, in the right place, at the right time.

By all accounts, my life *should* have been easy.

※

Captain Kōnane paces back and forth within her ready room, clearly about to lose her mind. Graying curls pull loose from her bun, and her intricately patterned 'ahu 'ula swings around her ankles with every turn.

I sit stiffly with my arms crossed behind my back. Despite being six feet tall myself, Kōnane practically towers over me in her rage. I've been here for a good thirty seconds, and the energy is already distinctly uncomfortable. And to make it worse, a giant gray reptile in a lab coat is fussing over the *minuscule* cut on my forearm. I just need to sit still, take the verbal beating, and keep my mouth shut. That's easy… theoretically.

The captain turns toward me suddenly. "Do you have anything to say for yourself?" she asks, deadly calm.

I let out a snort against my better judgment. "I'm surprised Kerresi isn't in here getting grilled out with me."

"Oh, believe me," Kōnane laughs humorlessly, "she's next. It's safe to say you're *both* on probation."

"Um." The doctor clears their throat, gingerly grabbing my arm between large dragon-like claws. "I should really bring Ensign Hōkū to sickbay—"

"Not now, Tern. They're fine," the captain says tightly.

Dr. Tern awkwardly shuffles away.

"Hōkū ... why did you have to do this?" she asks, exhausted. Captain Kōnane pulls out a seat at her desk and sits down. "You put the *'Oumuamua* at risk today for nothing."

"It's not... nothing," I argue. "We all heard Kerresi say the initial scans looked Imuni in nature! We found what looks like a data-holding artifact on a seemingly uninhabited planet on the verge of collapse...and managed to rescue it before it was destroyed forever. That's *huge*."

"So you chose your *friend* over a direct order?" Kōnane snaps. "You chose an ensign's theory over your captain? Just for her personal gain—or the gain of her species?"

"Are you even *listening?*" I sigh, biting back further words. The captain raises her eyebrows.

"If this really is an ancient relic, it could mean so much for Kerresi's people," I attempt to explain calmly. "They have almost no traces of their history pre-war. This could tell them about their past!"

"*If. Could.* I was not willing to risk the lives of over 150 individuals on this starship on a maybe, Ensign."

I swallow, mouth dry. "Sir, I know I disobeyed your orders to abandon the artifact for the ship's safety," I admit, in some sorry attempt at an apology. "*I knew* I could get to it in time, and I told you that, but nevertheless... I'm sorry."

I try to make my face look at least a little remorseful.

"Look, Hōkū." Kōnane sighs, her voice dropping in volume. "This is your third count of misconduct in the past two months."

My heart drops. I try not to look her in the eye.

"We both know there's no one better suited to fly this ship." The comment goes to my head a *little*. "Your skill definitely runs in your blood," Kōnane chuckles.

I deflate, biting my lip to keep my mouth shut. Here it comes.

"I was thrilled to have Admiral Kaulana's child aboard my ship!" she continues.

Blood rushes to my head, pounding furiously.

"But your behavior so far has been… disappointing."

My hands tense behind me, curling and uncurling. The dams break loose.

"Is that *all* I am to you?" I snap suddenly. "Did you even look at my exam scores or my Academy records before you offered me this position? Or did you just want the perfect carbon-copy *offspring* of my father?"

The captain's head snaps toward me, shocked. I can literally see my life flash before my eyes.

"I'm putting you on probation for a week," Kōnane says emotionlessly, staring me down with a brutal gaze. I lower my head. "You're still young, so I'll let you get off with a warning. But your father will be getting a full report of your behavior."

"You can't do that!" I protest, eyes widening. It comes out as more of a whine. "That's *cruel*."

"And effective. Also, yes I can." The captain stares at me coldly. "He's *your* admiral too. You're excused."

My mouth opens and shuts again. Nothing comes out. I tear myself out of the chair, face burning red, and storm out toward the exit. Someone clears their throat behind me. Dr. Tern's horns droop awkwardly as they try to duck their massive, seven-foot frame past a doorway. "Ensign, can I…" they ask politely, waving a medical tricorder in the vague direction of my arm.

"Yeah, yeah," I mutter, trudging my way toward sickbay.

"Have you seen Kerresi?" I ask frantically, pulling on the end of my cape with a newly healed arm.

The 'ahu 'ula has always been my favorite part of the officer's uniform, even if mine only reaches my chest as an ensign. When I was little, my father let me play with his floor-length admiral's cloak. He used to tell me in the ancient days capes were made out of feathers from birds like the ʻiʻiwi, and only chiefs could wear them. I suppose when Earth evolved beyond capitalism and status and scarcity, we took that relic from our past and regifted it to our current most prestigious members—our space explorers.

Calling the blank-staring ensign in front of me a "prestigious member of society" seems like a stretch, though. He points a wing toward the very back of the mess hall. "Should be over there," he grumbles, immediately returning to his sandwich.

I resist the urge to roll my eyes.

"Thank you," I mutter, then rush toward the pointed direction. I find her sitting at a table alone, picking at her plate. It's weird to see the little red-speckled Imuni, who's usually filled to the brim with energy, sit so still.

"Not under house arrest?" I say lightly, announcing my presence.

"Not yet." Kerresi moves her replicated food around the plate without taking a bite. Normally, she can eat twice the weight of her four-foot-tall, Menehune-sized body. "Haven't seen the cap yet."

"Hey." I swallow past a dry throat. "I'm sorry I dragged you into this mess."

Kerresi lifts up a maroon-spotted hand, waving me off. "Don't be. I was the one who wanted to retrieve the artifact in the first place."

I gingerly take a seat next to her. As we sit in silence, I catch my reflection on the glass table and choke back a sudden, inexplicable rush of shame.

My curly, shoulder-length hair reminds me of my dad's. The freckles that dot my warm brown skin come from my mom. Even my smile, which has always been a little crooked around the edges, can be traced back to my grandmother. Every part of me is a reminder of my family.

I've let them down today.

Commander Lin once told me the reason he has waist-length hair is because he sees it as a gift from his ancestors. It's no secret that our origins and cultures are a big source of pride on this ship. We come from all over, and since every officer feels the need to represent their respective homes, I've heard every story. I know that our Chief Engineer Tayanita is Cherokee, that Commander Lin is part Hakka Chinese and Taiwanese, that Lieutenant Commander Njeri grew up on a space station but has Kenyan roots, and, of course, that our Captain Kōnane is a fellow Kānaka Maoli hailing from Hilo.

Just like them, I love that I'm reminded of Hawaiʻi every time I look at myself. I hate that it makes me think of my family.

Kerresi's still quiet, so I try to break the increasingly awkward silence. "Well, it's not so bad to be on probation!" I finally say, with a fake air of cheeriness. I don't know if I'm trying to convince her or myself. "Weren't you just complaining about your shifts being too long?"

"I'm not worried about being kicked off the bridge for a week," Kerresi mumbles without looking up. "I'm worried about this going on my permanent record. It'll be a death sentence for my career unless I *somehow* pull off a bigger accomplishment."

"Oh." Honestly, I didn't even think about my record when I was being chewed out by the captain.

Kerresi pushes back her dish with finality and sighs. "It's not the same for you, is it?"

"What do you mean?" I ask, furrowing my eyebrows.

She shoots me a look. "Have you ever noticed that the *ʻOumuamua's* captain, commander, chief engineer, *and* head of security are all human? Tern and I are the *only* senior officers who are not! Humans make up, what, 10 percent of the Star Union? And yet you guys outnumber the rest of us nearly four-to-one on this ship." Kerresi heaves a breath, knitting her six-fingered hands together under her chin. "It's harder for us to prove our worth. In the Union, no one has *ever* expected anything out of me."

"I guess I've never thought about it before," I say numbly, completely stunned. I suppose she's right, but it's just… never crossed my mind.

"Humans rarely do," Kerresi says. There's a tinge of sadness in her eyes. "You don't even have to worry about your record. No matter what, people will just see your family tree."

I can't hear *that* enough. I laugh bitterly. "Yeah, that's the problem, though. My family tree is six generations of Star Union officers and pilots and leaders and whatever. I've always been perfect, because I have a legacy to maintain," I confess, words pouring out of my mouth in a solid rush. "But each accomplishment feels *wasted* if everyone only cares about who my family is."

I was insanely sure of myself when I was little. I knew I was māhū before I could speak and knew I wanted to be a pilot as soon as I could. But as I've gotten older, I've begun to feel lost and directionless. Kind of funny, since my job is to, y'know, *guide* and direct ships. I'm having a mid-life crisis, and I'm only nineteen.

But then Kerresi looks at me, and it's as if she's the only being in the universe who understands.

"You're the one person who made me feel ok with not being perfect," I admit.

Kerresi smiles quietly. "You're the one person who made me feel like I was already perfect."

"Aww, you're gonna make me cry," I say dramatically, covering up a few actual tears. She shoves me in the ribs, and I laugh and nudge her back, and just like that we're back to normal.

"Really, you probably aren't gonna get too bad of a punishment when you go into the captain's *lair*," I joke. "Hey, maybe we'll get to do community service together! We can chill out in the mess hall, or check out the junk lying around storage…"

I trail off the sentence, staring Kerresi dead in the eye. Thankfully, she seems to have caught on at the same time as me. "…where the artifact is," she says, finishing my thought. "It's a stupid idea," Kerresi adds.

I grin back. "Precisely."

We speed-walk through the halls, trying our best not to look suspicious. Which I've been told is my best quality.

"I overheard Commander Tayanita say on our next space station restock they're gonna drop the artifact off," Kerresi informs me under her breath. "To the Union Xenoanthropology department."

I groan, turning to the left. The Xenoanthropology department is historically slow and famously useless. "So they're gonna get to it in, what, *ten* years? No one is gonna be analyzing the data we risked our lives to get!"

"Hōkū—literally no one in the Union cares about alien artifacts! Remember, the Xenoanthropology department is basically all human." Kerresi rolls her eyes, quickly followed by a flash of determination. "We have to check it out now, by ourselves. Or *no* one is going to."

I have to admit that Kerresi's right, but what else is new?

"If we can rescue the artifact from security, we're gonna need the science labs to do the necessary analysis scans," she continues.

I glance surreptitiously around the hallway to make sure no one's nearby.

"We're *both* on probation," I whisper back. "We can't even access the high-security labs right now."

Kerresi tilts her head, thinking through our options. "If we have a high-enough ranked officer with us they can override our locks!" She pauses. "But I mean, like, *high* up. Lieutenant commander status or greater."

I frown. "Well, Captain Kōnane and Commander Lin are ruled out. For obvious reasons. That leaves us with… Lieutenant Njeri?"

"*Or* Doctor Tern," Kerresi reminds me. "They're technically fourth in command."

I make a face. "No way. They're so stuck up, they'd never break the rules for us."

"Njeri, then? I think she hates me," Kerresi says hesitantly.

"So? She hates everyone."

"Are you *sure* we should go with her?"

"Absolutely not," I round the corner to the lieutenant's personal quarters anyway. "Let's do this."

✶

I shower Lieutenant Commander Njeri with my best award-winning smile as she rubs the sleep from her eyes. I note the lack of her usual beaded jewelry and the normally pulled-back dreadlocks loose around her shoulders. Njeri looks… less-than-thrilled to see me and Kerresi after hours.

"Hello, Lieutenant! You look stunning today."

"What do you want," she says, unimpressed.

I cough and elbow Kerresi, who timidly lays out our plan.

The lieutenant stares at us blankly. "You want me to go against direct orders, endanger my place on the ship, and allow two *unexperienced* ensigns on probation—charged with second-degree ship damage—to analyze a piece of highly sensitive material?"

Kerresi winces, pointy ears drooping. "Well, when you put it like *that*—"

"Sure."

I blink slowly. "Sorry. *What?*"

"Sure," Njeri says plainly. "I'll give you access."

She starts toward the labs, and Kerresi and I scramble to follow her.

"Why are you helping us?" Kerresi asks suspiciously, half-jogging to keep up with the fast-paced lieutenant.

Njeri offers the first smile I've seen her give… *ever*. I didn't even know her face could do that.

"Because you're smart."

"I... what?" Kerresi sputters.

"Because you're *smart,*" she explains. "You two are both idiot troublemakers, but I know *you're* the brains behind the operation at least 50 percent of the time. And I know that you've been an ensign for *six* years, and there's no way you should still be one. Aliens are vastly underprivileged, and you deserve better."

Kerresi nudges me with an uncomfortably pointed elbow and raises her eyebrows. "See? I was right!" she whispers under her breath.

"Humans in the Union are treated *far* better than they should be," Lieutenant Njeri continues, unperturbed. She shoots me a sudden look over her shoulder. "Do you think Jianyu deserves his position?"

"Commander Lin? I—but he's not... dumb?" I protest.

"He's a thirty-year-old *commander,*" Njeri says with a roll of her eyes. "He wouldn't be able to make a cup of coffee without a replicator. He literally asked me if we could fly through an ion storm and 'be fine' the other day. Do you think *any* non-human with his... intelligence would ever be offered that position?"

"Fair point," I admit.

"We're here," she announces to no one in particular, tapping a string of commands into the door's holo-screen. I hold my breath surreptitiously, but Kerresi and I can enter the lab without any blaring alarms going off.

"Computer, beam artifact Alpha-228 from storage unit two into science lab four," Njeri commands. It teleports in front of us with a flash of blue.

I wince. "Will anyone know you did that?"

The lieutenant shrugs carelessly. "The captain never checks the logs. Typical human."

Kerresi giggles, and I roll my eyes.

Njeri ushers us toward the artifact. I've only seen it from afar before, and when we were using the tractor beam to haul it in from the planet it looked like a nondescript black orb. The actual sphere is *easily* ten meters in diameter—it's a good thing this science lab is massive. And every square centimeter of it, from top to bottom, is carved with intricate runes in a language I've never seen before.

Njeri runs a modified tricorder over the side of it.

"If Kerresi is right that the artifact is Imuni I can compile several dialects of ancient Imuni writing into a language algorithm to try to make sense of the symbols," Lieutenant Njeri considers. "It might take a while to decode, though."

"It's not like we're gonna miss work," I say dryly.

⁂

Two hours and several dozen wires hooked up to the artifact's mainframe later, and we're about to start decrypting the heavily deteriorated, foreign information.

"What do you think it is?" Kerresi murmurs, practically shaking from excitement. "Do the runes form…a book? Maybe a religious text?"

"It could be a Rosetta Stone-type object?" I chime in.

"Both of you are obviously wrong," Njeri announces from the other side of the room. Her hearing is *inhuman*. "Look at this."

We rush to her holo-screen, almost tripping over each other in our enthusiasm.

Kerresi takes a second to process and slams a hand over her mouth when she does. The little Imuni chokes back a sob.

"Ensign, remember when your scans from the ship sensed electromagnetic radiation?" The lieutenant says smugly, nodding toward Kerresi. "The artifact isn't just a storage device."

I stare at the screen in disbelief and whisper, "It's a *computer!*"

There's genuinely too much info on the holo-screen for my brain to process at once but I catch digital folders full of technological knowledge, medical knowledge, building schematics, old religious texts, folklore, ancient stories from all over the galaxy, and so much more. Terabytes of new information load in with every second.

"Thank you for believing in us!" I exclaim, wrapping an incredibly disgruntled Njeri into a hug. I'm a little dramatic, as always, but I mean every word. "We couldn't have pulled this off without you."

"Sure. Thank *you* two for being idiots with unwarranted confidence," Lieutenant Njeri responds dryly.

"No, really, thank you," Kerresi adds on. "I've never met a human who's so willingly helped an alien before. You're someone... really different."

I know Kerresi well enough to tell when she's being sly. "No *way*," I mutter under my breath. Njeri looks up at Kerresi slowly and holds her gaze for a while, basically confirming both of our thoughts.

"Wow, you got me. My big secret, I'm an alien!" The lieutenant rolls her eyes, but there's still something sweet about it. "Solid mix of half-human and half-Myrasku. I got 'lucky' with the genes, so my mom raised me on a Union space station as a purebred human."

I stare at her wide-eyed. Kerresi doesn't even try to hide her smugness.

"How would you *hide* that?" I blurt out. "Even if you look mostly human, your biological differences as an alien are bound to show up in the ship's med-scans! Unless you *literally* have a med officer cover for you—"

Njeri's eyes twinkle. "Tern isn't as stuck up as you all think," she whispers. "They aren't such a stickler to the rules. They've had to work just as hard as you, Kerresi, to get anywhere on this ship. We stick up for each other, right?"

Kerresi nods fiercely.

I'm still staring in disbelief, but I manage to look back at the screen. "This is a *find*," I announce. "We have to tell the captain about this!"

And then I sigh, remembering the events of the last twenty-four hours. Njeri shoots me a look, mirth in her eyes.

"Don't worry. I'll cover for you two," she smirks.

· ✧ ·

"...and the artifact's data storage basically functions as a computer." Kerresi's voice wavers a little on the last words. I give her an encouraging glance. Honestly, from the look on their faces, the captain and Commander Lin are too bewildered by the whole situation to be angry.

"Um, we theorized that given the language similarities, the civilization who created the artifact was an advanced race and recent common ancestor of the Imuni," Kerresi continues, starting to ramble. "Due to radiation on the device, we estimated it's about 15,000 years old. There are approximately 38.2 zettabytes of data—"

"Kerresi," the captain says, softly cutting her off. My friend swallows and nods back. "I already know that if *Chineye Njeri* decided to help you two out, this is important. What does this artifact mean to you?"

Kerresi pauses for a beat and then simply answers, "... everything." For the first time, her voice is steady as she talks to Captain Kōnane. "My people—the Imuni—are natural explorers! Barely any traces remain, but we used to be travelers jumping from planet to planet. And we were *incredibly* technologically and scientifically advanced, more so than what we've been able to replicate since."

The overwhelming pride in her voice drops suddenly. Kerresi takes a shuddering breath before she continues, somber. "Then, during our Great War thousands of years ago, we... lost it all. Less than 5 percent of Imuni lived through the genocide. Any survivors were sent back to the stone age."

We could have heard a pin drop in the ready room right now. The captain's eyes are trained on Kerresi.

"This artifact is... it's our forgotten past. Politically, culturally, medically, spiritually, it's a piece of our history that we've lost. This knowledge could save *lives*. I speak for every Imuni when I say that this discovery means *everything* to us."

Kerresi steps back with finality. I knock my shoulder against hers, grinning proudly.

The room is silent except for a loud sniff from Commander Lin. The captain clears her throat. If I didn't know better I'd say she looked teary-eyed, too. "And you can vouch for them?" Kōnane asks, directing her gaze towards Njeri.

She nods insistently. "I hate to admit it, but these two are the smartest and bravest officers I've ever worked with."

"Ok," Kōnane decides, offering the lieutenant a rare smile. "I trust you with my life, Chineye. You're never wrong."

The captain turns back towards both of us. "The Union thanks you both today," she professes sincerely. "You two took a risk in the message of exploration and learning, and it resulted in a world of difference for the Imuni people. I can think of no two better officers to have in the Union, or on the *'Oumuamua.*"

Kerresi breathes out a loud sigh of relief, and I can't stop my own grin from forming. Njeri shoots us a thumbs up from the back of the room.

"Does this mean we're off probation?" I immediately blurt out, unable to hold my tongue. The captain blinks at me and inexplicably starts to laugh.

"Yes, I'll pardon you two! The two-week community service is staying, though. After all, you both *did* still break direct orders—" I shoot a look at Kerresi that means, *I told you so* "—and Hōkū."

My gaze snaps back to her.

"Your father will still be getting a report of your behavior." I open my mouth furiously to complain, but Kōnane cuts me off. "I think he'd be interested to know… his child helped to rescue a culturally significant artifact and bravely, selflessly performed as a Union officer."

I shut my overactive mouth. She smiles at my dumbfounded look, and her voice softens. "He's going to be so proud of your actions today. As am I, and the rest of the crew of the *'Oumuamua*. Hōkū, you've taught me something about determination, skill… and trust. I'm glad to have you on board."

For the first time… probably ever, I can't think of a single word to say. "Thank you, Kumu," I finally manage.

Captain Kōnane ushers us out of her ready room, with mentions of throwing a celebration in the mess hall before setting a course to Imuni. The artifact is going to be returned to its rightful owners. Kerresi ends up walking by my side, and we talk and laugh all the way to the party our captain *insisted* on.

Twelve-thousand light years away from Earth and the Hawai'i I grew up in, the *'Oumuamua* is starting to feel like home.

△▽△▽△

MAUKA ON MARS

[a. a. attanasio]

"Mauka on Mars means toward the mountain." The tour guide directed the group's attention to the colossal shield volcano astride the wide, cratered land. "Olympus Mons. The largest mountain in our solar system."

Alpenglow lit the sprawling volcano, illuminating in pink pastels jagged rimlands along the caldera. "The first people on Mars remembered the greatest voyagers in terrestrial history, the intrepid navigators of Earth's largest ocean, and used their word to orient themselves on the Tharsis plains. Mauka on Mars is obvious. Rising twenty-two kilometers from the surface of the planet, Olympus Mons is as large as a volcano can get. If it were any bigger, the crust of the planet would collapse."

The guide communicated in clairvoyce, because the students' genus of humanity did not vocalize. This pack of students from Triton had been genetically designed to thrive at temperatures a few degrees above absolute zero. They wore billowing, full-body cowls of transparent film—soma|skins—to keep from vaporizing in the incinerating heat of Mars.

The tour guide, a zobot assembled from trillions of self-organizing nanoparts, had assumed a form similar to the body plan of the tourists it addressed but without the soma|skin: a tubular frame of segmented rings, alternating amber and gray.

The human beings from Triton seemed faceless as worms. The zobot, however, had been programmed to recognize emotions in the movement of the black sensory bristles atop the tubelike visitors' crest-holes. There, tucked among those lively whiskers, each of their eight pigment-cup eyes brimmed with iridescent intelligence—and boredom.

Sound didn't travel far in the tenuous nitrogen atmosphere of their homeworld, and Homo frigus had no ears. Huddling in their communal hives and assembly mills on the cryogenic plains of Neptune's largest moon, they conversed in thermal streams of aromatic compounds. Martian temperatures vaporized those olfactory signals. So, the guide had no choice but to use clairvoyce, directly inducing understanding in the students' brains through their soma|skin's neuronet.

Uncomfortable with clairvoyce and disinterested in the Martian tour, several students sidewised to the game arcades on Deimos. Chromatic freckles dotted the spaces where they had stood, fading slowly to pocks of crinkled space.

Another student flicked open a gill vent on their soma|skin, aimed it in the direction of the guide, and expelled a shrill whistle of tholins. The red plume of hydrocarbons from Triton flared violently in the warm atmosphere, kicking up gravel and gouts of orange dirt. A sharp cyclonic gust heaved the zobot to the ground so forcefully it burst to tiny jigsaw bits among the rocks.

Satisfied, the student sidewised to Ceres, joining a scavenger hunt in the asteroid belt. Other students followed, leaving a hot wash of rainbow pixels suspended in the wrinkling air.

"Sorry about my mates," the lone remaining student transmitted in clairvoyce to the scattered and shivering parts of the tour guide.

"They just want to spree before returning to Triton. Our program there is tombed labor."

"And you?" the shattered guide inquired. Its fragments dissolved into gray wisps of nanoparts, which swiftly knitted a cylindrical silhouette mirroring the visitor. "Don't you want to spree with the others?"

The lone student's eight eyes shaded to black rainbows. "Not yet." Surveying the planet's sepia distances, the tourist's crest-hole tilted southeast. They peered beyond the three Tharsis volcanoes in the distance, each ten kilometers high and evenly spaced seven hundred kilometers apart on the buckled horizon. "Earth is rising."

"There's a better view higher up," the guide advised.

"Mauka!" the student hailed and sidewised to the summit of Olympus Mons.

The abrupt change of altitude discharged a sharp hiss from the inflated soma|skin. A crimson haze of tholins seeped out of the suit's pressure valves and smudged away in the high wind, disappearing across horizons of smeared lava flats and scoria.

From the rim of the caldera, the famous veins of dried riverbeds appeared below. The rumor of floods chamfering rusty plains, grooving slurry floors with the toilings of water, fanned out and melted away into mantle beds of jet-black glass. "Deep time," the student marveled.

"Yes." The tour guide appeared alongside in tubular form. "This landscape is over four billion years old."

The student scanned the baked expanse of toppled blocks, tilted stone benches, and ranks of needle spires, all trembling like flames in the reverberate air as day slid into night. Throughout the rugged terrain, scattered among crater outcrops, green light palpitated. Remnants of the planet's shattered magnetic field lit pale, discrete auroras across the nightscape.

The tour had timed their arrival for twilight, to view the Martian blue sun. In an ethereal mauve glow, a small teal disc hovered like a flawless moon above barren vistas of oxide deserts and crenulated mountain ridges. The smoky blue sun blotted into the horizon, while overhead stars braided the Milky Way.

The student's clairvoyce whispered so softly it might have been a thought: "When lava flowed here, we were microbes there—in those oceans." Bristles pointed east, into the purple twilight above auburn deserts and rows of dead volcanoes. A large blue star flimmered far down the sky.

"Earth."

The student stood still, fixed to that moment and everything inside it. There! Staring avidly, cupped eyes discerned the star's planetary limn, azure oceans, and white-feathered weather.

Two students in radiant soma|skins sidewised onto the slope behind the tour guide. "Spree! Come on! The waze on Vesta is full-stop! Let's go!" They logrolled down a sandy scarp under a cloud of ruddy dust, then slid slantwise into the starry sky. Draperies of violet auroras parted as they vanished.

"They must be having fun," the tour guide conjectured. "Don't you want to join them?"

"They're here to forget," the student replied, all eight eyes trained on the brilliant sapphire low in the sky. "I came to remember."

"You're here to honor those who came before," the zobot understood, with a slash of humor, "—including the microbes."

"Especially the microbes." Bristles flared upright, stiff with reverence. "Those ancestors had no ancestors. Just water, sunlight, and iron patience."

"I sense that our tour is more than just informative or an amusement for you." The guide widened alternate eyes and splayed bristles in a gesture of attentiveness. "Will you share your thoughts with me? I'm interested in human experiences."

"A design imperative for tour guide zobots?" the tourist inquired, not budging attention from the blue world.

"Exactly so. I'm programmatically curious why one of a score of students would rather stand on a dark mountaintop than spree."

The student's crest swiveled about to confront the shapeshifting guide. "My mates are engineers. They work in the mills on Triton, designing and building components for the massive telescopic array at the boundary of the Oort cloud. This tour is a chance for them to have fun before getting back to construction of the Eye."

The tour guide pulled up a data array for that monumental undertaking—an observational sphere with a radius of three light years. "A millennial endeavor," the zobot noted. "Over a thousand Earth years of effort, less than one percent of the Eye has been completed."

"Yet enough to map all the worlds in our galaxy," the visitor noted. "I'm training to pilot one of the colonizing vessels bound for a Triton-like planet twenty light years away. Even with paralux pushing space at three times the speed of light, the journey will take four Martian years. In that time, any small invariance in the engine's spaceshaping field and—poof! At some unpredictable moment during the flight, our ship could fly apart, spewing our atoms across several parsecs."

"That kind of paralux catastrophe is rare."

"It happens." Sensory bristles trembled, and the iridescent eye-cups looked away. The twilit desert spread into fins of burnt orange rocks under silver threads of noctilucent clouds. "I'm here to remember all those who went before. All those with the courage to dare."

The student paused, making room for an occasion of insight. "The great navigators on Earth risked everything to cross the immensity of the sea, seeking islands they didn't know were there but that were always there, far out of sight, connected to the stars, wind, and ocean currents. Those first explorers met the mysterious outer world with their hearts, bravely. They won deep intimacy with the planet and its elemental powers—and with the islands that were always there."

"Their greatness thrived."

Bristles softly waved agreement. "Across the abyss, they found their way mauka. The direction out of the ocean toward the mountain. Toward new life."

"You're here to honor these intrepid seafarers."

"I'm here to remember them—and also the most fainthearted voyagers in terrestrial history, those timid navigators who hugged the coastline and whose word for mauka is anabasis. For them, that direction was a return from death—from the underworld."

The guide activated a traceroute through Ancient Earth History and recited in clairvoyce, "The Hellenes nervously navigated one of the smaller seas on the planet. In their minds, the ocean embodied chaos."

The student's bristles rippled, eagerly rendering thoughts into clairvoyce: "Anabasis showed the way up from chaos to the heights of reason, to the very apex of all that can be known. Anabasis is the peak of knowledge pointing our way to the stars. But it was mauka that gave humanity the courage to embrace the unknown and dare the perilous journeys beyond Earth."

"May I quote you to future tour groups?"

The student seemed not to hear. Their sensory bristles pushed against the soma|skin as if feeling through the transparent film and the intentful dark for the blue star. "I joined this tour to see for myself the planet-wide ocean that the greatest navigators mastered. On Triton, water is lava. Boiling water erupts dangerously from volcanoes on my world. We keep our distance. But down there—on Earth—water is life."

"Perhaps you will tour Earth and visit the great navigators' prize, the planet's most remote island chain." The tour guide didn't have to inform the student that, ages ago, most of the first people had uploaded their minds into virtual realities, so… "The archipelago appears pristine, eco-corrected for flora and fauna, exactly as the first humans found it after their three-thousand-kilometer ocean voyage. I can get you a license for a quick visit."

"Thanks, but no. This is as close as I can get without solar armor. And I've already taken the virtual tour, which is a lot more immediate than sightseeing in a shield suit." The student's clairvoyce dimmed, "I guess I'm just reaching. Reaching for connection."

The zobot drizzled away and coalesced into a large wooden frame of crisscrossing bamboo sticks.

"That's a wave-piloting chart," the student recognized in the wanting light, bristles alert. "Master navigators used these to model ocean currents and find their way among the scattered islands."

"It's a map of wave patterns," the guide elucidated, clairvoycing from within the frame. "More," the student suggested. "It's a map of the navigators' minds."

The dark had thickened, and bioluminescence pulsed with a frosty glow behind the cuticle segments of the student's body. Analyzing these additional biological data, the zobot more accurately read the visitor's inner state. "You're not just curious. You're feeling awe."

Recognized, the student's heart spoke a cherished dream, "Show me Tevahine and Tane."

The bamboo frame, leaning on a rock in the night shadows, dissolved. Two figures stepped from darkness, large Homo sapiens in their prime with strong features, waists girdled in bark cloth. The student recognized them from spun light recordings.

Centuries earlier, humankind had discovered how to view ancient light trapped inside the photon sphere of black holes. The immense gravity of collapsed stars captured rays from every direction in space and spun them in endless orbits, recording events across the universe for all time.

The Eye had gleaned the full history of Earthlight spinning around the event horizon of a black hole only 130 light years away. Everyone on all 186 moons and the four rock planets of the Solar Compact got to witness Earth's continents drifting and greening, early life squirming from the sea, and the emergence upon sky-wide savannahs of furtive human clans, refugees of fallen forests.

Early in training, the student had found and fixated on spun light recordings of the double-hulled outrigger canoes exploring Earth's largest ocean. Tevahine and Tane stood at the prow of the lead canoe in a fleet arriving at a snowcrest island. Landfall delivered them to the slopes of Earth's largest mountain, a shield volcano rising to stupendous heights from the ocean floor. The pair leaped together from the bow and ran splashing through sunstruck shallows hand-in-hand. Dogs and pigs thrashed behind. Spun light chronicles identified the couple as The Woman and The Man.

The life-size figures of Tevahine and Tane that the zobot generated stood half the height of the visitor from Triton. Surprise ricocheted off the student's memories of the first people. In spun light panoramas, they had looked larger.

The seafaring couple gazed up placidly at eight iridescent eyecups peering down. If the voyagers had been real, of course, nothing placid could possibly have transpired. Upon the deserts of Mars, terrestrials—for all their lucid intensity—existed as impossible creatures.

Abruptly, the student saw beyond dreams to the reality of the first people. They had mastered themselves and the elemental world. And they were gone. After a few generations, the great seafaring ended. Islanders on the most remote island chain lived in seclusion. Centuries witnessed more typical human behavior in conflict and combat among descendants—until the anabasis of the timid seafarers reached their shores.

"Greatness thrives in individuals."

Was that the tour guide—or the student's clairvoyce?

Tevahine and Tane had disappeared. No trace of the zobot remained. Clairvoyce had sheared to silence and left the student's mind vaguely thrumming with body noise. The tour was over.

Bioluminescence strobed serenely through amber and gray ring segments. For a limpid spell, the tourist from Triton remained unmoving atop the vast mountain. The parting thought from clairvoyce came laughing back. In the full history of life—microbes to ice worms on Triton—individuals thrived. Great or small, the thriving and the striving had always been and could only ever be personal—toward mauka within, invisible and perfectly clear.

Stars loomed in the Martian night. And Earth rose higher over expanses of bare stone flecked with ghost fire. Just standing there on the rimrock felt like a cosmic event.

Then, Phobos launched out of the western mountains. The oblate moon waxed brighter on its swift arc across the night. Its expanding illumination cast wheeling shadows from buttes and sent moony airs shimmering over canyon floors.

The student pivoted full circle. A tremulous halo of bristles framed eight eyecups, slimmed and gleaming with moonlight. Invisible and perfectly clear. Why else would the tour end alone atop Olympus Mons, where any step in every direction moved away from mauka on Mars?

HĀNAI

[GREGORY NORMAN BOSSERT]

Helena was high above Moʻokini Heiau in the morning shadow of Kohala when the swarm found her. She swatted the microdrones out of the way and kept climbing.

"Dammit, Helena." Izzy's voice was a tiny buzzing chorus from the scattered swarm.

"I want to reach the ridge before it gets hot," Helena said, "and Pololū before it rains. Which means walking, not talking."

Izzy regrouped the swarm just out of reach, the drones connecting themselves into a sort of flying speaker. "Some of us manage to do both at the same time," she said.

"Some of us are sitting on their ass in an office right now."

"I'm working. You might vaguely remember the concept. The Republic of Hawaiʻi doesn't run itself, even on a normal day. It takes all sorts of unique personalities."

It was beginning to sound like Izzy was working to a point, and that point might involve not making it to Pololū before the rain. Helena picked up the pace. Izzy sent the swarm after her and turned up the volume.

"The Sisters dropped in-system last night."

"So I saw," Helena said. The seven primary spheres of the composite ship had hung brilliant in the evening sky, haloed by their fractal cloud of companions.

"Wandering Willie D was on board."

"Well, you pick a name like that for yourself, you better actually do some wandering or folks will talk." Helena had talked about the lone alien's choice of names, back when the news feeds still sought her opinion as a xenoanthropologist, back before she'd become news herself.

"The *Sisters,* Helena."

"I heard you the—"

"—Which means he had to write a petition strong enough to persuade the most cautious and…"

"Pigheaded."

"…*ethical* of the five known starships to carry him here."

"I do recall the Sisters' rules, Isabella, thanks. I also recall explaining them to you in the first place. Look, he's the last of his species; that's a pretty persuasive argument. And he's always had a thing for Earth."

"Not 'here' Earth. 'Here' *Hawaiʻi*." The linked microdrones smacked the back of Helena's head. "Will you turn around already?"

Helena spun, one hand raised to fling the swarm into the dirt. "Dammit, Izzy, I'm not…Oh."

Maui was eighty kilometers away. The cloud-covered bulk of Haleakalā sprawled on the line between blue ocean and blue sky, and behind it was the twenty-kilometer-wide sphere of one of the Sisters' primaries, floating motionless in defiance of physics and sanity.

"She's sitting there over the ʻAuʻau channel just like she did in '52."

"When she picked me up," Helena said, reluctantly, knowing she was hooked.

"It's a convenient place to park if, say, you're an island-sized interstellar starship dropping your passenger off *in my office*."

Helena sighed. "Ok, ok, Counselor. What is Wandering Willie D, the last survivor of a dead alien race, doing in your damn office?"

Helena could hear the satisfied grin on Izzy's face through the buzzing feed. "Why, Kulikuli, he's asking for you."

※ ※ ※

Izzy's office was up the hill above the civic center, safe from the tourist crush of Lahaina's shorefront. Most days there was little traffic beyond government staff catching a little sun. But Helena was still two blocks away on her walk from the skimmer port, and the street was *packed*. And it was not just tourists on the lookout for aliens or gawking at the curve of the Sisters ship overhead; the crowd was equal parts camera crews, remote presence robotics, and drones of every size, from microswarms up to heavy armored quads that must have flown in from the base the U.S. still rented on O'ahu.

Helena turned right to skirt around the worst of the crush, considered turning around altogether. But Izzy was most likely already tracking her with a swarm, and anyway curiosity had always been her downfall.

"Well, Helena, that cat is already dead, so what do you have to lose?" she muttered and cut through the hospital parking lot toward Izzy's back door.

The answer, of course, was a peaceful solitude that had taken her a decade to achieve. Even though she pulled her frizzled bangs down and pushed her sunglasses up, there were cameras on her for the last ten meters to the door, and face recognition algorithms were not so easily fooled.

Izzy kept a small crew, now that she was counselor-at-large and less involved with the day-to-day functions of independent Hawai'i. Her legal aide and general factotum, Kai, was at the front door, talking with a couple of police officers, and her research assistant was gesturing emphatically behind a pair of AR glasses. Kai saw Helena over the cops' shoulders and waved her toward Izzy's office.

The windows inside had been dimmed, and it took a moment for Helena's eyes to adjust. Izzy, though small and dark, stood out thanks to her halo of white hair and her quivering energy. Wandering Willie D was easily a hundred-and-fifty kilos and over two meters; Helena only blinked him into focus when he stood up and stretched huge hands wide in greeting, the iridescent pannae of the webbing under his arms glimmering in the low light.

"Helena Johnson! Such a pleasure to meet you! Though Counselor Dasha tells me I may call you Kulikuli."

The keetea had stayed close to their aquatic roots. Willie looked like an upright manatee, with the wicked grin of a porpoise and wide whale eyes set in deep folds. His smooth brown skin draped in folds and was covered almost everywhere by the pannae, feathery scales in rainbow hues ranging from thumbnail width to palm-sized tufts down his back and along the width of the flat tail that skirted the back of his legs.

Helena shot a glare at Izzy and tucked her thumbs into her rear pockets. "Helena will do."

Izzy sat down in her desk chair and swiveled back and forth with a flash of death as bright as her hair. "It's a well-earned name, Helena."

"Which means 'Shut up.'"

Willie hooted and sat back down on the couch. His voice was a basso growl over which a counter-tenor whistle soloed in loose synch from the nostrils on the back of his head. His English was slow and swooping but easy enough to follow. "I have been known to go on myself. 'Long-winded' is your delightful phrase, yes?"

Helena leaned against the edge of Izzy's desk. "Mmm," she said.

"It's a useful trait for us swimmers. And you are an avid swimmer, or so the counselor informs me."

"When life gets strange…" Izzy said, with a wave toward the monitors on the side wall, half of featured coverage of the exterior of her office or the Sisters' ship overhead.

"And when is it not?" Willie said.

"…You can count on Helena to do one of three things: swim, dance, or put on her walking shoes."

"Ahhh, yes, the dancing. This is what has brought me here."

Helena had turned to give Izzy another glare. She blinked in surprise and looked back at the alien on the couch.

"I have greatly enjoyed your writings on the ethnography of motion arts. My research, ah, so many cycles ago, was on xenobiology, so I was reading as a layman. But I felt we were reaching for the same truths with our—" He wiggled webbed fingers. "—differing grasps."

Helena blinked again, tried to turn what felt like an expression of surprise into one of polite interest. "I, uh, see," she said.

"But that is not why I petitioned the Sisters to bring me across the galaxy to meet you," Willie said.

"I see," Helena said, with what now felt like a frown.

"No no no, I am here because of the *hula*." His whistling overtone played a whole melody over that last drawn-out word.

Helena gave up trying to figure out her own expression. Hell, she was out of practice talking to humans, let alone wandering alien lifeforms.

"I have heard, and your counselor Dasha confirms, that after your, ah, retirement and return to Hawai'i that you have become an ardent practitioner of the art of the hula."

"I, uh, well, yes. Under Zach, that's Kumu Ho'omana'o, my teacher at the Hālau Kakahiaka here on Maui."

Willie smiled his porpoise smile, revealing an irregular row of greenish teeth.

"But I'm an amateur. Not bad, maybe, for a kid from Oakland. But there are many others far more qualified, both through skill and heritage, here on the islands."

"Ah, but few with your background and insight on the role of dance in cultural tradition, yes?"

"Well, true, but…the kumu will be the first to tell you that I am also not much on the tradition thing when it comes to hula."

"This is also beneficial to my purpose."

Helena looked back again at Izzy, who shrugged. "We didn't get this far before you arrived," she said.

"Before I continue, though, I trust you will allow me one question." Wandering Willie D leaned forward, hands on knees and tilted his head to look at her from first one eye, and then the other. The pannae along his shoulders flared in iridescent waves.

A sudden premonition, or perhaps simply ten years of precedent, told Helena what the alien's next words would be.

"Why did you destroy the frescoes at Malae on Kepler-442b?"

Helena pushed herself up from Izzy's desk. She sent what she hoped was a devastating side-eye at Izzy as she turned toward the door.

"You trust wrong," she said, without looking back at the alien. Then she walked out and slammed the door behind her.

Helena floated on her back, half a mile off Olowalu, listening to the 'ua'u call of passing petrels and watching the layers of the midnight sky.

Apart from the birds, the first ten meters above her were relatively empty, with just the occasional stray insect and, once, a school of flying fish that almost brushed her nose.

Beyond that was a realm of small drones, messengers shuttling to and from the neighboring islands. And higher yet, larger cargo drones and passenger skimmers and a flock of deep growling quadcopters that might have been the U.S. military drones she'd seen outside Izzy's office on the long haul back to Oʻahu.

On most nights the next stretch of sky would have held commercial flights to the other islands and beyond, but that space was currently occupied by twenty kilometers of starship. The Sister ship was a perfect sphere; its spotless matte-white surface picked up the lights from the shoreline, the blinking beacons of passing drones, and a rim of light from the waning Moon. Clusters of the smaller Sister spheres revolved around the primary like moons of its own.

Between that ship and the Moon above were a thousand man-made objects, from fleet schools of netsats to the leviathan space stations. Dwarfing even those, of course, were the other six primary spheres of the Sisters and their countless companions, made by neither man nor any other known species, hanging motionless a couple of thousand kilometers directly overhead.

"Keeping an eye on your sister here, and on Wandering Willie D-for-Dingbat, and not me, I hope," Helena said.

She'd flown on the Sisters three times: once to Kino Beacon and back for a galactic conference and festival of motion arts, and once the one-way trip to the excavations at Malae on Kepler-442b. Travel via the Sisters required a petition every bit as tedious and exacting as an academic grant proposal, complete with essay, and only a fraction of those petitions were granted.

"Even if you're this close to be burned at the stake by a mob of enraged archaeologists and an entire alien government, isn't that right, you sanctimonious prigs?" Helena said to the ships overhead.

That refusal to bring her back to Earth after Malae was why the Sisters surely had no interest in her now.

Helena let out her breath and sank until just her face was above the water. The water was warm and still, the breeze gentle and filled with rich island scents and the occasional whiff of grilling fish from the shore. The stresses of the day, and of a decade of trouble that that day had recalled to mind, floated from her fingertips to drift down in the deep.

I can stay out here for another hour, Helena thought, *before I need to head back in.*

There was a flash that could have been lightning, if lightning was perfectly circular, deep purple, and bright enough to light up not just the vast curve of the Sisters ship overhead and the moon-sized spheres of the other six Sisters primaries above, but the dark limb of the Moon itself.

Something streaked from that flash, stopped a hand's span from the cluster of Sister primaries 2,000 miles above. The thing was much smaller than even one of the Sisters' primary spheres, not much more than a brilliant dot. But its sudden appearance meant it had to be one of the other four known starships in the universe, and its reckless approach and constantly shifting brightness and color were a dead giveaway as to which of those it was.

Without a sound or any sign of force, the Sister ship just overhead started to rise toward space, her small companions swirling upward in her wake.

"Dammit," Helena said to the universe at large and started swimming for shore.

"It's the Construct," Izzy said, thumping a monitor with her fingertip.

"Looks like it," Helena said.

On the screen a nested series of rotating polyhedra, formed out of what seemed to be brightly colored shafts of light, drifted back and forth in a manner both unpredictable and somehow nauseating.

"That's two of the five starships—"

"That we know of."

"*Two* of the five starships, Kulikuli, not just hanging over Earth but hanging over Hawai'i." Izzy continued thumping the monitor, even though the image had switched to a panel of commentators.

Helena thought of pointing out that the Sisters were technically many ships all on their own, but Izzy's raised eyebrow suggested that sitting down and being quiet might be a better approach.

"One of them the most liked and admired of the ships," Izzy continued, prodding a different screen that showed the Sisters, all seven primaries now reunited in space.

"Only because they condescend to speak with us."

"With *us*," Izzy said, with a gesture than apparently included herself and every other being in galaxy except Helena. Which was fair enough, Helena thought.

"And the other," once more poking the screen with the commentators and managing to hit the UN Special Envoy to the Galactic Community square in the nose, "is the least understood, least seen, and least trusted ship in the known universe."

"Can't really blame them for avoiding us," Helena said.

"Avoiding *us*," Izzy replied, with that gesture again.

"Well, Wandering Willie D is the last of his kind. I am sure even the Construct has some interest in what he's up to. Speaking of which, what *is* he up to, now that he's given up on me?"

Helena hoped against hope that that last bit would provoke Izzy into giving up some details on the alien's motives. But this after all was the woman who had overseen Hawai'i's fight for independence, not to mention bargaining the lucrative deal with an extremely aggravated U.S. for their continued use of Pearl Harbor. Izzy collapsed into her desk chair instead and rubbed her thumping finger.

"Right, let's count aliens," Izzy said. She tapped the still-raised finger; it looked like she'd broken the nail. "One is Willie." She raised the middle finger and looked between the two at Helena. "Two is the Sisters. And three is the Construct. And what do these aliens have in common, three, two, and one?" She lowered the fingers again as she counted down and shook her fist at Helena.

Helena drew a slow breath, but before she could say anything Izzy answered her own question.

"Helena Johnson is what. And that, in case you haven't been following along, is you. The only person to have been banned by the Sisters, the only person to have ever flown on the Construct, and the only person who the last surviving keetan is going to confide in, apparently, since all of my gracious charm and lawyerly skill has gotten me absolutely nowhere with him despite hours of trying while you were off paddling about in the ocean. So what are you going to do about it?"

Izzy slumped back in her chair and examined her broken nail. "And Kulikuli, you are my dearest, most precious friend and please please please don't tell me you are going swimming again."

"I am not," Helena said, and stood up. "I'm going dancing."

After more than a bit of grumbling, Izzy had lent Helena her little two-seater runabout. Its dimmable windows and swarm of anti-drone drones would provide her a bit of privacy. The two of them weren't the only ones to make the connection between the two starships; Helena's face was popping up on the news streams almost as frequently as Willie's, and every time with some variation of the phrase, "the disgraced xenoanthropologist who destroyed the frescoes on Kepler-442b."

The road down the South Maui coast to Mākena was quiet now that the big corporate reports had closed. Helena undimmed the windows and watched the rain fall from the Lono drones high above Kahoʻolawe.

When she saw the camera drones and remote bots hovering around Hālau Kakahiaka she figured they must be for her. She manually piloted the runabout as close to the door as she could and walked the few steps with one finger raised above her head. Three steps past the door, though, she heard the unmistakable boom and whistle of Wandering Willie D.

The alien was in the center of the floor, surrounded by her fellow students of the hālau, showing a dance step to Kumu Hoʻomanaʻoinākūpuna Zachary Pukui.

Helena had far too much respect for the kumu as a teacher, and Zach as a friend, to do anything but sit quietly and watch.

Willie repeated the move a few times, a step back and lean forward with a sweep of the arms that sent the webs under his arms flaring, the feathery pannae raised and shimmering, and then showed it in context of a longer section. In motion, the alien's sagging bulk seemed to float and glide with the underwater grace of a seal.

After a few minutes, Willie stopped, hooted a laugh, and slumped to the ground.

"I would blame the unaccustomed gravity here, but in truth it is less than that of my home. The wear and tear of time passing is, however, the same. This sequence I had from my grand-aunt," he inserted a series of whistles and clicks here that must have been her name, "who had it from <more whistles> and so on back into the tradition of their family. It is important for us…"

Willie trailed off for a second.

"It *was* important for my people to trace the teaching of these dances from family to family, and generation to generation."

Kumu Hoʻomanaʻo sat as well and nodded. Some of the students took this as a sign to speak quietly among themselves, something that was frowned upon during a lesson. "Observe with the eyes; listen with the ears; shut the mouth," was a key principle of the hālau.

"We say *Nānā i ke kumu,* which means 'look to your source,'" the kumu said in his quiet voice, that required one's full attention and silence to hear.

Willie said, "And we have <a long flowing series of harmonized tones>, which is 'know from where the current comes.' I should add, though, that though my great-aunt was adopted, in a way, into this other family and its ancient traditions, she brought our own family's techniques to their dance. And my family's style is far from traditional. This was the cause of great tension between the families, I confess."

"Here as well, the *hula kahiko,* the old traditions, versus the new *hula ʻauana. ʻAuana* means to wander or drift, and it has indeed drifted far and to strange waters. Helena here has helped me understand that."

Helena had been glaring at drones trying to peek through the shutters of the hālau, a moment of exasperation that the kumu must have caught. She sat up straighter, met Willie's gaze. There was a twinkle in those deep-set eyes all too like the one Izzy's got when she was about to make a winning point.

"That conflict between the stationary and the drifting can lead to great passions," Willie said.

"And so on Hawai'i with the traditionalists, like those on Kahoʻolawe, who feel that hula ʻauana is a capitulation to the haole, the colonizers. And yet Kahoʻolawe flourishes because of the drones that bring the rain. I was a traditionalist as a young man, and my understanding of hula was the lesser for it. This is also something Helena helped me see, with knowledge she brought back from space."

They all looked up toward the ceiling, and the starships beyond.

"Tradition evolves, our understanding of tradition evolves. This gift of knowledge I thank Helena for. Even if she does insist on dancing the men's forms."

Willie hooted, and climbed to his feet, as did the rest, Helena last of all.

The kumu looked up at the alien. He laughed, and said, "Hey, Joe Pahuhau, you might have met your match."

Joe was the biggest of the dancers, with arms like Helena's thighs and a torso like a tree trunk. And like Willie, his weight seemed to disappear when he moved. He stepped over now and proved to be almost exactly Willie's height.

"Bruddahs, brah," Joe said approvingly. "I gotta get some da kine, d'ough, ya?" he said, waving his fingers under his arms.

"The pannae," Willie said. "We say <two sharp clicks>." He spun to show the long feathers that ran down his back to the flap of his tail; the largest curled around the edges like peacock plumes, all of them in shimmering shifting colors that formed and unformed patterns as he moved.

"They're symbionts. Living creatures. They cannot live long without a host, and we would not care to live long without them. They are part of our heritage, part of our family."

Kumu Hoʻomanaʻo said, "We say 'hānai,' an adopted child."

"Exactly," Willie said. And to Helena, "They're a reminder that the very different can nonetheless join in common purpose."

The kumu looked back and forth between them. "The lesson is over," he said. "It's ok to ask questions. I'll start. Do you know Helena's nickname and how she got it?"

Willie grinned his porpoise grin at Helena. "Kulikuli, yes? I'm told it means something like 'be quiet.' I assume it's a reference to her well-known tendency to speak her mind."

Joe laughed and shook his head. "No, brah. She come back here from the way-up, face over all the streams, maybe de most famous person on the ground, maybe de most famous up there too, you know what she say the first six months she spend here in the Hālau?"

Willie tilted his head at Joe, who just smiled.

In his quietest voice, Kumu Hoʻomanaʻo said, "Not a word. She sat and listened."

Helena shut her eyes and said, *"Nānā i ke kumu."* Then she opened them again and said, "Ok. Ok, let's talk."

A look that might have been joy spread over Wandering Willie D's face. "Wonderful," he hooted. "Wonderful. Perhaps, though, we should find a more private place."

They all looked around. Several swarms of microdrones had made it though the shutters, and a hulking remote with the logo of one of the big streaming services had its cameras pressed to the glass of the door.

"Ah," Willie said.

"No problem. I know a girl," Helena replied.

"No problem" might have been an exaggeration. Izzy had built a safe-room under her old offices in Maʻalaea, back in the dangerous days of the fight for independence, and she'd kept an arrangement with the current occupants to get access when she needed it for her current government work. It was snug, particularly when one of the occupants was a hundred-and-fifty kilo keetan, but it was cozy enough, despite the metal walls and plain plastic furniture.

"No place for bugs to hide," Izzy explained.

That was less true, it turned out, for their own selves. The scanning equipment in the safe-room's antechamber turned up over a dozen microdrones or other devices secreted in their clothing, hair, or places even more personal. One was so deeply embedded within the sole of Helena's shoe that she tossed them into the trash of a nearby coffee joint and walked back barefoot, bonus coffee in hand. In that short walk back she managed to pick up two more drones for the scanners to find.

Once they themselves were cleared of uninvited guests, and the room and its airlock had been scoured by Izzy's anti-drone drones, they sealed themselves inside and Izzy prodded her tablet until she felt satisfied that they were free from eavesdroppers.

They sat in silence, then, for a while. Helena and Izzy exchanged thoughts via glances with forty years of friendship behind them, as Wandering Willie D collected his thoughts. He finally let loose a low whistle from his rear set of nostrils.

"It was rude of me to start by questioning you, when I have come all this way in search of your skill and knowledge."

Helena shook her head. "It was rude of *me* to take it as an attack. When I'm asked that question here on Earth, the person asking always already has their own answer, and has no real interest in my own. Just in watching me squirm."

"I promise you I am, as you say, all ears." The small pannae across his head and neck shook like leaves in the breeze. "But I must ask. Why did you destroy the frescoes at Malae on Kepler-442b?"

Helena could feel Izzy's anxious gaze. She stared down into her coffee instead.

"I had been on Kepler-442b for a few months when the frescoes were discovered, working on the art and engravings at other sites, or rather, on the pictographs depicted within them. Those pictographs were based on story-telling poses, a type of dance, if you will, of those ancient peoples. Poses that still had echoes in the dance of their descendants on 442b and the surrounding systems."

"The Axellos," Willie said. "A lovely tradition of the arts, if somewhat zealously guarded. I think you would call them a 'passionate' people."

"Passionate and heavily taloned," Helena said, rubbing her thumb over the scars on either forearm. "The frescoes at Malae were discovered accidentally. They were entirely covered by several layers of plaster contemporary to their making, and that covering had been renewed every few decades for centuries by resident monks, until the last of their order died and the government sent in the scientists. There was a political point in play, a question over the historical ownership of that entire continent. A technician was taking a core of the layers in the antechamber for dating purposes when an entire slab of the covering plaster came loose."

Helena took a sip of her long-since cooled coffee.

"I had a friend, an Axellan on the archaeological team, who got me in that night, while they sent for a scanner that could pick up the remaining frescoes through the overcoats. She worked to preserve the rest of the panel—the covering was just crumbling away at that point—while I deciphered what had been exposed. And…"

Helena blinked at the green enameled metal of the wall.

"And?" Izzy gently promoted, though she knew the story better than any else but Helena herself.

"And then I locked my friend out of the room, and took a laser excavator and burned every last inch of plaster from the walls of the entire chapel."

She glared at, or more precisely, *through* Willie. The alien opened his mouth, then shut it again.

"But your question wasn't what I did, which is public, very very public, record, but why. I've never discussed the reason publicly. I *couldn't,* not without invalidating what I had already done. I've only told Izzy, and Zach, and now you."

"I hope to be worthy of your trust."

"Trust is what this is all about, isn't it?" Helena said. "Here I am always feeling like it's me against the entire universe, when I have Izzy and the Hālau and my own world under my feet. And you, you're truly on your own in every way. It's me who needs to be worthy of trust. So here it is.

"The frescoes in the chapel's antechamber were a sort of prelude, a warning, an apology in the literary sense, for the much more extensive frescoes still hidden in the other rooms. Hidden deliberately and guarded over the centuries by the order that had dwelt there for just that purpose. Those frescoes, the prelude explained, told the history of the founding of the continent. A history told through a pictographic dance so powerful and evocative that I wept as I read them. A history so full of rage and disgrace, the artist had said, that the only hope for redemption was to purge the story from her people, via the act of capturing them through motion, then freezing that motion for all time in still images, and burying those images, her masterwork, from sight forever. Burying herself as well; she was the founder of the order that kept those frescoes hidden and never left the chapel again.

"My friend asked me why I was crying, and I said it was the plaster dust and asked if she could get me some water. I locked the door behind her and then sat there thinking about the artist and her despair, and of the passion of her descendants, who had already fought four wars over the 'rightful' ownership continent. And then I got up and found the laser."

Willie asked, "And was it not the right of the Axellos to make such a momentous decision regarding the work their ancestors?"

"The Axellos, both the government and the opposition, don't give a *damn* about their ancestors, except when they can be used to score points in some endless bloody game," Helena said, her voice reverberating in the tiny room. "And *I* wasn't making a call, I was following the clear, desperate desire of people for whom those frescoes were literally life and death." Helena was on her feet now. "It was an ethical imperative, and I'd do it again tomorrow, damn the Axellos, and government, and the Sisters too while you're at it."

There was a silence in the safe-room for a moment. Izzy reached over and patted Helena's chair. She took a step back instead and put her hand on the doorknob.

Willie sat very still, though the pannae across his body quivered. The expression on his face was nothing Helena could interpret.

"Thank you," Willie finally said, in a low whistling whisper. "Thank you for your trust now, and for your actions then. I have come across the galaxy on the sheerest hope that you would answer as you have."

And then in a voice closer to his usual boisterous growl, "I have three favors to ask of you, though they are each a burden I have no right to place upon you. I must trust your understanding, which is great, and your compassion, which as I suspected is beyond measure."

He shook himself until the pannae settled, raised a hand and swung it in a graceful arc. "There is a dance my people do, a defining tradition of the culture, and yet unique to each dancer. A duet between an elder and another, usually of another lineage, who thus becomes part of the family. We say <three rising tones over a low rumble>. Your kumu had a word…"

"Hānai," Izzy said.

"Yes. The dance is private, deeply so, a passing of a life's story from the one to the other. But the elements of the dance, the motions and their performance, are drawn from the legacies of both dancers. And so that story transcends the individual life and makes something new of those traditions. I would like you to be my <three rising tones over a low rumble>, my hānai, and help me work out the story of this last dance of the Keetae, and dance the dance, the <long falling notes> with me when the time comes."

"I..." Helena fumbled herself back into her chair. "I was thinking the chances were fifty-fifty that the Axellos had sent you to assassinate me, or worse, you were writing a book."

"She means, 'It would be an honor,'" Izzy interpreted.

Helena nodded vigorously. "But..." Helena added. "You said *three* favors. Unless there are three dances?"

"Just the one dance," Willie said. "I hope you will trust me just a little while longer regarding the other two matters."

"No sweat," Helena said, still looking a bit stunned.

"No sweat at all," Willie said, back to his jovial tone and with a hint of his toothy smile. "But I will require just a drop or two of blood."

"—exclusive footage of remarkable collaboration between the last surviving keetan and a hula dance troupe on the island of M—"

<beep>

"—illie D explains that the theory, known as 'panspermia', could explain the remarkable genetic similarities between humans, Keetae, and almost all of the other known alien—"

<beep>

"—ohnson, the disgraced anthropologist who destroyed the frescoes on K—"

<beep>

"—who goes by the unlikely name 'Wandering Willie D' is working with scientists at the University of Hawaiʻi on Oʻahu in a study of DNA from species across the galaxy, which might shed light on the amazing similarities betw—"

<beep>

"—do *not* need to be the big W-W-D to pull off these amazing moves, and I'm going to show you just how to do it! Start with your arms rais—"

\<beep\>

"—still hovering fifteen hundred miles above the island nation of Hawai'i, and within a few hundred miles of each other, the closest we've ever seen two starships approach one and—"

\<beep\>

"—the very same Helena Johnson who destroyed the frescoes on Kepler—"

Izzy waved the monitor into silent mode.

"It's been three months," Helena said. "Three full months of you, me, and Willie on our best behavior. Not a single suspicious move."

"Exactly," Izzy said, feeling around her feet for the bottle. "The suspense is killing them."

Helena held her glass out. "Them who?"

"Everyone who isn't you, me, or Willie D."

"Or the Hālau Kakahiaka."

"To the Hālau Kakahiaka," Izzy cheered, and raised her glass.

They both took a long sip. If you were looking for proof of a single common basis of galactic life, Helena had said the other day, one need look no further than Willie's excellent taste in whiskey. The alien had headed to O'ahu for a few days of work on the mysterious second favor, which somehow involved panspermia and far more than a couple of drops of Helena's blood. She and Izzy had promptly claimed the couch and the bottle, though the party had been somewhat moderated by Izzy's need to check the news streams every few minutes.

"*You're* not even on the streams," Helena grumbled.

"No, but Hawai'i is. This is work, love." She leaned forward to shout toward the door. "Hey, Kai, we stay working, ya?"

"Nah, it's seven-thirty, Aunty," Kai called back.

"Workin' *late*," Izzy said and sat back, satisfied. "Researching the global media presentation of the Republic of Hawai'i in regards to, oh *crap*." She sat up, knocking over the bottle, and gestured at the monitor to rewind a few seconds.

"What is that?" she said.

Helena frowned at the screen, and then back at Izzy. "Umm, the parking lot of the hālau?"

"No, *that.*" Izzy got up and thumped the screen with a nail still a bit crooked from her screen-thumping three months before. In the trees on the far side and half-hidden by the usual cloud of drones, was a tiny blur, barely visible against the sky behind it. Izzy zoomed in, but that just got them a larger blur.

"A cloud?" Helena said, squinting.

"No, too small, and too round. Hey, Kai."

"Aunty?" Kai stuck his head around the edge of the door.

"That image processing AI we're leasing for the astronomers, we've got access to the account, ya?"

※ ※ ※

Despite Izzy's best efforts to keep the safe-room free from clutter in which drones and bots might hide, the space had filled over the months: coffee mugs (take out cups were no longer allowed after the scanners had found transmitters hidden in them three days in a row), legal pads (covered with dance moves from the Keetae, the hula, and the traditions of a dozen other cultures on and off the Earth), a medical kit (for drawing blood), a Wandering Willie D action figure (for blocking out his part of the dance) and another of Wonder Woman (for Helena's), a woolen beanie and several shawls (the subterranean room could be cool in the mornings), and three hand fans (the room warmed up fast with the three of them at work).

Izzy had shoved it all to the back of the table and propped her tablet up against the pile. On the screen was the blur from the news stream after the astronomy AI had processed it: a perfect sphere, maybe ten centimeters in diameter judging from the trees around it, pale blue against the pale blue sky.

"That's the first one I saw, over the hālau," Izzy said.

She swiped to the next image, a green sphere nestled in a treetop. "Also the hālau."

A darker blue against an early evening sky. "Over my office, after our first meeting."

Smaller and mottled grey against a concrete wall. "Outside the lab at the U of H where you've been doing your DNA work, Willie."

A tiny brown ball tucked into wooden eaves. "The coffee shop down the street here."

Helena frowned suspiciously down into her mug. "The *Sisters* were bugging my coffee cups?" she said.

"Nah, two of those devices were U.S., one was Chinese," Izzy said. "If the Sisters have anything that small, then my scanners haven't picked it up."

Helena put the mug down and shoved it to the far side of the table.

"All of these are from news streams except the coffee shop, which came from a security camera. These next ones, though, came from a U.S. server on Oʻahu, never you mind how."

It was a video, this time, once again from the parking lot of the hālau.

"Those military quadcopters carry some nice gear," Izzy said. She zoomed in, and in, and in, until they could see through the gaps in the shutters, thin slices of Helena, Willie, and the kumu working through a step.

Izzy swiped through false-color variations on the same video. "Infrared, ultraviolet, ultrasound, I don't even know what that is but I'd love to get my hands on it. See anything suspicious?"

Helena shook her head, and Willie made a raspberry sound.

"It took a fancier AI than the astronomers have to catch it," Izzy said. She swiped again and zoomed into a red graphic frame overlaid on the image until it filled the screen.

Against the sky, not far from where Izzy had first seen the Sisters' camouflaged sphere, was…nothing that was ever clear on any single frame. Just a hint of an edge here, a point there. But over time, shapes emerged: a tetrahedron, a cube, something like a soccer ball, each one folding into the next.

Helena slumped back in her chair and stared upward. "Are you watching us or the Sisters?" she asked the ceiling.

"Given what we know about the Construct, which is pretty much nothing, I'd say—Willie, are you ok? You look…tired."

Willie had also slumped, which in his case meant the chair had disappeared under his bulk. A high rattling note hissed from his rear nostrils.

Without sitting up, he waved a hand at the table.

"The <long flowing tones>, this duet, this dance. This one last precious memory I hoped to salvage from the wreck of my species. An exchange between two beings as private and personal as any in our lives. For my own family, who turned from our planet-bound people to embrace the stars, the *one* tradition to which we held with a reverence close to holy."

He pulled himself upright and stretched his arms out. "And here we are in an underground room so small I can reach across it, planning what should be a joyous motion with paper and puppets. What is it that the people of Earth and elsewhere fear, to so appropriate our privacy? Do we plot against them?"

"Maybe we should," Helena said, with a sour laugh. "Can we go after the Sisters first?"

Izzy said, "The three of have all done things that extend well beyond our private selves. It's like the Sisters and their companion spheres, or me and my drones. Part of us is out there in *their* own spaces. It's no surprise that they wonder about the source."

Willie gave a mournful hoot, reached across the table to retrieve the two action figures and set them upright on the table.

"The dance is meant to take place on a high place or clearing under the open sky in the first light of the rising sun. Where will we find such a spot anywhere here on Earth? I was considering petitioning the Sisters to take us to some abandoned planet, even to my own dead and poisoned world. But we now know that even the mighty and mysterious starships will not grant us a moment of solitary peace."

Izzy had gotten an odd look on her face halfway through Willie's words, and that sometimes spooky connection that they had developed over the decades meant that Helena had guessed what she was thinking before Willie had finished.

"They're legally private," Helena said. "International agreements and everything, right? No drones, no cameras, no interaction of any kind without prior approval."

"That might stop the streaming networks. Not the scopes on those U.S. drones, or the satellites, or the starships," Izzy replied.

"Psssh, you'll figure something out for the rest of it. It's the best bet we've got, and it's right next door. Plus, they understand the hula."

Willie rapped on the table with the action figure's feet.

"Kahoʻolawe," Izzy explained. "The island southwest of Maui. The one you can see off the coast from Mākena, where the hālau is."

"Set aside by international law for Hawaiians of Polynesian descent who want to live by the old ways," Helena explained.

"Ho, Sistah Kulikuli, this is gonna be a tough one."

"Izzy's cousin is a kahuna there, in charge of relations with the outside world. They've got beef with her, ever since the Republic of Hawaiʻi was formed and she was first elected councilor."

Willie made the raspberry noise again. "Who could possibly debate the legendary Isabella Māhealani Dasha's qualifications to lead?"

"Oh, they're fine with Izzy being in charge," Helena said. "They just think she should stop playing with drones and be their queen."

Powered craft were banned from Kahoʻolawe, as were all electronic devices of any kind. The three of them plus Kai paddled over in a canoe that Izzy kept for that purpose and tried to use as infrequently as possible.

The trip could be done in about three hours each way, but they got an early start and looped around the volcanic cone of Molokini and its glorious garden of reef life.

A line of patrolling drones marked the edge of Kahoʻolawe waters. Izzy had given herself and the others clearance before they left shore, and the boat passed through without raising an alarm.

They'd been seen from the island, though, and by the time the boat reached the beach in Keoneuli Bay, a group of the inhabitants were making their way down a trail toward them. Izzy signaled a stop when they were still half a dozen meters offshore.

"Wish me luck," she said quietly. She slipped over the side of the boat and half swam, half waded the last stretch to shore. Kai kept the canoe in place with gentle strokes from his paddle, he and Helena straining to hear the conversation onshore.

The initial exchanges seemed civil enough. "Greeting greeting respect respect how's the family it's been too long la la la," Helena translated for Willie.

Next was a lengthy speech from Izzy, punctuated with gestures back at the boat and up at the sky.

"She's explaining who you are and where you come from," Helena said.

"She calls you 'a voyager into unknown waters,'" Kai added. "The bearer of the traditions of your people."

There was a bit of conversation among the locals, and a few long looks across at the boat, but the mood seemed positive.

"We do send a courier over once a month to carry messages on important issues, like problems with the Lono drones," Kai said.

"Or giant interstellar globes hanging over their island," Helena said.

"So they had already heard you were here," Kai finished. "Now she's reminding them that Helena was born on Oʻahu."

The conversation grew more vigorous.

Helena said, "And they're reminding *her* that my parents were both from the mainland, and worse, my dad was in the military. And that I was still child when my mom took me with her back to Oakland."

The satisfaction in Izzy's voice as she answered was clear even out on the boat. Helena grinned and said, "Izzy says that's exactly why it's important that when I came back home from my travels, I came back here, to Hawaiʻi. Because this my home, and these are my people. Which is true. And yes! Nice segue, Izzy. Now she's explaining why you came to Hawaiʻi. Your dance. Our dance."

There followed a long conversation that seemed to be going well at first, members of the group of locals asking questions and Izzy answering. But as the talk continued, the tone grew more edgy, one member of the group dominating the conversation.

"Ah, crap," Helena said.

"That's Helena's cousin," Kai said. "He's in charge of access to the island."

"And he's making it personal. He *says* he has no problem with you, Willie. He says he has no problem with me, though I don't believe him. But Izzy, he says, *is* a problem."

Kai blew out a sigh. "And now they're going down the same hole they always go down. She's reminding him that without her Lono flying above the rain shadow of Haleakalā to catch the moisture the island would be desolate, he's reminding her that roots of the Republic were in the Hawaiian traditionalist movement, she's asking him if all revolutionary socialists have been Hawaiian traditionalists or if it was just Marx and a few others, and—"

Izzy said something sharp and the shouting stopped like a switch had been thrown. Both Kai and Helena winced.

"Well, that's that," Helena said.

Izzy turned without another word and swam back to the boat, which Kai had already turned around. After a few minutes of silent furious paddling Izzy sighed and said, "That could have gone better."

Kai said, "Most of them were sold, or coming round. They'll keep talking. Give them a week, that's what you always say, Aunty."

Izzy grunted. They paddled on in silence, past the drone fence, past Molokini, within a mile from the Maui shore when Helena shaded her eyes and pointed forward. "Here come the drones. Let's just stay right here and let 'em gawk until they run out of juice and ditch in the ocean."

Willie said, "I fear that they will outlast us." He pointed into the sky overhead where a perfect sphere hung, blue on blue.

A week had passed, and then another two, with no word from Kahoʻolawe. The trio's regular meetings in the safe room alternated between work on the dance, increasingly absurd schemes to escape the onlookers, and what the locals called talking story. Izzy described her plans and fears for the fledgling island nation or told stories from the days of the revolution. Helena talked about her travels about the galaxy, and of the mysteries of the five known starships and their unknown owners. She'd flown on four of the five; her studies and her own experiences before and after Kepler-442b had left her in equal parts fascinated and mistrustful of the ships and their influence over the planet-bound species. She and Willie swapped stories of travel mishaps on distant worlds, and Izzy added hilarious insights from her viewpoint as the host to a constant stream of tourists. Willie had proven to be an excellent singer, with a fondness for the blues and similar styles from half a dozen species. They'd added a guitar to the clutter in the safe-room, and their meetings often ended with a few songs and red-faced squalls of laughter.

Helena was not laughing now, though. She came down the steps to the basement two at a time, to find the other two were already prepping the safe-room, electronics stowed in the box in the entryway. They had clearly not seen the news. She paced back and forth until Izzy had completed her scans, which had grown longer and more complex with each new discovery of a bug or bot. As soon as Izzy gave the all-clear, Helena shoved them into the safe-room and slammed the door shut.

"You talk about a respect for privacy, Willie. How about a respect for the privacy of my own damn genes?"

Willie looked at her in confusion, from first one eye and then the other. "We had full approval from both yourself and the authorities to research shared traits between human and keetan genetic materi—"

"My genes. Which the damn U.S. government now has."

"The team would never share data without clear—"

"It was a raid. FBI, military bots, armored drones, people in suits and ties in ninety degree heat. They shut down your U of H lab because *someone* was violating a dozen different international laws about DNA manipulation. I gave you my blood to *study*. Not to *change*."

"But, but <Low rumble>. The study of genetic material, of anything, really, requires taking it apart. It, we, I..." Willie trailed off with a few sharp clicks.

"Helena, this is the U.S. taking a shot at us," Izzy said. "At the Republic, I mean. It doesn't mean they were actually up to anything inappropriate."

"Then why is one of the scientists missing?" Helena snapped.

Izzy and Willie looked at each other.

"Did the reports say who?" Izzy asked.

"It wasn't on any of the reports," Helena said. "I was just back from my swim, getting changed, and one of the reporters from the BBC catches me in the dressing room and tells me about the raid, says the news about the missing scientist was being quashed while they tried to track her down. Leilani something. Gone and took the physical evidence. 'A case full of biological samples.' Trying to get a reaction out of me, I guess, but all she got was me looking baffled and a few words she can't stream."

"Leilani Anna Marcyas," Willie said. He sat on the edge of the table, which creaked under the strain and slid a few inches until it hit the wall, sending its contents scattering.

"Are you alright, Willie?" Izzy asked. "You look exhausted. Or like you're in shock. What can we do?"

Willie raised a hand, managed a few short whistles.

Helena started to say something, stopped and stared a moment, inhaled.

"Not tired," she said. "Sick. You're sick, aren't you?"

Willie slumped, his round porpoise nose lowered, head angled to look at them with one deep-set eye, pannae fluttering in waves. In that moment, he looked utterly alien.

"More than sick, I think." Helena said. "Willie, this is about trust, remember? Stop holding things back. Stop pretending."

Willie closed his eyes, stood up with a shivering motion that raised all the pannae and settled them flat again. Something in his posture, though, the slope of his shoulders, the forward thrust of his head, the flare of his flat tail, left him looking no less alien.

"I have not let myself stop pretending for some while," he said, and his voice was strange too, the vowels long and flowing, the consonants clicking. "Since long before I came to Earth to find you, I have been pretending, since I first learned the last few dozen of my kind on my home world were fading, since I first conceived this mad idea of finding some way, some *one*, <three rising tones over a low rumble>, to share my <long falling notes>. My legacy, my final dance. Which, yes, is done when the elder is dying. I am not sick. But I am very very old, and the damage my people did to their own genetics runs very very deep."

A beat of silence, then in parallel, Helena said, "We should have known, we should have done something." And Izzy, "I'm so sorry we didn't realize how much you were suffering."

Willie pulled himself upright, tucked his head back and his tail down, his appearance returning to its accustomed form, in no way human and yet more human-like. His voice, too, settled back into its usual cadence.

"Please believe that my silence *pretense,* is nothing to do with my trust for the two of you, which is absolute. The weakness is mine. There is a tendency, one of those traits shared across all species, even the Sisters, I suspect, to see something noble and flawless in a dying race. That we must surely have achieved some sort of grace and wisdom from our long past, or from our glimpse into the abyss of our future. But I am just a retired biologist and would-be explorer and occasional singer of the blues, from a minor and somewhat scandalous family, whose status as the last surviving keetan is no more than a fluke of genetics. I was frightened and alone and desperate to be accepted, even if it meant pretending to be something more acceptable. More human. I hope you can understand."

Helena and Izzy exchanged a long look. Then Izzy pulled the table back into position, pulled a chair up, and sat down. Helena slid another chair to Willie and sat down in the third. She set the action figures back on their feet.

"So, where were we?" she asked.

"At the second favor," Willie replied. "The project that I was working on with Dr. Marcyas under cover of the genetic research, the results of which she bears in that case, or so I hope."

He spread his arms and turned a graceful circle, the long feathered pannae down his back curling up in waves like an entire flock of bright tropical birds taking wing. Then he sat and held one arm out toward Helena, with the fingers of the other hand stroked the smaller, iridescent pannae that scaled his wrist.

"We say the pannae are a separate species, a symbiont, or as some of your streaming reporters would have it, a parasite. But the truth is more complex. The Keetae and pannae share large portions of genetic code, entire genes in common that are simply active or not in one species or the other. And that sharing is an active process, neurotransmitters and RNA and cells linked to the functions of learning and memory. At the hālau I said that we regard them as family. But our relationship is more than that. In a very real way, my pannae are part of my self."

Izzy made a quiet sound.

"A part of the <long falling notes>, my people's final dance, is the grafting of pannae from the elder to the one who has agreed to take on their legacy."

"Ah," Helena said.

"It would be madness to imagine that this could possibly succeed with you and I, if were not for two truths: the unlikely similarities between the genetics of Keetae and humans and most of the other known sentient species, and the equally unlikely bonds between the keetae and the pannae. Similarities so unlikely, and so deep, that some feel they must have been deliberately engineered. It was this belief about the origins of the pannae, in fact, that lead to my family's dubious reputation, and to my decision to become a biologist. But I dared not mention it unless I knew it was feasible, and if so, if it was safe for the recipient."

"Which is me."

"Which will be you, if you so agree. We've already attempted the transplant on a rat that, I confess, we named Kulikuli."

Izzy snorted. Helena shushed her and waved at Willie to continue. "And…"

"And both Kulikuli and the pannae survived the grafting with no obvious ill effects. I dearly hope that they escaped with Dr. Marcyas and will make their way here for you to meet."

"If that reporter wasn't just making that part up to rattle me," Helena said.

"And the U.S. hasn't grabbed her yet," Izzy added.

"She is quite resourceful. She gave me a messaging application that she assured me was secure," he said.

"The U.S., or any of the other big players, can crack pretty much anything on the net in an hour or two," Izzy said, standing up. "And goodness knows about the Sisters or the Construct. We need to be ready to go before we try to contact her. I'll send a secure swarm to my contacts inside the military, set up an extraction, get her into a boat inside a shipment of drone parts. We've done it before—no one thinks twice when it comes to me and dro..."

Izzy trailed off, staring over their heads, and slowly sat down again.

Willie tilted his head. "Now it is my turn to ask if *you* are alright."

"She gets that look," Helena said. "When she's though of something especially sneaky."

"I think I know how to get you your private sunrise," Izzy said. "But it's going be awful."

"Worse than having alien parasites grafted onto your skin?" Helena asked, with a bit of a shudder.

"Much worse," Izzy replied. "I'm going to have to go back to Kahoʻolawe and ask nicely."

As it turned out, Izzy didn't have to ask, nicely or otherwise. Willie convinced her to let him make his case directly, with Kai along to translate. Meanwhile, Izzy worked on retrieving their missing scientist, and Helena had her own mission at the hālau.

Willie and Kai had padded back to Mākena by late afternoon. Helena picked them up in the runabout, and they met up with Izzy at the safe room. Against all odds, they had each been successful.

Helena played a clip from one of the streaming channels still stubbornly lurking in the parking lot of the hālau:

Helena stormed out the door of the hālau, followed by Kumu Hoʻomanaʻo, Joe, and some of the other dancers. She swept her hand at the surrounding drones and bots, and shouted, "See? They're not going to go away, not as long as I am here."

"It's fine, Kulikuli," the kumu replied in his quiet voice. "After all, we're training to perform for an audience."

"An audience of people, of locals, not a bunch of virtual tourists buzzing overhead day and night!"

"Da kine more quiet da sistahs at one festival," Joe said. "No problem."

"It's a problem for me, Joe," Helena said. "I'm sick of it, and I'm sick of dragging my mess into your lives. I gotta take a break from it. Just a week or two. I promise."

"You'll miss the celebration for Wandering Willie D," the kumu said.

"I'll see it on the streams," she said, waving at the cameras again. "With my feet up and a glass of something cold. I'm sorry guys, but I need this."

Kumu Hoʻomanaʻo nodded slowly. "We'll be here when you are ready. Aloha, Helena."

"Shoots den. Have a bottle for me," Joe said with a wave.

"Zach and Joe deserve an Oscar for that performance," Helena said. "And I walk them through the rest of it inside. Honestly, the streaming services are getting bored of showing us dancing, particularly when Willie and I aren't there together. Even the creepy Sister sphere is only there half the time."

Izzy reported that the extraction plan for Dr. Marcyas was ready to go that night. It meant potentially blowing the cover of one of her spies, a naval shipping clerk who would approve the shipment of a large crate of "replacement quadcopter batteries."

"He'll come across on the same boat," Izzy said. "Better to pull him than risk his getting caught, and anyway he's earned some time lying on the beach. It's time to call your doctor, Willie, and hope she's still there to answer."

While Izzy set up the connection, Kai described the trip to Kahoʻolawe to Helena.

"We get there easy before noon. Willie knows how to pull a paddle, and the broddah talks some seriously funny story. And the traditionalists, of course they're there waiting on the beach for us, and not at all sure what they think about it just being me and Willie. I think they were all fired up for another round with Izzy, ya? I went through the whole explanation again, about Willie and your dance and the tradition and the privacy, and that Willie wanted to make his case himself. And then Willie, he slips over the side of the boat, and they all get real serious, like he's going to come up onto the beach, one alien invasion, and they weren't sure if they could fight him off. But no, Willie stays by the boat and… I guess you'd call it dance swimming or swim dancing, but not like the stuff with the rubber caps and everyone in synch, no this was like the hula, like he was telling a story. And it was one sad story, too. Beautiful, but heartbreaking."

Kai shook his head.

"And then Willie climbs back in the boat and asks me to tell them that he understands what they've lost, and what they can lose, and that he gives them this dance of his people as a small thing to fill some of that emptiness. And then he gives me this big wink with those crazy sideways eyes of his because we both knew he'd done it. Even Izzy's cousin was wiping his eyes. "They're only letting the two of you on the island, though, no one else, and they went on about no recording equipment or anything like that, even though we told them, you know…"

"That's kind of the whole point," Helena said, and surprised Kai with a backslapping hug.

And then she stepped backward straight into a hug from Izzy. "We're on," Izzy said. "This Dr. Marcyas is as sharp as Willie said. She's been lying low at the apartment of some cousin too many times removed for the mainlanders to suspect, right in downtown Honolulu, while the U.S. has drones sweeping the bush and scanners at all the airports. She on the way to meet my contacts now. If all goes well, they'll be here sometime after midnight."

All went well. By 4 a.m. they'd gotten the crate to the safe room. While Kai drove Izzy's agent to get some well-earned rest, the others unpacked the scientist and her precious cargo.

Doctor Leilani Anna Marcyas was short and slender, with teal hair as bright as Willie's pannae and skin as dark as Helena's. Despite having spent six hours in a crate on a cargo skimmer with a case half her size and an anxious rat in a cage, she was cheerful and delighted to meet Helena and Izzy. And to introduce Kulikuli to her namesake.

The rat was white with a pink nose. Once out of the cage and given the chance to investigate her new surroundings, she scampered to Willie, who picked her up and cradled her in his huge hands.

On either side of Kulikuli's back, just behind the shoulder blades, was one of the pannae, about a finger's length and half as wide. The one on the right was shades of yellow and orange, and on the left a rich green with a shimmering iridescence. They flapped slowly as the rat stretched out in Willie's palms, for all the world like tiny wings.

Helena gently stroked the rat's back, ran a fingertip over the lines where the pannae entered the rat's skin.

"There's an orifice, a sort of mouth," Dr. Marcyus explained. "It develops when the pannae are removed from their old host. Once they're attached to the new host it expands to allow a number of new organs to develop and integrate themselves with the host's circulatory and nervous systems. Their ability to adapt to the specific host is fascinating. I've never encountered anything like it."

Helena felt a shudder coming on again at the thought of mouths, but Leilani's enthusiasm was contagious.

"But there must be a risk of some sort of immune response, a rejection or worse, anaphylactic shock," Izzy said.

"Ah, so, see here?" Dr. Marcyus gently rolled the rat onto her side and touched a small bump under her hip. "This is the real focus of Willie's and my work. It's a sort of nanofactory that monitors the immune system and can produce hormones and targeted viruses to moderate any severe reactions. It also produces some essential nutrients that the pannae require the human, or in this case rat, body does not produce. It's extraordinary technology, as much a living organ as a device. We've been working on similar technology for a decade or so, based on descriptions from the Keetae, but the advantages of working with an actual keetan biologist is...how can I put it? When we can go public with this data—after your and Willie's dance, that is—the impact on the treatment of immune disorders will be nothing short of revolutionary."

Izzy sat down. "And here I was thinking the excitement here on Hawai'i was just about over."

Dr. Marcyus gave Izzy a wicked grin, and a gentler smile for Helena. "You'll probably have to keep one of these embedded for as long as the pannae live, which could be as long as you do. And your life could be longer, much longer, with the nanofactory than without. At the very least, you'll never need antihistamines again."

Willie said, "I have many of these devices embedded, countering the genetic damage my people did to themselves. It kept all of us alive. Until it didn't. But fear not, this application is far more simple and stable than ours, and Dr. Marcyus will be here to refine it, as will I, as long as I am able."

"Any questions?" Dr. Marcyus asked and yawned. "I mean, that we can answer here and now, and then I think maybe I need to take a nap for a day or two."

Helena sat down next to Izzy and scrubbed her fingers through her curls. She looked at Izzy for three long breaths, then up at Willie and Dr. Marcyus. "I guess there's just one question left. When?"

Willie gently set Kulikuli into Helena's hands. The rat promptly curled up and fell asleep.

Willie set himself into a chair and sighed.

"We have all earned a little rest," he said. He stroked the pannae on his head smooth with somewhat shaky hands. "But I feel the time coming."

Muku, the old month "cut away," the new moon, past midnight. Wandering Willie D and Helena swam under starlight.

Five hours earlier, Willie had gone in the front door of the hālau, Izzy on his arm, under the eyes of a couple dozen drones and camera bots. The press had been welcomed in this time, for a performance of the hula in honor of Willie's interest and support.

In the dressing room, Izzy and her microswarms kept a running scan for watchers, while Willie, the kumu, and the rest of the crew assembled an elaborate series of brightly colored headpieces, veils, and cloaks onto the wide frame of Joe Pahuhau.

"Braddah, your folk really put all this on this foa go a show, back in the day?" Joe asked.

Willie gave one of his sharp-toothed grins. "One thing about being the last of your kind, is that *anything* you do is a tradition."

"Sweet," Joe said, somewhat muffled as the last veil was lowered.

Izzy spent a few minutes hooking up the sensors and jammers laced through the costume. Nothing would block government, or alien, tech for long. But all the broadcasting equipment crammed into the performance area would provide some additional interference. And anyway they just needed a distraction of an hour or so for Willie to get away and into the water where he should be near impossible to track.

The fake Willie was paraded out to the place of honor, Izzy and Kumu Ho'omana'o nudging Joe along on either side since he couldn't really see through the layers. The real Willie was wheeled out to a catering van in a rack that had held drinks and pūpū platters.

Meanwhile, Helena was down on Mākena Beach, helping Kai open up crates of drones. These were the Lono, the palm-sized copters that flew above the 3000 meter rain shadow of Maui's volcano to catch moisture from the trade winds and shower it onto the otherwise barren slopes of Kaho'olawe. The Lono flew themselves back to Maui on rotation for repairs or replacements, but now they were preparing to release all the off-duty ones at once. Kai had sent out a press release about the advantages of a new swarm software algorithm which could increase vapor capture rates by up to half a percent or more, thus guaranteeing that they were ignored by the press in favor of the hula performance up the hill.

Dr. Marcyus had sacrificed her teal bob for a black-died crew cut, and with great glee had added a fake mustache to complete the disguise in order to help them with the drones, and to give the pannae on Helena's shoulders one last check. The grafting process had been as challenging as Helena had expected, particularly as their exposed mouths gaped in search of a new host once removed from Willie's chest. The pannae had been prepared for the transplant by a process of raising them and stroking their underside over several days. "And they seem to know, somehow, that the time is coming," Willie had said.

With another keetan, the pannae would have been placed and allowed to attach themselves, but Dr. Marcyus had made starter incisions, four on the back of each shoulder, as well as implanting a pair of nanofactories into the flesh above Helena's hips.

There had been no adverse reactions in the four days since the graft, beyond a little itching, and both Helena and the pannae seemed healthy. Helena had spent hours looking over her shoulder in the mirror, watching the pannae drift and curl, brilliant shades of blues, greens and yellows that shifted with the light.

On a keetan, a group of eight of the pannae was more than enough to spread, reproducing by cloning off buds that would latch onto an adjacent spot. Neither Willie nor Dr. Marcyus could predict if that would happen with Helena. Dr. Marcyus was looking into lab cloning as well. But for now, the pannae's survival beyond their original host species seemed assured.

It was already dark when the catering van drove straight onto the beach and pulled up next to the crates of drones. Willie emerged from the back, and after a brief greeting and thanks to the others, he and Helena got into the water. Everyone had agreed that the boat seemed too risky; they'd swim the five miles across open ocean to Kahoʻolawe.

Willie had been moving slowly these last few days, taking frequent breaks during their last preparations for their dance, and more likely to let his adopted posture and voice slump into their native forms. But now in the water he came to life, stopping for impromptu spins and somersaults when he got too far ahead of Helena, or diving deep to sing at distant whales. She swam in his wake, pulled ahead by the currents he dragged behind him, and laughed for joy as he frolicked. The pannae flowed against her shoulder blades as she swam, already beginning to feel like part of herself.

A steady stream of Lono drones zipped overhead, on their way to join their siblings already high over Kahoʻolawe. That passage was additional cover from any spying eyes, which had with luck already been thrown off by the evening's masquerades.

They stopped a couple of hours into the swim to rest and hydrate and watch the stars, both natural and artificial, that filled the wide ocean of sky.

And so they were looking upward when one of the Sisters' great primary spheres started to descend.

"You damn meddling busybodies," Helena growled. "Can't you just give us this one moment?"

Willie trilled a series of frustrated clicks. "We can still hope that Izzy's plan provides us the cover we require."

"Against one of their little spheres, sure. Against a hundred, maybe. But against that thing? It's wider than Kahoʻolawe."

The sphere had gone from moon-sized to three times that in just a few seconds. But it was not the only thing moving in the heavens. The Construct began to drift and sparkle. It was almost impossible to judge its size or shape, but it seemed to be tracking the Sisters' ship.

More clicks from Willie, and a low wailing. "What hopes can our little band possibly hold against *two* starships?" he moaned.

"Wait..." Helena said. "I'm not so sure they're on the same side."

The Construct had gotten closer and closer to the Sisters' sphere, and now was clearly underneath it, between the other and the Earth below. And then it stopped moving.

The Sisters' ship stopped as well. There was a long quiet moment, Helena and Willie floating motionless in the calm water, the two ships hanging still overhead.

"I've always felt that the Sisters are worried about what we, meaning all the planet-bound species, might do," Helena said. "They want us to ask nice, and then they pick and choose who can travel where. They say they are concerned *for* us, but that goes hand-in-hand with being concerned *about* us."

The Sisters' sphere dropped a bit lower. The Construct did not budge.

"The Construct, though, who can tell? The entire time I was on their ship I sat on a platform hanging in the dark in a space so large I couldn't see the walls, while little geometric shapes folded themselves out the dark and back into it again, all around me. Should have been terrifying, but I never felt threatened, never felt like *they* felt threatened."

The Sisters' ship moved a little to the side. The Construct matched its motion.

"I just felt that the Construct is—I can't in any way back this up with science, and wouldn't have believed it before being on that ship—the Construct is *curious*. Curious about me, about what all of us *could* do."

Helena looked over at Willie. His eyes reflected the entire sky back at her.

"And what I've learned about curiosity, from my travels, from Izzy and Zack and Joe and Kai and Dr. Marcyas, from you, Wandering Willie D, is that curiosity always wins."

And so they were looking at each other, instead of the sky, when the Sisters' ship started to retreat. It was almost back in place with her six sister primaries when they looked up again. The Construct stayed where it was, a thousand kilometers overhead, unmoving, while they swam the remaining miles to Kahoʻolawe.

Izzy's cousin and a few others met them on the beach of Keoneuli Bay, and led them up the steep trail to Puʻu ʻO Moaʻula Nui, the peak that faced east toward Maui and the distant horizon. Helena was better at understanding Hawaiian than speaking it, and she feared that English or pidgin would have been disrespectful. There was no tension in the silence, though, but rather a sense of ceremony. When they reached the top of the hill, Willie gave a graceful bow. Izzy's cousin nodded, and then the locals withdrew.

The Lono drones had brought the rain to Kahoʻolawe, which had in turn brought trees and shrubs to the barren island. There was not really such thing as native vegetation on Hawaiʻi, raised by volcanos so far from any continent, but the traditionalists had encouraged those plants that had come with the first explorers from distant Polynesia.

The top of the hill, though, was still bare, just a few stubborn bushes clinging here and there to the rock. Willie and Helena paced out a clear space for the dance, drank some water. Kumu Hoʻomanaʻo had given Helena a skirt made of long feathers in colors that matched her pannae. She took it from the waterproof pack now and put it on, folded up her swimsuit and put it into the pack along with the water bottles, set it to the side. They sat in the center of the circle to wait for the dawn.

They both looked upward now and again, in case the Sisters had made another attempt despite the protection of the Construct, but the view overhead was entirely black. The Lono drones, their numbers reinforced, were building a cloud like a thunderhead over their heads. No rain fell there on the peak, but they could hear its patter, smell the scents it woke from the rock as it began to trickle down in a circle all around the hill.

"Three favors, you said, Willie. In that first meeting in Izzy's office, you said you had three favors to ask. The dance, the pannae, that's two, unless I am missing something."

Willie hooted a laugh. "And in that same meeting, Counselor Dasha said you could be counted on to do three things. Swim. Dance."

"…Or put on my walking shoes." Helena finished.

"Life is motion, Helena Kulikuli Johnson, and you have been still for too many years."

Willie gestured up at the growing storm.

"What new moves are out there to discover in the beyond? What people wait to share in those steps you have gathered? What were the terms for the hula the kumu used?"

"Kahiko, 'auana," Helena said. "Tradition, wandering."

The Lono were spiraling down now, bringing the cloud with them, and the rain. The stars, the lights of Maui, the growing light on the horizon to the east, all of Kahoʻolawe beyond the spot on which they sat, were lost behind that cloak.

Willie sang for a moment, a melody both sad and peaceful. Then they helped each other to their feet. Willie shook himself out, his pannae flaring up, their brilliant colors catching a growing light. Helena stretched and felt her own pannae do the same.

A sudden dizziness hit her, a sort of déjà vu, a doubling of her vision and then a doubling again and again, as if she'd stood ready for this dance not just once before, but countless times. Was it a reaction to the pannae, a glimpse into the alien memories they held? She almost said something, but the feeling was already fading, or rather settling deep into her. And anyway, it was time.

The swirling wall of drones and clouds had thinned to the east. Now it parted in a narrow gap, leaving a sheet of rain so thick it resembled glass.

The sun's first rays hit that glass and shattered into light.

Helena and Wandering Willie D looked at each other, and then back into that light. Together, they began to dance.

CONTRIBUTORS

a.a. attanasio lives alongside Ka Iwi Nature Preserve on Oʻahu and wrote this story, like most of his fiction, while sitting at a boulder inside a volcano: Koko Crater, a botanical garden near his home. "Mauka on Mars" first appeared in Issue #122 of *Bamboo Ridge, Journal of Hawaiʻi Literature and Arts*, "Snaring New Suns, Speculative Writing from Hawaiʻi and Beyond."

Gregory Norman Bossert is an author and filmmaker based just over the Golden Gate Bridge from San Francisco. His story "The Telling" won the 2013 World Fantasy Award; other stories have appeared everywhere from *Asimov's Science Fiction* to the *Saturday Evening Post*. When not writing, he wrangles spaceships and superheroes for Lucasfilm's Industrial Light & Magic.

About "Hānai" he says, "Growing up in New England, Hawaiʻi seemed as fabulous and distant a place as the planets and mythical kingdoms of my favorite books. In the years since, I've discovered the reality of the people and landscape of Hawaiʻi is much more complex and wonderful. I hope I've captured some of that feeling in my story."

"Hānai" first appeared in the November/December 2021 issue of *Asimov's Science Fiction*.

CONTRIBUTORS

ALAN BRENNERT fell in love with Hawai'i on his first visit in 1980 and has since become a chronicler of island history through his bestselling novels *Moloka'i*, *Honolulu*, and *Daughter of Moloka'i*. But he also has deep connections to the field of speculative fiction: he wrote for the 1980s TV revival of *The Twilight Zone* and won a Nebula Award for his short story "Ma Qui." "Puowaina" was written for Carol Serling's 50th Anniversary *Twilight Zone* anthology as a kind of homage to Rod Serling's script "The Time Element" (also set in Honolulu) but rooted in the Hawaiian mysticism that often finds its way into Alan's novels. He wishes that he was able to live in the islands, but he and his wife reside in Malibu, California, which he calls "a pretty good second choice."

C.B. CALSING is an editor, author, and graduate of the Creative Writing Workshop at the University of New Orleans. Her work has been published in journals and anthologies as well as online. Currently she lives on Hawai'i Island. "Beneath the Ironwoods" was inspired by Mrs. Calsing's work with students on the autism spectrum and the time she's spent snorkeling at Richardson Beach in Hilo. News and reviews can be found at cbcalsing.blogspot.com.

JOHN CHAMBERS is a software developer and horror writer from Austin, TX. He is the author of *Scourge Ship*, a gross-out novel set on the high seas. His work has appeared in *Cracked* and in the horror anthology *WTF*. His favorite snack is Hawaiian macadamia nuts.

A.M. DELLAMONICA'S first novel, *Indigo Springs*, won the Sunburst Award for Canadian Literature of the Fantastic. Their fourth, *A Daughter of No Nation*, won the 2016 Prix Aurora. Alyx has published over forty short stories in tor.com, *Strange Horizons*, *Lightspeed*, and numerous print magazines and anthologies. They were the co-editor of *Heiresses of Russ 2016*. Their most recent works are the solarpunk thrillers *Gamechanger* and *Dealbreaker*, written as L.X. Beckett, which take place in a near future grappling with the 21st century carbon crisis. "The Sweet Spot" first appeared in issue 26 of *Lightspeed*.

SOLOMON ROBERT NUI ENOS is a Native Hawaiian artist and illustrator based in Honolulu, Hawaiʻi. He grew up on the Waiʻanae Coast in a family dedicated to cultural preservation and community building. This upbringing gave him ample inspiration for stories based on the legends that was shared with him in his youth and in the time he spent in the taro fields of his ancestors. With art as a medium, Solomon has gone on to make a career based on visually translating his culture and an ancient sense of wonder, passed down through the land and the waters of his youth.

Eager to look for contemporary shells to inhabit, like a hermit crab, Solomon has also drawn upon a bit of H.P. Lovecraft to depict this Kupua on the cover, a magical creature from an ancient ocean, as an anthropomorphic anemone. The narrative is left up to the viewer to cultivate, as its origins are as much a mystery to the artist as it is to his audience. The responsibility for translation continues with the viewer, as Solomon aspires to do with all his work.

SAM FLETCHER is a writer, reporter, and editor (and diver!) in Honolulu, Hawaiʻi. "Blues of Eu" is the confluence of 1915 newspaper clippings surrounding the sunken F-4's unprecedented salvage, the legend of the Molokaʻi shark god Kauhuhu (particularly his sacrifices-turned-sharks), and some imagery in "Hua, King of Hāna" by King David Kalākaua. As for the name Moʻoaliʻi, Hawaiian speakers will recognize this is closer in meaning to King Lizard than King Shark, though it is the name Kalākaua used in several of his stories of the (likely shapeshifting) shark god, and Sam especially liked the king's description of Moʻoaliʻi's entourage of black sharks.

CONTRIBUTORS

Born and raised on Hawai'i, the Big Island, DENAROSE FUKUSHIMA always held a deep respect for Hawaiian Culture. She grew up with stories of Pele's power and Māui's resourcefulness and enjoys adventuring in Volcano National Park and the occasional trip to Punalu'u Bakery. Her love of mythology and deep connection to her own family spurred her to write "Lehiwa and the Name Thief," the first of her stories to take place in Hawai'i. She currently resides in Japan, where she hopes to broaden her knowledge of culture and mythology. "Lehiwa and the Name Thief" first appeared in *Myriad Lands Volume II*.

TOM GAMMARINO'S speculative works include the novel *King of the Worlds* and the novellas *Jellyfish Dreams* and *The Yellows*. Shorter works have appeared in *Interzone*, *The Writer*, *American Short Fiction*, and *The New York Review of Science Fiction*, among others. He has been awarded a Fulbright Fellowship in Creative Writing and the Elliott Cades Award for Literature and has a PhD in English from the UH Manoa. Recently, he served as co-editor of *Snaring New Suns*, an issue of Bamboo Ridge focused on speculative work from the Pacific. He teaches Science Fiction, Magical Realism, Jazz Lit, and Creative Writing at Punahou School. tomgammarino.com

"What We Yield" originally appeared in *Tahoma Literary Review* and was nominated for the Pushcart Prize. The author had this to say about the story: "I'm hardly the first to observe that writing fiction about climate change poses some unique challenges. On the one hand, there's the risk of writing mere disaster porn; on the other hand, the scale of the crisis has a way of exploding the usual loci of meaning, making dramas of the human psyche feel trifling, even indulgent. 'What We Yield' is my attempt to split the difference. If rising seas, mass extinction, and billions of climate refugees risk exceeding our emotional grasp, surely a hike in the price of coffee can still command our attention."

CONTRIBUTORS

DARIEN GEE is the author of five novels that have been translated into eleven languages. Her collection of micro memoirs, *Allegiance*, won the 2021 IPPY Bronze Award in the essays category. She is the winner of a 2019 Poetry Society of America Chapbook Fellowship Award for *Other Small Histories* and a 2015 Hawaiʻi Book Publishers' Ka Palapala Poʻokela Award of Excellence for *Writing the Hawaiʻi Memoir*. She is the executive editor for the anthology, *Nonwhite and Woman: 131 Micro Essays on Being in the World*. She lives and writes from the Island of Hawaiʻi. "Pele in Therapy" first appeared in the anthology, *Don't Look Back: Hawaiian Myths Made New* (Watermark Publishing, 2011).

ALAYA DAWN JOHNSON is a Nebula award-winning short story writer and the author of seven novels for adults and young adults. Her most recent novel for adults, *Trouble the Saints*, won the 2021 World Fantasy Award for best novel. Her debut short story collection, *Reconstruction*, was an Ignyte Award and a Hurston/Wright Legacy Award finalist. Her debut YA novel *The Summer Prince* was longlisted for the National Book Award for Young People's Literature, and the follow-up *Love is the Drug* was awarded the Andre Norton Nebula Award. Her short stories have appeared in many magazines and anthologies, most notably the title story in *The Memory Librarian*, in collaboration with Janelle Monáe. She lives in Oaxaca, Mexico. "A Guide to the Fruits of Hawaiʻi" first appeared in the July/August 2014 issue of the *Magazine of Fantasy & Science Fiction*.

JEFFERY RYAN LONG lives in a book-polluted apartment in Honolulu, Hawaiʻi and is enrolled in the English PhD program at the University of Hawaiʻi at Manoa. His fiction has been published in *Bamboo Ridge*, *Hawaiʻi Review*, *Vice-Versa*, *Euphemism*, *The Spectacle*, and *Midway*. Jeffery's collection of short stories, *University and King*, was published by Aignos Press in 2014. He is also an incorrigible jazz DJ at the University of Hawaiʻi's radio station, KTUH.

CHRIS MCKINNEY is a Korean, Japanese, Scottish American writer born in Honolulu, Hawaiʻi. He is the author of *Midnight, Water City*, book one of the *Water City* trilogy. It was named a Best Mystery of 2021 by Publisher's Weekly and a Best Speculative Mystery of 2021 by CrimeReads. Book two, *Eventide, Water City*, will be released summer of 2023. He has written six other novels: *The Tattoo*, *The Queen of Tears*, *Bolohead Row*, *Mililani Mauka*, *Boi No Good*, and *Yakudoshi: Age of Calamity*. In 2011, Chris was appointed Visiting Distinguished Writer at the University of Hawaiʻi at Manoa. Over the years, he has won one Elliot Cades Award and seven Kapalapala Pookela Awards. Chris currently resides in Honolulu with his wife and two daughters.

LEHUA PARKER writes speculative fiction for kids and adults often set in her native Hawaiʻi. Her published works include the award-winning Niuhi Shark Saga trilogy and *Sharks in an Inland Sea*. Her short stories have appeared in *Va: Stories by Women of the Mona*, *Bamboo Ridge*, and *Dialogue*. An advocate of indigenous voices in media and a graduate of The Kamehameha Schools, she is a frequent speaker at conferences, symposiums, and schools. Connect with her at LehuaParker.com.

About "Pili Koko" she writes, "Growing up in Hawaiʻi, we knew our ancestors stood guard between us and entities that wished us harm. Like most of my stories, 'Pili Koko' started with a question: what if a child couldn't tell the difference? And then Ahe started answering…"

As his father was stationed in the Pacific with the navy, GREG PATRICK'S earliest and fondest memories have been among the incomparable Hawaiian Islands. After learning to swim before he walked, he went on to extensively dive the vibrant reefs of every Hawaiian Island. He has encountered many of Hawaiʻi's fascinating sea creatures on his adventures, especially its many sharks while diving with conservationists. A student of Polynesian history, culture, and traditions, he has taken special inspiration in the fearless and matchless Polynesian seafarers and navigators.

CONTRIBUTORS

His readings of the armed struggles of leprosy-infected rebels evading capture and exile to Molokaʻi inspired "The Last Chieftain of Molokaʻi." Also of inspiration was his own almost fatal experience with a condition in early teenage years that left him emaciated and close to death. The author divides his time between his residence in Maui, Europe, and the west coast of the States.

JOSH POOLE is a visual artist and writer working out of a small town in Virginia. His sculptures and paintings focus on environmentalism, and his primary medium is soda cans. He's worked as a gag cartoonist since high school, venturing into writing much later. "What Grows May Burn" is a co-authored piece with Travis Wellman, and the two frequently collaborate with works of science fiction and fantasy. Josh's work has been published in *Air Mail Magazine*, *The Woody Creeker*, *The Rockbridge Advocate*, and dozens of other publications.

RHIANNON RASMUSSEN is an author and illustrator interested in monstrosity and the persistence of hope. Graduate of Mililani High School, currently in the PNW, but with Hawaiʻi always in the heart. "Charge! Love Heart!" was thought up lying in bed, listening to the truck brakes echoing through Kīpapa Gulch. The story first appeared in *The Sockdolager*. Rhiannon's other fiction has appeared in publications including *Lightspeed*, *Evil in Technicolor*, and *Magic: the Gathering*. Visit rhiannonrs.com.

PHILLIP RILEY came to Hawaiʻi in the '90s quite by accident and became a Special Education teacher in Waipahu. In his career he taught Civics, Modern Hawaiian History, American History, English, and many areas of Special Education. He is drawn to the ecology in Hawaiʻi as well as its history and cultures. The characters in his stories are creatively spun from people he has met or worked with in Hawaiʻi.

CONTRIBUTORS

JAMES ROSENLEE is a UH Mānoa student and an English major who's been writing short stories since he was young. More than anything else, a life-long love of Star Trek inspired him to write "Mawaena Nā Hōkū." Although James is a diehard fan of all things science fiction, he's also noticed the lack of stories involving people of color in mainstream sci-fi. And so, "Mawaena Nā Hōkū" was born—a short story that combines elements of classic science fiction, ancient Hawaiian culture, and a hopeful view of our contemporary society.

MELISSA YUAN-INNES believes that of all the places she's visited on earth, Hawai'i feels like a sacred place. She wrote "Eating Rainbows" after driving the road to Hāna, challenging herself with yoga on the Big Island, and soaking up rainbows. Melissa recently released two speculative fiction collections, *Chinese Cinderella, Fairy Godfathers & Beastly Beauty* and *Dog vs. Aliens, Grandma Othello & Shaolin Monks in Space*. She also writes award-winning Hope Sze thrillers as Melissa Yi.

GEORGE S. WALKER is an engineer and writer in Portland, Oregon who has fond memories of vacationing in Hawai'i. This story was inspired by his love of Hawaiian history, jetpacks, and volcanoes. His stories have appeared in *Abyss & Apex*, *Andromeda Spaceways*, *The Colored Lens*, and elsewhere. Anthologies containing his work include *Mothership: Tales from Afrofuturism & Beyond*, *Bibliotheca Fantastica*, and *The Best of Abyss & Apex (Vol. 2 & 3)*. His website is sites.google.com/site/georgeswalker. "Kites and Orchids" first appeared in *Electric Spec*.

TRAVIS WELLMAN is the Operations Manager of the Stonerose Interpretive Center and Eocene Fossil Site where he plays with fifty-million-year-old fossils. His step-aunt has long lived in Pearl City on O'ahu, and she has regaled him with stories during her visits. Travis drew upon those stories when working with Josh Poole on "What Grows May Burn." His writing has been published in *The Woody Creeker*, and *The World of Myth Magazine Anthology IV - Dark Myth Publications*.

KRYSTLE YANAGIHARA lives on Oʻahu and knows no other home. Her family roots go all the way back to the plantation days, and she is also part Kānaka. "For All The Hearts We Buried" was written as a way to channel the grief she was feeling during her grandmother's death anniversary, and is inspired from her experiences growing up as a hānai child. She loves milk tea and can always be found with one in her hand. This is her first published work and, hopefully, she'll finish the novel she's currently writing.